The Lightless Dome

Douglas Hill was born and raised in Western Canada, but has lived in Britain for more than thirty years – mostly in London, and mostly working as a freelance writer. He has written about twenty non-fiction books, including works on history, folklore, and popular science, but he is best known as an author of children's science fiction and fantasy: the *Last Legionary* quartet, the *Huntsman* trilogy, and many others including a two-part fantasy, *Blade of the Poisoner* and *Master of Fiends*. Now his latest departure into new fields brings him his half-century: *The Lightless Dome*, his first full-length fantasy novel for adults, is also his fiftieth book.

DOUGLAS HILL

The
Lightless Dome

Book 1 in the Apotheosis Trilogy

PAN BOOKS
LONDON, SYDNEY AND AUCKLAND

First published 1993 by Pan Books Limited

This edition published 1994 by Pan Books Limited
a division of Pan Macmillan Publishers Limited
Cavaye Place London SW10 9PG
and Basingstoke

Associated companies throughout the world

ISBN 0 330 33166 3

3 5 7 9 8 6 4 2

A CIP catalogue record for this book is available from
the British Library

Phototypeset by Intype, London
Printed and bound in Great Britain by
Cox & Wyman Ltd, Reading, Berkshire

For
GRAYDON GOULD
across a farther Continent

PRELUDE: ONSET

In the winter night the moon rose late, half-way through its turn, sharp-edged and frigid as a fragment of yellow ice, and shreds of cloud drifted across the sky as if the cold made them sluggish. The sea was a bright pewter-gray, sliding like thin oil on to the sand and away again, endlessly, all along the desolate shore. At one point a spit of land thrust out into the water like a small peninsula – almost entirely covered by an immense and featureless structure. It loomed like a vast, misshapen hemisphere, its curved surface gleaming blackly. On that wild shore it seemed grotesquely unnatural, like a gigantic swelling from some infection, shiny-dark and monstrous.

Inside, also, monstrosity was being prepared.

Nothing passed through that huge black half-sphere, not winter's chill nor thin moonlight. Within, darkness ruled – saved for one blemish. A window, flickering orange-red from the upper portion of a building made of dark stone, high-roofed, solid, and grim. Like a mansion with aspirations to be a castle, it had a tall tower at each corner, rising almost far enough to touch the inner surface of the over-arching sphere. The lighted window, slit in one of the towers, opened from a high-ceilinged chamber extending its full breadth. It was bare save for a few hangings on the walls and a raised area at one end. On this area stood two luxurious divans with backrests and a solid, thick-legged table loaded with manuscripts and parchments, flasks and vials, and other strange devices and implements. In the centre was a tall striped candle.

Beyond its reach the uncanny darkness, almost palpable, owned the room: it rippled in the corners like vapour over a marsh, drifted thickly along the ceiling, lapped like black silent surf at the edges of the small island of light.

But the man standing at the table was oblivious to the darkness. He was a tall man in a high-collared robe, his bony face showing the lines of middle age, with a greying beard and a mane of silvery hair. Studying a stained, flaking parchment, he muttered aloud in a harsh baritone. Then he glanced at the candle, nodded briefly, and took up a bulbous flask. A sudden faint phosphorescence gathered around his fingers as he reached with the other hand for a small pouch, from which he took a pinch of powder and dropped it into the flask. He spoke one low, sharp-syllabled word and fumes arose – thick and acrid.

'May this give me strength enough, tonight,' he said, his voice echoing in the silent chamber.

Then he bent forward, face into the fumes, and inhaled. He quivered slightly as he filled his lungs – and when he raised his face again his face was flushed and his eyes were unnaturally bright.

Stopping the flask, he glanced at the candle once more before striding to the edge of the dais. As he lifted his hands, the eerie glow still playing among his fingers, the drifting darkness fled back, leaving the floor bare. Taking a deep breath, hands raised high, he began to chant.

His voice as it lifted grew more harsh and grating, speaking words in the incantation that were of no human language but an ugly, guttural tongue never meant for the mouths of men. As the chant went on he became hunched and taut, as if straining beneath some awful weight. His glowing hands began to shake: his arms quivered as if they had grown too heavy to be held aloft. Sweat burst out on his skin, streamed down his twisted, drawn face. Yet still he chanted, voice rising and falling in a complex pattern of minor keys and discords. As it rose steadily higher, its dissonance growing wilder and more raucous, the man's hands flexed into claws, spreading wide. The chant became a cry, a howl – his eyes bulged, his face darkened, his every muscle and tendon vibrated with unbearable strain.

The chant rose until he was screaming the words at the upper limits of his larynx. Abruptly he stopped – for a resounding instant of total silence – before the climax of the incantation. A final word erupted, in an appalling shriek that seemed to tear his throat in agony. As it echoed around the chamber he lurched, found his balance, lowered his arms as if they pained him, and staggered back towards the table. There he fumbled to open the flask, half-choking as he gulped another huge breath of the thick white fumes.

But he did not take his gaze away from the centre of the room.

Above the blank floor a swirling haziness appeared. Unlike the black fog of the darkness, it glittered coldly, seething. Within its depths an image began to form.

Vague and blurred at first, it quickly became recognizable. Two pairs of tall pillars or columns, ghostly but unmistakable, supporting a broad, smooth-surfaced pediment. Between the pairs of columns, below the pediment, the opening presented itself, an entrance, a doorway . . . a Threshold.

The entire rectangle was outlined in a lurid green light, as if the perimeter of the threshold was formed of luminous gas. Beyond it more shapes were slowly forming: a series of shadowy arches that supported a long, flat surface glittering as coldly as the haziness from which it was emerging. Like a Bridge, stretching away from the threshold, its farther end invisible as it extended into the haze.

When threshold and bridge seemed fully formed, the man by the table moved again to the edge of the dais. The second inhalation of the fumes had steadied his step and eased his trembling, but he looked no less tense and haggard. And something else showed in the set of his jaw, the glint of his eyes – the look of a man who is clutching hard at his courage, steeling his will. Reaching the edge, he stopped, his face twisting in a grimace that might have been apprehension.

Before him, beyond the threshold, along the bridge, something moved.

It had appeared out of the haziness as if materializing. But it did not glitter like the haze. It seemed to be formed of shadow, hues of grey and black. Yet it was not truly formed at all, for its dark mass was shapeless and intangible. And immense. As it flowed along the bridge it towered high as the threshold's columns, broad as the pediment. Its planes and surfaces were in ceaseless motion, twisting, folding, roiling, never finding shape or substance. Yet it was an entity with undoubted material presence – an awareness that, as it reached the threshold and halted, bore down on the man like the gaze of a ghastly eye. No words or thoughts or other identifiable communication issued from it, yet the man cowered and flinched. Uncontrollably he stepped back a pace as he experienced – even through the protected threshold – the impact of its power, immeasurably old, incalculably evil, augmented by the cravings of an indescribable hunger.

The monstrous presence moved forward slightly farther. A shapeless portion of it touched the threshold like a terrible hand. The green perimeter pulsed wildly as the hand pushed and probed, seeking a weakness. And behind it the man sensed the ravenous hunger, mounting, an immense force that was shrieking soundlessly with a murderous desire to rend and crush, to devour and drain.

The man stumbled back another pace, his face ashen. 'No!' he cried, his voice cracking. 'There is no need . . . ! The barrier will not fall – and your hunger will soon begin to be fed, even as I promised you!'

The shadow gave no sign of understanding or acknowledgement, but the terrible pressure withdrew – perhaps merely because the luminous shielding of the threshold had thwarted it. For an endless moment the being remained where it was. Then, abrupt and soundless as before, it flowed away, back along the bridge, and vanished from sight amid the haze.

The man's body sagged with relief as he watched bridge and threshold fade into mistiness and finally nothingness. When he turned away he was stumbling and trembling as if on the edge of collapse, yet his lips curved in a smile of fierce satisfaction. And that smile widened and grew more savage as he sank down on the nearest of the two divans, let his head loll back, and raucously laughed aloud.

'I *did* it!' he said to the empty chamber, his voice raw and quavering. 'I *can* perform the Invocation, even at my present level! It *will* answer my summons!' Again the croaking laughter rose. 'So now all is in place! Now dreams will become realities! Now I may *begin*!'

PART ONE

THE OUTLANDER

ONE

When the assistant director announced that they would be going for a second run-through, nearly everyone on the set reacted with the usual chorus of groans and muttering. But then the technicians and crew began to busy themselves with the sort of things they always seemed busy with, while Red Cordell and one of the other actors went back to doing what actors always seemed to have to do – killing time, while waiting. In their case, time was killed with a pack of cards and an endless game of gin rummy, which did not prevent them from glancing over now and then at another actor, the *star*, in prolonged conversation with the director himself.

Watching the director take a few steps, with gestures, as if in demonstration, Red smiled a mocking smile. 'It'll take more than that to turn Loopy into an actor.'

The other man grunted. 'Just so he remembers his lines,' he said.

Red laughed, but his eyes were thoughtful. 'They ought to try to brighten up the scene, while they're at it.'

'Don't say that. We got enough extra days' shootin' already.'

'Extra days are extra pay.' Red peered briefly at the discard pile. 'And the scene is a *dud*, Karl.'

'Maybe.' The other man, Karl, was staring at Red dubiously. 'An' maybe it don't matter. So don't you go . . .'

Whatever warning he was about to voice was interrupted by a shout from the assistant director and a sudden extra bustle as everyone settled themselves for the second run-through. Red grinned at Karl and rose, gathering up the sheathed sword that he had set aside during the break. And with a worried frown Karl picked up his own sword and followed.

Both men were dressed in someone's romanticized idea of

3

the garb of ancient warriors, from some unspecified era. Their sleeveless leather jerkins displayed an abundance of bare chest and arms, while otherwise they wore close-fitting trousers, boots, short cloaks flung back, and of course their sword-belts. Red was clearly the younger of the two, perhaps in his late twenties, with good facial bones, pale blue eyes, and a shock of russet-red hair. Though he was fairly tall, with the hard, lean muscles of an athlete in peak condition, he looked almost slight beside the older man. Karl was a little taller and far heavier, his bulk solid and fleshy rather than athletically muscular, with the beginnings of a belly and tinges of grey in his hair.

As they moved towards the set itself, they were joined by the star, similarly clothed. He was the most powerfully built of the three, the overdeveloped muscles of his upper body bulging from his jerkin with impressive definition, looking as if they had been oiled. He also had long black hair, slightly close-set eyes, and a large jaw that was set in a look of determination.

'Places, everyone!' cried the director, oblivious of the fact that everyone was already assembled in their places. He wore an ill-fitting safari jacket, was bony and balding, and his face was mottled with a semi-permanent floridity. '*Do* let's try to get it *right* this time!' he added, both his tone and his accent sounding slightly affected.

'Oh, *do* let's,' Red muttered – earning a half-smile from Karl and a scowl from the star.

Then the three of them walked forward, on to the set. It was a scene from a grimly arid land – powdery grey sand underfoot, dead trees standing skeletally here and there, great outcrops of rock or heaps of crumbling boulders looming around them. The only element it lacked was the typically relentless sun of such a landscape, for the batteries of mighty lights around the set would not be switched on for a mere run-through.

As the three advanced, Karl was staring worriedly around at the rocks and trees. 'Thagor!' he said in his gruff baritone. The others turned to him enquiringly.

'Are we wise,' Karl went on, 'to travel here so openly?

4

By now the Soulless One will surely know that Thagor the Invincible has entered his realm.'

The big black-haired man heaved immense shoulder muscles in a shrug. 'It matters not to me what he knows,' he replied, his voice flat and stilted.

'But if he sends his troll-creatures . . .' Karl said.

The one called Thagor shook his head stiffly. 'We have to reach the Citadel, my friend. There is no choice. We must simply be watchful.'

During the exchange Red had remained silent, letting one hand stray to his sword-hilt while he looked around warily. Then the three moved off again.

They had taken no more than a few steps when roaring horror erupted from behind the nearest outcrop.

It was a giant, taller than a tall man, with legs and arms like tree-trunks and purple-grey skin as thick and ridged and knobbly as armour. It had three huge staring eyes, curved yellow fangs in its roaring mouth, and a club studded with spikes in one vast hand.

Red was closest to the charging monster, standing as if paralysed with terror. But when the vicious club swung down, it struck only empty air. Its intended victim moved with startling speed, flinging himself into a flat sideways dive – and a controlled dive, so that as he struck the sand he rolled once and came smoothly to his feet, having somehow in the same motion drawn his sword.

The monster was clumsily wheeling towards him, raising its club, when the sword flashed through the air. Strangely, the blade did not shine with the silvery brightness of ordinary steel, but glimmered with an ever-changing variety of luminous colours. But its edge was not in doubt when it parried the enormous club, nor was the strength of the blade. It neatly sheared off most of the club's length, which bounced in a rubbery way as it fell to the ground.

The monster stumbled back awkwardly. 'God's *sake*, Red!' it said, sounding shaken.

At the same time another voice raised itself, from the edge of the set – the voice of the director, sounding not shaken but decidedly irate.

'Cordell!'

Karl looked at Red with an almost weary shake of the head. The star, bunching his deltoids, looked at Red with an angry glare. But the younger man merely sheathed his sword with a resigned smile, amusement brightening his pale blue eyes.

Near by, the towering monster reached up to pull back the head of its costume, revealing the lantern-jawed face of a very skinny and obviously unusually tall man. The man poked a foot at the portion of the club on the ground, severed by the strangely colourful sword.

'That'll take some fixin', Red,' he said mournfully.

'Sorry, Al,' Red replied. 'I didn't think the blade would be so sharp.'

By then the director was striding angrily up to them, face more floridly mottled than ever. 'Cordell!' he barked. 'What the bloody hell was that all about?'

Red smiled brightly. 'It was about believability, Dick.'

'The name is *Dirk*!' yelled the director.

'Right,' Red said. 'Sorry. Don't know why I always think of you as a Dick.'

The muted ripple of laughter among the people around the set served to darken the other man's face even more. 'Never mind! I want to know what you think you were bloody *doing*!'

Red gestured vaguely. 'I'm supposed to be a warrior, aren't I? Who's just been told to be watchful? It seems stupid to get myself killed without even reaching for my sword.'

The director was taking deep breaths as if trying to contain a towering rage. 'Cordell. The script says that the monster comes out and clubs you, and you die. That's all. Nothing more.'

'But it's not—' Red began.

'Cordell!' the director shouted. 'This is for *children*! Kiddies don't care about believability! You get killed, that's *it*! No sword, no gymnastics, nothing!'

'Anyway,' the huge Thagor suddenly interrupted, 'if someone's doin' fightin' tricks an' stuff, should be *me*.'

Red glanced at Karl, standing stolidly next to him. 'Tricks?' he murmured. 'He needs a stuntman to help him draw his sword.'

6

'I mean,' the huge man went on, apparently not hearing, '*I'm* Thagor the Invincible.'

'Thagor the Unconvincing,' Red muttered.

'Right, Lupe, right,' the director said reassuringly to Thagor. 'But we don't want too much in this scene. The troll kills Cordell, you kill the troll, then you and Karl take off and get picked up by the Sand Witch.' He glanced around, then at his wristwatch. 'But it's all taken too long now, today. We'll have to shoot the scene first thing tomorrow.'

The rest of the crew turned away with another general chorus of groans, while the director swung around to glower again at Red Cordell.

'The cost of replacing the club will be deducted from your pay, Cordell. And another thing – where did you get that sword with the rainbow blade?'

Red shrugged. 'Found it in Props. I thought it was kind of unusual.'

The director snorted. 'Kind of hokey, is what it is. Like something from a cereal packet. Get something that looks like a *sword*, for tomorrow.'

'Whatever you say, Dick,' Red replied.

The director's nostrils went faintly white as his face tightened. 'Stop pushing your luck, Cordell,' he snapped. 'It wouldn't be hard to get another actor for your few scenes. If we have to.'

Red's eyes glinted as he began to reply. But Karl, next to him, clamped a firm hand on his shoulder. 'Leave it, Red. It's never worth it.'

Red stopped, clenching his teeth with a grimace, turning away from the director who stalked off with a victorious smile. But then the giant Thagor, or Lupe, took a lumbering step forward.

'You had to play games,' he grumbled at Red. 'And now we got to do the damn thing tomorrow.'

Red smiled tightly. 'What's wrong, Loopy? Afraid you'll forget your lines by morning?'

The bigger man bunched his fists, swelling all the muscles of his arms and shoulders. 'Someday,' he growled, 'somebody should smash in that smart mouth of yours.'

7

Red did not appear to move. Yet a feeling came from him of springs coiling, and his pale eyes acquired a light that looked like eagerness.

'If you want to be that somebody, Loopy,' he said evenly, 'just say the word.'

The big man blinked, seeming to lean back slightly, something like doubt showing for an instant on his face. 'Yeah, well,' he said at last. 'Just watch it.'

As he wheeled and lumbered away, perhaps a little too quickly, Red's mocking smile reappeared. 'Mr Universe runner-up,' he said idly. 'Body of a gorilla, balls of a gnat.'

'They ain't all like that,' Karl told him. 'An' he's right, too. Someday bein' a smart-ass *is* gonna get you into trouble. No matter how tough you think you are.'

'I've *been* in trouble, Karl,' Red said lightly. 'Beats being bored, any time.'

Karl sighed. 'Sure, sure. I prob'ly said stupid things like that myself, when I was your age. Maybe you should go back to stunt work, Red. Get rid of all that excess energy.'

'Not me,' Red said as they turned to walk off the set, with the troll-monster man trailing behind. 'Acting pays better, and no broken bones.'

Karl shook his head. 'It don't pay better when you got to cough up for wrecked costumes. Or if you get fired.'

'I won't get fired, Karl,' Red told him. 'Tomorrow I'll be good and let Al here kill me just like the script says.'

The troll-monster man came up beside them at the mention of his name. 'You guys wanna get a beer, when you're changed?'

'Not this time,' Red said. 'Got a date.' He grinned at Karl. 'You probably did things like *that*, too, when you were my age.'

The older man grunted. 'It's a nice life, ain't it, kid? All fun an' games – pick a fight, laugh at the boss, a few girls on the side, never a care . . .'

'That's it, Karl,' Red said easily. 'Fun and games. Without them, life wouldn't be worth living.'

And none of the others noticed how, with those words, most of the amusement faded from the pale blue eyes.

*

8

Some while later, he was still looking unamused. In fact his expression had been thoroughly glum while he had stared at himself in the dressing-room mirror. He always hated it when people like Karl – older people who had been around and knew a few things – started getting serious. He hated it because lately he had started to suspect that they might be right, in their implied or spoken criticism of his life-style. Or at least that they might be right in pointing out that he couldn't go on like that – being aimless and irresponsible, two of the words most often used – for much longer. He wasn't far away from the watershed age of thirty. And after thirty, as far as he had always understood, the fun and games started coming to an end.

Sighing a deep sigh, he turned away from the mirror, pulling on a T-shirt to go with the jeans and Reeboks that were his normal street wear. As he tucked the shirt in, his gaze fell on the long slimness of the sword that he had carried, which was resting against the wall where his costume hung. His expression brightened a little as he picked it up, sliding the blade partway from the sheath, admiring the luminous, delicate play of colours on the metal.

Hokey? he thought, remembering the director's dismissive word. Never. It's beautiful. Strangely light and perfectly balanced, for all its length. And how had the makers done that, making it seem to glow, making the colours seem to move *within* the steel?

Smiling a half-smile, he reached up to where he had hung the short, midnight-blue cloak that was part of his costume. He remembered the cluttered corner of the Props room where he had been idly rummaging, at the studio, when he had found the sword. If it had been left under all that mess, he thought, it clearly hadn't been used for a long time, if ever. It would never be missed.

Right, sword, he said silently. If you're not wanted here, you can come with me.

Wrapping the cloak around the sheathed sword, in order to carry it on to the bus that would take him home, he sauntered smiling out of the dressing-room.

TWO

When she awoke, she found that she was lying in near-darkness on a heap of evil-smelling straw. At first she thought she might be in a stable, but the odours were wrong. So, too, was the shape of the room – if it *was* a room, she thought. The walls and the low, rounded ceiling seemed to have been carved from bare rock, except for part of one wall, made of heavy planking with a blank wooden door, where dim reddish light seeped in through the cracks. And rivalling the stink of the straw was the dankness of the stone around her, musty and stained, belying the fact that it had been a warm late-spring day in the city from which she had been taken.

She shivered briefly, less from the stony chill than from the memory of the icy, incredibly strong hands that had clamped on her throat from behind, skilfully compressing windpipe and arteries, plunging her into unconsciousness before she could bring any of her powers or her own lithe strength into action. She felt the lingering soreness in her throat – and with it a rising fury in her spirit. But since there was no one around to vent her fury on, she controlled it, setting it aside within her, to be brought out as a fuelling source when – *if* – anyone did appear.

Meanwhile, she lay still and considered her position. She had clearly been robbed, and left wearing only her light chemise. But more important, she was bound: heavy metal manacles, fastening her wrists uncomfortably behind her. And she knew that they were no ordinary manacles. She could sense a warmth deep within them – not a physical warmth that affected her flesh, but an unnatural essence at the very heart of the metal.

Warded, she thought, her heart sinking. And powerfully, so that the metal would not respond to her at all. But, even worse, the warding power uncannily reached *out* from the manacles. She could sense it surrounding and enveloping her to muffle and constrain her own powers, rendering her doubly helpless.

She wriggled to bring her legs beneath her, raising herself to a sitting position, carefully testing the strength of the irons on her wrists. I know someone possibly skinny enough to slip out of these, she thought. But not just yet. It was a time for waiting – to learn who had done this, and why, before she took steps to free herself and, perhaps, impose a proper punishment on her captors.

So she sat still, calming herself, smoothing out her tensions as she might another time have smoothed her hair. It was a rich, tawny blonde, though just then in something of a tangle since she had lost the jewelled combs and pins that had held it in a careful coiffure. If she had been standing, it would have waved and rippled down past her hips, soft and luxuriant. Her skin was also tawny in its own way, smooth as honey, glowing like soft bronze. Her eyes were emerald-green, wide and clear, her mouth was curved and generous, her hands were slim and shapely. And the thin chemise revealed a body that was in its splendid prime – exuberantly rounded, yet with a trim waist and long, shapely legs.

A few small lines appearing at the corners of her eyes, the edges of her mouth, the long sweep of her throat, showed that she had left her girlhood behind her. But otherwise the honey-bronze skin was almost unblemished – save for a peculiar mark in the deep cleft between her breasts, revealed by the chemise's low neckline. The mark looked slightly ridged, like a scar or perhaps a brand, and had certainly been placed there  by design. It consisted of two vertical curved lines coming to a point at the top, like a stylized image of a drop of water or a candle flame, in a simple circle.

For a long time she sat on the foul straw, composing and readying herself. As well as she could in the dimness she studied the details of the room, especially the planking of the door with its iron hinges. Of course it would be locked and barred – but she knew that if she could free herself from the unnatural restraint of the manacles it would offer her no more of a barrier than the straw. So she sat unmoving, waiting – ignoring the ache in her wrists just as she ignored the chill, the stink, the rustling of vermin in the straw. She even dozed now and then, brief drifting catnaps.

But she came fully awake, watchful and ready, when with a creak and a crash the door was suddenly flung open. There was a flare of torch-light that made her wince and blink. Then, through slitted eyes, she examined the six people who crowded in through the door.

Five of them seemed to be a little less than average height, but she could tell nothing more about their bodies. They all wore long heavy cloaks, with deep hoods and full sleeves, that covered every part of them, hiding their faces and hands, their shapes and gender, everything. Only the sixth person came in uncloaked so that she could see the details of his appearance, none of them pleasant or reassuring.

He was a tall, bony man with pale skin and long, lank, yellow hair. He wore narrow dark trousers, low boots, and a black leather tunic trimmed with a liverish green. Green, too, was his belt and the two sheaths fastened to it, one obviously containing a sword, the other a short sword or long dagger. And one side of the man's narrow face was ridged with shiny scar tissue as if it had been burned.

But the scarred one had one thing in common with his five companions. The hooded ones all had strange designs imprinted here and there on their cloaks – mostly abstract patterns, oddly disturbing to the eyes – and they also wore heavy metal amulets, with similar designs, on chains around their necks. A similar pendant hung from the scarred man's neck, and similar markings showed on parts of his clothing and weapons.

More wards and protections, she knew, obviously aimed at shielding them from her powers if she were somehow to free herself from the manacles. But we will see, she told herself fiercely. When it is time.

She watched expressionlessly as the scarred man stepped towards her. The man had seen her survey of the designs that covered him and the others, and he showed stained teeth in a cruel smile.

'See the magics we got on us?' he said. 'Feel the power in your irons? You'll get none of your witchings past that.'

She raised one eyebrow, coolly. 'Are you so sure of your sorceries?' Her voice grated slightly from the soreness of her throat.

'Not mine.' The man's short laugh mocked her. 'I got different talents – and your throat's likely reminding you of some of them. You maybe even heard of me. Name's Vanticor.'

If the name had been intended to unnerve her, it almost succeeded. Her eyes began to widen before she could control her expression, and she fought down a shiver. 'I have heard the name. A notorious assassin who prefers a blade in the back, a garrotte from behind.'

The man laughed again. 'Good to know the Sisterhood keeps in touch with things.'

'Sisterhood?' she repeated, raising both eyebrows.

The ugly smile twisted. 'Don't play games. I know your ring.' He held up his left hand, where on the smallest finger gleamed a delicate gold ring, the metal twined into a complex knot. 'And everybody knows about the witch-mark.'

He reached down to pull at the top of her chemise, exposing her breasts and the strange ridged design on the skin between them. But she did not move, or react in any way. She had seen the ring on his hand before he showed it, and she had assumed that he would have seen the mark on her skin. It did not seem to her that his knowing what she was made her position any more dangerous.

As long as he did not know – and he could not – *precisely* what she was.

The man, Vanticor, looked irritated by her lack of response. And behind him the hooded figures had begun to stir as if growing impatient. Releasing her, he stepped back, the smile becoming a snarl.

'Right, then, witch,' he rasped. 'It's good and dark now, no moon yet. So we can get going, out of here.'

'To where?' she demanded sharply. 'Why are you doing this?'

13

The man snickered, a grisly sound, but without replying turned to the others and muttered something inaudible, with unmistakable gestures towards her, the door, the unknown areas beyond it.

'Tell me where you're taking me!' she demanded again, her voice ragged as tension and fear threatened her self-control.

Vanticor turned back to her, eyes glinting orange in the torchlight. 'We're taking you for a ride in a cart – an ordinary farm cart, waiting outside. Something nobody'll look at twice. It'll get us all out of the city and along the river a ways, where we got boats waiting. And that's all you need to know right now.' His grin was savage. 'Nobody'll see you in the cart – nobody'll hear you, 'cause you'll be gagged. And if you try to make a noise, or to get away, you'll be hurt. I'll *maim* you, if I have to, to keep you still.' The orange-lit eyes roved over her. 'My orders say just keep you alive. Nothing says I got to keep you in one piece.'

Though her flesh crawled at the cold viciousness of the threat, she kept her gaze and her voice as steady as she could. 'What do you *want* with me?'

Vanticor laughed his mocking laugh. 'Me? Nothing. I'm just taking you to someone. But what *he* wants, lady, is just about everything you got.'

The words echoed in her mind, doom-laden, as Vanticor reached down and roughly drew her to her feet. Drawing from within his tunic a slim, wicked dagger, hiltless like a throwing knife, he gestured towards her, the dagger's point impelling her to stumble through the straw towards the door. The cloaked figures had preceded her, and beyond the door, in what looked like a low tunnel hacked from the rock, she saw the five of them hurrying on ahead, only vaguely visible in the half-darkness that did not seem to slow them down.

Behind her, with the torch and the dagger, Vanticor urged her on. Briefly she tensed her muscles against the grip of the manacles, half-frowning with intentness – while the mark between her breasts began eerily to glow as if lit from within. But then she let her arms go limp behind her, the glow on her skin faded, and she allowed herself to be driven forward, bare feet stumbling now and then on the tunnel's stony floor. Their route took them into another, wider tunnel, and then another, where a chilly, foul-smelling wetness also covered the floor. Finally they came to a shadowed place where the torch-light showed a vertical shaft stretching up into the blackness, with steps cut crudely into its sides. She knew that she could not climb the shaft without the use of her hands – but then Vanticor shouldered past her, jammed the torch into a crevice, grabbed a thick handful of her hair and began to climb ahead, hoisting and dragging her up the steps behind him with amazing strength.

The pain from her hair, and from her bruised feet as she scrambled for footholds, combined with the fear flooding through her, threatened to swamp her spirit. She fought that inner battle all the way up the climb – until at last she found herself with relief on level ground with a fresh warm breeze blowing around her.

There Vanticor found another small torch from somewhere and fumbled to light it. Its flame showed her that they were in a small, empty building that looked deserted. And when he pushed her out ahead of him, knife in hand, she saw the dim shapes of other low, shabby buildings all around them. And before her, on the broken remnants of a once-cobbled alley, she saw the shape of a small farm cart with a horse or mule harnessed to it.

Which was to take her out secretly through a city gate, Vanticor had said. And then on to some kind of boat. Clearly her captors would not risk taking her to the city's waterfront, which was always awake and populous even late at night. So they were going this way to a less visible, more private stretch of river. And from there . . .

Fear was still clamouring along her nerve-ends, but her battle with it was being aided by a resurgence of her anger. She would *not* go quietly, she affirmed to herself, whatever they threatened. There would be a moment. There had to be. When they would relax, thinking her helpless, defeated. If she appeared immobilized by fear, that moment might come sooner. She guessed that her focus on her inner struggle with fear had already given the impression that she was cowed and unresisting. So she remained that way as a soiled cloth was bound roughly over her mouth and a larger cloth smelling of horses was wrapped around her body. Then Vanticor lifted her into the cart, which she found was partly full of a sweet root vegetable that was among her favourites. The familiarity of the fragrance almost brought tears to her eyes.

But she quelled them, feeling the cart sway and tremble as the five cloaked figures climbed silently in, presumably while Vanticor took the driver's seat. The mule clopped away, the cart creaking and wheels rattling over the broken roadway. One of the hooded ones pushed her down flat, then they all heaped the vegetables over her. Half-buried, she lay fighting her fear, focusing her anger. In a moment she began to make soft, almost inaudible sounds that, if they had been heard over the cart's noise, would have been taken for sobs.

But she was not crying. She was singing.

She knew – or desperately hoped – that her captors would grow bored and inattentive. And she was preparing. Of course she could not complete the song, the incantation, in that position. The warding power within the manacles still enveloped her, and would restrain and stifle the incantation, preventing it from extending out from her. At the same time, she felt that she could probably free herself from the manacles – but then she would have no time to sing the whole of a complex incantation. So she was preparing. She had begun the song, begun the shaping of magical forces. When she freed herself from the manacles, she would need merely to sing the final phrase – to bring herself what she would need.

Her problem then would be the wards her captors wore, protecting them from her witch-power. So she had decided, unflinchingly, that she would fight her way to freedom another way. Before trusting to her fleetness of foot, she would fight not with witchery but with a physical weapon. The incantation, the song, would bring her the weapon she would need.

Because of who and what she was, she knew just where to seek it – a very special, very effective weapon that she could wield with ease. And a muscle jumped in her jaw as she prepared herself, half-buried in the rattling cart, and sang her song.

The incantation took only a few minutes to complete, save for the final syllables. She could feel it within her, an internal pressure, a small concentration of indefinable power, waiting for release. The cart by then was rolling over smoother stone: they had come to undamaged streets, no doubt drawing closer to the city gate. From somewhere near by she heard the muffled sounds of voices raised in song or argument or bellowed laughter, unmistakable sounds that had to emanate from behind the doors of a tavern that knew no such thing as closing time.

A tavern, she thought, where there might be men who would help a woman in trouble. Especially if she were attractive and wearing only a light chemise. So let it be now, she prayed. If there are gods listening, let the moment I need be *now*.

In the next moment it seemed that her vague and undirected prayer had been answered. She heard the heavy tramp of boots on stone, and a voice raised in an authoritative shout.

'Stop, there – you in the cart!'

Around her the cloaked figures stirred tensely. Hardly breathing, she heard Vanticor's cold voice replying to the challenge, heard the boots of men gathering by the cart.

'Step down,' she heard the other voice say. 'We are searching vehicles that approach the city gates – by the prince's order.'

Militia, she thought, hope flaring within her as she listened to Vanticor explaining that he was merely conveying a group of pilgrims from a rural order, for whom he had been acting as guide during their trip to the city . . . Within the cloth that wrapped her she could see the bright torchlight around the cart, could hear the mutters about 'a lot of monks' from the militiamen. Then her hopes surged higher as the cloaked figures were again ordered out of the cart, and as they slowly began to obey.

She took the chance then to lift her head, to wriggle silently up out of the covering of cloth and vegetables. As far as she

17

could see, there were only four or five militiamen by the cart – but they were all armoured and helmeted, well armed with crossbows and swords, looking tough and watchful. And the cart had indeed been stopped only a long stone's throw from the door of a tavern whose apparently large and noisy clientele she had heard enjoying themselves.

There would be no better moment. Her good fortune was astonishing, but also energizing. She felt the power of the incantation quiver within her, awaiting its completion. But for a moment she set it aside, sitting up slowly in the cart. First she had to reach within herself for another magical process, one that was very special and familiar, and one that she could perform even in the cart, because it did not need to reach *beyond* her own being, and so could occur within the constraint of the warded manacles. To free her, she hoped, from their grip.

And then she would complete the incantation, and do battle with the weapon she would call to her . . .

THREE

It was early evening by the time Red Cordell reached the large, ramshackle house where he rented a room, as did several other young hopefuls who were seeking to fulfil ambitions or realize dreams. By then the tensions and angers of Red's working day had more or less evaporated, and his thoughts were full of what awaited him that evening. Some inexpensive food, some ditto drinks, and the otherwise gratis attentions of a lissom aspirant actress. And how'll *that* do for using up excess energy, he said silently to the absent Karl.

Inside the gloomy old house he closed the door and bounded up the broad staircase. He was only half-way up when he was halted by a raucous voice. A woman's voice, from the back of the house mostly occupied by a kitchen of generously old-fashioned size.

'That you, Red? Want a coffee?'

He smiled to himself. Coffee would be welcome, as would the continuing motherliness of his elderly landlady. She offered the strongest coffee and the most kindly nature of any landlady he had ever known, and was the least likely to turn sour when he let the rent slip a little during times of unemployment. Besides, he liked her. She was someone he could really talk to.

Some day, he thought, the smile growing sardonic, I'll get a shrink to tell my troubles to, like all the stars do. Till then, I have a landlady.

'Down in a minute!' he yelled, and ran the rest of the way up to his room.

His tenancy gave him use of the kitchen, for his infrequent cooking, and a share of the bathroom with the other residents. So his own room, itself, was not a large room, and was minimally furnished with bed, table, chair, tiny TV, and an abundance of books and clothing. There were shelves for the

19

books and a closet for the clothes, but most of them had none the less come to rest on the floor. Stepping through the clutter with practised ease, Red dropped the long narrow bundle of the sword on his bed, glanced at himself assessingly – as actors do – in the full-length mirror on the wall, then turned to go back downstairs for his coffee.

'Can't stay long, Ryla,' he said as he breezed into the kitchen, where a steaming cup awaited him on the scrubbed pine table. 'Have to be at Eve's by eight.'

The old woman by the counter, pouring herself a cup of the glutinously black fluid that she called coffee, gave a laugh that was almost a cackle. 'Make her wait. She'll appreciate you more.'

Red blew on his coffee, sipped, winced, grinned. 'She appreciates me enough. If I make her wait, she may not pay for supper.'

This time the laugh was definitely a cackle as old Ryla hobbled to the table. Red knew that she had once been something of a dancer, which explained why she rented rooms to young folk with theatrical ambitions or pretensions. And she had been something of a beauty, as well, which still showed in the handsome bones of her face. Red had no idea exactly how old she was, but obviously she was old enough to be white-haired, stooped, excessively wrinkled, and bone-thin to the point of appearing withered. Yet her hazel eyes always sparkled with life and humour, and her energies were as boundless as her fascination with her young tenants' lives. Perhaps especially Red's.

So he sipped his potent coffee and regaled her with the excitements of his day. She laughed at Red's intentional mistake over the director's name, but she grew more serious as the rest of the tale unfolded.

'You be careful, sonny,' she said at last. 'You'll find the work harder to come by if you get a reputation for being difficult.'

'It's Dirk the Dick who has the reputation – for being a jerk,' Red said lightly. 'No one'll listen if *he* badmouths me.'

She shook her head, her thick white hair remaining immobile in its complex arrangement, held up by countless pins and combs. 'He's a *director*. Some people will listen. Maybe they'll be right to do so, as long as you keep playing the fool.' She smiled with fondness and concern. 'Red, it's an old saying but a true one. Nobody survives in the business without HBT.'

'And what's that?' he asked, as he was supposed to do.

She grinned, dentures gleaming. 'High Bullshit Tolerance.'

As he leaned back, laughing, her grin faded. 'It's funny, but it's true. You have to learn to put up with a *lot* more than you do. Like everyone else.'

'Sure.' His smile twisted into a sardonic grimace. 'Everyone up to their necks in it, trying not to make waves.'

Ryla sighed. 'Maybe it is like that. Or . . . maybe Karl was right, Red. Maybe you should go back to stuntwork, while you can.'

'Ryla!' He grinned ironically. 'I would have thought you'd tell me to stay away from all those dangerous deeds.'

The old hazel eyes regarded him steadily. 'But isn't that what you're always looking for, Red? The excitement of danger?'

He held her gaze for a moment, then his eyes dropped. 'Are you going to start on that again?'

'It's time,' she told him firmly. 'You're at some kind of crossroads here – I can feel it. Maybe you'll never be an actor, because you won't take the crap. But you were *good* at stuntwork, and you could be one of the best. From what I know of you, Red, it's like your whole life has been designed to aim you in that direction.'

He frowned. 'I've wanted to be an actor since I was a kid.'

'Have you? You've told me what you were best at, in drama school and after. *Action*, Red, not emotion. Movement and gymnastics. Riding horses. Taking falls. Studying all that martial art stuff.'

'You forgot fencing,' Red said lightly. 'I got fairly good at that too.'

She nodded. 'As I say. All the *physical* side.'

'You need that stuff too,' he said defensively, 'even for Shakespeare.'

Ryla waved a dismissive hand. 'You *may* be a good actor. You've never had a part big enough for anyone to know. But

21

really, Red, down deep, you've never wanted to be an actor. You want to be a hero.'

He dropped his gaze again, staring silently into his coffee-cup. And the old woman reached over with a bony hand and tousled his russet-red curls.

'Poor boy,' she said softly. 'Another day you might have put on a lovely uniform and ridden off to a glorious war, all horses and swords and swashbuckling. But nobody swashes buckles any more.'

'Actors do.' His voice was as quiet as hers. 'Maybe a pretend hero is better than nothing.' He forced a grin. 'Maybe some-day *I* can get to be Thagor the Invincible.'

'Quite an ambition,' she said flatly.

For a fleeting second the expression on his face went bleak and empty. Then he found his grin again, gulped the rest of his coffee and got to his feet.

'Anyway, thanks, Ryla. For the coffee and the peptalk. I'll see you tomorrow night and tell you how much of Dirk's bullshit I was able to tolerate.'

Some while later, Red was wandering back to his room after his shower, wearing only a towel tucked around his waist in the usual unconcerned way of Ryla's tenants. He had stayed a long time under the shower, keeping it fiercely hot, as if trying to scald something out of his system. Something like the aftermath of Ryla's words. More home truths, making the same demands on him that had always been made, by parents, teachers, instructors. Straighten up. Settle down. Be sensible. Learn discipline. All that. And while he knew that they said these things because they wanted to help – and that they were probably right – still he resisted.

From his earliest teens, his watchword had been: There has to be more to life than this.

So he had spent his youth upsetting and annoying people by being wild, irresponsible, restless, foolhardy, and the rest. He had good looks, charm, tireless energy, and athlete's reflexes and co-ordination, and not a drop of anything resembling caution. He was always ready with a laugh, an escapade, a challenge. He had never lacked for company in his hell-raising or for female company at other times. He had been admired, loved, sought after, fought with, wept over. He had had a terrific time.

But more recently, with the big three-oh looming towards him, he had begun to take stock of himself a little, now and then, and not to like it much. His parents were dead, he had no siblings, he had no close friends or confidants except maybe Ryla, and his so-called career kept being stalled by his own behaviour. He felt that he was adrift, aimlessly, on treacherously thin surfaces. And often he seemed to hear a clear-sighted part of his mind repeating his old motto with an entirely new emphasis: There has to be more to life than *this*.

Inside his room he slammed the door and looked around for something to divert his mood. He knew that later on he would feel better, aided by a few drinks, supper, and the compliant body of that night's partner. But he didn't like to start off a night in an evil mood. So when his eye fell on the sword, lying on his bed, he grinned with relief at the return of lightheartedness, recalling the end of his day's work. He unwrapped the narrow bundle and flung the short cloak around his shoulders. Turning to the full-length mirror, he grinned more widely at the incongruity of the old-style cloak fastened with a narrow chain at his throat and the fluffy striped towel still wrapped around his hips. Drawing the glowing sword, he struck a mock-heroic pose.

'Thagor the Invincible,' he said aloud, making his voice sonorous. But from nowhere came an echo of old Ryla's words. *Quite an ambition.*

He felt the lightheartedness start to drain away, and fought to retain it. Brandishing the sword, he lowered his voice to approximate the rumbling bass of some beer commercials.

'Thagor the Towel-butt,' he intoned. 'Red the Unready.'

That brought some of his smile back. Also, the new pose had somehow altered the play of colours within the metal of the swordblade. They seemed to be shifting and shimmering at a quicker rate. Really pretty, he thought, watching them in the mirror.

Until he noticed that it was the air around the sword that was shimmering. His reflection, too, was wobbling and

23

shivering, like the way heat-waves make things look shivery through a telescopic lens.

He blinked, turned his head, and suddenly felt not a heat-wave but a rush of cold that goose-pimpled his half-naked body. The whole *room* was shivering. And everything within it – trembling and growing hazy . . .

And then the room disappeared.

For an instant it felt as if he was falling down an endless shaft, a bottomless well. The instant seemed to last longer than all the other instants of his life put together, yet even so he did not have time to draw breath to scream. Only to start opening his mouth.

To find himself standing in semi-darkness on a street in an unknown city.

Or so he gathered, after his first dazed look around. The darkness was relieved only by guttering torches, not by any sort of civilized light. The street under his bare feet was not asphalt or concrete but made of wide, flat blocks of dirty stone. The buildings looming vaguely through the darkness looked like no buildings he had ever seen. Foreign, but more than foreign. And some distance away, half-lit by other flickering torches held on posts like lamps, he saw what looked like a high, ponderous stone wall, with an immense wooden gate barred and braced by gleaming metal.

Then his disbelieving glance focused on what lay directly in front of him. A primitive cart, with a horse or something. People inside the cart, and other people standing at the side.

And some of them had *swords*, for God's sake. And . . . were those crossbows?

Then one of the swordsmen, also holding a torch, shifted his light a little, and despite the warmth of the night Red felt cold again.

The people with the swords and crossbows and torches looked like some kind of soldiers out of history, with weird helmets and body armour. Facing them was a tall, bony character with a scarred face whose hands rested tensely on the hilts of *two* swords, it seemed, at his sides. And climbing

24

out of the cart were some very spooky-looking types in long-sleeved robes with hoods that hid their faces.

Red took an automatic step closer, trying to see more clearly, trying to hear what was being said. Two more of the spooky hooded figures were in the cart, preparing to climb down, seemingly absorbed in what was going on with the others. No one, the hooded ones or the soldiers, had apparently noticed Red's materialization on the street.

But someone else had.

A third person in the cart, lying low in shadow. A woman, he saw, raising her head and pulling a cloth away from her face – whose eyes went wide, jaw dropping, as she caught sight of Red. Startled in his own way, he stared at her, seeing that she was a very old woman who looked a little like Ryla, his landlady. This one also had lots of thick white hair, hanging down around her in a wild mass, with a deeply wrinkled face and an incredibly skinny body.

As he stared, she closed her mouth, glanced carefully at the two figures in the cart with her, saw they had their backs to her, and began slowly and stealthily creeping towards the back of the cart. Red just watched, unmoving, still half-paralysed by the shock of finding himself impossibly where he was. He was obviously dreaming, he thought, though he couldn't remember falling asleep. Or maybe Ryla had put something hallucinogenic into his coffee, as an unlikely practical joke.

At the same time he was peripherally aware of other things around him – the warmth of the night, the mixture of the unfamiliar and unlovely stinks drifting on the breeze, the nearby sounds of loud talk and laughter and bottles clinking that spoke of a bar or pub in full flow. But his primary focus remained on the scene in and around the cart – especially on the aged woman's slow, furtive movements.

She's *escaping*, he suddenly thought. And all his nerve endings twitched as that realization made him at last aware of the atmosphere around the cart, the tension, the potential violence that hovered over the group.

He took another step forward, unconsciously tightening his grip on the hilt of the sword that he still carried, its scabbard in his other hand. The old woman came to the edge of the cart, slowly and cautiously turning to clamber down. But as she did so from somewhere on her person came an audible *clank* of metal on metal.

The sound made the two hooded figures in the cart with her start to wheel around. And then Red became certain that he had somehow been plunged into a hallucinatory dream.

The old woman at once sat up, showing that she held in one hand what looked like primitive handcuffs, two curved wrist-bands linked by a short iron chain seemingly too large to hold her narrow hands and bird-like wrists. And while the two hooded ones were still turning towards her, every part of her body from head to foot started to tremble and blur with some kind of impossible vibration.

Then she was gone.

Where she had been, there sat a staggeringly beautiful woman with long wild hair like dark gold. A woman wearing only something short and filmy like a slip.

Red gaped, feeling chilled by the thought that he might have toppled into delusion or delirium. *No*, he thought. It's not possible. I just didn't see her clearly before, in the shadows.

By then the two hooded figures in the cart were reaching for the woman with hands hidden in the sleeves of their robes. But they did not make contact. The woman came smoothly to her feet and struck at them – wielding, Red saw with another jolt, the metal cuffs that the old woman had held. The hooded ones dodged the blow, but the cart heaved and jounced with the sudden movement so that they stumbled into one another. And while they were off balance the woman sprang from the cart, towards Red, her face taut with mingled fury and desperation.

'Give me the sword!' she yelled at him.

By then the others at the side of the cart had seen her sudden leap. Red heard the scar-faced man shout something like 'bitch' or maybe 'witch', and start after her with the other three hooded ones. But with shouts of their own the armoured soldiers tried to block their way – and metal glinted as they and the scarred man drew their weapons. Suddenly they were

26

in a wild mêlée, with yells and curses and the ring of steel on steel. Above it all Red heard the scarred man yelling 'get *away*!', presumably at the hooded ones, who started to move back from the brawl. But the two from the cart were instead leaping down in pursuit of the woman, with strange loping bounds.

Dream or delirium, it no longer mattered. The sudden flare of violence brought adrenalin flooding through him, flushing away his near-paralysis. He moved forward, his eyes oddly bright, echoing the brightness of the sword. The woman glanced back at the hooded pair coming after her, then whirled to confront Red again, her hair swirling wildly around her.

'Give me the *sword*!' she cried.

Red smiled. 'Not a chance, lady,' he said – and brushed past her to face her pursuers.

FOUR

They slowed as they saw Red move to oppose them, then crept forward, crouching, moving apart. Red swept the sword from side to side warningly, standing balanced and ready. At once the two of them leaped, both trying to get around the sword to reach the blonde woman. Red swung the sword at once, who dodged back, then pivoted smoothly to drive a flashing kick into the groin of the second one.

It was a powerful and precise kick, but instead of howling and doubling up with pain, the hooded figure seemed merely jolted as his rush was stopped, only grunting slightly as he moved back and away. Balls of steel or none at all, Red thought, as the two stood still for a moment before him. He was only distantly aware of the continuing mêlée by the cart, the bellowing and clanging metal – but then he and his opponents were distracted by another tumult and an eruption of light, behind Red, showing him the reflected glitter of eyes deep within the dark hoods that faced him.

The new tumult contained a great many voices, male and female, yelling and laughing. Instantly the two facing Red turned and fled, running for the nearest shadows in their weird crouching lope. And Red then saw the other hooded ones, and the scar-faced man, also in full flight from their battle – leaving two of the soldiers on the ground, bleeding, with their comrades stooping over them. Turning, Red saw that the burst of light and noise behind him came from the bar or pub whose sounds he had heard, and whose occupants had been drawn out by the fight. on the street. And the scantily dressed blonde, Red saw, had gone to meet them, and was talking intently to a bulky, broad-shouldered man, while the rest of the crowd went to stare at the four soldiers or just milled around.

Red went to join the woman, irresistibly drawn to her,

noting that she was as oblivious of her semi-clothed state as of the occasional leer from men in the crowd. Clearly she was describing the night's adventure to the big man, holding up the manacles and rattling them, while he shook his head gravely. Red saw that he was leaning on a straight stick about as tall as he was, like a hiker's staff or perhaps a quarterstaff – except that it glinted in the light as if it was made of metal. But he shifted it lightly enough to his other hand, to take the manacles from the woman and inspect them.

'You did well to escape from these, my lady,' he was saying as Red approached them. The man's voice was deep and hoarse, and surprisingly muted to have issued from that vast chest. For as he drew closer Red could see that the man was not merely broad-shouldered. Within his loose tunic and baggy trousers he was enormously broad in every way. Almost inhumanly so, for the proportions looked unnatural – since he was only a little shorter than Red but about three times wider and more massive. Even his face was broad, what could be seen of it beneath a thatch of steel-grey hair and above a straggle of dark beard. But his wide-set eyes were visible enough, large and dark – and bright with merriment as he turned to regard Red, with a grin that was as broad as the rest of him.

Red returned the grin, but his gaze was drawn as by a magnet from the bulky man to the blonde beauty beside him. He had to force himself to raise his eyes and look at her face – seeing then that her eyes were startlingly green and were studying him quizzically yet with an impish humour. There were a thousand things he might have said, or asked. But by then he had begun to revel in the hallucination or dream, enjoying it as if it was a film or a stage play in which he had a part. And what was the point of asking questions in a dream? So he merely made his grin shift a little, to become more nonchalant and slightly roguish. He let his gaze drift down to her body and up again, noting but ignoring the oddly shaped weal or scar in her cleavage. And when he spoke, it was in his lightest and easiest manner.

He merely said, 'Would you like to borrow my cloak?'

The impish amusement on her face grew brighter and more

wicked. She laughed once, a throaty chuckle. And her gaze swept up and down over Red as boldly as his had examined her.

'I think you need it more,' she said in a melodious contralto.

And only then did Red realize that while he had arrived wherever he was wearing a cloak and a towel, in the flurry of action he had managed to lose the towel. He tried to wrap the cloak around himself, realized he was still holding the sword though he had dropped its sheath somewhere, clutched at the cloak with his other hand. The woman laughed again, the bulky man gave a hoarse snort that must also have been laughter, and from the crowd near by several others joined in.

'An unusual costume even for an outlander,' the bulky man said.

'Oh, he is no outlander, Krost,' the woman said. She was still smiling, but the quizzical look remained in her eyes – along with something that might have been concern. 'He is from an even more distant place, and not by his own wish. He is going to need a great deal of explanation.'

'And some trousers,' the man named Krost said merrily.

That caused more laughter from those onlookers who had not wandered back inside to resume drinking. Red flung them a glare, seeing as he did so that the two uninjured soldiers were marching in their direction with looks that said they had serious, official questions to ask. Wait'll they hear *my* answers, Red thought, looking around for his sword's sheath so as not to confront officialdom with a naked blade. As he looked, he glimpsed a convulsive movement from the midst of the shadows some way beyond the torchlight.

From there flew something small and glinting, some kind of metallic missile hurled with vicious force, either at the woman or at the larger target of Krost.

Red never had moved so swiftly in his life. He flung himself at the other two, hands slamming against them to push them out of the way. The woman staggered back, half-falling with the jarring impact. But when Red's other hand struck the bulky man's shoulder, it was like trying to push a cliff. The

30

massive body did not shift by the tiniest fraction – as if he was rooted, or composed of lead, immovable.

Even so, the missile did not strike him – because Red's arm was in the way. A hammer-blow was followed by sudden electric agony, and then Red was staring at his forearm where something seemed to have sprouted like a ghastly growth. A knife, with a slim haft and no crosspiece on the hilt, a throwing-knife whose narrow blade had speared entirely through his arm.

He felt his legs grow rubbery. The knife had grazed bone as it stabbed through his arm, and the pain was ferocious, on top of all the other shocks of that impossible night. He felt Krost's huge hand grip his good arm, to steady him. Then he felt the soft hands of the woman – and new agony exploded in his arm as she drew out the blade.

'Explanations and things can wait,' he heard her say in a matter-of-fact voice. 'Let's get him inside.'

He felt himself sag. But Krost hoisted him up, one-handed, as easily as Red would have lifted an infant. 'Right,' he heard Krost say. 'What he needs before anything is a *drink*.'

First, though, they had to deal with the two soldiers, returning after having dashed off in pursuit of the knife-thrower and finding nothing. After the blonde had taken them aside and spoken to them briefly, the soldiers began a good deal of deferential saluting and bowing. Then she and Krost took Red into the noisy tavern. Krost held Red's uninjured arm all the way across the room, towards an empty table, and several times his feet left the floor although Krost showed no signs of strain. Finally seated at the table, trying to deal with the blazing pain from his wound, Red merely stared at his two new companions in dazed silence. And with some disbelief – as when a waiter in stained shirt and breeches arrived with drinks and tried to move Krost's metal staff, leaning idly against the table. The waiter was no small man, yet he needed both hands to lift it and even then he was struggling, although Krost had been waving the staff around as if it was bamboo.

And then Krost, whose unnatural weight had already shown itself, proved it again when he sat down on a huge

31

solid bench made of thick reinforced planking – and it creaked and bent like wickerwork beneath him.

But that was nothing, in terms of disbelief, compared with what the woman did. When Red was seated, clutching his injury with blood seeping through his fingers, she peered at his ashen face and said: 'I'll get something from the kitchen for him.' And then she did the unbelievable thing that she had seemed to do before. Her splendid body began to blur with a weird all-over vibration, and suddenly Red was looking at the withered, white-haired old lady that he had seen in the cart, stooped and frail, wearing a floor-length dress of some heavy grey material. As if the lovely blonde had *turned into* the old lady.

She didn't even say *Shazam*, Red thought wildly. He could feel hysterical laughter trying to rise within him, and to quell it he reached shakily with his good hand for one of the drinks, in a tall pewter mug, and gulped. The brown fluid inside smelled and tasted like strong ale, with a bite like battery acid and a bitter, grainy after-taste – and it did wonders for the different kinds of shock assailing him. Including the disturbing fact that Krost had seemed wholly unsurprised by the woman's transformation, just as people at neighbouring tables had merely glanced over with mild curiosity before returning to their drinks. Thinking about that, Red returned to his, gulping again, feeling pain and shock being thrust back a little. That gave him the strength to try a crooked grin in the direction of Krost, who was watching him with interest over the rim of his own mug.

'This's one helluva dream,' Red said, lifting his drink in a half-toast.

'It is not a dream, friend,' the big man rumbled.

'That's what people in dreams always say,' Red told him.

Krost shrugged. 'You will come to know, soon enough. And for one who thinks he is dreaming, you did well out there tonight – taking the knife meant for Aurilia or me. We are in your debt, for that.'

Red lowered the mug, starting to feel slightly muzzy. 'My pleasure,' he said wryly. 'And that's her name – Aurilia? Or do I say *their* names?'

He heard a short laugh like a cackle, and turned to see the old woman hobbling up to the table, skinny arms laden with several objects including a pair of dirty, much-patched trousers. 'These come from a stable lad, about your size,' she said, dropping the garment on Red's lap. 'But first, give me that arm. And take a pull of ale against the pain.'

Red needed no more prompting – but needed to empty the mug, as the old woman bathed his wound with some fluid from a jug she had brought. A herbal infusion, she said, which she had mixed in the tavern's kitchen. It was steaming hot, with a sharpness in it that bit like acid down to the core of his wound, so that it took every speck of Red's will to remain silent, as he was determined to do in that company. But then the old woman, Aurilia, bandaged the wound, and the pain receded to an almost bearable level of burning and throbbing.

Aurilia patted him on the shoulder with a wrinkly smile. 'That was brave – but you could have groaned a little. You have already proved your courage well enough tonight.' Her bony hand tightened on his shoulder. 'I will not forget how you defended me.'

'Me neither,' Red said, slightly slurring his words. 'But then I often remember my dreams.'

'He is certain he is dreaming,' Krost put in drily.

'Or insane, or on a weird acid trip,' Red said, almost to himself. 'Or in a film studio where someone's playing a very elaborate joke.' He grimaced. 'Or maybe I've died, and this is some kind of purgatory or limbo.'

Aurilia shook her white head slowly. 'I don't know what some of those words mean,' she told him, 'but you must believe me. You are not dreaming or having delusions. You are . . . in a different reality.' She paused, her eyes – as green in that form as the other – softening with concern. 'And I believe I know why. Will you . . . will you tell us your name?'

Red blinked. 'Right, sorry – we haven't been introduced. My name's Cordell. Red Cordell.'

Her face went very still. 'As I thought. As I feared. And yet . . . could there be purpose behind misfortune?'

Krost, frowning, announced that he did not understand,

and Red thought that made two of them. So Aurilia began explaining, with a lot of mystic gibberish about other Spheres, and how he had been brought to that Sphere from his own by a sort of freak accident. He was somehow linked to the *sword*, she said, and it was the sword that she had wanted. But she had accidentally got them both, when she had reached out to bring the sword to her – with what she called a song of summoning.

Magic.

And that was where Red stopped her.

'Enough,' he said harshly. 'I don't need all this. Now I *know* it's a dream or some kind of really crazy game. So let's just move on to whatever's next, before I wake up.'

Aurilia studied him with an odd sympathy. 'So you come from a Sphere that denies magic. That will make it harder for you . . .'

'Just *leave* it!' Red snarled.

'Cordell.' Krost leaned forward, his dark eyes intent. 'Let her explain things to you. We mean you no harm. This is the city of Quamarr where the prince has his palace, and we are acquainted with him. You can trust us. There is nothing to fear . . .'

'Fear?' Red repeated tautly. 'I'm not *afraid*. Just confused and shaken up, like people get in these kinds of dreams.' He waved a hand slightly unsteadily, with a half-grin. 'Just let me get dressed, and then we'll see what happens next.'

It was something of a struggle, pulling on the shabby trousers with only one hand, but the other two left him to it. Aurilia turned to Krost, saying something more about the sword, but Red resolutely refused to listen. Because he knew that beneath the bravado he *was* afraid – and growing more so.

It was the oldest, most deeply rooted, most primitive human fear of all. The fear of the unknown. The fear of Mysterious Powers, dark, mighty, unfathomable forces that made helpless pawns out of ordinary people. And the fear arose from the fact that he was in the midst of equations that could not be worked out, impossible paradoxes that could not be resolved.

34

On the one side, all the unbelievabilities about Aurilia and Krost, plus her casual talk about Spheres and magic and so on, meant that it *had* to be unreal – a dream or a delusion. But on the other side . . . Red had never known a dream that seemed so consistent within its own terms, with none of the surrealism, the jumbled jump-cuts and illogicality of dreaming. Nor had he ever known a dream in which all the tastes and smells and textures were so vivid. The grainy bitterness of the drink, the coarse cloth of the trousers on his skin, the unabashed stinks around him of sweat, spilled beer, and oily smoke from the many lamps and braziers. Not to mention the undeniable throbbing of his wound.

And if it all turned out instead to be a joke or a game, it would be an absurdly expensive one in terms of sets and players. And one that had become seriously unfunny, out on the street, with the confrontation and swordplay, and that knife coming out of the darkness.

So if it wasn't a dream or game . . . But once again his mind circled around and sheered away from the conclusion. It *couldn't* be real. His mind would not make that prodigious leap to a place where he could accept the unacceptable.

He was aware of Aurilia turning towards him, but he ignored her, letting his gaze drop. That did not help, for he merely then saw the supposed cause of his trouble – the luminous sword, on the floor at his feet, returned to its sheath which Aurilia had presumably retrieved. Closing his eyes against the sight of it, he let his head sink down on to his arms, welcoming the new fire that the pressure sent through his wound. He could deal with mere pain – but he could not deal with the other feelings, where his mind seemed to be crouched on the lip of a chasm, assailed by undeniable impossibilities . . .

'May I intrude?'

Red thought that the interruption, in an almost childishly treble voice, had come from another waiter. Blearily he lifted his head to encourage the ordering of more drink, with its promise of oblivion. But he became aware of a tension within his two companions – and then he saw the one who had spoken, and gaped with surprise.

35

He saw a small, balding man with a funny tall hat in his hand and a smile on his face. It was a cheerful smile, though just then also a diffident one. Red almost felt like smiling himself at the little man's smooth pink cheeks and froth of receding white hair, his overlong blue coat and wrinkled blue trousers, and his general air of boyish innocence and kindliness and good humour.

Except then Red saw the newcomer's eyes. Which had to be the eyes of another dream figment – because the irises were a deep rich purple, and the pupils were a pure, shocking white.

The little man inclined his head in a polite almost-bow to Aurilia and Krost. 'Forgive me,' he said quickly. 'I understand that the young man has been injured, and is an outlander – perhaps feeling a little overwhelmed by the events of this night . . .'

'How is it your concern?' Aurilia said carefully, with an edge of curiosity.

The little man looked abashed. 'Forgive me,' he said again, 'for not making that clear. I am a healer. I hope I am not wrong in assuming—' he glanced at the bandage on Red's arm— 'that you, my lady, do not include healing hands among your many gifts?'

Aurilia paused, sorting through the syntax. 'You're not wrong,' she said with a cool half-smile. 'You claim that ability, do you?'

'Indeed.' The little man nodded, smiling. 'I am Hallifort, my lady, Hallifort the Healer. I have had some dealings with some of the Sisterhood, in the past – perhaps you know of me?'

She shook her head. 'No. But if you can help our friend, we shall be grateful.'

But as the little man turned towards Red, Krost leaned forward, one great hand clenched into a fist like a boulder. 'And if you intend any treachery,' he rumbled, 'you will regret it.'

The warning sounded even more ominous because it was spoken so quietly in that hoarse bass. But the little man merely widened his smile, showing tiny white teeth. 'I have no doubt of that, sir. But I wish only to heal.'

He reached out with a small hand and placed it gently on the bandage on Red's forearm. Red started to wince and draw away, then stopped. The hand seemed oddly hot, even through the bandage, but its touch did not hurt in the slightest. Nor was there any pain when the little man slipped his other hand under the injury, lifting the arm slightly between both hands. To Red it felt as if his arm had been gently dipped into some incredibly soothing analgesic. The burning and throbbing simply died away. Even the livid core of the pain, where the knife had gashed the bone, faded and vanished.

No less gently, the little man unwrapped the bandage – and Red gaped, dumbfounded. Just as the pain had disappeared, so had the wound. The skin of his arm was unmarked, the flesh renewed, made whole.

More damn *magic*, Red thought, and jerked his arm out of the little man's grasp.

The man, Hallifort, shook his head gravely. 'It is a dangerous battle that you are trying to fight, young man. You must not seek to deny the undeniable. This is reality, not dream or delirium. You are truly in this place. And it is truly a place where magic is real and widely practised.'

'How do you know so much of his inner battles?' Aurilia asked suspiciously.

Hallifort's smile was tinged with regret, and an odd shadow moved briefly across his strange eyes. 'I have some experience, my lady, of being lost in a strange land, and I recognize the symptoms. Besides, a healer must be able to perceive the true nature of that which is to be healed.'

Aurilia glanced at Krost, who shrugged silently. 'Then you can also heal inner, mental afflictions?' she asked Hallifort.

'In some cases, yes,' the little man said calmly, reaching out to place his hand like a benediction on to the russet tangle of Red's hair. Red turned so that his gaze met Hallifort's, and for a moment something like the pure gleam at the heart of a diamond seemed to spin, in the depths of the little man's inhuman eyes. It felt to Red as if the soothing sensation that had come over his arm was spreading through his entire being. His eyes drooped and began to close, and he felt himself sagging in the chair.

'This sleep will benefit him,' he heard Hallifort's high voice saying, 'more than one that is drink-induced. When he wakes, he will be restored and calmed – more able to accept this reality.'

Red heard Aurilia offer thanks and payment, heard Hallifort politely refuse the latter. But the sounds faded rapidly as sleep brought a comforting darkness and wrapped it around him.

FIVE

He awoke slowly, blinking against a shaft of brightness, savouring the last moments of total relaxation. He was lying
naked under a single cover – a little threadbare but clean
enough – on a narrow, lumpy bed in a room with a sloping
ceiling. Sunlight poured past an ill-fitting curtain over a case-
ment window set deep in the whitewashed plaster of the wall.
Propping himself on an elbow, he saw his cloak, the borrowed
trousers, and the sheathed sword laid out on a low-backed
chair next to a stand with a ceramic basin and a ewer of water.

This is a room in the same tavern, he said to himself. And
it would have been Krost who lugged me up here. Probably
with one hand.

The sight of the ewer made him realize he was thirsty, with
a sour-metal taste in his mouth left by the ale of the night
before. He climbed out of bed, glanced at the narrow door of
the room to be sure it was shut, then tried the water, finding
it cool and fresh enough. After a gulp or two, he padded over
to the window and pushed the curtain aside, blinking at the
cloudless sky, enjoying the sun on his skin. All in all, he
thought, he felt pretty well. Relaxed and rested, in good
shape . . . He glanced at his left arm, at the unblemished
skin, and smiled wryly. Some healer, he thought – and then
his smile vanished as he realized to his astonishment that he
was feeling entirely untroubled. All the shock and tension
and fear of the night before had drained away. Even when
he recalled the details, dwelt on them – the spooky hooded
figures, the improbable city, the shape-changing woman, the
healing of his wound – he remained unaffected. He knew,
calmly and without doubt or fear, that he was not dreaming,
that what was happening was true and that the place he had
come to was *real* – despite all the . . . the . . .

'*Magic*,' he said aloud, tasting the word. 'I'm in a place where magic is as real and natural as . . .'

He couldn't think of an adequate comparison. In any case, he was enjoying the welcome absence of dread. He merely felt interested, puzzled, and excited. And that's because of more damn *magic*, he thought with a smile – Hallifort's magic, wiping away the fear. So now I can handle this place, with all its mysteries. I may not know what the script says or where the action's going, but I can ad lib with the best of them.

Continuing to smile at what he thought was a fairly neat metaphor, he reached for the shabby trousers. Time to make a new entrance, he thought as he pulled them on. See what's happening, find a little breakfast . . . He left his cloak where it was, but took up the sheathed sword, reluctant to leave it unattended. Opening the door, he stepped out into a narrow hall where he saw another door opposite, and at the end of the hall the top of a flight of stairs.

He was moving towards the stairs when he heard a sound from behind the other door. A woman's voice, not speaking but singing – melodically enough, yet in an unknown language and in eerie minor keys that lifted the hairs on the back of his neck.

He felt fairly sure that it was Aurilia's voice. And that intrigued him enough to draw him to the door, hand raised to tap against the wood. But just then the singing voice stopped, trailing off on a high weird note that sounded like a wail or a cry of pain. Suddenly unnerved and anxious, Red decided against knocking. His grip tightened on the sword's sheath as he turned the handle and warily pushed the door open.

Beyond it he saw a room much like his own, with no one in it but Aurilia, stooped and grey-gowned in her old-woman shape, standing with her back to him. Before her stood eight small receptacles on a stand of smooth wood – eight cups without handles, reminding Red of tulips in their soft bright colourings. They seemed to be candle-holders, for within each cup a small slender flame burned quietly, like the heart of the flower. Aurilia, who had not noticed Red's entrance, was bent over the cups and their flames, hands extended. And she seemed to be *speaking* to them, very swiftly, too quietly for him to hear the words.

Then his skin prickled and goose-pimpled with a cold wash of shock. Because some of the candle-cups seemed to be *replying*.

The other voices were even quieter than Aurilia's, their words even less audible. They were tiny murmurings and whisperings, like a breeze through small leaves or the distant hum of insects. But it was a conversation, in which Aurilia listened intently, replied, listened again. And Red saw that a flame would shiver and flicker when a voice was issuing from its particular cup.

He was too dazed with shock to see much more, or to make sense of the eerie conversation even if he could have heard it. And, in the course of trying to grasp what he was seeing, he must have moved his feet, as if seeking any sort of available balance. A floorboard creaked under him – and instantly Aurilia gasped, fluttered her fingers at the candles, then whirled. Each of the eight flames winked out, leaving not a trace of smoke as a candle would. And at the same time Aurilia herself shimmered through another of her changes, becoming her younger form again, in a long green dress that matched her eyes.

At once she relaxed, seeing Red. 'I hope I didn't disturb you,' she said calmly.

Red had no idea whether she meant the word in the sense of *awaken* or *alarm*, but he was unwilling to ask. 'No,' he said, gesturing vaguely. 'I'm all right.'

She studied him for a moment without replying. And Red in that moment had the unfamiliar experience of feeling both ill at ease and speechless. He saw himself as a clumsy trespasser, one who had foolishly spied on sights he should not have seen, powers he dared not ask about.

But then she smiled, warm and friendly, and his tension dwindled. 'The healer did well,' she said easily. 'If you'd seen all this last night you would have refused to believe it.'

'I suppose so,' he said, trying for a lightness of tone to match hers, still unable to bring himself to ask about what he had seen.

41

She nodded as if he had said something meaningful. 'I was going to come and wake you soon,' she said. 'To bring you some clothes that I've gathered for you.' She gestured towards a small leather satchel at the side of the room, and her smile grew impish. 'I think they'll fit. I got a good idea, last night, of your measurements.'

He blinked, registering the nature of her smile. Then tension and unease vanished and he laughed aloud.

'That's very thoughtful,' he told her. 'Nice of you to look after me.'

'It's only right that I do so,' she replied, 'after last night.'

He made a small self-deprecatory gesture. 'About last night . . . I'm sorry for starting to fall apart like that.'

Her smile softened. 'No, Red Cordell. I'm the one to apologize, for having caused you to be brought here.'

Vaguely he recalled what she had been telling him about his arrival, before he had stopped her. 'You said you just wanted the sword, wasn't that it? And I got in the way?'

'There is more to it,' she said quietly. 'I can't say that I understand exactly how the Translocation could happen. But it must be to do with . . . who and what you are.' She paused, as if seeking precise words. 'I believe you are a *correlate*, Red, of the man whose sword it once was.'

Red frowned. 'You didn't say anything like that last night.'

'No – because you stopped wanting to hear. But I can tell you now.' She paused again, gathering her words. 'The sword is a special weapon, Red, created many years ago for a special man, a hero. Created by the Sisterhood, to which I belong.'

'Sisterhood?' he echoed. 'Like some society of sorceresses . . . ?'

'No. Not that term. The Sisterhood is pledged to the Earth Magic, not the Higher Magic. Certainly not to any darker Powers, so we are not sorceresses. Call us witches, enchantresses . . .' She broke off. 'But we were talking about your sword.'

'More yours than mine,' Red said.

'I don't believe so,' she said, surprisingly. 'The sword was made for a particular hero, as I said, who vowed to use it to defend the Sisterhood in times of need. Its blade is protected, so it is unbreakable – and its edge is sharper than the most perfectly honed razor, and can never be blunted.'

Red glanced down at the sword that he still held, remembering how it had sheared through the club of the imitation troll on the film set – a very long time ago, it seemed. 'So how did it get to me?'

A tinge of sadness darkened Aurilia's green eyes. 'The hero grew old, as people do. Yet he sought to achieve some final adventure, one last quest . . . on which, at last, he died. And when the Circle of Nine that rules the Sisterhood reclaimed the sword, they chose to remove it from this world, lest it fall into evil hands. They flung it by magic out through the Realms and Spheres, to a world where it would not be recognized and so not misused. But, just in case, they attached a line of power to it, so it could be summoned, retrieved, if a need for it arose.'

Red frowned, trying to take it all in. 'So you summoned it when you were in trouble. And got me too.'

'Yes. But I believe the song of summoning would not have gathered you up as well if you were not a correlate, as I say, of the man who once owned the sword. It means a kind of . . . echo,' she explained as Red frowned again. 'Not an exact duplicate, but a sharing of qualities. You in your Sphere were probably much like the hero of this Sphere who wielded the sword. No doubt that's how you and the sword came together, there.'

'I doubt if I'm much of a hero,' Red said wryly.

'No?' Her eyes stared into his. 'You acted as one on the street last night. You are surely some kind of warrior, in your Sphere.'

Red shrugged. 'I've studied some kinds of combat . . .'

'As I thought,' she said. 'And you are similar to him in other ways, though he was somewhat heavier in his later years, when I knew him. But the main proof is in your name. He who wielded the sword bore the name of *Corodel* – known, because of his hair, as Redmane.'

Red stared, 'That's *my* name – the full name. Redmayne. It was my granny's maiden name, and I got it when I was born with this hair . . .'

43

'Very suitable,' she said. 'And whether Cordell or Corodel, it's a good name – for a hero.'

He laughed. 'Better than Thagor the Invincible.'

'Who?' she asked, puzzled.

'Private joke,' he said. 'So . . . I'm here because I have some tie-up with a dead hero, and you wanted his sword. But just what was going *on* last night? Who was that bunch you were aiming to fight?'

Her face was sombre. 'That is indeed the question, Red. I was taken captive earlier yesterday by the scarred man you saw, whose name is Vanticor, and the mysterious others in their robes and hoods. They were trying to get me out of the city unseen when the militia stopped them. Which allowed me to complete the song of summoning.'

Red shook his head, bewildered. 'But who were they? Why did they want you?'

'I know only Vanticor, the assassin,' she said. 'Not who those are who serve him – or whom *he* serves – or why they took me. Except . . . Vanticor made it clear that they wanted me *because* I am of the Sisterhood. He took the ring that I wore, which is one emblem of our community, and he knew this other emblem, that I bear.'

As she spoke, she calmly opened the top buttons of her bodice, exposing the firm upper curves of her breasts. Admiring them, Red saw with equal interest the mark that marred the honey-coloured skin of her cleavage. He had glimpsed the mark the night before, but daylight showed more clearly the formation of the shape within the circle.

'The four symbolic elements of the Earth and of the Earth-magic,' she said quietly. 'At once a tongue of fire and a drop of water, with the air and the earth itself expressed by the surrounding circle. Most folk know the mark, and who wears it – as did Vanticor and his helpers, when they captured me. Nor am I the first Sister to be taken. Many have been disappearing, in this city especially, since the turn of the year. I am just the first to get away.'

'Then you're lucky,' Red said.

The green eyes flashed. 'It wasn't entirely luck. Vanticor did not know . . .' She paused, then continued: 'I spoke before of the Sisterhood's ruling Circle of Nine. They are quite powerful, magically, with abilities reaching well beyond those of most ordinary Sisters. And I am one of them, Red. One of the Named Nine.'

Nine, he thought dazedly, trying to take in this new revelation. And there had been eight of the weird flower-like candles, that spoke . . .

She saw it in his eyes and nodded. 'Yes – I was communicating with the others of the Nine, through these—' she gestured at the small empty cups on their stand— 'when you came in. Consulting with them about last night, and what it all might mean.'

He looked at her for a silent moment. Like a magical conference call, he thought. But the attempt at flippancy failed to ease the sense of near-awe that he was beginning to feel, as he saw more clearly than ever the special quality that she had in both of her forms. It was a sense of *power*. Being with her was being in the presence of some awesome potency that was barely being held in check – or in readiness. Red had felt the same when once he had stood on a dam looking at the immensity of water being retained by its wall – or when he had once gazed into the unreadable eyes of a tiger, through the bars of a zoo's cage.

He swallowed, then took a deep breath. 'Why . . . er . . . why the *Named* Nine? Don't ordinary Sisters have names?'

'Of course. But the Nine bear special names as well, symbolic of their roles and responsibilities.' Abruptly she stopped and frowned, shaking her head. 'This is strange . . . The Names of the Nine are secret, and must be so, for there is power in a Name. Yet . . . I feel a strong compulsion to tell you mine.'

Red managed a shrug. 'Go ahead. Who would I tell?'

'Yes . . .' She was still frowning, thinking fast. 'It may be a kind of bond has been produced by the Translocation . . .' She nodded decisively and looked directly at him. 'Very well. My feeling says you should know, so you may. My Name is *Auriflamme*. It says that I am a representative of the Circle of Nine to the outside world. Their emissary, and standard-bearer.'

'Quite a name,' Red said, feeling awed all over again. 'Auri—'

At once she was close to him, fingers cool on his lips. 'Beware, Red. I told you there is power in a Name. Do not speak it lightly.' She took her hand away, her eyes intense. 'But *do* speak it, if there is ever . . . *need*. I believe there *has* been a bond forged between us, Red, somehow. And if you speak my secret Name, while you are in this Sphere, I will hear you and I will strive to come to you. Wherever you are, whatever stands in the way. If there is need.'

Red shivered slightly, partly because of the eeriness of her words, the shadow of the supernatural in her eyes. But partly also because of her nearness, and the delicate spicy perfume of her hair . . . He turned away, trying to make the movement casual, to regain control, to break free of the magnetic power that she seemed to wield so easily. And he saw a hint of her impish smile begin to reappear.

'Anyway . . . er . . .' he said jerkily. 'Thanks for telling me. I promise to keep the secret.' He dredged up some of his actor's skill, to appear at ease. 'I wish I had a secret name to tell you in return. But I'm just Red Cordell, real name and stage name.'

'Stage name?' She took a gliding step towards him.

'I'm an actor, where I come from.' The unease had not entirely left his voice. 'Mostly out of work. A long way from a hero with a magic sword.'

'Yet you *have* the sword.' She moved closer, her eyes luminous.

He blinked. 'I have it *now*. But I'm not *keeping* it. Surely it'll stay here when you send me back.'

She drew even closer. 'Are you so eager to go back?' she murmured.

He swallowed, throat suddenly dry. 'You have to send me sometime. After all, it was just the sword you wanted.'

'Last night, yes,' she said. 'But today . . . may be different.' Her smile was wide and brilliant. 'Besides, it's not so easy. I could bring the sword here, and you with it, because the line of power was already in place, needing only the summoning. But to *construct* a Translocation, a movement between

46

Spheres, in order to replace you at a specific point . . . I do not have that level of power. It would need a very High Adept, or a conclave of lesser mages – or a full convening of the Circle of Nine.'

Red looked stricken. 'Are you saying I can't go back?'

'No, no,' she reassured him. 'But *I* can't send you. You will need to wait a while, till we can seek the aid of those who have the power to do so.' She took another slow step towards him. 'Meanwhile, I don't think your stay will prove . . . uninteresting.'

She was very close to him again, her scent enveloping him. And her tawny blonde hair, which had been pinned up in an elaborate arrangement, had seemed to come loose by itself, so that it tumbled down in darkly golden waves past her shoulders, past the slender waist, the curve of hip . . .

At that moment Red could see no reason at all why he should be in a hurry to leave the Sphere, or indeed that room. 'Er . . . that's fine,' he said hoarsely. 'As long as I *can* get back . . . eventually . . .'

'Of course.' Her voice was soft, her eyes were warm, her lips curved in a smile that no longer held impish laughter. 'But not too soon. There is some fateful reason for the accident that brought you, Red. Just as there is some meaning in the impulse that made me tell you my Name. If there is a bond between us, as it seems, it exists for a purpose, and we would be unwise to ignore it.'

She reached out to him, her fingertips like fire and ice as they trailed over the muscles of his bare chest.

He took a deep, shaky breath. 'Aurilia . . .' he began, husky-voiced.

'Are you feeling reluctant, because we are strangers?' she asked. 'Or because you think I'm really an old hag wearing a false shape?'

'I . . . er . . .' Words deserted him under the impact of her touch.

'You may be sure that this shape is not an illusion,' she went on. 'See for yourself.' She took his hand, placed it on the upper swell of her breast where her bodice still remained unbuttoned. 'And I have a cure for reluctance, if need be.'

47

Red thought he saw a strange glow between her breasts, as if the mark of the Sisterhood had uncannily begun to shine with a light of its own. But then his gaze was diverted as one of the fallen strands of her hair suddenly lifted, coiling and swaying upwards like a live thing, reaching for Red's hand where it lay on her breast. Before he could react, the strand of hair twined around his wrist, twisting back and over in a complex knot. Red half-tried to pull his hand away, failed, then no longer wished to try.

The sensation storming through him was irresistible – like a molten current sweeping from his wrist out along every vein. He was instantly aroused, to a pitch of sexual hunger that was almost an agony. Desire enflamed his entire being, a craving the likes of which he had never known. His left hand, which had all the while been clutching the sheathed sword, flung it aside as he reached to grasp Aurilia . . .

Somewhere far away, or so it seemed, he heard a thump and a clatter. And then he staggered, almost crying out, because the overpowering sensation had been suddenly, brutally, cut off – as Aurilia stepped back from him, the strand of her hair whipping away from where it had been knotted at his wrist.

The noise had been someone knocking at, then opening, the door to the room. In the doorway stood a stout woman with a mop of grey-brown curls. She stopped abruptly, staring, then let a knowing grin overtake her face as she inspected the beautiful woman with her hair tumbled down and the half-naked, flushed young man.

'Beg pardon, I'm sure,' she said brightly.

Aurilia smiled calmly and nodded. 'What is it?'

'Landlord says t' tell you food's ready in the taproom, just as you ordered, m'lady.' The stout woman's grin widened. 'I'll tell him you might be a while yet.'

She turned away, closing the door with a firm thump, and Aurilia smiled up at Red's slightly glazed eyes. '*Will* we be a while?' she asked softly.

Red seemed to shake himself. 'I don't . . . Maybe it's not such a good idea.'

She raised a lazy eyebrow, a strand of her hair twitching and coiling. 'Do you think you could prevent it?'

'Maybe not,' Red said hoarsely. 'But I might not be pleased, after. I might not like . . . being forced, by your magic.'

'*Forced*?' The green eyes blazed for an instant. 'The love-knot can have little effect where desire does not *already* exist. But never mind. I know how men hate to feel in thrall to a woman's power.' She smiled her impish smile. 'So go and put on your new clothes, Master Cordell. And then, if you wish to come down and take breakfast with me, I will be a skinny old woman again and you will be quite safe.'

'Right,' Red said stiffly, disturbed to find that he had some-how managed to make himself feel a total fool. 'Good. Fine.'

Picking up the satchel and the sword, he moved towards the door, and was ushered out of it by a ripple of melodic laughter.

Back in his room, he realized that despite everything the thought of food was greatly appealing. So he used the rest of the water in the ewer for a quick wash, finding that the satchel provided by Aurilia contained not only clothing but such useful necessities as a crude straight razor and a wooden comb. After a cautious shave and a painful attack on the tangle of his hair, he put on the clothes – dark-grey trousers and a midnight-blue shirt, both well tailored from good cloth, along with a pair of boots and a belt that accommodated the sword's sheath as if they had been made for each other. Everything fitted perfectly, as Aurilia had indicated they would, which brought a slightly rueful smile to his lips. And then, with the cloak thrown across his shoulders, he took a deep breath and went down to breakfast.

Aurilia was indeed in her guise of the old woman, seated in the taproom at a table full of covered dishes and bowls that smelled inviting, along with mugs of fragrant herb tea. Her smile seemed quite matter-of-fact, though Red detected a gleam of leftover laughter deep in the green eyes as she removed a few covers to display assorted meats and breads, cooked cereal and fruit, inviting him to help himself. He sat down, reached out, then paused.

'I've only just thought,' he said. 'The drinks last night, the room, this food . . . Are you paying for all of it? Or don't you use money here?'

She chuckled. 'We do. But I have more than enough for your needs, and I'm sure Krost has as well. You will be our guest while you're here. I owe you that at least.'

Red shrugged, nodded his thanks and reached for something that looked like a sweet roll. 'Where is Krost?'

Her smile turned into a pursing of wrinkled lips with faint disapproval. 'Krost is very fond of ale, and was still here quaffing it when I finally left him and sought my bed.'

He grinned. 'Quite a character, Krost. What's his story?'

'I will answer your questions however I can, Red,' she said quietly. 'But Krost's story is not mine to tell. Nor would you be advised to ask him. Not till you know him better.'

'If you say so,' he replied, raising an eyebrow. 'Then let's try other questions. Like – where the hell am I?'

'Ah, the most imponderable of questions,' she said, smiling. 'But easily enough answered, this side philosophy.'

And, succinctly, she told him. He was in the city of Quamarr, she said, principal metropolis of a large continental island called the Four-Cornered Continent. The city stood in a rich interior named the Central Grasslands, while around it were the Four Corners – the Northern Moorlands, where Aurilia had been born and where the Sisterhood had its base; the Southern Highlands, where Krost came from; the desert Eastern Wastelands; and the wild, partly swampy Western Woodlands. The Continent's greatest river, the Tenebris, bisected the Grasslands as it flowed past the city of Quamarr . . .

'Wait, wait!' Red said desperately. 'Enough geography!'

'You asked,' she smiled.

'All right. Let me ask another.' He sorted his thoughts. 'One things seems just about weirder than anything – the fact that everyone here speaks my language.'

'We don't,' she told him. 'It is just that we understand one another.' She held up a bony hand to stop his startled interruption. 'It is how it happens, with a Translocation – especially from one *human* Sphere to another. No one really knows why, though there are many theories. But if you bring someone magically across the Realms and Spheres, they arrive in your Sphere able to communicate.' She smiled again. 'An Adept I once knew said that such movements should not be called Translocations, but literally *translations*.'

Red shook his head. He had read his share of tales in his own world where wizards summoned spirits or demons, like Faust and Mephistopheles, and in them too there never seemed to be a language problem. Anyway, though he was sure he would never know how it worked, he was glad it did.

'If you say so,' he replied at last. 'Let's try another question. If you and Krost come from other areas, what are you doing here? Do you work in the city?'

'No,' she said gravely. 'I have come from the Fastness of the Sisterhood, in the Northern Moorlands, to find out what I could about the disappearances of Sisters during the past months. But also I am here to respond to a more recent summons – from Prince Phaedran, the ruler of the Continent, whose palace is here.'

'Yes, Krost mentioned him.' Red leaned forward interestedly. 'What does he want?'

'I don't know yet. I've only arrived lately, and haven't yet been to the palace. My summons came indirectly, sent to the Circle of Nine, saying only that the prince sought our help in some urgent but undisclosed matter. And Krost, too, told me that he has been called with the same urgency and secretiveness, to the prince's aid.'

But then she stopped, for as if on cue a shadow fell across their table. The immensely wide shadow of Krost, leaning on his iron quarterstaff, grinning cheerfully down at them – though the cheer was marred slightly by a tinge of redness in his eyes.

'Good day,' Krost said, his voice hoarser than ever with the after-effects of ale. 'Can you spare a roll for a hungry man?'

Whereupon he sat down, on another heavy bench that groaned beneath him, and put away five rolls while Aurilia and Red brought him up to date on how Red was feeling and what he had been told – omitting some of the more private details of their encounter that morning. And Krost chewed and listened, and sipped carefully at a beaker that a serving-woman brought him, which smelled very much like ale.

'I am glad you are feeling more at ease here, my friend,' Krost told Red at last, lightly squeezing his shoulder, which went numb. 'It is a fine city, and a fine land. You should stay a while.'

'Seems I *have* to stay a while,' Red replied. 'Might as well make the best of it.'

Krost grinned, swallowed another gulp from his beaker, then turned to Aurilia. 'There has been a message from the palace. Phaedran welcomes us, but regrets . . . what did he call it? The *disturbance* of last night, which he heard about from the militia. He wants us to go and be his guests at the palace – Red as well. He will send a carriage for us at sundown today. And he will be able to receive us tomorrow, to say why he called us.' He glanced at Red. 'Aurilia told you . . . ?'

As Red nodded, Aurilia sniffed. 'I'll be glad to have the mystery cleared up.'

Krost leaned back expansively. 'The prince's servants will collect our belongings from here. So, before we need to make ready, we have some hours to pass.'

'I'm not sitting here all day,' Aurilia snapped, 'watching you pour down mugs of ale.'

'No, no,' Krost said, pretending to look hurt. 'My thought was that we could continue Red's education. We could take him out and show him something of Quamarr.'

They decided to take their excursion on foot, which made Krost look only a little pained. And before they left the tavern Aurilia went through that blurring vibration which meant another shape-shift. Red watched with interest, marvelling quietly at how he was starting to take such exhibitions of magic for granted. He also marvelled when the youthful Aurilia appeared in a new costume – a high-necked tunic and a flowing split skirt over low boots, in a silky leaf-green material, all very unrevealing and demure. She had even contrived a wide hat to perch on her high-piled blonde hair.

'That's a good trick,' Red said lightly, 'changing clothes when you change . . . yourself. Saves on baggage.'

She smiled sweetly. 'I like to be suitably dressed, in either form.'

'Naturally,' Red said, keeping his voice casual. 'Do you . . . ever take other forms?'

'Such as a wolf or a bat?' she said, laughing. 'No – I am restricted to the two forms you've seen.'

'And . . . er . . . which is the *real* you?' Red asked.

Her smile grew even sweeter. 'Why, Red, I thought you understood. They *both* are.'

Krost hooted with laughter. 'She will never tell you, my friend. It is like any of the secrets of the Sisterhood – a mere man must simply accept his ignorance.'

'In any case,' Aurilia added brightly, 'the distinction between the real and the illusory has baffled great minds all through history.'

Red gave her a wry grin. 'I can't win, can I? You're always one step ahead of me.'

She touched his arm lightly. 'We are not in a competition, Red Cordell. I would not be so unkind.'

And she strode away, leaving Red trying to puzzle out whether her last remark was a reassurance or an insult.

Their route from the tavern first followed a twisting back street, paved with rough cobbles, with no separate pavement at the sides for pedestrians. The buildings on either side huddled close together, seldom rising above two storeys, mostly made of wood and crude plaster, some low and narrow and mean enough to be called hovels. They seemed to be homes rather than shops, with tired-looking women visible in some doorways, scrubbing floors or front steps. Otherwise there were only a few dour men moving along the street or idling at the corners of side streets, along with some blank-eyed old folk sitting in patches of sunlight and troops of barefoot children shrieking up and down, or stopping to stare at the well-dressed trio walking past.

'I hope these are just the slums,' Red remarked wryly, 'and the rest of the city gets nicer.'

'It does,' Krost told him. 'But this is just a poor area. The true slums lie across the river, and are called the Rookeries.'

'Home to the worst of the city dregs,' Aurilia added, 'thieves and cutthroats and the like.'

'And kidnappers?' Red asked pointedly.

She shot him a quick glance. 'Very likely. Vanticor would not be the first villain to seek a lair in the rat-warren across the river.'

'Sounds an interesting place,' Red murmured. And it seemed that Krost was about to agree, with some enthusiasm, when he was halted by a glare from Aurilia's green eyes.

'If you want to explore low and rowdy areas,' she said firmly, 'where we are now is quite bad enough. For myself, I'll be glad to get out of this area.'

'But you stayed at the tavern, in this area,' Red reminded her.

'Because I was weary,' she said, 'and because you were there and I felt . . . responsible for you. My belongings, and my horse, are at a far more pleasant inn in a much nicer part of the city.'

'We can go that way and collect them, if you like,' Krost said soothingly.

54

So they walked on, at a fair pace, gradually leaving the shabby area behind. Before long they came to a wide, attractive thoroughfare, which did have pavements on either side, where riders on horseback or in wheeled carriages streamed past on the roadway, where the well-dressed adults were stout and cheery rather than haggard and dour and where the few children on view were too well behaved to stare at anyone.

'This is Merchants' Avenue,' Krost said, waving his quarter-staff at the length of the thoroughfare. 'Big houses, rich people, lots of well-stuffed shops where one lot of traders go to be cheated by another. Not a good tavern anywhere. And closer to the river, there—' another wave of the staff— 'are warehouses and storehouses, no one there except storemen and porters.'

'And thieves at night,' Aurilia added, 'running footraces with the militia.'

They crossed the great avenue and walked on. And as his guides explained more urban geography to him, Red began to understand that Quamarr was shaped more or less like a lady's fan. The prince's palace and its extensive grounds formed the focus at the bottom of the fan, the narrowest point. Several broad, imposing thoroughfares – including the Merchants' Avenue – reached out from that focal point like supporting ribs of the fan, dividing the city into sections and taking their names from professions or occupations that were or had been centred there. So besides Merchants' Avenue there was Craftsmen's Boulevard, containing skilled artists and artisans of every sort – Healers' Highway, where you could find legitimate physicians or quacks, as Krost put it, along with magical healers like Hallifort – Priests' Row, where religions, sects, and cults had their headquarters – and some others.

The entire city was enclosed by a substantial wall, a bit of which Red had glimpsed the previous night. And near the top of the fan-shape, where the city was nearly at its widest, the River Tenebris flowed across its width, providing a natural line of demarcation. Beyond the river, between it and the wall, lay the supposedly dangerous slum area of the Rookeries.

Which, Red thought, Aurilia sees as being out of bounds. But his view was decidedly otherwise. In his experience, the less civilized and sanitized parts of a city – any city – usually held the more interesting and lively goings-on. And, unless he was misjudging him, he thought Krost felt that way too.

The three of them seemed to be walking crossways through the city, on a complex route along some of the interwoven side streets and back streets that lay between the great arteries. Since they were still in a well-to-do area, those streets were dominated by fairly large buildings, mostly constructed from stone of varying hues and textures. Whether the buildings were private homes, commercial enterprises, institutions or whatever, they all seemed to Red to exhibit an architectural style that could be labelled Ostentatious Gothic – except for those which looked more like Random Lunacy. Every structure displayed endless arrays of burdensome elaboration and ornamentation. The larger the building, the more wildly abundant were its columns and pilasters, its arches and cornices, its statuary and gargoyles, its moulding and scrolling . . . Any one sizeable frontage could boast a profusion of openings, from vast rose windows to tall mullioned windows to jutting oriel windows to small inset windows like portholes, all flung together in patternless discord. And from what Red could see of the tops of the buildings – a wilderness of towers, spires, domes, cupolas, castellations, and more – he imagined that overflying birds would be too dazed and confused ever to find a place to land.

Shortly they came to another of the great thoroughfares that fanned out through the city, and again Krost waved the staff sweepingly, as if it was a conductor's baton. 'Scholars' Way,' he announced. 'Many old schools and academies and so on, containing most of the city's learned men, who know the names of stars and fishes and can recite verses by the bucketful, and sometimes need help to put their boots on the right feet.'

Red laughed. 'Any Colleges of Magic? Maybe I could take a course.'

'The power is inborn, a gift of the gods,' Aurilia told him quietly. 'It can only be trained where it already exists – so a youngster with the gift will become an apprentice to an older Adept, to learn the nature and uses of spells. But one without the gift cannot acquire it.' She smiled faintly. 'In any case, a College of Magic is unlikely. Wizards and sorcerers tend to be solitary, suspicious folk, more given to rivalry than community.'

'Like film directors,' Red muttered – to himself, for the others had walked on.

Soon more side streets had led them to a junction of four roadways, as they entered another slightly poorer section. The junction was crammed with people, riotously so, as well as with small carts, hand-barrows, horses, mules, dogs, and much else. It was a street market, Red saw – though more like what his world would call a flea market, with countless heaps of shoddy, well-worn junk being offered by hopeful vendors, mixed with stalls laden with stringy vegetables and fly-specked meat.

Red brightened at the sight of the noisy, surging crowd, and the presence of life and activity after the succession of overblown buildings and uneventful streets. And Krost, too, seemed more at home there, cheerfully marching through the throngs of people who seemed all too willing to step aside from his bulk. Red followed with Aurilia, gazing around with a smile, enjoying the sonorous cries or rapid-fire patter of the stallholders as they tried to attract buyers. They paused for a moment to watch a small rubbery man entertain onlookers with a stream of amazingly filthy jokes, all aimed at selling vials of a liquid that was, he claimed, the ultimate cure-all, for everything from a bald head to a broken heart. He was doing good business, too, as was a dark-eyed woman selling lengths of exotic cloth . . . and a youth blithely butchering a succession of shrieking fowls in front of an amused if blood-spattered audience . . . and a fat man offering delicately fili-greed silver jewellery – and more and more, all of which Red revelled in.

Aurilia was smiling, watching his enjoyment. 'If there is anything you wish to buy . . .'

Red shook his head quickly. 'You're spending enough on me.' He glanced once more around the market. 'I'd like to take a souvenir back with me, if I can – but probably not from here.'

'No,' she agreed firmly, 'not from here.' Her voice softened. 'I'll think of something suitable . . . for you to remember us by.'

'If you like the market, friend Red,' Krost rumbled, 'I know another place you would like even more.' He grinned at Aurilia's slight frown. 'Near Craftsmens' Boulevard? The Players' Green?'

'Players?' Red echoed interestedly.

Aurilia was gazing steadily at Krost. 'A green where, as I recall, there stands a substantial and popular tavern.'

Krost assumed an innocent look. 'Aurilia! I only thought Red would like it, since he is an actor . . .'

'I would!' Red said eagerly. 'Where is it?'

It turned out to be a fairly long trudge from the site of the street market. And while Red was growing a little footsore in his new boots on the uneven cobbles, he found that the walk was well worth it. The Players' Green was a small enclosed park, boasting little actual greenery beyond some patchy, half-dead grass and three drooping saplings. But even that greenness was made nearly invisible by another crowd, not visibly different from the throng at the marketplace – except that this one stood mostly in silence, paying absorbed attention to a makeshift stage formed by four flat-bed wagons pulled together on which a swarm of performers declaimed, cavorted, sang, and sometimes broke into flurries of dancing or acrobatics or even mock battle with wooden swords.

Red was delighted, although Krost and Aurilia confessed that they had no idea what was being performed. But a toothless old man was willing to inform them, between scenes, that it was a historical pageant, to do with some ancient time of conflict and upheaval in the Continent known as the Mage Wars. That still meant little to Red – yet he watched with pleasure, delighting in the performers' physical skills and smiling at their oratorical ones. Until at last all the actors and dancers and acrobats together stormed around the stage in a climactic, neatly choreographed mock-battle where just about

58

everyone died, melodramatically – before leaping up again to join in a jolly chorus that proved to be the finale.

As the crowd lustily bellowed its appreciation and flung showers of coins, Krost grinned at Red. 'A good troupe!' he said. 'And there are many such, in the city and travelling the Continent.' His grin widened. 'You might find work with one of them, Red.'

He laughed, and Red joined in; but he wondered just what it would be like to be a wandering player in such a land. Gazing around, he told himself that he had played to more fragrant houses but never to a more appreciative one.

Then he went very still, his body tensing. His gaze had encountered a dark and malevolent glare – from the eyes of a man in black and green, with a scarred face and lank yellow hair.

'Krost!' Red hissed. 'Look – the creep from last night!'

Krost and Aurilia whirled, following Red's gaze. 'Vanticor!' Aurilia said – and they all started forward.

But at their movement, Vanticor also moved – sliding away like a snake through the crowd that was only slowly beginning to disperse. Red snarled with frustration as his way was blocked, while Krost looked as if he was about to start flinging people out of the way. But Aurilia held them back.

'Don't,' she said. 'You won't catch him now.'

The two men subsided, knowing she was right. 'Do you think he is following us?' Krost asked. 'To try to take you again, Aurilia, or seek revenge?'

'He'll not take me again,' Aurilia said flatly.

Red was peering in among the crowd, one hand on the hilt of his sword. 'I hope he does try something,' he muttered. 'I'd enjoy a little revenge myself, for that knife I took.'

Krost looked at him with approval. 'That is just what Corodel might have said. You are growing into the part, my friend.'

There were few other alarms or excitements that afternoon. They did repair to the tavern by the Players' Green for a rest and a bite to eat – with which Aurilia sipped a light wine, Red made a careful approach to a small beaker of ale, while

Krost threw back four huge foaming mugs of the potent brew and seemed all the better for it. Finally Aurilia prised them out and took them determinedly on another walk, along many more streets which ended at a small ivy-covered building that was the inn where she had taken a room before being abducted. There she gathered up a pair of substantial valises, showing that not *all* her possessions came by means of her magical shape-shifting, and from the stables reclaimed a stately gelding of purest white. When it was saddled, with the valises strapped on to its substantial haunches, she reverted to her elderly form and rode in dignity all the way back to the poorer area and seedier tavern where they had begun their day.

There she vanished to her own room for her own purposes, while Red joined Krost in the taproom for another mug of ale and for the pleasure of pulling off his boots and easing his aching feet. But sundown and the prince's carriage were both approaching, so Red made sure to restrict himself to one mug, not wishing to be half-drunk the first time he met royalty. His abstention drew a smile of approval from the aged Aurilia, when she rejoined them – and so did the royal vehicle when it finally arrived.

It was a high-wheeled open carriage pulled by a matched pair of chestnuts, with four equally matched men in attendance, two on the driver's seat and two behind, all wearing identical grey-blue uniforms. Bowing, they ushered Aurilia and Red on to the carriage's cushioned seats. But Krost, unwilling to impose his weight on the vehicle's springs, briefly disappeared before returning mounted on a horse that was the equine version of himself. A dapple-grey beast, fairly short of leg but immensely broad of chest and beam, looking powerful enough to pull a city-full of royal carriages by itself with strength to spare.

'This is Wolle,' Krost told Red, slapping his mount on its powerful neck, a blow that would have felled any man but that the grey did not seem to notice. 'He is a Highland pony from the South, where I come from,' Krost went on affectionally. 'My sturdy little friend.'

Some pony, Red thought. Like a short Percheron on steroids. And he glanced back as the carriage rolled smoothly away, watching the squat, massive horse bearing its bulky rider with a springily muscular trot that it looked like it could keep up all year.

The carriage heaved and swayed a good deal, like a small boat in rough water, making Red even more glad that he had not over-indulged in the ale before leaving. They first traversed more of the grimy streets near their tavern, then emerged on to the breadth of Merchants' Avenue – trundling down the centre of it at a considerable rate, while other drivers and riders made way, offering respectful salutes to the royal livery.

Before long they were rolling up to a vast sweep of velvety grass with colourful shrubs and flowerbeds, divided by a curving drive where immaculate white gravel crunched beneath the carriage's wheels. It led eventually to an edifice that had to be the palace, which made the largest building Red had seen in the city that day seem reticent. Immense columns soared up to overarching pediments, a profusion of spindly towers thrust up above them topped by turrets or belfries, with sturdy parapets and battlements stretched along between them. The immense mass of the main structure, in a creamy stone that bore no stain or blemish, was buttressed by wings that trailed off to either side, with more towers and gables and sudden steeples jutting up at the corners like afterthoughts. And smaller extensions grew out from the wings, and smaller ones still from those, all rambling sideways and backwards like parasitic growths leeching on to the central body.

Taken as a whole, it was overpowering. But it was also overdone and overwrought, Red felt, with all those cluttered additions on either side forming a farrago of bits and pieces that created the effect of unharmonious disorder. Still, as the carriage pulled up at the foot of graceful, creamy steps leading up to tall doors gleaming with polished wood and flawless decorative bronze, and as more liveried flunkeys hurried down to greet their arrival, Red made sure to keep a straight face and to look suitably impressed.

If only Ryla could see me now, he thought. And then he

was struck, again, by how far away and oddly unreal his other life, his own world, had begun to seem.

By then he and his new friends had dismounted and started up the splendid steps. And for a moment he did feel legitimately impressed by the tall figure awaiting them at the top, wearing a perfectly tailored uniform of the same grey-blue but with abundant gold braid and decorative insignia. The man was tall, balding, strong-jawed and bright-eyed, and for a moment Red wondered if this was the prince himself, come in person to greet his guests. But the balding man began to bow respectfully, murmuring his welcome to 'Lady Aurilia' and 'Master Krost' – and Red realized that he was some kind of senior servant even before Aurilia turned to introduce him.

'Red, this is the Lord Seneschal of the palace, who keeps it all running smoothly,' she said. 'Seneschal, this is our new friend, Red Cordell.'

Red began to hold out his hand, but the seneschal was bowing again. 'Indeed,' he said courteously, 'the outland gentleman of whom the prince has heard so much. Welcome, my lord.'

Red wanted to point out that he was no lord, but the seneschal was turning away to usher Aurilia in through the great doors, and Red could only trail along.

'I must stable Wolle myself,' Krost said, hanging back. 'He has no liking for strangers. I will find you in the palace later.'

He marched back down the steps to deal with his pony, and Red joined Aurilia in time to hear the seneschal apologetically saying that the prince, not he, must be the one to tell her why she had been summoned. Red paid scant attention, too busy studying the immense vaulted ceiling of the entrance hall, bearing a colourful painting of some apparently stylized battle and supported by fluted pillars and smooth stone walls bright with tapestries. They set off up a vast curving staircase of gleaming stone, Red still trailing behind, staring around at the sumptuous carvings in wood, marble, and sometimes silvery metal that stood in niches in the wall or adorned the shiny banisters. When they reached the first landing, with a carpeted corridor stretching away on either side, Aurilia and the seneschal were still ahead, talking in low voices like old acquaintances with much gossip to catch up on. But then the seneschal turned to Red with another half-bow.

'A footman will show you to your suite, my lord,' he announced, 'which has been readied for you on the floor above.'

And, again before Red could speak, he offered another small bow and turned away with Aurilia along the corridor. To *her* suite, I suppose, Red thought, feeling a little deflated when Aurilia did not turn, as if she had forgotten about him entirely.

But a liveried footman had appeared, waiting patiently, and so Red followed him up another sweeping arc of the great staircase and along more very similar corridors and finally to a polished wooden door with gleaming brass fitments, which the footman opened for him to enter.

Beyond it Red found a sizeable sitting room, comfortably furnished to approach opulence, with a high ceiling and tall, elegant windows. It contained sofas and chairs and small tables, lamps and chandeliers, mirrors and ornaments on the walls, a sideboard offering fruit and sweetmeats and another bearing interesting-looking flagons and slim goblets. Through another door Red could see a room nearly as large, dominated by a richly covered and canopied bed. And beyond that was a small anteroom with what looked like a fairly primitive water-closet. But he took all that in with just a glance or two – because most of his attention was being given to the young woman on the far side of the room.

'This is Nellann, sir,' the footman murmured, gesturing to the young woman. 'She will attend you here, while you are a guest in the palace.'

'Will she?' Red asked, bemusedly. The young woman seemed barely out of her teens, with curly brown hair and large brown eyes, small but curvaceous in her grey-blue dress that seemed a size too small for her. And she was surveying Red with equal interest as she offered a sketchy curtsy.

'Er . . . thank you,' Red said at last to the footman.

'My lord,' the man said, bowing. And before Red could correct him he had marched out of the room and closed the door.

Red turned to confront Nellann's smiling appraisal. 'I'm no *lord*,' he said firmly, determined that someone in the palace should be made aware of the fact.

'Aren't you, sir?' Nellann said brightly. 'That's good. 'Cause I'm no lady.'

There was little that Red could say to that, so he busied himself instead with looking around the suite, now and then glancing at the sway of Nellann's hips in the tight dress, as she accompanied him. He found that his satchel, which Aurilia had brought to him in the tavern, had preceded him to the suite, resting at the foot of the sumptuous bed, its meagre contents already neatly unpacked into a nearby chest of drawers. He had the feeling that the bed would have filled his entire room back at old Ryla's rooming house, and when he pressed down on it a faint flowery fragrance rose from its soft covers. Then, as he straightened, he felt very little surprise to find Nellann standing quite close, with the top two buttons of her dress undone.

'Is there anything I can do for you, sir?' she asked, touching her upper lip with the pink tip of her tongue. 'Anything you want?'

Red smiled down at her, enjoying her disregard of subtlety, enjoying the view as well. 'Not now, Nellann,' he told her. 'I'll just . . . get settled in.' And find out a little more, he said to himself. About customs and taboos in this place, the proper protocol regarding guests and maids. Though if Aurilia and Nellann are anything to go by, this world doesn't suffer from puritanism.

'Very good, sir,' Nellann said, looking only a little disappointed as she bobbed another brief curtsey. 'But if you should want me later, for anything—' she gestured to a bell-pull by the bed— 'just ring. Any time.'

She left the room with another hip-swivelling display, as if to indicate to Red what he was missing. And he watched, and smiled, then turned his attention back to his surroundings. Luxury, he thought. Better than a five-star hotel. Unbuckling his sword-belt, he tossed it and his short cloak on the bed before wandering back to the sitting room, where he poured a gobletful of a pale fluid that turned out to be a delicate dry wine and went to gaze out of the window.

Twilight had descended by then, but he could see a collection of outbuildings obviously at the rear of the palace. They were mostly stables, with numerous horses and people still working around them, grooming them, tidying their stalls. This can't be the *best* suite in the palace, he thought with a faint grin, with such a view. But he had no complaint, for he liked horses, liked looking at them and riding them. And beyond the stables he could see a wide swath of the palace's estate extending away from the city, with grassy swales, patches of woods, and what looked like bridle paths.

I wonder if I'll be here long enough to go riding, he thought idly. Or to get anywhere with Nellann . . . or with Aurilia. I wonder what's going to happen – and *why* all this is happening – and what the prince wants. I wonder when we get supper, and where. I wonder what I'm supposed to *do* . . .

He felt a wave of gloom and impatience, mingled together, sweep over him. I feel like some helpless tourist with no mind of his own, he thought angrily. Being directed here and led there, never knowing what's coming next. I need to do something for *myself*. I need to get some control, somehow, over what's happening to me and what's going to happen.

And first of all, he thought, swinging away from the window, I should find out when and how I can go back . . . Then he paused, astonished by the unexpected, unmistakable surge of *reluctance* that arose at the thought.

SEVEN

Some while earlier, the silver-haired sorcerer in the high-collared robe entered a chamber in the shadowy mansion, or castle, that was his home. The chamber was at the top of another of the building's four towers, which stretched up almost to touch the inner curve of the immense black shell looming so unnaturally on that far western shoreline. The man moved through the chamber with absent familiarity though it was crowded and cluttered with furniture and equipment, and was uncannily dark, there as elsewhere in the castle. The darkness seemed to have acquired a physical substance, swirling and drifting as if the shadows had become palpable as smoke or black mist. But it kept its distance from the end of the room where he went to stand.

He stood very still, his eyes glittering in the light emitted from a shiny, circular surface jutting slightly from the wall at eye level. The surface – flawlessly smooth and tinged faintly yellow – was a large carved portion of semiprecious stone, set seamlessly into the dark stone of the wall.

And on its surface moved tiny images of Aurilia, Krost, and Red Cordell, as they had been while walking up the steps towards the door of the prince's palace.

'See, there she is! Aurilia, the hag, trying to seem as if she has never flaunted herself in her other form!'

The sudden exclamation came from one side of the chamber – from a young woman sitting on the edge of one of the divans. She was slim and pretty, with long dark hair falling around her heart-shaped face, elegantly dressed in a gown bright with embroidery and decorative pearls. But her youthful beauty was marred by her expression, as she stared at the images on the wall – an expression mingling resentment with anxiety, echoed in the tension of her posture, and of her hands that twisted within one another or plucked aimlessly at the folds of her dress.

'So,' the silver-haired man said, 'it is as I thought. The fool Vanticor sought to take one of the Nine, and then allowed her to escape.'

The young woman's eyes brightened. 'What will you do to him?'

He shrugged. 'He is still useful to my purpose. I could find none better. And he would say in his defence that he could not have known her status. As you know, my dear, they do not flaunt *that*.'

'He could have known,' the young woman insisted. 'He should have known!'

'How?' The tall man turned to her with an edge of impatience in his voice. 'He cannot communicate with me directly. I can only *watch* him, not speak to him, with the scrying stone. I have explained all this to you before.' He held up a hand as she seemed about to speak. 'In any case, the important matter here is that the witch – Aurilia, you say? – is about to meet the prince. Along with the one called Krost, and with this young unknown swordsman she has collected somewhere, who seems to be bearing the sword of Corodel that was thought to be lost. Clearly Phaedran is planning something – and I shall need to labour with my scrying to learn what it is.'

She stared at him, still plucking at her gown. 'Is that not . . . worrying?'

'Not at all,' he told her. 'At least Vanticor managed to get the others away without allowing them to be revealed. Phaedran may plan what he likes with whom he likes – it will avail him little until he can discover who his enemy is.'

'Until?' she repeated. 'Then you expect that he will discover it?'

The man gestured, his hand for a moment glowing faintly as if becoming phosphorescent, and the images vanished from the shiny section of the wall. 'In time, my dear, of course he will. Unless his tame mages are totally witless.' He laughed, deep in his throat. 'But it will be of no use to him. Even when he knows who and where we are, he cannot reach us.'

Her eyes brightened again, and she laughed in a high-pitched giggle.

'Furthermore,' the man continued, 'we shall become even more invulnerable, after the next enhancement of my power.'

The young woman leaned forward almost avidly as the silver-haired man raised his hand again to bring another image into being on the scrying stone: the image of a woman, heavy-bodied, well past whatever bloom of youth she might once have possessed. She was crouching on a bare stone floor within a room whose inky-black walls seemed to glitter, as if an unseen light source was being reflected from dark glass. The woman was wearing only a skimpy garment like a night-dress, torn in several places so that it exposed most of her thick flesh. She crouched in an awkward squat, knees drawn up against large breasts, arms around her knees, eyes wide and unseeing, mouth sagging, a line of drool bright on her chin.

'Fear has broken her mind!' the young woman breathed.

'It is a form of withdrawal that we have seen before,' the man said, with a thin smile. 'But she lives, her life force remains intact, and she will surely scream loudly enough to gratify you, my love, when her time comes.'

The young woman smiled as well, staring at the image of the wretched figure.

'I wonder if even the Sisterhood will miss this one,' the man went on. 'She is the ugliest yet. Vanticor might try to choose ones who are more physically appealing.'

The young woman's mouth twisted. 'They have always *all* been ugly to me – parading their magic in front of those who have been unjustly denied it . . . I would have them *all* dead. I *long* for the day when I gain my own powers and can kill them myself.'

'That day will come before long, my love,' the man told her, as she looked up at him hungrily. 'This one will bring us closer to it. I have calculated the aspects and alignments, and they will be suitably positioned tomorrow night. That is when this one will be Offered.'

The young woman moistened her lips. 'And so you will have to stay away from me?'

'Indeed, as I always must, for a full day before an Offering.'

With a wave of his hand the image vanished from the stone. Then he moved to stand over the young woman's divan, gazing down at her. She leaned back, eyes bright, smile inviting, as he reached down to trail the fingers of one hand along her throat, down to the curve of one small breast. His expression grew almost feral as she parted her lips, as her flesh trembled and flushed.

'So,' he went on at last, his voice grown rougher, 'we must make full use of the time available, my beloved.'

At the palace the following morning, Red was seated on a stiff-backed chair in an austere, windowless room that was a waiting room of sorts, where ordinary mortals passed the time before an audience with the prince. Next to him sat Krost and Aurilia – once again in her aged, grey-gowned form – silently lost in their own thoughts. Red had managed not to make irreverent remarks about the absence of old magazines as in dentists' waiting rooms, and was passing the time with some inward musings of his own. Mostly about the previous night.

Then, the twilight gloom that he had been feeling lifted a little when a servant had come to say that Lady Aurilia sought his company for supper in her suite. That had sounded promising – but Red had been disappointed to find that Krost had been invited too, and that Aurilia was still in her aged guise. And Red had then begun to feel left out when their conversation grew not only serious but speculative, about why the prince had called them there. Uneasy speculations, too, for even Red was aware of the atmosphere in the palace, a troubled tension that was everywhere.

'It must be something to do with Evelane.' Aurilia had been showing tensions of her own, eating little, occupying herself with shredding soft rolls into crumbs without seeing them.

Krost nodded. 'I thought we might have seen her.' He had been making steady inroads into a number of flagons of wine, with no visible effect.

'You know how moody and difficult she can be,' Aurilia sighed, fragmenting another roll. 'She might be in one of her withdrawals, staying in her rooms, seeing no one.'

As Krost then sighed as well, shaking his head, Red asked the obvious question. 'Who are we talking about?'

'The prince's daughter,' Aurilia said gloomily. 'Princess Evelane. She . . .' Another deep sigh. 'Krost was in the prince's employ for years, and knows some of this tale better than I. He should tell you. You should know something of Phaedran before you meet him.'

And so, in a voice made even more deep and hoarse with sadness, Krost had told Red what he needed to know about Prince Phaedran and his daughter.

It was a sad tale, Krost began, though it had its roots in happy times. In those times, more than twenty years earlier, Phaedran – then just past his thirtieth birthday – simultaneously succeeded to the throne and took to wife the lovely and well-born young woman named Ellemar, who was also a powerful enchantress with a high position in the community of the Sisterhood.

'Approaching the highest,' Aurilia interjected. 'She was being prepared to take a place, when one became vacant, in the Circle of Nine. But then, out of love for Phaedran, she gave it all up – to take on those other responsibilities, as High Princess of the realm.'

'And she discharged them well,' Krost said. He told Red how Phaedran became renowned as a wise, just and generous ruler, and she as his gentle and beautiful equal in those qualities. Together they delighted the people by being so obviously, besottedly in love – and then delighted them more with the announcement that Ellemar was to bear a child.

'I never saw two more joyous people. And their joy spread over the Continent. There seemed to be some sort of feast or fair, somewhere, every day for the full nine months. And the whole of the land seemed to hold its breath when Ellemar began her confinement.'

'But something went wrong,' Red guessed, seeing the darkening of Krost's eyes.

He nodded. 'The birth was difficult and long, and in some way damaging to Ellemar. The child, a daughter, was fine and healthy – but Ellemar never recovered.'

As she faded and worsened, he went on, Phaedran almost

went insane trying to halt her decline. He turned to armies of physicians, healers, alchemists, wizards, the Sisterhood's Earth-magic . . . everything. But nothing helped. Over days and weeks, Ellemar's life flickered and dwindled like a candle flame. Until, finally, it went out.

And Phaedran nearly went out of his mind. He plumbed bottomless depths of grief and desolation that seemed as if they would continue endlessly, threatening to destroy him. And when, in time, through his own inner strength and the aid of friends and healers, he began a recovery, began to regain control of his life and his reign, it was never to be in the same way.

'He was like another man. All warmth and light and laughter had dried up inside him. He still ruled well, with wisdom and justice, but his rule became like his new nature – cold and bleak and grim . . .' Krost shook his great head sadly. 'People still respect him and feel loyalty to him. But while Ellemar was alive, he was *loved*.'

'Must have been hard on the little girl,' Red said.

Krost looked at Aurilia, offering her the narrative, and she nodded slowly. 'It was, but not as you might think,' she said. 'I believe Ellemar had some prevision of how Phaedran would be affected by her death. Only a few days before she died, she requested – almost demanded – that the child, Evelane, be taken by the Sisterhood, to be cared for and educated until she reached her majority.'

'So the girl's an enchantress too,' Red said.

Aurilia sighed. 'No. And that is much of her difficulty. She *should* be, for the Earth-magic is inherited from the mother. But by some rare mischance Evelane did not inherit the smallest scrap of her mother's considerable power. She has no more magic in her, of any sort, than has . . . an earthworm.' She sighed again. 'Yet the Sisterhood accepted her, willing – as Phaedran was – to obey Ellemar's last wish, and raised her in our Fastness in the North. And it was soon clear that she had inherited little of her mother's nature, as well. I knew Evelane well in her later childhood, and she was ever sad and trying – tense, overwrought, stormy, with a terrible guilt-ridden belief in her own worthlessness. Because her mother

71

had died from bearing her – because unlike the other Sister-hood children she had no magic – because her father had, as she thought, rejected her and sent her away.'

'Poor little neurotic princess,' Red murmured.

'As you say,' Aurilia went on sadly. 'She wanted only to be loved. And though the Sisters showered affection on her, along with help and counsel, it was useless. The love she wanted was that of her father, whom she scarcely knew – and who had become a cold and aloof man to whom love was a stranger.'

'So when she reached her majority and returned to the palace,' Krost added, 'she and Phaedran lived as strangers, wretched and solitary and remote from one another. She is quite pretty, Red, and should be lively and happy with singing and laughter around her. But she skulks around the palace like a shadow, melancholy and withdrawn, as if she feels she has no right to be alive.'

'And brooding still about her lack of a magical gift, I'm told,' Aurilia said. 'So much so that it seems to be . . . affecting her reason. Several times she has sent messages to the Sisterhood accusing them of conspiring to deny her the gift of magic, refusing to confer one on her. Yet she must know as we all know that it can't happen, it can't be given to one who lacks it.'

That brought the tale to an end, so that the two of them went gloomily back to their silent crumbling of rolls and emp-tying of flagons. And the sadness of the tale had revived Red's own gloom – so that he soon claimed weariness after a long day and found a footman to guide him back to his own suite. There he briefly looked at the bell-pull by the bed and wondered if little Nellann's presence might not improve his mood. But he was still unsure about the propriety of such adventures, there, and so sought other diversion. He glanced at the array of flagons, but felt disinclined towards any more drink. He found himself wishing for a television, and was able to smile ruefully at himself. How, he wondered, could he be feeling so depressed and miserable on only his second night in a land of magic and mystery?

But he knew the answer well enough. It was the way he

always felt when he was being forced to be inactive, when his restlessness was being constrained. That perception brought another rueful smile, just as his gaze fell on a few leather-bound books tucked away on a high shelf. He dragged them down, half-hoping that he might find some record or tale of his new namesake, Corodel. But instead he found that it was a multi-volume history of the Continent's royal dynasties. Better than nothing, he thought – and, flinging off his clothes, he climbed into bed to read. He had managed only three pages, about the remarkably uneventful reign of a Prince Intaxipol II, before he slid into a heavy sleep.

Dreams came later to mar that sleep, including images of shadowy cloaked figures, faceless under heavy hoods save for the glint of their eyes. Which, uncannily, were the inhuman white-pupilled eyes of Hallifort the Healer. But they vanished when he awoke with a start, gritty-eyed and sour-mouthed – to find his candles burned down and Nellann in his room, flinging back the curtains on a sunlit morning before bringing a laden tray to his bed. He sat up, blinking, as she leaned over to place the tray on his lap, allowing him a view down her well-filled neckline. A view that displayed, between her round breasts, a familiar mark on her skin, a circle with two wavy vertical lines within it.

'You're in the Sisterhood!' he blurted.

She giggled. 'You know the mark, sir? From seeing Lady Aurilia's, I shouldn't wonder.' She stepped away with another giggle. 'I've not much of a gift, myself, but enough. Herbs and things, mostly. They say my love potion works *wonders*, sir.'

Red glanced suspiciously down at his tray, which held portions of bread, fruit and some unidentifiable meat, along with a steaming, aromatic mug of tea. Nellann smiled brightly.

'Your breakfast's safe enough, sir,' she told him. 'I'd never think a vigorous young gentleman like *you* would need the potion.'

Red grimaced, wondering why it was that the women he'd met in that world always seemed friskiest in the morning. Which was never his best time.

But Nellann surprised him, moving briskly away from the

bed with little of the hip-swaying invitation of before. 'Water's there for washing, sir,' she said, gesturing at the anteroom holding the water-closet. 'And you should hurry and get ready. Seneschal sends his respects and says the prince will receive you and your companions this morning.'

Then she left, without indicating *when* it would happen, that morning. So Red raced through his meal and his ablutions and threw on his clothes, just buckling on his sword-belt when a footman arrived to show him to the waiting room where Krost and Aurilia had preceded him. And there they had been sitting ever since, in their different silences, while Red had let his mind drift over the events of the previous night, including the sad tale of Princess Evelane. He was wondering vaguely how best to behave with a prince who was as cold and grim as Phaedran had been described when he was startled as the door at the far end of the room was flung open.

Another footman stood there, bowing as a man strode past on his way out. The man was dressed in a blue-grey uniform much like those of the militia who had been on the street where Red had first arrived, except that this man's armour looked very light, as if mostly symbolic, and he was much decorated with insignia that surely indicated high rank, as did the jewelled hilt of the sword at his side. He seemed to be a man in middle age, greying, not tall, angular and wiry. And, to Red's surprise, a strange smouldering anger leaped into his eyes as he saw Aurilia and Krost.

'Marshal,' Krost said easily.

The uniformed man stiffened slightly, replied with the curtest of nods, then stalked past them out of the waiting room.

'Marshal Lenceon,' Aurilia quietly told Red as they got to their feet. 'Commander of all the militia, who keep the peace in Quamarr and throughout the Continent.'

'Doesn't seem to like you two much,' Red commented.

'Jealousy,' Krost rumbled succinctly. 'He would like to be the prince's *only* confidant and adviser. And . . . I have annoyed him before, in other ways.'

But then they dropped the subject, approaching the door where the bowing footman waited to usher them in. And, straightening his back, composing his features, Red strode forward with his friends to be received by royalty.

The room beyond the door did not disappoint Red's expectation of splendour. It was long, high-ceilinged, airy and light with tall windows, its walls bright with paintings and rich tapestries. Decorative bundles of long-bladed weapons like pikes stood gleaming in the corners, clusters of ornate furniture – cushioned chairs and sofas, polished cabinets and low tables – stood here and there on the spotless floor. At the far end, on a bright marble dais raised a step above the floor, Red saw an immense unoccupied chair, high-backed and heavy-legged, rich with decorative inlays some of which had the pure muted glow of gold.

'Throne room?' Red whispered to Aurilia, indicating the chair.

She shook her head. 'That's only used for state ceremonies. This is one of the Receiving Halls.'

Red wondered how many such Halls one prince needed – but was unable to ask, since they were approaching one of the clusters of furniture where a man was sitting talking intently to the balding figure of the seneschal. From the deference in the seneschal's posture, and from the fact that there was no one else in the room aside from the footman, Red deduced that he was looking at the prince. Who seemed quite imposing, he thought, if not as overpowering as his palace.

Red saw a man of average height, solidly built, with a high forehead and a strong beaked nose, wearing a severely plain tunic and trousers. His short hair and trimmed beard were grey-white, his face was drawn and lined with deeply etched creases, his eyes glinted dark and frigid from beneath strong brows. As the seneschal stepped back with a bow, Prince Phaedran rose to his feet, glancing with keen interest at Red before turning to his companions.

'Greetings, Lady Aurilia,' he said in a voice as flinty as his gaze. 'And my faithful Krost il Hak. Thank you both for attending me so swiftly.'

Aurilia bent a knee in an age-stiffened curtsy. 'Highness.

75

Luckily I was in the city when I received your message. I only hope I can be of service.'

As Krost bent his great neck respectfully, muttering an echo of those sentiments, Phaedran turned his gaze again to Red.

'And this,' he said, 'will be the young man of whom I have heard?'

Aurilia drew Red a step forward. 'He is Red Cordell, Highness, from another Sphere, brought here by an unexpected dilation of a summoning I performed – to recall the sword of Corodel.'

Phaedran raised his eyebrows, glanced down at the sword, then looked thoughtfully back at Red. 'I am told you acted valiantly last night, Red Cordell. Yet it is unfortunate that you should have had such an introduction to our land. You must find it all very strange and troubling.'

'Strange, yes,' Red replied. 'Sir. But I'm not as troubled as I was at first. It all seems . . . very interesting.'

Phaedran produced a wintry half-smile. 'No doubt – as I should surely find your Sphere of interest. I would have sought to learn something of it from you, were these more peaceful and leisured times. But as it is . . .' He gestured vaguely. 'In any case, you will no doubt wish to be returned to your own world without delay?'

Red felt taken aback, as if he was being rushed into something that he needed to think about. 'Aurilia tells me it may be a while before that can happen. And . . . I'm not in a hurry to leave. Your Highness.'

Phaedran nodded distantly. 'Then we may yet be able to talk together, when I have . . . overcome my present difficulty.'

'Highness,' Krost broke in firmly. 'What difficulty? What trouble is it that made you summon us?'

The prince's eyes went dark and bleak, like the depths of a winter night. 'I am troubled by *loss*, my friend – a loss almost as grievous as any I have known.'

'Oh, no,' Aurilia breathed, her wrinkled face chalk-white. 'Not Evelane . . .'

Stiffly, as if the muscles of his neck were in spasm, Phaedran nodded. 'Yes – Evelane. Although not what you may think, Aurilia. My daughter is not – I pray to the gods – ill or dying. But she is gone from me.' He stared around at them all with his icy, tormented gaze. 'The princess has been *abducted*. Stolen away, some weeks ago. And I cannot discover where she has been taken, nor by whom.'

Some days later Red was again standing at his sitting-room window, staring out at the palace stables and the sweep of the estates beyond them, warm in the afternoon sun. And, as had been the case often in those days, he was lost in random and disjointed musings that were no longer concerned with his own edgy restlessness but with the abduction of a princess.

During the first meeting the prince had told them that Evelane had been riding in the palace's outer estates, with a retinue of ladies-in-waiting and guards. But she had galloped away from the others – or else her horse had bolted. And when the others had caught up with the horse, near one of the dense stands of trees on the grounds, Evelane had disappeared.

The grounds were searched, over and over. The prince had questioned Evelane's people, over and over. But nothing was found, no one knew more than they had said. The princess was, unaccountably, gone.

Everyone suspected that she had been taken by sorcerous means, but there was no proof – and no message or ransom demand of any sort had arrived in the weeks that followed. Phaedran had mobilized all the resources of his throne, including wizards, without finding the smallest clue as to her whereabouts or the identity of the abductors. In the end, even though he insisted on secrecy within the palace to prevent a general alarm across the land, Phaedran sought help from outside. He contacted the Sisterhood, who sent Aurilia – and who by that time had sent quiet orders to Sisters all across the land, to watch for signs of the princess. But Phaedran had asked for Aurilia for another reason, the same one that had led him to summon Krost.

'I need your strength and support,' Phaedran had told

them. 'But especially I will need you with me when we find my daughter – because you both have known her and loved her and can help to care for her. And we *will* find her. I have pledged it.' His voice had crackled hollowly. 'And when she is found, and her abductors known – then we shall *all* be there, with as powerful a force as need be. And I shall exact my vengeance in blood.'

The speech had left Red feeling chilled, mainly because of the prince's icy emotionlessness while promising bloodshed and death. But at the same time Red had been excited by the prospect of some *action*, which made him even more reluctant to be hurried back to his own world.

The trouble was that the action looked like remaining only a prospect, indefinitely. In the days that followed, Krost had been mostly closeted with the prince, who seemed to place great reliance on his solid common sense; and when Aurilia had not been in her suite making whatever magics she needed in order to consult at long range with the Sisterhood she had been closeted with them too. So Red had been left to his own devices – and, at first, he had very few of them.

He had spent a while exploring the opulent corridors of the palace, regularly getting lost, until one imposing chamber began to look much like every other. But he had found an interesting room that was a gallery or museum, including a collection of some fascinating weaponry. That had absorbed him for a time, trying to put names to various shapes and sizes of swords, spears, bows – and trying to identify weirder weapons. Such as one with a narrow haft of polished wood, about a foot long, with a needle-sharp spike of metal jutting from one end and a cluster of feathers fanning out from the other. Like an oversize dart, he thought, and wondered idly about the dartboard.

But after a day or two his wanderings had been interrupted by the seneschal, who had discovered his morose restlessness and had some forms of diversion to offer. Those entailed vigorous exercise as well as time-killing, and Red relished both. The seneschal introduced Red to the palace guard, who wore only slightly different uniforms from the city militia and who saluted him respectfully and stared openly at the sword he carried. They welcomed him into their exercise and training sessions – grinning when he told them, once the seneschal had departed, that he was not a lord and did not wish to be treated like one. They then put him through the fairly gruelling paces that were normal for them, and he had a fine time.

He had made them all laugh by his inexperience with the crossbow, but he silenced their laughter by proving his competence with the sword – using a blunt practice weapon, not the magically sharp sword of Corodel. He had shown that he could sit a horse with the best of them on wild gallops around the bridle paths, riding a long-legged roan that had been found for him. And for the fun of it he had also shown his new soldier-friends some of the basic moves and strikes of his world's martial arts, which had left them amazed and bruised.

So his days in the palace had become brighter and more exhilarating – although he could often be startled when he paused to think how at ease he felt after such a short time in such a remarkable place. And then he would marvel again at the eerie power of the little healer, Hallifort, who had made his swift adjustment possible. But with the enjoyable days there were also the nights, when he was usually alone, finding no consolation in the musty books, finding himself time and again looking thoughtfully at the bell-pull by his bed and visualizing Nellann in her tight dress.

But he had not rung for her. Nor had he ever responded to any of her overtures, when she was in his suite bringing his meals or tending to other chores. And his reluctance was only partly due to his unsureness about custom and propriety. He had found that, whenever he felt tempted by Nellann, part of his mind summoned a rival image that displaced all other thoughts – the image of Aurilia on his first morning in Quamarr, tawny-gold hair tumbling down, body ripe and inviting in its low-cut gown.

When that vision struck him in solitude, he tended to go back to staring out of the window, just as he was doing that afternoon. His friends among the guards, that morning, had been full of news about the impending arrival of important visitors – who, they said teasingly, would probably be unlike anyone that Red, the outlander, would ever have seen. That interested Red, but he had spent the rest of the day up to then on his own again, which left him feeling thwarted and annoyed, imagining that the visitors might well have come and gone.

What I'd really like, he thought, is to go and explore the city some more. But others, Aurilia especially, had discouraged that notion. He wasn't to go wandering in the city, she had told him – not with the assassin Vanticor out there somewhere, and who knew what other possible enemies connected with the prince's troubles. The message had been that because he didn't know his way around he should stay home and be sensible.

It was quite the wrong message to give to Red Cordell. True to his nature, whenever he was chafed or constrained, his automatic response was to break free, to kick over the traces, to rebel. Mock combat and exercise with guardsmen could only go so far towards appeasing him. That afternoon, irritated and disconsolate, his nature asserted itself. To hell with propriety, he snarled to himself, and strode away from the window to yank at the bell-pull as if he would tear it from its fastenings.

Within moments a soft knock came at his door. But when he called out and the door opened, he saw that it was going to be a completely frustrating day. Instead of a smiling Nellann, he was looking at a small, young and diffident footman.

'I rang for Nellann,' he said testily.

The footman wriggled, gazing at the floor. 'Nellann is not in the palace, my lord.'

'Not . . . ? Where is she?'

Another wriggle. 'I . . . No one is sure, my lord.'

Red glowered. 'Come on, kid. I'm not a lord, and you can talk to me. What's going on?'

The young footman looked up, seeming even more uneasy with Red's informality. 'Sir . . . Nellann was reprimanded by the seneschal. She was overheard saying . . . making suggestions, about you, sir, to the other maids.' He swallowed, saw Red was half-smiling, and took courage. 'The seneschal was *very* angry, sir. She was crying . . . And then *she* was angry – and she rushed out of the palace – and she hasn't returned, sir.'

. Just my luck, Red thought. I wish her scolding had been for what she'd *done*, not what she said . . .

'May I serve you in her place, sir?' the young footman asked.

Not in a million years, Red told him silently. 'No . . . that's all right . . .' he began.

But then he was interrupted as the door crashed open and Krost strode in, past the young footman who bowed, looking slightly puzzled, and departed.

'Red,' Krost said without preamble, 'come and join us. The prince has important visitors—'

'So I hear,' Red broke in drily.

'They are wizards – three of the most notable Adepts in the city – who have been trying to find Evelane or find out something about her. Aurilia thought you would like to meet them.'

'I would,' Red said at once. Wizards, he thought happily, following Krost out. Will they have long funny robes and tall pointy hats and carry wands or something?

The visitors were obviously already in with the prince, in the Receiving Hall where Red and his friends had first been greeted. Aurilia in her aged form was waiting in the narrow waiting room – but as Red and Krost joined her the seneschal himself opened the door to show them into the Hall. And this time the prince was seated on the throne-like chair dominating the Hall, listening intently to three men standing before him, who broke off their talk as the new arrivals entered.

None of the three fitted Red's image of a wizard. One of them was short and thin, wearing a long well-tailored tunic over tight trousers. The other two – one bony and bearded, the other heavy-set and florid – wore elaborate garments like frock coats and matching trousers. And all three regarded the newcomers with something like disdain in their expressions.

'Lady Aurilia, is it not?' the small one said.

'Wretifal,' Aurilia said shortly.

82

'You know me?' the wizard said, affecting surprise. 'Then you must know my colleagues here – Ahnaan, Inchalo . . .'

'How unexpected to find *you* here,' said the heavy-set one, Ahnaan. 'I thought you higher Sisters preferred to hide yourselves away in your northern Fastness.'

Aurilia glanced towards the prince, who was poring over a clutch of papers obliviously, then turned her scowl back on to the wizards. 'I am here because the prince sought aid from the Sisterhood, as I'm sure you know.'

Ahnaan laughed. 'I can't image what use the witches thought it would be, sending only *one*.'

The bearded one, Inchalo, snorted. 'I don't know what use it would be if they sent a *hundred*.'

'Perhaps,' Krost growled, 'your lordships would tell us what use *you* have been, so far, to help the prince.'

Ahnaan turned to stare at him. 'And who is this? A servant of yours, Aurilia?'

'No, no,' said Wretifal with a smirk. 'You remember, Ahnaan. He has been employed in the palace before. The dwarf from the Southern Highlands.'

Red glanced with surprise at Krost, who hardly looked like anyone who could be called a dwarf. Krost was bristling, immense shoulders hunched, one hand white-knuckled on the iron staff.

'You are free with your remarks, my lords,' he growled, 'here where courtesy keeps you safe.'

'We say what we like where we like,' said the red-faced Ahnaan. 'Flex your muscles as you will, Highlander, you lack the power to threaten our safety anywhere.'

Krost looked as if he was about to test that theory, but a gesture from Aurilia stopped him. 'Let them talk. Petty spite and sneering is as natural to wizards as poison to vipers.'

That drew a glare from Ahnaan and Inchalo. But Wretifal, no longer paying attention, had begun gazing at Red with undisguised interest.

'While we are all becoming acquainted,' he said, 'may we know the name of this young man? Your plaything, Aurilia?'

Anger brought sudden tension to Red's body, but he too was halted by a gesture from the old woman. 'He is an outlander, a warrior and a friend, Wretifal,' she said levelly. 'You would do well to guard your tongue. His name is Red Cordell.'

The mage's eyes narrowed. *'Corodel?'*

'Just Cordell,' Red snapped. 'And nobody's plaything.'

Aurilia smiled slightly. 'But his sword is Corodel's.'

Wretifal stared for a moment, then suddenly began to laugh. 'So the witches have reclaimed the sword of Corodel, and have found a pretty boy to wield it! Will he ride off to rescue the princess single-handed?' His laughter rose, joined by the other two. 'Where did you find him, Aurilia – herding goats?'

'His origins are no concern of yours,' Aurilia said, her sharp tone cutting through the hilarity.

Wretifal smiled brightly. 'A *secret*, is he? I might have known. How the witches love their secrets. If you only knew how *transparent* your mysteries are to higher Adepts – how easily they can be plumbed. It is an amusement, to look in on the foolish prattlings of your Circle of Nine. What pettinesses you spend time on, Aurilia. Or shall I call you by your *secret* Name – *Auriflamme?*'

He smiled at her as he pronounced the Name. But then his smile began to wilt. Though she had restrained Krost and Red, Aurilia herself was suddenly blazing with fury. Nothing about her altered, except for her eyes, where emerald lightning flashed. Nor did she move, other than slowly straightening from her stooped posture. None the less, somehow, confronting the wizards, it was as if she *loomed* – while an invisible power seemed to gather and build within her and around her, ominous, highly charged, immense.

'You *dare?*' Her voice was all the more menacing for being low and controlled. 'You dare to spy on the Sisterhood? You dare to learn the Names of the Nine, and to *speak* my Name, openly?'

'I do as I please,' Wretifal snapped. But his voice quivered a little, his eyes were wary, and Red saw a peculiar pale phosphorescence forming at his fingertips.

Aurilia saw it too. 'You would use magic here, now? You pathetic little man! My Name that you dared to speak marks me as Standard-bearer, emissary of the Sisterhood. If you challenge me, you challenge the Nine, and every living Sister with them. Is that what you want?'

Wretifal looked like one who wanted to step away and pretend nothing had happened, yet who also wanted not to lose face by such a retreat. But the impasse was abruptly resolved. The prince had emerged from his absorption with the papers to see the intensity of the confrontation, and his glare was glacial as he suddenly slammed his open palm down on the chair's heavy arm.

'Enough!' he said harshly. 'Conduct your rivalries elsewhere, Wretifal! Lady Aurilia and Krost are here at my command, and you will show them respect when you are in my presence!'

The mages flinched, and Aurilia relaxed, looking slightly abashed. 'My apologies, Highness,' Wretifal said quickly. 'It was just . . . She was . . .'

'I also apologize, my lord,' Aurilia said quietly. 'There are more urgent needs for our powers.'

'Quite so,' Phaedran said icily, fixing the mages with his glare as he brandished the sheaf of papers. 'I have read through this overblown account of your endeavours, and I find that it fails to answer the only question of any moment. So I ask it again, now. *Where is my daughter?*'

'Highness . . .' Wretifal writhed helplessly. 'I *deeply* regret . . . we cannot say.'

'*Cannot?*' Phaedran echoed, glowering.

'My lord,' Ahnaan put in, 'we have plied all our scrying powers till we are exhausted – we have ranged the Continent with spells of seeking and of sensing . . .'

A wave of the prince's hand closed the mage's mouth with a snap. 'That is what you have done,' Phaedran barked. 'What you have *not* done is find my daughter! Can you think of a reason why I should not banish all three of you and hire other Adepts?'

'Highness!' Wretifal cried, looking stricken.

But the bearded Inchalo inclined his head respectfully. 'You may dismiss us, lord, of course, but I feel it would avail you little. We have *driven* ourselves to do your bidding, my prince, to the limits of our strength. I do not believe other Adepts could do more.'

Phaedran glared. 'I hope you do not speak from jealousy and false pride, Inchalo. The fact is that you have not succeeded.'

'Not *yet*, Highness,' Ahnaan said. 'But it is only a matter of time. Our scrying and our spells will soon have examined every grassblade and clod of earth in the land!'

'And the Nine are doing the same, even now,' Aurilia added.

Phaedran nodded stiffly, his glare subsiding. 'Very well. I am sure all these efforts are valuable. But – my daughter may be in danger at every moment, while all this scrying and seeking goes on in vain.'

He surged up from the great chair, stalking a few paces away to stare unseeingly out of a window. And Red found himself feeling sorry for the cold-blooded prince, as he did for the unknown girl in captivity – or worse – somewhere in the land. But he felt most concern for his new friends, Aurilia and Krost, who were watching their prince with expressions of pain and distress. I wish I could help, he thought. And then he took a startled mental step back, examining that thought and its implications.

The prince wheeled back to stare imperiously again at the wizards. 'Did you seek to locate the one I mentioned,' he snapped, 'who might well be a suspect for such a crime? My old enemy, Talonimal?'

Red saw Aurilia's eyes widen in surprise as the small mage, Wretifal, nodded quickly.

'I did seek him, my lord,' Wretifal said. 'We know that years ago he went to make a solitary home for himself on the coast of the Western Woodlands. But–' he spread his hands in a gesture of defeat– 'my seeking there found nothing, no trace of the man. He must have moved elsewhere and covered his tracks magically – and as yet I have not located him.'

Phaedran scowled. 'Continue seeking him. I still firmly believe that Evelane was taken by sorcerous means, and that he is a likely suspect.'

Wretifal was still nodding eagerly. 'Indeed, Highness. We

have also looked at many of the more powerful Adepts, especially those who have withdrawn into solitude, as some mages do. We even tried to peer briefly at the mighty one, the Magister, who now dwells in a forgotten valley in the Southern Highlands. But . . . we did not detect the princess in any of those places.'

'Then continue,' Phaedran said hollowly. 'Use every scrap of your magical strength, to your limits and beyond. Examine every step of the Continent – and the outlands beyond its shores – and anywhere else that your powers can reach.'

The wizards bowed, mumbling reassurances.

'We might look especially here in the city,' Aurilia said suddenly, 'where magical seeking will not be weakened by distance.' She held up a bony hand to stop the mages' interruption. 'Some days ago, my lords, an attempt was made to take me captive – in the way, I believe, that other Sisters have lately been vanishing. It's possible that Evelane too may have been taken as part of . . . whatever plot is behind those disappearances.'

'But the princess is not one of your Sisters,' Ahnaan said doubtfully. 'She lacks any magical gift, I understand.'

'And she was taken from the grounds of the *palace*,' Inchalo added, 'not from some witch's hovel.'

'True,' Aurilia agreed coolly. 'She is not a Sister. But she was *raised* by the Sisterhood. Her abductors may have believed she is one of us.'

'Even if that were so,' Wretifal asked, 'how does that help us?'

Aurilia smiled fiercely. 'Because the man who led those trying to abduct *me* felt sure enough of himself to reveal his name. He is Vanticor – the known assassin.' She nodded as startled recognition showed on the mages' faces. 'He also spoke of his "master", who must certainly be an Adept – for Vanticor and his henchmen wore powerful wards and amulets.'

Understanding was dawning on the wizards. 'So this Vanticor . . .' Wretifal began.

'He has been seen in the city since, by Master Cordell here,' the prince said. 'My militia have been scouring Quamarr for him without success. But now Lady Aurilia has hit upon it. Wretifal, you and your colleagues must ply *your* skills to seek him. Use your spells, gentlemen, to find Vanticor – who may lead you to his master.'

'Who may well be the one holding Evelane,' Aurilia said grimly.

After that, Red's attention began to wander. The prince and Wretifal went into a separate huddle, to do with the one Phaedran had called his enemy – the sorcerer Talonimal – and where he might have gone. Meanwhile Aurilia and the other mages, their enmity set aside, began discussing magical processes that might find Vanticor and backtrack him to his employer. It all grew complicated and intense, and again Red felt very left out. He edged closer to Krost and nudged his elbow.

'Is there some way I can get out of here?' he muttered. 'I feel totally useless.'

Krost nodded. 'As do I. I have nothing to offer a meeting of mages.' He winked elaborately. 'Do you feel at all thirsty, Red?'

'Never more so,' Red said with a grin.

So they both offered vague excuses and took their leave – with a preoccupied gesture of permission from Phaedran and a scowl from Aurilia that spoke volumes about the need for sobriety and prudence.

'I feel like a kid escaping from an overprotective mother,' Red said wryly as they strode away through the corridors.

Krost's laughter boomed. 'She feels responsible for you being here, Red, and concerned for your welfare. But I doubt if she feels at all *motherly* towards you.'

That made Red smile a twisted smile, and almost made him broach the subject of particular customs and proprieties in Quamarr. But then instinct suggested that it might not be in the best of taste, in Krost's view. Especially if Red broached the subject in terms of Nellann, not Aurilia. So he walked on with Krost in silence, coming at last to the palace's great outer door, where another of the ubiquitous footmen bowed them out. Nodding in friendly fashion at the guardsmen on sentry duty outside the door, they marched breezily down the steps and away along the long gravel drive, which was being darkened slightly by the encroaching shadows of sunset.

Too bad we can't hail a cab, Red thought. But it's not *that* big a city, and it feels good to get out.

'Where shall we go, then, my friend?' Krost asked, sounding as pleased to be out of the palace as Red felt. 'Back to the Players' Green, and that excellent tavern?'

Red thought about that – and suddenly knew without doubt exactly where he wanted to go. 'Krost, I don't just want a drink. I want some fun, some life. Let's go across the river.'

Krost turned to stare at him. 'The Rookeries?'

'Don't tell me there aren't any taverns there.'

'There are many,' Krost replied. 'Many with well-kept ale. But, Red, the day is waning. And while the Rookeries are bad enough at any time, they are at their *most* dangerous after dark.'

'Are they?' Red grinned his eager grin, left hand resting lightly on his sword-hilt. 'Well, so are we, friend Krost. So are we.'

This is more like it, Red thought happily. Like coming out of a museum into real life.

They were strolling along a narrow, dimly lit, dirty back street, lined with rickety low-roofed buildings that were perfectly matched in squalor to the street. And Red was enjoying it all hugely, as he had done increasingly since they set out. He had particularly enjoyed getting to the riverside – taking in the great wharves, the vessels tied up, the foul-mouthed watermen busy at their tasks. He had studied the river itself with interest, since Krost had told him that it rose in the Ebony Mountains far to the south-east of the city, and its waters were stained by those dark crags so that the river was as inky-black by day as it certainly looked that evening.

Then as the twilight darkened they had crossed the river and plunged into the Rookeries. Yet despite the reputation of the place, the most dangerous thing Red had encountered on those grimy streets had been one or two outstandingly memorable stinks.

The street they were on, according to Krost, would lead them to the heart of the Rookeries and, inevitably, a tavern that he knew. Like most roads in Quamarr the street was cobbled, but there was a variety of litter and unrecognizable messes strewn or smeared over the rough stones. Down its centre ran a shallow gutter containing a thin brown rivulet that had to be raw sewage. And any light along that shadowy way came from windows in some of the narrow buildings on either side, which tended to lean in towards the street and sometimes to have gabled extensions stretching out from their upper floors that almost touched the ones opposite.

But though the general air of poverty and squalor was worse even than the area around the tavern where Red had spent his first night in Quamarr, there was in the Rookeries none of its dismal dreariness. The Rookeries were awash with life – as noisy, vibrant, and colourful as any sensation-seeking visitor might wish, and rather more filthy and foul-smelling than many might prefer. Red had been thinking of films he had seen and worked on that had tried to recreate the raw and jostling life in famous slums of the past. Even if those films got the costumes and bustle and all the visual richness right, Red realized that they never caught the authentic level and variety of noise – and of course they never got the stink at all.

On that one stretch of narrow street alone, they had passed the reeking corpse of something that might have been a dog but that had become a shapeless swarm of maggots – yet just next to it had been a doorway from which drifted the wonderful smell of freshly baked bread. And overlaid on to both those odours, and all others, was the unmistakable variety of reeks – sharply acid, sickly sweet, rancidly sour – that came from the endless flow around and past them of people.

In among the throngs of Rookeries folk, generally looking thin, ragged, unwashed, but rarely downtrodden, Red saw assorted startling characters who were obviously strangers to the city visiting the slums for reasons akin to his. Krost pointed out a stocky old man in a wide-brimmed hat and several layers of stained clothing whose sun-tan apparently showed him to be a prospector – for gold or precious stones, along the edges of the wild and deadly Eastern Wastelands. Later they passed two tall men who were also darkly bronzed, but Krost identified them as Northerners, from the area near where Aurilia was born. And a crowd of half-drunk men in thigh-high boots and greasy fur jerkins were, Krost said, fisher-folk from the north coast of the Western Woodlands – brave folk, he added, for they lived on the fringe of forests where all of the denizens were bloodthirsty and none of them was human.

The crowds might have made Red think that the whole population of the Rookeries was out on the streets that night, had he not heard the shrieks, bellows, laughter, clattering, and so forth from the decrepit buildings along the way, offering a counterpoint to the seemingly endless din from the streets. And the people around them seemed to grow even noisier as the darkness deepened, full of raucous laughter and coarse jokes as if in anticipation of the night's amusements. Many of the jokes were at the expense of the various strangers wandering through their midst – though the jokers took note of the size of Krost and his quarterstaff and the sword at Red's hip and kept all jesting at their expense on the right side of insult.

So Red merely smiled at the coarsely cheery cries aimed at him and Krost, as they walked on. But then he was smiling delightedly at nearly everything. At the street-sellers, for instance, still busy and noisy with their cries drawing attention to their trays or hand-carts heaped with wares – dubious foodstuffs, rags trying to be garments, assorted junk, but also quite a range of efficient-looking hand weapons. Red even smiled at the beggars who shambled towards them half-naked and filthy, all too ready to display amazing disfigurements.

But for all his enjoyment Red did not fail to notice that, as the night deepened, there were fewer and fewer of the shabby aproned women and scrawny urchins to be seen. And the men on the street were becoming different, as if one part of the Rookeries population was making way for another – for what Red's world would have called night people. Some of the new population were rough-looking slouchers with cudgels, some were swaggerers with heavy swords, some were pale slitherers with no visible weapons at all. The jokes became fewer, no one seemed to make eye-contact, all left plenty of space as they passed each other. And Red's smile grew more alert, yet more amused, as they progressed – walking warily around the well-armed ones, stepping carefully over the more numerous drunks snoring on the cobbles. They even managed not to stare too curiously at the body of a man crumpled in the mouth of an alley, knife-wounds staining the roadway crimson.

'Starting to get lively,' Red remarked quietly.

Krost grimaced. 'You are being well introduced to life in the Rookeries.'

'My kind of place,' Red said with a grin.

By then he was also grinning to see that a quite different

sort of woman was beginning to appear on the streets or at some windows. Not wives in aprons, those, but women whose profession needed no explaining. Most were coarse-featured and broken-toothed, with too much of their doughy flesh exposed by slit skirts and open bodices. But one or two were younger and prettier – and Krost saw Red's attention being drawn to them.

'Do not be tempted, my friend,' the bulky man said with a smile. 'Many evil diseases await the unwary man, from that quarter.'

Red shook his head. 'Don't worry – I'm just sight-seeing. But I hope there'll be no diseases on offer at this tavern you know. I could do with some supper as well as a drink.'

'The tavern is clean enough, for the Rookeries,' Krost assured him. 'I have eaten and drunk there often.'

'Maybe diseases don't have the nerve to attack you,' Red said drily.

Laughing, they strode on, turning again and again along more back streets and side streets, until Red knew that his sense of direction had completely given up and he was wholly lost. He had known urban areas in his time that were complexes of twisting streets and interwoven alleys. But the Rookeries was nothing less than an immense maze – a labyrinth without pattern or reason, where a street might branch into several alleys, where an alley might again become a street or might vanish into a narrower passage like a tunnel or into a dead end. Where all the roadways of all sizes crisscrossed and intersected and overlapped, at all angles, always over-complicated, always unpredictable, like the tangling branches of some vast overgrown plant.

'If we got separated,' Red said lightly to Krost, 'I'd never find my way out of here.'

'You might not,' Krost said solemnly. 'Many strangers to the city have vanished in the Rookeries. Probably because they lost their lives as well as their way.'

That thought silenced Red briefly. But around the next corner Krost turned to lead the way through the door of a one-storey wooden building that looked like a run-down stable from the outside but that was filled with the aroma of cooking meat and the fragrance of good ale. It was also fairly basic inside, designed solely for eating and drinking with no thought for decor. It was cool and smoky and dim, with a few small lamps flickering here and there. Red saw that the walls were greasy and smoke-blackened, that the plain wooden tables had no shortage of stains and blotches and moulds, as did the crude chairs and benches. But even so the taproom was nearly full, resounding with cheerful noisy talk and laughter and the clatter of drinking vessels and plates of food.

Over that noise Red could hear Krost's great belly rumbling with eagerness as they found a table by one wall where a solid, reinforced bench looked able to take Krost's weight. And it became clear to Red that his companion was well known in that place. Even as they sat down the tavern-keeper himself, a paunchy man in a soiled apron, appeared with two foaming mugs of ale and a cheerful greeting for Krost. Krost then asked the man for 'my usual stew' and recommended to Red that he try the meat they could smell roasting. Red's unease at not being able to pay was waved aside by Krost as unimportant. And as Red expressed his thanks he noticed that the tavern-keeper had begun staring at him, open-mouthed and wide-eyed. But then the man gulped, shook himself and hurried away.

Krost chuckled. 'He must think he is seeing a ghost. This was one of Corodel's favourite taverns.'

Red raised his eyebrows. 'Am I so much like him?'

'In some ways,' Krost replied. 'Not that I knew him well – and in his later years he was of course more weathered and heavier. Certainly he had less of a sense of humour. But I would say you resemble the *young* Corodel closely enough. There is no doubt you have the same air, the same devil-may-care spirit that got him into trouble often enough.'

'Once too often, from what Aurilia said,' Red remarked, as Krost paused to take a mighty gulp of ale.

'So it seems. He heard some fool's tale, some fiction about an unknown tribe of mysterious beings somewhere in the Eastern Wastelands. And even in his late middle age he could not resist the adventure, had go to seek the tribe. When the

Sisterhood finally went searching for him, because they had a special fondness for him, they found only his bones, and his sword, on the side of a dune in an empty desert.'

Red felt an eerie shiver along his spine, and touched the hilt of the sword that suddenly seemed strange to him. 'I'd better try hard,' he muttered, 'not to follow in his footsteps.'

Krost snorted. 'Try as you will, you would not be here at all if you were not like him. And you will not have to travel East to prove it.'

'Let's drop it,' Red said, feeling the shiver again. 'I'm just Cordell. Not a hero or an adventurer, just a traveller far from home. And a hungry one,' he added, as a serving-girl appeared at the table burdened with platters of steaming food.

The girl also glanced nervously at Red and his sword, showing that the tavern-keeper had been talking about him. But then Krost cheerfully changed the subject by chatting to Red about his food – succulent venison, it seemed, from the semi-wild herds of yellowhorn deer that roamed the Central Grasslands. And with the meat came a few vegetables, small round tubers like turnips and green knobbly things like spherical cucumbers.

'Terrific,' Red announced, taking up the heavy knife and fork provided. Then he leaned forward, seeing that Krost's plate held quite different things. 'What've you got?'

Krost raised his dark eyes with an odd look. 'Different vegetables – tubers, greens, legumes, herbs and spices . . .'

'No meat?' Red asked idly, his mouth full.

'My people eat no meat,' Krost said, still looking at him almost watchfully.

Red was only vaguely interested, since vegetarians were nothing new to him. And he failed to register the look, being involved in cutting another chunk of the venison. Then Krost's first two words got through to him, making him look up.

'Your people,' he repeated. 'Of course – you're from the south somewhere, aren't you?'

Krost nodded carefully. 'My home lies among the plateaux and peaks of the Southern Highlands. I am properly Krost il

Hak, of the Hak-illan tribe, the second most numerous of the plateau tribes.'

By then Red had registered the peculiar wary tension of his large companion. 'Interesting,' he said slowly. 'I've always liked mountains, myself. Do you . . . go back often?'

'Often enough. But I also spend long periods away.'

Red studied him, frowning slightly. 'Would I be getting too nosy if I asked why?'

'I had thought Aurilia might have told you,' Krost said.

'She said it was your story to tell,' Red replied.

'That was gracious. But there is no reason why you should not know.' Krost looked away, the darkness of old pain showing in his eyes. 'This is a large Continent, Red, containing many different kinds of . . . creatures. Including in some places beings that are not animals, are like men – but are not men. They come in many forms – some in Southern valleys, some in Western forests . . . perhaps some too elusive ever to be seen, like the tribe Corodel sought. And *my* people, Red, are such beings. Though we resemble humans in almost every way, we are not entirely human.'

'Not?' Red asked edgily. 'Then what?'

'Giants.' Krost's voice was empty of all expression. 'My people are giants.'

Red blinked. 'All right – I suppose you're big enough . . .'

'No.' The great head jerked in an emphatic negative. 'My people, the tribes of the high plateaux, are more than twice the height of a normal human. And as huge in bulk, and weight, and strength, as they are in height.' He was looking past Red, into the distance, into another time and place. 'Some are herdsmen, many more are miners – or stonemasons. I have watched them build a house from stone, cutting and shaping boulders that would half-fill this tavern, then lifting them and setting them into place by hand, *one* person to each rock. A rock that ten men of Quamarr could not budge. Those are my people – the giants of the Highlands. And among the giants, I was born . . . as I am.'

Red was staring, incredulous. 'Then *that*,' he said softly, 'is why that wizard in the palace called you . . .'

'*Dwarf*.' Krost's face hardened. 'Yes. I have been called that

96

often. In my tribe I was "the little one" to those who would be kind, but the crueller ones taunted me with names like runt or gnome . . . or dwarf. I was of course a disappointment to my family, never strong enough for the work or the life. So . . . I live apart from them, much of the time. Here, among men, I am of normal height, though I am stronger than most and my weight has surprised many. But there, among my own people and the mountains that I love and dream of, I am small, weak, useless. A freak. A dwarf among giants.'

He stopped, and they sat silent for a moment, Red watching the patterns of pain shifting across his friend's broad face. 'Thank you,' Red said at last, 'for telling me.'

'I felt you would understand . . . since you too are an exile, here. And it eases the old ache, a little, to tell someone.'

Red nodded. 'I wish I could think of something to say to ease it some more.'

'There are no such words, I fear.' Then Krost found a half-smile from somewhere and slapped a large hand on to the table, which groaned. 'Come – these sad memories raise a thirst. Another ale, my friend?'

Red managed a half-grin of his own. 'I could probably force another down.'

'And anyway,' Krost went on, waving the iron staff to beckon the serving-girl, 'it is not all sad, the story of my life. I have seen remarkable things and met remarkable people, which I would not have done if I had stayed in the Highlands.'

'People like the prince,' Red remarked, as two more brimming mugs were delivered to the table.

'Like the prince,' Krost agreed, diving into his mug, surfacing with a smack of lips and half the contents drained. 'I have known Phaedran since his happiest days when his wife, Ellemar, still lived. And he has taken me into his service in the past, as now, for special occasions, special tasks. As he did for those times when little Princess Evelane was travelling between the palace and her other home with the Sisterhood in the North. Phaedran would send *me* with her, to protect her.'

'Good choice,' Red murmured.

Krost nodded with quiet pride. 'I pledged my life to her

protection, and she was never at risk. I only wish I had been at hand when she was taken . . .' His great fists clenched. 'But I am grateful to Phaedran for asking me to join in her rescue.'

'Good choice again,' Red said. 'I hope you find her.'

They sat silent then a while, plates empty and mugs of ale being emptied, thinking their own thoughts about far away people and places. But as the ale made itself felt they resumed their talk, on lighter subjects, with good cheer and laughter and even a growing hint of boisterousness.

Until the cold draught of remembered evil fell across their merriment.

Red felt it first, for he was sitting at an angle that showed a view of the door. As people will, he had glanced casually across every time a new customer entered. But his casual glance became sudden tension when the door opened, then, to admit a newcomer in black and green, with a scarred face, shaking back his lank yellow hair.

'It's *him*!' Red hissed. 'Vanticor!'

Krost whirled on his bench, gripping the great quarterstaff. And perhaps the scarred killer saw the movement of those immense shoulders – or perhaps he was merely warned by some animal instinct. He peered through the dimness, saw Krost and Red, stared wildly for an instant – then spun in a blur of speed and vanished back out through the door.

And by then Red was also a blur, clutching his sword to his side, leaping across the taproom to that door.

'Red!' Krost bellowed after him.

But Red did not slow or turn. 'Krost, come on!' he yelled – and sprang through the door to pursue his enemy.

TEN

The narrow street outside the tavern was even more thronged than before, with more of the Rookeries night-people emerging from their homes and hideaways. And the crowds proved a benefit, for they hampered Vanticor's flight and also hid the fact of Red's pursuit. He had not made much ground when Red hurtled out of the door of the tavern, glanced around and spotted the green and black costume. And a moment later, when Vanticor glanced back to see if he had been followed, Red was shielded by a fat man with a voluminous cloak and his equally obese female companion.

Red's first instinct was to catch up with Vanticor and take some sort of reprisal for the assaults of his first night in Quamarr. He did not think twice about the risk of challenging a known assassin on what was surely the killer's home territory. But as the mass of people on the street slowed his first rush, he realized that being held back was a good idea. If he merely *followed* Vanticor, to see where he was going, maybe even where his hideout was – who knew what might be learned?

A vision arose like a film clip in his mind, making him smile at himself as he twisted and dodged through the crowd. A vision of himself returning to the palace in triumph, bringing with him the beautiful Princess Evelane whom he had single-handedly rescued from some foul Rookeries rathole.

As he hurried on, sometimes able to break into a quicker stride or even a jog when Vanticor rounded a corner and when the crowds thinned a little, he still kept a sensible distance behind his quarry. And stayed alert, for Vanticor was still glancing back occasionally, like a nervy wild creature checking for predators. Each time he did so, Red's reflexes saved him, letting him step into shadow or dodge behind an obstruction without being seen. So Vanticor visibly began to relax, to look around less often, confident he was not being followed. And the chase went on, along a twisting, angling route through the filthy back streets that left Red even more disorientated than before. But it was too late, he told himself, to worry about being lost. He had to go on, and trust to luck, as he had done so often in his life.

Luck seemed to be with him, in the end, when he realized some moments later that they were heading for the waterfront – as he was told by the odours of sewage-fouled water, wet wood, a tarry tang from boats. At least he knew that he could find his way home – to the palace – from the river, when it was time to do so. And he hoped briefly that Krost, who might still be sitting in the tavern, would not waste time scouring the Rookeries for him.

By the time he glimpsed the river itself, looking like shiny black metal, he was travelling on darker and less populous streets, and had dropped further back – glad that Vanticor's yellow hair picked up what light there was from occasional flickering torches. But shortly the assassin's route took him into a dark alleyway that offered no light at all, save the faint glimmering of stars. And when Red had crept as stealthily as he could along that alley, he found he had entered an area where there were no other people, and where he had lost sight of Vanticor.

It was a riverfront area that had clearly suffered some calamity, probably a fire. The starlight showed that most of the buildings were roofless and derelict – jumbled piles of broken plaster and charred beams – while others were simply patches on the ground of dark ash and rubble. And nothing, not even vermin, seemed to be moving among those broken, ghostly leftovers.

Red stood silent, hardly breathing, his head averted slightly to let his night vision operate at the corners of his eyes where it functioned best. He felt sickened at the thought that his pursuit had come to nothing, that Vanticor had escaped him, but he continued to wait, unmoving. And finally he was rewarded. In the blackness ahead – shockingly close – he heard the scrape of a boot on bare earth, then another scrape like metal on stone. Steel on flint, some instinct told him, and he dropped behind a chunk of crumbled wall just as a flare of light appeared, ahead, steadying into a flickering orange glow.

Peering warily past the broken wall, Red saw Vanticor with a small torch flaming in one hand, staring carefully around. After a moment, convinced he was alone, he moved away – with Red following slowly, as noiseless as any of the shadows cast by the torchlight. Within a short distance he turned into one of the ruined buildings, with its walls still standing though the roof had fallen in. The torchlight dimmed within the building, remaining in one place as if Vanticor was standing still. Then, abruptly, it went out.

Red moved forward, fervently wishing that he had a light of his own, or even a nice bright moon, to show him the way through the rubble underfoot. Finally, with every nerve vibrating, he stepped through the doorway of the building where the other man had vanished. And with the starlight failing to reach past the tops of the broken walls, he found himself in the most total darkness he had ever known. It was so dark that he felt stifled, as if his chest was being compressed, and also dizzy as if no longer sure where the ground was. He had no idea if Vanticor was waiting for him in the dark, or if something worse was lurking there. In his blindness, sweat bursting out on his skin, he wondered if he had the courage to step forward, or if he was going to turn and run.

But then something twitched in his memory, and he almost laughed in his relief. He was carrying a very useful source of light. The sword of Corodel, whose blade glowed with luminous colours.

Drawing the sword in itself did something to ease his tensions. Then the blade's radiance drove the dark away, and Red regained his orientation and his breath – and saw the place where Vanticor had disappeared.

Even by day, it might have looked to a casual glance like simply the darkened opening of a fireplace against the wreckage of a wall. But the light from the blade probed deeply into it, and showed that it was not a niche for a fire, but a hole.

101

Where the grate would have been was an opening like the entrance to a narrow, nearly vertical mine shaft.

Red stared at it consideringly, muscles jumping in his jaw. He had tried pot-holing in his own world as he had tried most of the exciting, danger-filled sports that he could afford to try. And while he had always preferred the clear air and wild winds of mountaineering, he had had some exhilarating times as well in the underground realm of constricting tunnels and hidden caverns. He had no claustrophobia, and was not afraid of climbing down into a hole in the earth even at night.

Except that he had never gone pot-holing with no equipment other than a luminous sword, and with an armed killer and who knew what else lurking somewhere below.

All the same, he could not walk away. So he began a short version of a karate breathing exercise, designed to gather his inner forces and centre them, to summon his adrenalin and his will even as it strove to relax his tensions. And finally, when he was ready, he stepped lightly forward and climbed down into the shaft.

The interior walls of the shaft were hard-packed earth solidly bound by dampness and by the flinty stone packed firmly into it. The sword's light showed a number of small crevices crudely chopped into the side of the shaft all the way down, narrow crevices offering ladder-steps, and Red climbed down fairly swiftly, the sword's light reaching around and downwards comfortingly, without provoking any challenge or attack or cry of warning. There was only silence, and the smell of musty earth, and the waiting blackness below.

At the bottom of the shaft, he saw that he was in a tunnel: its roof was low, forcing him to a crouch, and the floor was scattered with puddles of foul, stagnant water. He tried to step around them as he moved slowly forward, listening for any sound of Vanticor or other life ahead. But all remained silent as he continued on. He came then to another tunnel angling sharply off, carved out of solid rock yet roomier and higher, with the foul water channelled into gutters along the sides. It was a relief to stand straight again. But it was no relief at all when it began to sprout smaller branches along the way, on either side. Red knew that Vanticor might have dodged into any one of them, to take some other underground route. But though he began to grow despondent, more and more certain that the scarred man had got away, still he kept grimly on, refusing to admit defeat so soon.

At the mouth of each side tunnel he paused to listen, hoping for a hint of sound that might reveal his quarry's position. But none of them ever did. And his heart sank even further, some distance on, when the main tunnel that he was following appeared to reproduce itself – extending out to become three separate tunnels like a huge horizontal tripod. And as they led away through the rock into the relentless dark, many more side tunnels could be seen branching out from them.

At the juncture of the three tunnels Red halted, glumly, to consider what to do – and, feeling exposed at that underground crossroads, sheathed the sword to find a moment's concealment in darkness. Too many alternatives, he thought. I'd toss a coin if I had one, but it wouldn't do much good. So it's the end of the line. Let the prince send his militia to search these tunnels. And I'll bet Vanticor will be long gone when they do.

He began to turn away. But then he went very still, blinking slowly. At the edge of his vision, with his head partly turned, he could see something in the black depths of the left-hand tunnel. A faint hazy patch of reddish-orange, flickering but stationary – like firelight.

He reached for his sword, drawing it only part-way so that a narrow ribbon of light shone out from the portion of bared blade. Silently he crept forward into the tunnel. The orange glow grew brighter as he stealthily drew near, until he could see that it came from one of the smaller side tunnels ahead. Sheathing his sword again to hide its telltale gleam, he inched along it, every muscle and nerve-end poised and ready.

When he reached the end he saw two slabs of rock leaning against each other, offering a space between them like a rough triangular doorway. A bright doorway, too, with plenty of flickering firelight beyond it – along with a number of unsettling sounds. Sounds like movement, but also like croaking and growling, as if there was an underground menagerie there.

Crouching, Red moved up to the two slabs of rock, edged forward and peered with one eye around the edge of the slab.

To confront nightmare.

For a desperate instant Red tried to tell himself that the ten or eleven figures in the torch-lit cavern were just ordinary men with unfortunate deformities. But he knew otherwise. They were man-sized and man-shaped, but they were not men.

Some wore long cloaks and heavy hoods, showing Red at last just what it was that he had confronted on the night he arrived. But the cloaks were open and the hoods thrown back, and others in the group wore no clothing at all, so Red saw them all too clearly. They were squat and sturdy-looking, with long arms, and large hands and feet that had a slight webbing between fingers and toes. Their naked skin was grotesque, thick and scabby and wrinkled and a corpse-like greyish-white, with wiry tangled hair growing in patches over their torsos and groins. Their heads were small and flat, their faces were dominated by bulging eyes that looked blank and dark and soulless – until they blinked, showing that the blankness was a transparent membrane over narrow pupils that looked eerily reptilian. The lower part of their faces jutted slightly, like snouts, with slit nostrils and lipless mouths where small serrated teeth glittered.

Red stared at them, feeling cold sweat on his skin again. Like a cross between a gorilla and a gila monster, he thought shakily, trying for flippancy to combat his shock. But it did not entirely work – especially not when he spotted the oddly shaped pouches slung on thongs at their hips, which seemed to hold peculiar bouquets. But they were not flowers, he realized. They were feathers. And his mind dredged up the memory of the oversize dart that he had seen in the palace's weaponry display – the hardwood haft as long as his forearm with the vicious spike at one end and the flight of feathers at the other.

In that moment of realization Red felt even more chilled as he understood what danger he and Aurilia had truly been in, on that first violent night. And he was trying to gather himself, to start creeping quietly back the way he had come, when the monsters all fell silent, turning to a narrow opening on one side of the cavern, then baring their teeth and croaking and snarling in obvious interest. Vanticor was stepping through the opening, followed by two more of the monstrous beings supporting another figure between them.

The sight flung Red into a new depth of horror mingled with anguish that almost made him cry aloud.

The figure that was being supported was quite small, wearing a dress that was ripped and gaping open in front where buttons had been torn away. So it revealed the pale skin and rounded shape of a young woman, sagging as if unconscious in the grip of her captors.

Nellann.

'. . . in case she comes round and tries to get away,' Vanticor was saying as he entered the main cavern. Red, staring wildly at the slumped figure of Nellann being borne along by the two monsters, heard the assassin's voice as if from a distance and registered his words only vaguely.

'Use the Rookeries gate instead of going under the river like last time. Too many militia, that side of the river. Keep her covered up – yourselves too. And don't stop for *anything*.'

The two creatures holding Nellan stood silently, as if having heard it all before.

'And when you get there,' Vanticor went on, 'tell the master this. Tell him we've got to get out of Quamarr and hunt other places for a while. It's got too risky here. One day soon, somebody'll think of searching the Catacombs.' He leaned forward, eyes narrowed. 'You understand?'

One of the two creatures grunted, then snarled tonelessly. It took Red a moment to realize that the snarls were not more of its own bestial tongue, like their earlier noises, but were a recognizable human word, being repeated several times.

'Un'stand . . . un'stand . . . un'stand,' the monster said, blinking its reptilian eyes.

Vanticor stepped back with a curt gesture towards the triangular opening of the cavern. At that doorway, Red rose from his couch. He had no idea what he could do against all the armed monsters and the human killer who stood between him and Nellann. But he was about to start doing something.

As he rose and the luminous sword leaped from its sheath a reptilian head turned towards him, then a second. One of the creatures howled, an eerie animal cry, and pointed. And the creature closest to the opening plucked a dart from its pouch, in the fastest movement that Red had ever seen, and hurled it.

But shock and fury had brought Red's own reflexes to hyper-pitch. He was just able to twist aside to let the ugly weapon hiss past him and clatter against the rock behind. Then a monster was leaping at him, another dart raised to stab, with the rest crowding behind, howling. Yet only one at a time could pass through the narrow triangular opening, and Red easily evaded the stabbing dart of the first attacker and chopped at the creature with the sword. He had never fought in earnest with a blade, and was appalled at the ease with which his magical sword bit into its flesh. It stumbled back shrieking into the path of the others, pale blood gouting from its shoulder. And Red heard Vanticor's voice raised in fury.

'Kill him! *Kill* him! You can feast on him if you kill him!'

Red had a brief glimpse of Nellann lying crumpled where she had been dropped. But then the other monsters were lunging at him again, darts in hand, and he knew with a sick certainty that she was beyond his reach. If he remained a second longer, he was looking at sudden, savage death.

Oh, God, Nellann, he thought, in a despairing inward cry. And then he slashed furiously at the monster nearest to him, turned, and ran.

A dart hissed past him, then another. But the monsters were jostling and crowding in the small tunnel behind him, and their aim was not true. A bend in the tunnel briefly hid him from their darts, and he burst out of the small tunnel – sword held high to light his way – and sprinted along the main tunnel for some distance before his pursuers emerged behind him.

They did not try to hurl darts while running, but simply came after him, in their weird crouching lope that looked, to

Red's swift backward glance, powerful and tireless. But he ran on, soon coming to the end of the rock-sheathed tunnel, splashing wildly through the puddles. When he came to the shaft, with its crudely cut steps leading invitingly upwards, he sprang up it. At the top he looked back and saw that the monsters were starting to climb after him, spiked darts now clenched in their teeth. He leaped out of the shaft, plunged over the rubble of the derelict building, and away into the silent darkness beyond.

He vaguely knew the direction he should take, keeping the river behind him. But as he ran, sword still held high, he realized that he had no idea where to find the particular alley along which he had followed Vanticor. He slowed, hearing the croaking snarls behind him as the monsters gained the top of the shaft, frantically turning this way and that to find his escape route.

And there was the alley, ahead, to the right. Gasping with relief, he leaped towards it just as a dart speared his shadow. He hurtled into the depths of the alley, safe again for a moment from their deadly missiles.

And then he skidded to a halt, cold terror clawing at him.

It was not the same alley. This one led to a building that might once have been large and grand, whose ruins were still fairly imposing, with broken chunks of a splendid portico supported by wooden pillars that stood like oversized grave markers. But beyond the ruined building stood a wall, not at all ruined, and solidly barring his way at the far end of the alley.

The wall contained an iron-barred gate, dirt-streaked and rust-stained. But it too was still sturdy, locked or rusted shut, resisting Red's desperate shakings and kickings.

He was in a dead end. And as a flying dart struck sparks from the stone of the wall next to him, he knew despairingly how accurate a term it was.

He leapt sideways, flinging himself behind one of the wooden pillars, hearing another dart thud into the wood. And then he heard the monsters, their bestial voices rising with what sounded like grotesque laughter.

'He trap,' one of them said clearly.

And the others echoed it, with more laughter, croaking and snarling. 'Trap . . . trap . . . trap . . .'

He risked a quick look around the post, felt another dart slam into the wood a hand's breadth from his face, saw as he jerked back that at least ten of the creatures were advancing slowly, darts ready in their hands.

'Move roun',' he heard one say. 'Kill quick, two sides.'

There was a general snarling of assent. 'An' sword,' said another. 'Take bright sword for masser.'

Red guessed that they were speaking the human tongue so that he would hear and be overcome by fear. But he was not – just as he was not being overcome by the certain knowledge that he was going to die in that stinking alley. There was even a light in his eye as he planted his feet and took a firm grip of the sword-hilt. I'll take a few with me, for Nellann, he thought fiercely. They can have the sword – right in the guts . . .

That was when the impossible scream burst out behind him, making him leap like a hooked fish. It was a metallic shriek, filling the alley with its echoes, and as he whirled the icy sweat of terror washed over him again. Something looming and immense stood by the wall at the alley's end – something four times his height, massive and scaly, with red eyes like coals and claws like knives, with flame licking like bright tongues from the gaping, fanged maw.

He heard the reptilian creatures who had pursued him howling in terror, and he turned back to see them scrambling frenziedly away, driven faster by a ground-trembling roar from the towering, flame-mouthed monstrosity.

But when Red finally gathered himself and looked behind him again, sword held tremblingly at the ready, he saw only a small white-haired man in an overlong blue coat, smiling a hopeful smile, with eyes that had purple irises and pupils of an unnatural white.

'I do hope I didn't alarm you,' said Hallifort the Healer.

Red stared, his throat working but producing no sound through the speechlessness of shock and disbelief. 'How . . .' he managed to choke out – then stopped, unable to think of what to ask.

'That was an illusory shape,' Hallifort said, answering the unasked question. 'I felt it would serve to frighten them away.'

'Where . . . did you *come* from?' Red finally managed.

The little man waved a hand airily. 'I happened to be in the vicinity.'

Red squeezed his eyes shut and shook his head as if to dislodge something. In the *vicinity*, he thought. A dead-end alley in the Rookeries at night . . . Coming through a gate that was rusted shut . . .

But when he looked again at the little man's cherubic smile, he felt a complete certainty that he was not going to be made any wiser, that night, about the hows and whys of Hallifort. So he simply nodded, with a slightly edgy half-smile of his own.

'Then . . . thanks,' he said. 'For happening along.'

Hallifort made another small gesture as if to say it was nothing. And in that instant memory struck Red like a spear through the after-effects of terror and rescue.

'Wait!' he said wretchedly. '*Nellann!* We have to get help . . .'

Hallifort shook his head sombrely. 'The man Vanticor will have made his escape with her, through the tunnels. She is beyond our help, now.'

Ignoring the fact that Hallifort seemed to know a great deal about the details of that night, Red took an agonized stride towards him. 'But aren't you some kind of wizard or something? Can't you . . . ?'

'No,' Hallifort said quickly, his voice trembling with what sounded like pain. 'I cannot reach her, I cannot intervene. I am only a *healer*, my young friend. I have no power otherwise – beyond the small ability to assume illusory guises . . .'

Red sagged, only half-listening, feeling hopelessness and horror twisting like knives in his guts.

110

'I am so sorry.' Hallifort's treble voice seemed far away. 'But when my healing cannot help, I must merely . . . accept. As you must, now. She is gone.' He closed his weird purple-and-white eyes for a moment, then opened them again. 'Your friend the dwarf-giant is seeking you, meanwhile. Leave the alley, turn right, follow the next street that you find, and you will come to him. And . . . fare well, Red Cordell.'

He turned away, stepping through the opening where the iron-barred gate stood. Behind him the gate swung smoothly and silently closed, as if the age and rust that had bound it shut, before, had somehow been . . . healed. Red stood staring for a moment, as the little man moved out of sight beyond the wall. Then, still clutching his glowing sword, he wheeled and sprinted headlong down the alley as if an army of dart-hurling monsters was close upon his heels. At the end of the alley, however, when he came to an area where there were other people, with torches to dispel the darkness, he had to slow his pace. Shock and exertion had taken their toll on his strength so that he moved along the street in a kind of stumbling lurch, sweat-streaked and wild-eyed, still gripping the luminous sword. The Rookeries folk, having some experience of drunk, drugged, or crazed swordsmen, moved calmly out of his way, so that he was not impeded as he retraced his steps, back the way he had come, until at the intersection of three back streets he found Krost.

The bulky man was standing with iron quarterstaff in hand, talking to another man. And the other, jowly and blubbery with an enormous belly, was sweating and whimpering in fright – because Krost was holding him up in the air, one-handed, at arm's length, as he spoke. Nor was he straining at all to lift that considerable weight, but was lifting him with arm muscles only, and even shaking him a little.

'I asked you a civil question,' Krost was saying, 'and I am in a hurry. So I ask it again. Did you see a yellow-haired scarface being chased by a red-haired man?'

As the fat man shook his head rapidly, gabbling denials, Red saw another man – tall, stoop-shouldered, perhaps the fat man's friend – creeping up behind Krost, raising a heavy cudgel to strike. But Krost needed no help or warning. Half-turning, still effortlessly holding the fat man aloft, he swung the iron staff in a swift backhand as if swatting at an annoying insect. The staff smashed into the cudgel, flinging it out of the stooping man's hand in a shower of splinters. As the man was only beginning to widen his eyes with shock, Krost tapped him on the top of the head with the staff, which caused him to fold and drop like a discarded garment.

'I hate skulkers,' Krost said conversationally to the whimpering fat man. 'Now, you were saying?'

'Krost!' Red yelled.

Krost jerked his head around. 'Red!' he bellowed joyously, letting the fat man drop into an ungainly sprawl on the cobbles. But as Krost hurried towards Red, and saw his condition more clearly, his happy grin was erased.

'In the name of the Lighter Gods, Red!' he growled. 'What has happened?'

Quickly Red told him, his voice shaking a little at some points in the narrative. And Krost's dark eyes widened, and narrowed, and grew grim and angry as the brief tale unrolled.

'*Barachi?*' The hoarse voice sounded incredulous. 'The swamp-crawlers, here in Quamarr?'

'Krost,' Red said desperately, not knowing or caring what the big man meant, 'they've got Nellann . . .'

Krost nodded unhappily. 'I know. But your friend Hallifort was surely right. Vanticor will have wasted no time. She will have become another disappeared Sister, as Aurilia nearly was . . .' He peered at the agony in Red's eyes. 'My friend, you must not torment yourself. You could not have saved her, there in the Catacombs. You would merely have died with her . . .'

Red shrugged wearily, but his eyes were still tortured. 'Maybe so. But I wish I could have done better . . .'

'It may be, Red,' Krost rumbled, 'that you could get another chance – to do better. If you want it.'

As he made that cryptic remark, he was gazing around at the still crowded street, where other passers-by were giving them a wide berth, like a river passing on either side of a rock. Then Krost smiled with satisfaction, for a short distance away a man had just climbed down from a small wagon laden with firewood, pulled by two sturdy horses.

'Come, Red,' Krost urged, taking Red by the arm. 'We must return to the palace swiftly with this news. We will borrow transportation.'

The firewood-seller turned to stare with disbelief as Krost and Red clambered on to the wagon. 'Here,' he snarled, 'get off there!'

'Collect it at the palace tomorrow,' Krost told him, gathering the reins. 'You will be rewarded . . .'

'I'll reward *you!*' the man roared, lunging forward with a long knife that he had produced from under his coat. But then he halted, for he was staring into a pair of wild-looking pale blue eyes belonging to a man holding a glowing sword at his throat. The firewood man stumbled back, Krost lashed at the horses with the reins, and they were away.

It was a frenzied, manic gallop, that crossing of the city, and Red quickly sheathed his sword and clutched the seat of the wagon with both hands. They scattered the people on the Rookeries streets, set a shaky bridge to trembling as they hurtled across it, then stormed on through the emptier streets on the more civilized side of the river. Shortly they were flying down the nearly deserted length of one of the great thoroughfares that fanned out from the palace. And though Red's mind was a riot of questions, intermingled with continuing tortured thoughts of Nellann's fate and his own forced retreat, he had no chance to speak above the thunder of hooves and wheels on stone, the hoarse roaring of Krost and the slap of reins on the horses' rumps. Several times they nearly overturned as a horse half-stumbled or a wheel struck a hole in the roadway. Often Red was sure that the groaning, sagging wagon would give way beneath Krost's weight. But miraculously they remained upright and intact as they charged along the curving drive leading to the palace and came to a skidding halt with the horses squealing and gravel spraying from under the wheels.

Red saw white-faced guardsmen by the palace door levelling crossbows as he and Krost leaped down. But the two of them leaped up the steps without pause, ignoring the sentries

113

even as they were recognized. Krost slammed a mighty hand against the door, flinging it open so that it nearly crushed a footman rushing to see the cause of all the noise.

'Where is the prince?' Krost bellowed.

'In . . . in his chambers, sir,' the footman stammered.

'Come, then – we must rouse him!' And Krost spun the unfortunate man around and gave him a hearty push.

But within a few strides the seneschal appeared, looking quite unruffled, and took charge. He sent a footman racing on ahead to prepare the prince, sent another at Krost's suggestion to collect Aurilia, then led them himself to the private chambers of the prince. They entered a sitting room only slightly smaller than the Receiving Hall, and rather more luxuriously furnished. And there Phaedran awaited them, scowling and perturbed at all the upheaval. He was scowling more darkly by the time that Aurilia joined them, to hear the rest of Krost's and Red's tale of that night's adventures. And when the tale was done, the result was uproar.

'*Barachi?*' the prince raged, his face twisting. 'Barachi from the Western swamps, in Quamarr? With this *man*, this Vanticor, leading them? Seneschal!'

The balding official instantly appeared at the door, and the prince pointed a rigid finger at him. 'Summon Marshal Lenceon!' Phaedran roared. 'I want the Catacombs searched by the militia, every step of them, before this night ends! I want all gates watched and guarded – the whole length of the river through the city examined . . .'

'They will be long gone by now, Highness,' Krost rumbled.

'No doubt,' the prince snapped. 'But we must make certain.' He swung around to the seneschal again. 'Send someone to rouse those mages and bring them here! And tell Lenceon to present himself to me as soon as possible after sun-up, with a full report!'

As the seneschal bowed and withdrew, Aurilia – in her aged form once again – came over to Red, looking concerned. 'You are not harmed?' she asked.

'Not a scratch,' he said bitterly. 'More than can be said for Nellann.'

She put a thin hand on his arm. 'Don't go too far down

that path, Red. Hallifort was right. What we cannot alter we must accept.'

'I know.' He sighed, his eyes haunted. 'I'm just . . . It was quite a night. I still don't really know . . . What *are* these Barachi?'

Before replying, she glanced around. The three mages were then being ushered into the chamber, and the prince was directing Krost to bring them up to date. So, in that moment of respite, she told Red what he needed to know.

The Barachi were a primitive race of not-men who lived in the Western Woodlands, mainly in the swampy areas near the southern coast. And they, even more than the swamps, were the reason why so much of the West remained wild, unpopulated by humans, save for scattered settlements of fisherfolk on the northern shores.

'Barachi and humans have fought whenever they have met,' Aurilia told Red. 'Expeditions have been sent into the Woodlands to hunt and destroy them, but always they failed, defeated by the creatures in the swamps that are their home. Nowadays the Barachi are more or less left alone, and in turn rarely show themselves outside their own realm.'

'Just as well,' Red muttered. 'They're not much to look at.' Ugly memories of that night stirred within him – including the recollection of how Vanticor had spurred them on to pursue him. 'Are they cannibals or something, too?'

Aurilia nodded. 'It is thought that they eat human flesh.'

'So,' Red said, looking sick, 'they could be having Nellann for dinner, now?'

'I think not,' she said quietly. 'She was taken as I was nearly taken, as so many Sisters have been taken. I believe she will be kept alive to meet some other fate, elsewhere – perhaps at the hands of Vanticor's mysterious *master*.'

Red stared beyond her, feeling chilled and revolted by the thought of some dark plan spawned by some unknown power, requiring the sending of horror monsters to abduct magical women. Trying to clear that ominous shadow from his thoughts, he asked other questions – and learned that the tunnels, the Catacombs, where Aurilia had also been held, were a leftover from a time when the Continent was sometimes riven by war. Back then the people of Quamarr created the system of tunnels as a hidden route under the river, and a storehouse for food, in case of siege.

'They haven't been used for generations,' Aurilia added. 'Few people would still know where they lie, or where their various entrances are placed.'

Red grimaced. 'So they'd be perfect for Vanticor. And nice and mucky for his swamp-things.' He shuddered faintly, remembering the wild chase through the tunnels, the dead-end alley.

Aurilia tightened her hand on his arm, the green eyes grave in the lined old face. 'You were reckless and foolhardy tonight, Red, following Vanticor down there alone. And while that may be your nature, as it was Corodel's, you must not give it free rein. There are places and beings in this land more dangerous than you can possibly conceive.'

'So I gather,' he said, trying for a light tone. 'I know just how close I came to being the main course at a Barachi feast.' He smiled tensely. 'I owe old Hallifort quite a lot.'

'Indeed,' she said thoughtfully. 'It might be well to find out more about Hallifort the Healer.'

'So it might!' The interruption came from the large red-faced wizard, Ahnaan, lumbering up to them. 'Too much mystery about the man!'

Red looked at him with dislike, remembering the mage's discourtesies to Aurilia. 'Hallifort's one of the good guys as far as I'm concerned,' he said tersely. 'Anyway, you're supposed to be a star wizard – why can't you solve his mystery?'

Ahnaan glowered. 'I have heard his name, of course, and some tales of his healing prowess. Perhaps I *will* turn my attention to him, when there is time. Meanwhile, His Highness wishes to speak to us all.'

He turned away, with Aurilia and Red following, to join his two colleagues. Wretifal and Inchalo were standing very still and listening nervously to the prince, who was addressing them in tones that went beyond firmness, while Krost stood by with a grim smile.

'You will turn your *full* attention to the Western Woodlands!' Phaedran was ordering. 'You will examine every tree

116

in the forests, every pool in the swamps! You will begin this very night, and you will not cease until I give you permission!'

'Highness,' Wretifal replied, 'I have already scoured the Woodlands with scrying and seeking . . .'

'Wretifal!' The prince's glare was fiery, his voice glacial. 'We now know beyond doubt that the Barachi are involved in abducting Sisters. We know that the Barachi and the man Vanticor are acting at the behest of an unknown master. We know that the Barachi come from the *West* – the very region where my long-time enemy, the sorcerer Talonimal, went to hide himself. So now – you will *look for him*!'

Wretifal had grown pale, but there was stubbornness in the set of his small jaw. 'Highness, in all my magical searching there has not been a trace of the man, not the smallest hint of his continuing existence.'

'*Wait!*' Aurilia stepped forward, fixing Wretifal with fierce green eyes. 'Your pardon, Highness, but there is something wrong. Wretifal, you say "*I* have scoured" and "*my* searching". Do you mean to say that you *alone* have sought Talonimal?'

The sudden appalled look in the small mage's eyes was answer enough.

'You pathetic *fool*,' Aurilia raged, her old voice crackling with emotion. 'Working *alone*? Have you forgotten how spells and scrying are weakened by being extended over great distance? Or did you refuse to augment your power in conclave with these others because you wanted the glory for yourself?'

'*No!*' Wretifal cried, as icy storm-clouds gathered in the prince's eyes. 'It was just . . . there was so *much* to do, so much ground to cover . . . and only the three of us . . .'

Aurilia snorted. 'And do you really feel that your own magic, alone, is great enough to know the difference, over distance, between a seeking spell that finds nothing and one that is *deflected*?'

The prince turned his frozen glance towards her. 'Explain that, Aurilia.'

'Sir,' she said tensely, 'your enemy, Talonimal, may well be a likely candidate for the author of these evils afflicting us. We cannot yet know. But we can be reasonably sure of two things. First, our enemy is almost certainly a sorcerer of some power. Second, he almost certainly has his base in the West, if he is recruiting Barachi. Yet Wretifal says he has searched the West, to no avail. So – either those two near-certainties are mistaken, or our enemy *is* in the West but is protecting himself against discovery. By warding against it. By setting up a magical shield, a barrier.'

Phaedran turned his glare on to the white-faced Wretifal. 'This possibility did not occur to you?'

'Of course, Highness, of course it did!' The mage threw a sidelong, hate-filled glance at Aurilia. 'But I am sure my powers would have detected such a barrier, if there were one! I am sure I would *know!*'

'Yet now it seems you might not, since you worked alone, over such distance,' Phaedran said, and even Red shivered at the wintry fury in his voice. 'So you will try again, Wretifal, in conclave with these others, and with still more mages if need be. You will begin at once – and you will not cease until you can prove to me, beyond all doubt, that your combined searching has been fruitless!'

All three mages bowed deeply, mumbling assurances, then hurried away after a few more furious glares at Aurilia. And the prince, looking suddenly old and weary, turned towards her where she stood with Red and Krost.

'Aurilia, I thank you for your perception,' he said. 'Mages can be such fools, with their squabbling and posturing.'

'Even so, my lord,' she said gravely, 'they may not succeed. Even if there is a sorcerer in the West, behind a barrier, for whom the Barachi are stealing Sisters, he may not be the abductor of the princess.'

'I know it,' the prince said, rubbing his hands across his face. 'Yet I feel more hopeful now, tonight, than I have felt since Evelane was taken.'

'And I,' Krost rumbled. 'It would be a strange chance indeed if there were *two* villains abducting women.'

'Quite so,' Phaedran said. 'And I am grateful to you again, old friend, for your part in this discovery.' He turned his gaze on to Red. 'But you have my special gratitude, Red Cordell.

Had you not risked death to pursue Vanticor, we would still be fumbling blind and helpless in our search.'

Red bowed, not sure what there was for him to say.

'What can we do now, Highness?' Krost enquired.

'Rest, if we can,' Phaedran said, 'after such a night of alarms. We can gather again after sun-up, when the marshal comes to report on his militia's searches. And when, if we are fortunate, the mages too might have something to report.' He looked again at Red. 'I hope you will join us then, as well. I am aware that much of this may be . . . unclear to you, but tomorrow will be a better time for explanations. And, if the gods smile upon us, for plans.'

'I'll be there,' Red agreed. 'Sir.'

A thoughtful glint lightened the prince's gaze as he studied Red. 'Some whim of fortune has brought you to be a part in all this, Red Cordell. Tonight it proved to be a vital part. Perhaps it was an auspicious whim – not only returning the sword of Corodel to the land, but also bringing a hero's arm to wield it.'

TWELVE

Later that night Red was standing in the bedroom of his suite with a goblet of wine in his hand, watching two footmen scurrying around doing his bidding, and trying not to think of how much he would rather have watched Nellann. When he had left the others to seek his own rooms he had known that he was too tense to sleep. Also he had been running and fighting and being terrified for some hours, and his clothing was stiff with dried sweat. Wishing that the plumbing of the palace could run to steaming showers, he had requested a bath. The footmen had brought a high-backed metal tub to his bedroom and were filling it with hot water from large coppers, adding a little scented oil and setting out a block of fragrant soap and several large soft towels. When they were done, Red peeled off his clothes so they could be taken and washed, and as the servants bowed their way out of his suite he sank gratefully into the tub, wine still in hand.

The water felt wonderful, at once beginning to soak tiredness and tension from his muscles. But he knew that there were deeper tensions that neither hot water nor wine would dispel. And they mostly arose from the inescapable memory of Nellann, slumped in the grip of the two Barachi. He knew that he would in time learn to apply Hallifort's wisdom, accepting the inevitability of what happened, but he also knew that that image would never be wholly erased. He had barely known Nellann, had never touched her, and yet he knew he would think of her with sadness and regret and a feeling of failure all his life.

But another thought was troubling him in his mental turmoil. It came from the echo of the prince's last remark, before they had all parted. The prince had sounded very much as if he thought Red was going to sign up: to join in, waving the

120

sword of Corodel, if or when everyone set off with some wild plan for rescuing the princess.

And the *real* trouble was that Red was beginning to feel that it would not be a bad idea.

He knew he must be mad even to be thinking about taking part in such an enterprise, if it ever happened. He could remember Aurilia's warning, that there were things in that land more dangerous than he could imagine. But still he could not resist the attraction of the idea – that he might ride off on some fairy-tale adventure, wielding a magical sword in heroic battle. Against that notion, the idea of returning to the hum-drum triviality of his own world seemed not only unappealing but downright cowardly.

Interesting choice, he thought sourly. To be crazy, or to be chicken.

As if to drive away the dilemma, and the apprehensions that it stirred, he surged up out of the bath, dried himself perfunctorily, wrapped a towel around his waist and went out to the sitting room to pour himself another drink. Where he stopped short, staring.

'That seems to be one of your favourite garments,' Aurilia said, smiling her impish smile.

She was standing next to the sideboard that held the drinks, a slim goblet in her hand. And she was in her youthful form, in an amazing new costume. The dress was the colour of a summer mist, and about the same texture – high-collared at the back, low-cut in front, swirling around her lush body as if in constant motion, clinging and then withdrawing to cling elsewhere.

'You have a great future in burglary,' Red said lightly as he moved towards the drinks. 'I didn't hear a thing.'

She stayed where she was, so that they were standing quite close as he poured his wine. And she shrugged delicately, causing the dress to ripple even more amazingly, while her faint spicy perfume drifted around him.

'I thought I would bring you a drink, in your bath,' she said.

'Nice thought.' He tried to keep his smile ironic. 'And that's the only reason you're here?'

121

Her smile faded, and the green eyes grew intent. 'You have been through a night of fear and violence, Red. And sorrow, for the fate of the girl, Nellann. And I know beyond any question that more fear and violence and sorrow, more blood-shed and death, lie ahead – for the prince, for Krost and myself, perhaps for much of the Continent. Knowing that, Red, sensing shadows of unknown horrors on the future, I . . . I thought we could bring comfort to one another, now.'

Red swallowed. 'Yes. I'd like that.'

'It can be an interlude,' she went on softly, 'of shared peace and warmth, before the storms. Without obligation, or im-position, on either part.'

She reached up to touch something at the front of her dress – and the garment fell away. She wore nothing beneath it, and Red stared hungrily down at the flawless honey-bronze of her skin, the firm breasts, the sculpted thighs.

'Do you feel threatened – or troubled by thoughts of my other form – or uneasy in any way?' she asked, smiling.

'Nothing like that at all,' Red murmured, watching the sinuous play of muscles in her legs as she stepped out of the fallen dress.

'Good,' she breathed. And the tawny sweep of her hair fell away from its high coiffure, tumbling down the length of her naked back – with one strand lifting, snaking out, reaching to twine around Red's arm in the love-knot that she had put upon him before.

But he drew back. 'Don't,' he said huskily. 'Don't use your magic. You don't need it.'

She let her gaze drift downwards, then up again, her smile becoming a wicked grin. 'No,' she said. 'I see that I don't.'

As her hair drifted back and away, she reached out and took his hand. Together they walked into the bedroom, where Red flung aside his towel. And there they lowered themselves to the softness of the bed's coverings, and embraced.

Some time later, as they lay side by side, hand in hand again, their breathing returning to normal, Red marvelled at how many more of the tensions afflicting him had been swept entirely away. A magical woman in every way, he thought peacefully – and propped himself on an elbow, smiling down

122

at her smile, trailing his fingers down over the velvety skin of her belly.

'Which is the real you?' he asked suddenly. 'Won't you tell me? Is this your real form?'

'I told you before,' she said, smiling. 'This is my real form at this moment. Will you not just enjoy the moment?'

He sighed, then nodded. 'All right. It's been a very special moment.'

'It has,' she agreed. 'Perhaps better still because I didn't *force* you, as you once put it, with the love-knot.'

Red laughed ruefully. 'I wouldn't think you'd ever have to force any reasonably healthy man. So you can save your love-magic for a time when my capability shows signs of failing.'

As he spoke he let his stroking fingers slide further downwards. She gasped, then chuckled and put her arms around him.

'I wouldn't think,' she murmured, 'that I'll need the love-knot for a long time.'

At almost exactly the same time, far to the west, the silver-haired man in the dark robe moved with grim purpose through the darkened ways of his home. His movements, which did not entail the use of doors or corridors, led him swiftly to a narrow but opulent chamber filled with dark furniture where the slim young woman sat, wearing another embroidered gown, her pretty face taut with anxiety, her fingers tapping the arm of her chair in an erratic tattoo.

'It is as I thought,' he said without preliminary. 'The scrying stone confirms that Vanticor has been discovered – and the Barachi have been seen – in the Catacombs.'

'Then everything will be *known*! Now you *must* punish Vanticor. Flay him alive and give him to a Barachi feast!'

'He was not to blame, my dear. It was an unforeseeable accident. And I always anticipated that the prince would learn the truth eventually.'

'But now he will . . . he will . . .' Her voice trailed off as she twisted at the fabric of her gown. 'What will he *not* do? He has the militia – and so many mages to command – and the Sisterhood . . .'

'Let him do what he will do. Our protection will withstand any magical attack launched from Quamarr. And if his mages choose to come nearer, to intensify their power, they will face the forest, the swamps, the Barachi . . . No, my sweet. They cannot reach us. And even if they could – I would oppose them even now with a magical strength greater than they would expect.'

'If only . . .' she began. 'If only *I* had the power now, that I should have had. To stand at your side . . .'

'Patience, my love. You have had my promise. And it will not be too long before I am powerful enough to fulfil it. After today, remember, I shall be another stride towards the Apotheosis.'

She blinked, then brightened. 'Oh, yes. Is it time?'

'It is.' He smiled a twisted smile. 'And, my dear, Vanticor whom you would punish so severely is even now on his way here with *another* juicy titbit from Quamarr. To provide me, in time, with a *further* stride.' He reached a hand towards her. 'But now – for the one who is already here – the Tower of Invocation stands ready.'

As she took his extended hand and rose to her feet, he gestured with the other hand. Eerie phosphorescence formed and writhed around his fingers – and instantly they both vanished like quenched flames.

They reappeared in a quite different chamber, with a high ceiling, bare stone floor, and walls where hangings here and there partly covered narrow window-slits, although darkness like black fog drifting through the castle obscured everything. At one end of the chamber stood a slightly raised area like a low stage, with broad steps leading up to it at one side. On it stood the only furniture – a heavy table next to two richly upholstered divans, each with one end curving up to form a cushioned backrest. The table was covered with manuscripts and parchments and a variety of implements, devices, and containers, along with a few candles that were the only illumination.

The young woman took up a half-reclining position on one of the divans, watching the man expectantly as he strode to the table, glancing at the flaking pages of an ancient parchment, then at one tall candle marked with strips that were divisions to show the passage of time. Nodding to himself, he looked again at the parchment, while the strange phosphorescence reappeared to flicker around the fingers of both hands.

'We may begin.'

He reached out to gather up some small vials from the table, along with a short slim-bladed sword whose hilt was carved with weird symbols. Turning, he strode down the steps to the centre of the chamber's floor. A flick of his glowing hand drove back the drifting black haze, exposing the bare stone. Carefully he scattered the powder of two vials, while in a low voice muttering harsh rough words from an inhuman language. He drew the tip of the sword lightly over the floor in a complex pattern, muttering still, and the lines glowing faintly as they formed and reflected in the glitter of his eyes. Still speaking in the harsh tongue, he raised a third vial and with a jerk of his hand flung its contents like a spreading shower of sparks out over the floor. As they settled on to the glowing lines, he barked a single strident word.

From the lines on the floor, instantly, a fire sprang up.

It was no normal fire. It rose directly from the bare stone, burning no fuel, never altering in height or breadth, emitting no sound, giving no heat. And its narrow, twisting tongues of flame shone an uncanny silvery-blue.

He nodded sharply and strode back up on to the raised area, looking at the young woman with a thin smile.

'The Offering fire awaits,' he said hoarsely.

She wet her lips, her breathing quickened. 'Would you . . . bring *her* to watch, while you perform the Invocation?'

His smile grew cruel. 'If it pleases you.'

He gestured, with both luminous hands. At once a figure materialized near the edge of the low stage. A figure that was weakly struggling, as if gripped by some unseen force, yet sagging as if unable to stand upright. The heavy, middle-aged woman in the torn night-dress, over whose image the man and the young woman had gloated, before, in front of the scrying stone.

The man gestured again. The woman stiffened, still sagging

125

but suddenly immobile, as if the invisible force that gripped her had tightened to hold her still. Then her feet left the floor. As she rose into the air her face grew contorted with increased terror, and from her mouth came a weak, high whimpering like the distant crying of seabirds.

He lifted his hands and her body drifted slowly forward until it was hovering in front of the unnatural fire. He twitched a glowing finger and his victim's flimsy covering was flung away into nothingness. For a long moment his gaze roved over her naked body, seeming to probe like fingers at the drooping breasts, the fleshy belly, the patch of greying hair where the thick thighs joined. At last he glanced aside, at the time-keeping candle – seeing its flame dwindling, trailing dark smoke.

Once again the man began to speak – more loudly than before and in a rhythmic, incantatory tone, but still in the ugly, guttural alien tongue. The chant rose and fell in a complex, dissonant pattern while the man slowly raised his blazing hands high, his body tightening. Yet he seemed to experience little of the undue strain that he had suffered during his first Invocation, performed in the depths of the winter so many months before. Nor did he need to inhale the fumes of a drug or seek any other artificial reinforcement of his magical strength. The only sign of exertion, as the incantation went on, was a faint sheen of sweat appearing on his brow.

Dampness also showed on the skin of the young woman as she leaned forward, biting her lip, raptly watching as the man's hands flexed into claws. His incantation rose higher, his voice crackling with the ever more raucous sounds, his hands spreading wide. Before him the eyes of their naked victim where she floated in mid-air bulged from their sockets and saliva streaked her chin, while before her the silver-blue flames leaped higher, and power grew vibrant and resonant in the air.

The last spark of the time-keeping candle faded and died. The man's chant reached a rasping climax like a shriek of pain. At that instant, on the farther side of the fire in the centre of the chamber, a haze formed, seething, pale and cold and bright. Slowly images began to appear, gathering clarity.

Tall columns supported a broad pediment to create an entranceway, a portal . . . a threshold, with a line of greenish incandescence like a frame all around its perimeter. Beyond the columns appeared a long series of arches, with a flat surface resting on them. A bridge, beyond the threshold, stretching away endlessly into nothingness.

In the silence that fell the three people stared at threshold and bridge. The young woman, pale and motionless, blood beading her bitten lip, her eyes avid. The man, slowly lowering his hands, his sweaty, drawn face alight with a feral eagerness. And the naked victim, suspended in mid-air, no longer even whimpering though spasms shook her flesh and horror twitched in her eyes.

As they watched, something moved on the bridge. A towering shapeless grey-black shadow, its insubstantiality twisting and writhing in ceaseless motion. It moved to the very edge of the threshold and halted, gigantic and ghastly, its awareness falling upon the humans like an unbearable eye. Emanations of its nature and its force reached them even from across the protected threshold, wave upon wave of incalculable power mingled with unimaginable hunger.

The quivering victim clamped her eyes shut and screamed: a scream that rose up and up, piercingly, echoing around the vaulted chamber, finally trailing away at its shrillest level as if the terror that impelled it had grown too great for sound.

At that moment the silver-haired man extended his glowing hands before him and croaked a final phrase. The naked woman, still open-mouthed in her silent scream, drifted downwards through the air and slowly sank into the fire.

As the flames took her, her body seemed to grow translucent. Slowly the flesh moved and slid, drooping in great stretched hanging gobbets like melting wax. The flames were silent still as her flesh dripped away from her bones, as the bones cracked, crumbled, disintegrated, and were gone.

Yet something remained, held in the the midst of the flames where her body had been. Some insubstantial essence, not material, just visible as it hovered within the tongues of silvery-blue. It fluttered for an instant, swirling this way and that as if seeking escape, yet never leaving the flames. Then finally it swept away, past and over and somehow *through* the figure of the silver-haired man, whose face contorted with wild joy, whose body shook within his robe.

Then the essence moved towards the misty columns of the threshold – more slowly, as if trying to resist the power of the monstrous being that waited there, that seemed to be compelling it, drawing it irresistibly towards destruction. As it finally slid through the green-bordered entranceway, the entire shadowy mass of the being surged around it, engulfed and devoured it.

A moment later, the being retreated along the bridge. And when it could no longer be seen, both bridge and threshold dimmed, blurred, and disappeared, and the fire vanished from the unmarked floor. On her divan the young woman lay back, trembling slightly, looking both elated and appalled. And her smile was expectant as the man turned to her, his gaze impaling her. No sign of strain or fatigue showed in his face and posture, while his expression mingled a grisly satiation and a near-maniacal triumph.

'Stronger and yet stronger,' he said, his voice grating.

She wriggled her hips in a small sinuous motion, a flush darkening her throat, her mouth softening. 'Bring me your strength, Talonimal,' she breathed.

Smiling his feral smile, he raised a still phosphorescent hand. Her rich gown vanished, leaving her naked. His gaze probed her hotly, as it had probed the nakedness of his victim's body, and she moaned slightly and let her thighs sprawl apart. When he gestured again, his own garments disappeared.

'One day soon,' he murmured, leaning over her, 'I shall be strongest of all, my Evelane.'

Aurilia was gone when Red woke, but traces of her subtle perfume remained behind, along with the new wealth of his memories. He lay back luxuriously and savoured them, relishing the absence of so many of the tensions of the night before. But soon his idling was interrupted by a hurried footman, who announced that his presence would be welcomed by the prince and that breakfast would be served to the gathering. Power breakfasts even here, Red thought with a smile – then sprang up, dressed in his newly clean clothing, strapped on his sword, and went to join the others.

They were gathered in the Receiving Hall where he had first met the prince. Phaedran was not this time being formal on the great throne-like chair, but sat tensely by a table in one of the clusters of furniture, where Krost and Aurilia also sat, with the seneschal hovering and other servants offering platters of food. Red managed a reasonable half-bow for the prince, a nod and a wink for Krost, and then grinned at Aurilia – who was in her aged form, and who offered him a non-committal smile in return. Discretion all around, he thought, taking a place next to Krost and opposite Aurilia, instantly receiving a plateful of breakfast delicacies from a servant. Looking around, he saw something new – a large map on the wall, lavishly coloured and decorated, which according to its inscription depicted the peninsula that was the Western Woodlands of the Continent. Red studied it briefly, but felt more immediately interested in the food on his plate – a small glazed fowl, slices of sweet golden bread, segments of pale fruit. Some power breakfast, he thought idly, watching as the prince muttered something to the seneschal with an intent frown.

Phaedran clearly had no appetite, Red saw, and seemed on the edge of a taut impatience that even his chill control could barely restrain. And he jerked in a nervous spasm when the door suddenly opened, and a footman announced the arrival of a new guest whose name Red had heard before. Marshal Lenceon, commander of the militia.

The marshal looked as lean and trim as before in his much-decorated uniform. And as before, his expression still revealed a simmering anger when, after a bow to the prince, he surveyed the rest of the company. He really resents our presence, Red thought, watching as he nodded curtly to Aurilia, let his eyes drift indifferently past Red, to glare finally with clenched jaw at Krost.

'Master Krost,' he said, almost a snarl. 'I might have expected you to be here – again.'

Krost smiled slightly, though his eyes did not. 'The prince requested my presence, Lenceon. Again.'

The marshal sniffed, swinging his angry gaze to fix it on Red. 'And this is the outlander of whom I have heard?'

'Red Cordell,' Krost said. 'Who bears the sword of Corodel.'

As Red nodded coolly, Lenceon sniffed again. 'You would do well, outlander, to wield the sword with half its true owner's skill.'

'I wouldn't know about that,' Red said flatly. 'Never met the man.'

'Come, Lenceon,' the prince broke in. 'Address the matter that concerns us. What of the Catacombs?'

The marshal turned, inclining his head. 'They were searched thoroughly, Highness. Two hundred men walked every step of every tunnel, while others swept the riverbanks on both sides, far out on the plain beyond the city. And we found *nothing*, sire, to confirm this . . . *tale* of Barachi. Nothing except the remnants of fires, probably lit by some of the dregs from the Rookeries. And a few scattered bones, gnawed by rats.'

'Human bones, Marshal?' Aurilia asked pointedly.

Lenceon glanced at her with distaste. 'Of course not. The bones of Grasslands cattle, and some of yellowhorn deer.'

Aurilia nodded. 'Do you then suggest that those whom you call Rookeries dregs have somehow come to afford to buy good meat? Or that they went *hunting* on the Grasslands –

not something that Rookeries folk are noted for – and roasted their kills in the Catacombs?'

The marshal's expression grew angrier. 'I suggest nothing. I merely report what was found – and what was not found. We did *not* find any trace at all of the Barachi who the outlander apparently claims were infesting the place.'

Red stirred in his chair, smiling a small smile. 'Do you doubt me, then, Marshal?'

Lenceon glowered. 'I only say what was not found.'

'No one here,' Phaedran said sharply, 'doubts Cordell, Lenceon.'

Aurilia nodded firmly. 'Red had never seen Barachi, or even heard of them, Marshal. Yet he described them in detail, unmistakably. And my own near-abduction, earlier, is further confirmation.'

'We are convinced that Barachi were there,' the prince added, 'with the man Vanticor. Clearly they have fled, as Krost expected they would. Even so, we have gained valuable knowledge. We may gain more when the mages have concluded their efforts.' He gestured. 'Come, Lenceon, take some food, and let me tell you what possibilities have come to my mind.'

As the marshal went to take his place by the prince, looking almost happy for the first time since entering, Red turned to Krost. 'The Marshal seems in a worse mood than ever,' he murmured.

Krost grimaced. 'Lenceon cannot believe that everyone else is not as ambitious as he is. He resents anyone whom the prince seems to favour. And he has never forgiven me for being given the task of guarding the princess instead of his militia.'

Red smiled. 'You did say you'd annoyed him in the past.'

'Not for that reason alone.' Krost grinned. 'Back then, when I was guarding little Evelane, I grew weary of his enmity and challenged him to prove that his militia could be better protectors than I. He accepted, and sent a squad of his best men to pretend to take the princess from me, to teach me a lesson.' His chuckle was a deep growl. 'I did not hurt them very badly.'

Red laughed, and the marshal looked around with a vicious glare as if he suspected what they were talking about.

'He seems to have taken against me as well,' Red said, sounding untroubled.

'Rumour is spreading your name through the palace and the city, my friend,' Krost told him. 'And you are here at the royal table, having earned the prince's gratitude. Oh, yes, you will now be high on the list of the marshal's hates . . .' He broke off as the door was opened once again. 'But now things will happen. Here are the mages.'

Red turned to look, and saw at once that in fact things *had* happened. The wizards, dressed more or less as before, looked entirely different. They seemed exhausted, of course, as they well might after having laboured through the night at the prince's order. But they looked wretched beyond mere fatigue. Bearded Inchalo seemed bent and hunched as if in pain, Ahnaan's red face was blotchy and flaccid, and little Wretifal was so pale that he was green.

They weren't just tired, Red realized. They were terrified.

'Wretifal?' the prince barked. 'What have you to report?'

For a moment a quivering silence fell, as everyone watched the little wizard take a deep, ragged breath, eyes half-closed, as if rallying his spirit. Then he clenched small fists, straightened his back and opened his eyes to meet Phaedran's gaze.

'Your Highness,' he said in a low voice, 'we have done as you asked. Together in conclave, through the night, we have examined the Western Woodlands – by scrying-glass and by spells of seeking and sensing.' He twitched briefly, glanced at Aurilia, then continued. 'And we found . . . We found what Lady Aurilia . . . suggested might be there. We discovered a place where our spells were balked and deflected . . . by a barrier.'

No one seemed to be breathing as another ominous silence fell. And Wretifal, still gazing directly at the prince, squared his narrow shoulders. 'It is entirely *my* fault, Highness, that this was not discovered earlier. I . . . I accept full responsibility.'

That took guts, Red thought, feeling impressed. But the

prince's expression was unfathomable – a cold, blank stare that held the three mages fixed like insects on an icy pin.

'Very well,' Phaedran said in his most frigid tone. 'You are wise not to have lied to cover your error. But pray that the princess can be recovered, Wretifal, despite this delay. Otherwise – you shall not escape punishment.' As the mage's face went shiny with sweat, Phaedran rose abruptly to his feet, staring at the map on the wall. 'Now show me the place of this *barrier*.'

Wretifal moved to the map, reached up with a shaking finger. 'There, my lord. Claw Point.'

Peering at the map, Red saw a small spit of land jutting out from the southern coast of the peninsula, looking very much like a curved and sharp-pointed hook or claw.

'And what more can you tell me?' Phaedran demanded. 'What is the nature of the barrier? Who erected it? Is there any sign of Talonimal's presence?'

Wretifal looked desperate. 'I . . . we can add nothing, Highness. The barrier simply thwarted our spells, revealing nothing of itself or its creator – except that it arises from a powerful spell of shielding, or perhaps from several. But . . .' He looked at the other mages as if for help. 'We know something of Talonimal, sire, by reputation at least. He is a sorcerer of some recognized ability. It is not beyond credibility that his power could erect such a barrier.'

Phaedran turned away, his face tight and darkened. 'It is he! I *know* it! I feel it in my very marrow – it is *he!*'

Aurilia peered over at him, a concerned frown adding more lines to her old face. 'Highness,' she said carefully, 'I too know about Talonimal mostly by repute. Why are you so sure that he has done this – that he is your enemy?'

The prince turned, staring at her for a moment before nodding slowly. 'Yes,' he said emptily. 'You should know. You must all understand his enmity, if you are to aid me.'

The others settled to listen, warily intent.

'I knew him first when we were both young,' Phaedran said. 'When I had first succeeded to the throne, and when . . . when my Ellemar and I were first wed. In those days the palace housed a court mage, an elderly Adept who had served

133

my father – and who had taken as his assistant a promising young mage, Talonimal.' The prince was staring beyond them all, at unseen images of the past. 'He too took up residence in the palace. And therefore, in time, something of his . . . nature became known to me. Perhaps I was the last to know, as can be the case. But eventually I realized that he was a man driven and obsessed by several things. By a desire for success and wealth and acclaim. By a desire for power, as well, in both magical and mundane terms. And also, it seemed, by mere *desire* itself – an unnatural level of physical lust.'

Red might have smiled a little at that, if the prince's face had not contorted with remembered pain.

'I was not particularly concerned, at first,' Phaedran went on, 'leaving the matter of his discipline to others, including the old mage who was his master. I chose to be indifferent to what he did among the maidservants or the women of the city. More foolishly, I disregarded how deeply ambitious, envious, and spiteful was his nature.'

Red thought he saw the smallest twitch from the marshal at those words, and at that he did smile, inwardly.

'I was to regret my indifference,' the prince said. 'Because . . . the old mage died, one winter, in suspicious circumstances. And when I spoke of my suspicions to my Ellemar, she told me . . . she said that she had long suspected the evil within Talonimal. That he had many times made . . . overtures to her, almost flaunting his lustful hungers. And even when she repulsed him, and warned him, he would not be deterred. She was so beautiful – and he was drawn to her beauty, with an obsessional desire to possess it and to sully it, as the worm is drawn to the most perfect fruit.'

He wheeled suddenly and stalked to the window, concluding his tale with his back to the others, in a voice that creaked and grated.

'I had no proof of his guilt concerning the old mage, but I needed none. In a rage, I imprisoned him and threatened to have him slain. But Ellemar intervened – too soft-hearted earlier to reveal his insult to her, too wise and good to permit his death without firm evidence. I remember his smirk as she spoke against the execution . . . So I banished him – from the palace, from Quamarr. I banished him to the wilderness, putting an end to his ambitious dreams of wealth and renown. And I can still feel the heat of his fury, the force of his hatred, when he threatened me. When he said that I would come to regret my action, that banishment, for the rest of my life.'

Phaedran turned back to face his audience, his expression bleak and frozen. 'So now he has made good his threat. I am more sure of that than of anything. He has taken his revenge – by taking my daughter.'

'Highness . . .' Aurilia began, soothingly.

He seemed not to hear her – raising a fist before his face as if to strike out at something only he could see. 'But now,' he rasped, 'now that he is discovered . . . I shall seek him, and find him, and exact *my* revenge!'

'I wish I *could* take a course in magic,' Red said to Aurilia. 'I don't understand most of this at all.'

They were strolling along a palace corridor, later that day, considering what had gone on at the prince's 'power breakfast'. The prince, following his fierce promise of vengeance, had ordered the three mages to find out all they could about the strange barrier in the West, and had stalked out, leaving behind a gathering of anxious people.

'What don't you understand?' Aurilia asked Red. She was still in her aged form, hobbling slowly beside him, and so able to take his arm and hold it tightly without any apparent unseemliness.

'All that about the prince's enemy, Talonimal,' Red said. 'It seems a pretty flimsy case against him – that he may have gone to live in the West and the Barachi come from there . . .'

'It's not conclusive,' she agreed. 'But Talonimal is a good suspect, since he hates Phaedran so much. And he can't be found anywhere *else*, so he may be hiding behind that very suspicious barrier. Though what I can't work out is why Talonimal would want to abduct all the Sisters, as well as Evelane.'

Red looked unconvinced. 'Or why he should send Barachi to do his abducting, if he's such a great sorcerer.'

135

'Not *great*, Red. He is certainly not one of the premier Adepts of this land.'

'Good enough to put up a barrier, maybe.'

She gestured dismissively. 'Constructing a major spell of shielding would be one thing. Reaching across the Continent, magically, to capture Sisters, would be quite another thing. The power of a spell is diminished by distance, always. So he *would* need to send others, like the Barachi.'

'But everyone seems to think that he *did* reach out, from where he is, for Evelane. Maybe . . . maybe he's got stronger, since he was banished.'

'No,' she said firmly. 'First, we don't know that Evelane was spirited away by magical means. But if she was, her abductor may have come to Quamarr in person, secretly, to do it. Second, it is quite *impossible*, Red, for any mage's magical gift, his personal powers, to be increased. *It cannot happen.* A person without a gift cannot acquire one, a person with a gift cannot enlarge it. It's like a natural law – or a supernatural one. Each of us, Adept or enchantress, has only the gift he or she was born with. We can improve our *use* of it, by study and so on, but we cannot expand it.' She shivered briefly. 'There have been tales of sorcerers in the past who thought they found some dark way to grow more powerful. But the tales say every one of them either vanished totally or died hideously, without exception. Apparently it is not a law that can be bypassed.'

Red shivered a little, too, at that, deciding that he had heard enough for a while about the spookier side of magic. 'All right. Then what if it isn't Talonimal, or some other evil-doer, out there on the coast? What if it's just some poor magician who wants to be alone? And what if someone else has taken Evelane, for reasons that have nothing to do with Talonimal – or Vanticor, or the Barachi, or anything?'

Aurilia's green eyes clouded beneath the white eyebrows. 'Those are many what-ifs, my dear, all of them unanswerable. We can only hope that Wretifal and the other mages can learn something, now they know where to look.'

Red nodded. 'Right, let's hope. And if it turns out to *be* old Talonimal behind the barrier, he's in trouble.'

136

'Indeed,' she said, looking troubled. 'Phaedran will then go, in a cold fury, to seek his daughter. And if he finds her, within this barrier on Claw Point, he will show no mercy.'

'There is no doubt of that,' said a hoarse voice behind them, and they turned to see Krost coming to join them. 'It may already be beginning. The mages say they can find no way past the barrier, from this distance – and Phaedran wants you, Aurilia, to come back and consult with them.'

Aurilia looked surprised. 'That will not please Wretifal.'

'No matter,' Krost growled. 'I believe that Phaedran has made up his mind to send a force of men, and mages, to investigate whatever it is on Claw Point at first hand.'

'Then we had best go and consider these warlike urges,' the old woman snapped, and hobbled away along the corridor.

As they began to follow, Krost glanced at Red with slight unease. 'Your role in this so far, my friend, may lead to something that might not please you. I think the prince will ask you to come with us.'

Red's smile twisted. 'You don't mean just coming along to join the discussion, now, do you?'

'No,' Krost said soberly. 'I mean come *with* us. Joining the prince's force, with your courage and your wits . . . and your sword. To help us find out if Evelane is in this place in the West, and to bring her back, however we can.'

Inevitably, when they were all gathered again in the prince's presence – in his sumptuous private chambers, this time, not the Receiving Hall – Red was not paying the closest attention to what was happening. Krost's words had stirred up all the doubts and amazements and indecisions that had been troubling him the previous night. So it could really happen, he was thinking. I may get invited along, to join an armed attack on some kind of magical fortress.

His memory produced the words of old Ryla, his landlady back in his own world, when he was last with her. 'Another day,' she had said, 'you might have ridden off to a glorious war, all horses and swords and swashbuckling.'

And now, it seemed, if he wanted to, he could. But did he want to?

Once again he confronted all the ambivalences in his mind that arose whenever he thought about staying in Quamarr, and once again he found that they were less obvious. The images in his mind of his own world had been growing steadily more indistinct, like a dream on waking. But also the images of his 'real' life simply couldn't compete with what he had found in the Four-Cornered Continent.

A cluttered little room in a boarding-house, or a luxurious suite in a prince's palace. A collection of burdensome and mostly valueless possessions, or the liberation of owning only what he stood up in, but which included a magic sword. The company of various actor-acquaintances who mostly whined or moaned about their careers, or of a new friend who as some kind of outcast dwarf-giant had plenty to moan about, but didn't. The favours of several pretty but vain and self-absorbed girls – or those of a staggeringly beautiful and sexy woman who was also a powerful enchantress.

Even the city was better, he thought. Yes, Quamarr was smelly and primitive and not too strong on plumbing, with some seriously dangerous areas. But the supposedly *modern* city where he had lived contained its own unlovely range of stinks and squalors, its own versions of the Rookeries – where the predators carried weapons more lethal than knives or cudgels.

So he debated with himself, in the midst of the intense discussions around him. He tried to think about what would be happening in his own world – who would notice his absence, who would care. His lips twitched briefly as he thought of the rage of the director, Dirk, when Red failed to show up to be killed on the film set. When it comes down to it, he thought, only Ryla will care. Only she will wonder if something happened to me – or if I just skipped out on the rent.

I'm all right, Ryla, his mind called, half-humorously. I'm just in this other weird place, where I'm actually at last going to be a hero . . .

He stopped, jolted. *Am I?* Have I already decided, without admitting it? Do I really want to step into the role of an adventuring hero, like Corodel, galloping off to rescue a damsel?

As he asked the question he felt again as he had felt pursuing Vanticor in the Rookeries – felt the tingling of adrenalin in his veins, the small eager smile on his lips.

He leaned back in his chair at the edge of the chamber, amazed to find that apparently his blood and bone and spirit had already made the decision for him, even while his mind was still weighing pros and cons. Almost in self-protection, then, he pushed the whole tortuous debate away, and tried to concentrate on the others around him, deep in their talk.

'It is impractical, then, it seems,' the prince was saying, 'to lead a large army into that region. The logistics, as Lenceon has shown, would forbid it. Far better to take up his idea of a smaller, faster-moving force, including our three mages, to sweep past the Barachi before they can muster against us.'

Lenceon was looking pleased with himself. 'I have officers who know the West, Highness. They will find a swift route from the lower river to the coast.'

'Draw up your plans, then, Marshal, with all speed. And give orders for the readying of my barge . . .'

'Is it wise for *you* to lead the attack, Highness?' Krost asked.

The marshal flung Krost a look of venomous hatred, which seemed to Red a very strange response to an ordinary remark. But apparently no one else noticed. Phaedran merely smiled a wintry smile and nodded.

'I intend to be there, Krost, when we find my daughter. And when we deal with the abductor as he deserves.'

Aurilia leaned forward. 'Would it be of value if I were to gather a company of the Sisterhood, to join us?'

'Thank you, my lady,' Phaedron said, 'but no. Wretifal assures me that he and his two colleagues will together be more than a match for Talonimal or whatever enemy we will face. Your own powers, added to theirs, should provide a formidable magical force.'

As Aurilia nodded, a little doubtfully, Phaedran looked around at them all. 'So it is decided,' he said, sounding brisk and eager. 'A highly mobile force, sailing down-river to the heart of the Woodlands, then riding through the forest to

139

Claw Point.' He surveyed them again – Krost and Aurilia, the marshal and the mages, Red sitting to one side. 'And all of you will sail with me, on the royal barge.'

The marshal looked startled. 'The outlander too? *He* is to go?'

Phaedran looked at Red. 'He has not been asked, yet. We owe him much, for the discovery of the Barachi above all – and if he wishes now to return to his own Sphere, he is of course free to do so. But . . . I would welcome your presence, Red Cordell, and your sword.'

Before Red could reply, the marshal curled his lip. 'The sword, certainly. But we might wish there was truly more of Corodel in the wielder.'

Krost shifted, his chair groaning beneath his weight. 'Have a care, Lenceon. He is like Corodel in more ways than his name and his sword.'

'If I can get a word in,' Red said sharply, glaring at the marshal, 'I'd just say that I . . . I've been thinking for some time that I might stay around awhile.'

Aurilia nodded, her smile unreadable. 'I knew it. He is young and reckless and hot-blooded – and he has found *many* things here that suit him.' Red gave her a sharp look at that, but she blandly ignored it. 'I knew he might want to stay, to seek adventure like his namesake.'

'I knew it last night,' Krost growled, 'when he set off after Vanticor. That was like Corodel.'

'So you've got me all figured out,' Red said drily. 'Fine. But the fact is, I'd better go along with this expedition just to help keep you two out of trouble.'

The prince was smiling almost warmly. 'I said that I would welcome you, Cordell. But beyond that – if you join us, on top of the service you have already performed, I would *reward* you, amply.'

'Reward?' Red's eyes brightened. 'Why, then, your Highness – how can I say no?'

'Oh, yes,' Krost muttered. '*Very* like Corodel.'

FOURTEEN

Red's first indication of what a prince might mean by reward came the following morning. He had spent the rest of the previous day mostly on his own, since Aurilia had been busying herself with various preparations while Krost remained with the prince – to try, as he put it, to stop Marshal Lenceon thinking that *he* was in sole charge. And Red found the day dragging on heavily and emptily, for even his friends among the palace guards were caught up in the hubbub of readying the expedition. For the *war*, Red thought, although it seemed to be viewed by most of the people in the palace as just another princely enterprise.

After whiling away the day, Red had spent the evening alone as well, vaguely hoping that Aurilia might come to him again, not sure he could find his own way – which discretion would require – to go to her. Solitude probably contributed to his restless inability to sleep, that night, along with his lingering amazement that he had actually, readily, enlisted in the prince's force. Not that he had any regret or a wish to recant. He soberly told himself that he owed it to his new friends and his royal host. But behind that, more truthfully, the prospect of riding off with a company of bowmen and swordsmen led by a prince, including wizards, a witch, and a dwarf-giant, to do battle with a sorcerer, simply filled him with a wild inner glee and the keenest excitement he had ever known.

Next to that, the prospect of the reward that the prince had offered seemed incidental. But it seemed less so when Krost appeared at his door that following morning, grinning broadly, inviting him to come out for a stroll.

'What's up?' Red asked, studying his friend's grin a little warily. 'Has the bad guy surrendered already?'

Krost chuckled. 'Nothing like that. It is just that Aurilia and

141

I suggested to the prince that he might give you some of your reward in advance – and I want to show you what he is offering.'

And, ignoring Red's questions, Krost led him away through the palace and then outside, to the extensive outbuildings that included all the stables. Where Red was introduced to a horse.

More specifically, to a mare – a glorious, golden creature whose mane and tail were so blonde as to be almost white. With an arched neck and shapely head, a healthy and glossy hide, a long-legged muscularity that spoke volumes about speed and grace and stamina, and intelligent eyes that surveyed Red with serene enquiry.

'She is yours,' Krost said, his grin widening at Red's open-mouthed amazement. 'One of the prince's finest.'

'He's very generous,' Red said breathlessly. 'Thank you and Aurilia . . . for the suggestion.'

He laid a hand on the mare's silky-warm shoulder, slid it up along the wonderful sweep of her neck, then finally, carefully, stroked the delicate texture of her nose. The mare snorted very softly, lifting her head a little, never taking her eyes from his.

'Her name is Grilena,' Krost said. 'I think she likes you.'

From behind them came a rasp of cackling laughter, and Red turned to see Aurilia in her old-crone form. 'You don't think she may be too much woman for you, young Red?'

He grinned. 'They have an expression where I come from, Aurilia. Blondes have more fun.'

The old woman cackled wildly at that. 'Fun, is it? Take your blonde for a gallop while you may, my lad. The time for *fun* is nearly over.'

And she hobbled away, cackling to herself, muttering 'blondes have more fun, indeed' under her breath.

So Red followed her advice, after Krost produced a gold-embossed saddle that he said was also part of the prince's gift. The mare seemed as keen on the idea of a getting-acquainted ride as she did. And when he swung up on to her back she whickered once, softly, with what sounded like enjoyment. Krost by then had decided to go along and had saddled his massive dappled pony, Wolle, who seemed to regard Grilena with considerable interest. As the massive weight of Krost settled on to the pony's back, Red reached over casually to pat his shoulder. For an instant it felt like touching a warm statue of a horse, for the mounded muscle under the dappled hide was as hard and unyielding as if it was bronze or marble. Then Wolle's head snapped around, and Red jerked his hand back from the clash of its teeth.

'Your horse is more of a meat-eater than you are,' he complained.

Krost laughed. 'Wolle does not like the touch of strangers. But he will get used to you.'

'Don't let him go to any trouble,' Red said sourly.

He nudged Grilena forward – and knew at once just how special she was, how little time they would need to grow used to one another. In the next short while, as they rode, it was confirmed. They trotted and cantered and walked, even galloped briefly. They wheeled sharply in circles to the right and left, backed up, even frisked elegantly sideways. Whatever he asked her to do, she did it with only the most feathery touch of knee or heel or rein. Mostly she seemed to anticipate him, moving with his gestures and not from them, as a skilled dancer will anticipate the movements of the partner who leads her.

'She does like you,' Krost said at last, having tried with some difficulty and laughter to keep pace.

'It's mutual,' Red said softly, stroking the mare's silken neck. 'It's like riding a telepathic cloud.'

He spent most of the rest of that day with Grilena, wandering here and there over the expanse of the palace grounds, extending and enjoying the rapport that had so instantly been established between himself and the beautiful mare. Krost soon left them to it, perhaps feeling that Wolle and he were an intrusion. Eventually, returning to the stables, Grilena seemed as reluctant as he felt when he dismounted. But he spent a while more with her, brushing her and tending her after unsaddling her – tearing himself away at sundown with difficulty, certain that he heard the same feeling in her soft farewell whinny.

143

All in all, it had been an amazingly peaceful time, he thought, for a day that had begun with his decision to go to war. And for him the evening continued on the same lines, when Aurilia came to his suite to join him for the evening meal, bearing the news that preparations were well advanced and that they would be leaving Quamarr, by water, at noon of the following day. That brought Red a few tremors of anticipation, though not enough to limit his appetite for supper. And they had no effect, either, on his appetites when Aurilia then decided to stay the night, proving in her younger form some of the truth in the adage about blondes that Red had quoted.

In the morning, the prince's expedition was mustered.

It had been decided to assemble the militia at the waterfront itself, before dawn, as quietly as possible, so as not to brew rumour and alarm through the city. But at the palace itself, the frantic turmoil and uproar that accompanied the preparations reached new heights of chaos as last-minute complications inevitably arose. Red spent his time staying well out of the way, with Grilena, which pleased them both. She seemed quite untroubled by the excitement, or by having Red's satchel strapped on her back behind the saddle. And she snorted with what seemed like satisfaction when they rode away for another peaceful, communing canter beyond the stables.

But then a servant ran to collect him, and he rode around to the palace courtyard at the front to find Krost and Aurilia waiting. Aurilia in her youthful form was wearing a modest knee-length tunic and leggings of soft buckskin, for riding, seated on her tall white gelding and looking as excited and eager as anyone. Even Krost's Wolle was champing at the bit impatiently, being reined in by his grinning rider. And Red – who had never been a soldier save as an extra in a low-budget war film once – wondered if it was always like that, going off to war. Always quivering outward excitement and impatience masking the questions and doubts that were raising themselves inwardly. About which of them, if any, would still be there to ride together when the enterprise was done. Or if they would be riding at all, he thought dismally, reaching to touch the neck of his Grilena.

But forebodings fled from his mind when with a rumble and a clatter an ornate open coach rolled into view from the side of the palace. Sunlight glittered on its gold leaf and bright paint, the driver and his mate in rich livery rode in front while two blank-faced footmen in livery rode behind. Following the coach rode the three mages, looking less than comfortable on glossy grey horses. And in the cushioned heart of the vehicle sat prince Phaedran, staring fixedly ahead, in a gorgeous blue-and-gold uniform with a jewelled sword at his hip.

Red stared at the resplendent vehicle as it rolled slowly towards them. 'He can't be serious. Going to war in a royal coach?'

Krost laughed. 'No, just through the city. The prince must ever provide a ceremonial show when he moves among his people. Things will be more sober and warlike when we are on the river.'

As the coach came up to them, and they made their bows, Phaedran surveyed Red on his new mount, with another almost friendly smile. 'Do you like her?'

'She's beautiful,' Red said fervently, then reached for more formal language to express his feeling. 'No man could receive a greater gift, Your Highness, or be more grateful.'

Phaedran nodded. 'But I am grateful too, to have you ride with me. So each gives to the other, Corodel.'

And the coach rolled on before Red could find a polite way to remind the prince of his actual name.

Aurilia nudged her gelding towards him. 'Take position on the other side of the coach,' she said, pointing. 'The people will enjoy having a look at you, too – Corodel.'

As Krost chuckled, Red scowled at her, receiving an innocent smile in return. Then Red swung Grilena to the left-hand side of the coach, like an outrider, while Krost took up position on the right and Aurilia dropped back to ride with the mages. In that way they paraded down the gravelled drive and out on to the breadth of Merchants' Avenue.

The people of Quamarr seemed to have advance notice of the event, proving the efficiency of the rumour-grapevine even in a city without advanced forms of mass communication. A sizeable crowd was waiting expectantly by the palace gates, greeting the coach and riders with a burst of cheers that alerted others along the avenue ahead. So the thoroughfare was lined with people several deep, staring, pointing, cheering, as the small parade advanced. And amid the noise and movement Red could see many a finger pointing at him, and could hear the name sweeping through parts of the crowd. 'Corodel . . . Corodel . . .'

I've got a starring part at last, he thought wryly. Under another man's name, with another man's sword, a bit overshadowed by my companions – but still a featured player. And he smiled his insouciant smile as he sat the beautiful mare, one hand idly on his sword-hilt, and was Corodel for all he was worth along the way to the river.

The Marshal was awaiting them, on a coal-black stallion with a wild eye. 'Everything is in readiness, sir,' he said at once as the coach rolled to a stop next to him. 'All the supplies and horses and arms were loaded during the night, and the men went on board just before dawn, as you ordered.'

His tone implied that it had been an unduly long time to keep his militiamen in such a position, but the prince merely stared wordlessly towards the boats that the marshal's stiff gesture indicated. And Red looked as well along the succession of great wharves, wood-slabbed and stone-aproned, where a number of heavy vessels lay in their berths. The crowd gathering near by to gawp from a respectful distance would see only a few rivermen moving on the decks of the vessels, no alarming sign of a warlike force.

'The men can emerge to take their ease when we are away from the city,' Phaedran said at last. 'How are they distributed?'

'Sixteen pack-boats,' Lenceon replied, 'twenty men with their officers to each boat.'

The prince nodded. 'Then we shall board my barge and cast off without delay.'

That drew Red's attention to the vessel tied up at a wharf in the other direction. The pack-boats, as Lenceon had called them, seemed more to deserve the term *barges*, for they were vastly broad of beam, considerably long, and fairly low in the water, with clumsy square-rigged sails on stubby masts and provisions for giant oars as well. The other vessel, the so-called royal barge, was entirely different, more like a large yacht. Narrower than the pack-boats and immeasurably more graceful, it wore a proud bird-of-prey figurehead at the bow and a tall mast with tightly reefed sails held like a pair of arms spread eloquently wide.

When everyone had dismounted, crewmen hurried from the royal vessel to take charge of the horses and other gear. The coach with its two drivers turned to retrace its steps to the palace, leaving Phaedran with only the two footmen to attend him, who at once began organizing the transfer of the prince's considerable baggage to the barge. Just two servants, Red thought, raising a mocking eyebrow in Aurilia's direction. He's really roughing it.

But Aurilia was otherwise preoccupied – having noticed that some of the crewmen were watching her and the mages with visible unease. And Lenceon, too, had noticed it.

'Your crew seems unhappy, Highness, to be conveying a witch as well as mages,' he said with some satisfaction. 'No doubt they see a bad omen in it.'

The prince frowned. 'I care nothing for their superstition, Lenceon. If they grow too unhappy, as you put it, I shall dismiss them and turn over the sailing of the barge to you and your men.'

His frigid tone carried effortlessly to all the nearby crewmen, who instantly grew very busy and assiduous, while the marshal wilted slightly, bowing with a twisted half-smile. And Aurilia did not miss the chance to twist the knife.

'If it's omens you seek, Marshal,' she said sweetly, 'look for them in the swift running of the river's current, and the fresh breeze blowing from the East to speed us on our way.'

That earned her a glower of distaste from Lenceon, as they all made their way to the barge. And Red was feeling uneasy at the talk of omens, and Aurilia's careless assumption of *good* ones. Touch wood, my lady, he told her silently – and did as much himself as they went up the broad gangplank of the barge.

Perhaps it was an actor's impulse, then, that made him turn to look back at the crowd – his audience – that was still milling around on the cobbles. But the look became at once sharply focused, for on one side of the crowd's main mass he saw a familiar figure. Small, white-haired, cherubic in his overlong coat – Hallifort, again, regarding Red steadily with his eerie white-pupilled eyes.

Red turned to draw Aurilia's or Krost's attention to that unusual onlooker, but they had gone on ahead. And when he glanced back at the wharf again the little man was no longer in sight.

By then the royal barge's crew – seven men and their captain – had cast off the vessel's lines and were easing her away from the wharf. Four of the men were using the enormously long, heavy oars, two to an oar, to push the barge off, while the others began to make sail. Then Krost took one of the oars, lifting it as if it was feather-light, his strength impelling the vessel away with such a rush that Red felt he could probably pole it all the way like a punt. The sails flowered out from the wide yardarm, filling with the east wind. They looked to Red like two great wings, arched and white as a seagull's, straining to break away from their lines and stays and take flight. Ballooning taut with the wind, they spread their huge double canopy far on either side of the barge – and the vessel surged ahead with a chorus of creaking and groaning like sounds of thankful release.

Red had done a share of pleasure sailing in his own world, mostly small craft on lively coastlines. But there, with the royal barge virtually taking wing on the bosom of a broad, inky-black river, he felt another of the rushes of exhilaration, almost exaltation, that he had been feeling at times since his arrival in Quamarr.

But even in the midst of his excitement a cooler part of his mind was asking what kind of *omen*, good or bad, could be read in his glimpse of Hallifort's eyes.

PART TWO

THE OFFERING

The valley was deep and remote, tucked between the granite battlements of mountain ranges. Under drooping rainclouds the valley floor was almost entirely blanketed by forest – but a forest like no other. The trees were gnarled, twisted, sometimes splintered or broken, and all entirely dead. Yet they stood firmly, solidly, for they had petrified where they stood, root and branch transformed into rough grey flaky stone. No leaves grew on those unnatural branches, no dead leaves lay on the ground. And no other plants grew there – no shrubs or ferns, no vines or flowers, except for smears of yellow-green lichen on the stony trunks, puffs and bulges of fungi on the limbs or on the dank bare ground, and patches of grey-white moss at the trees' bases or on the sides of rock outcroppings.

Yet through the desolation, indifferent to the squalls of chill rain, living beings moved. Weird and unsightly, they resembled crude caricatures or travesties of the human figure, their naked skin as coarse, grey, and flaky as the surface of the stony trees. Thick-bodied and heavy-limbed, they moved in graceless lurches, now and then pausing to tear up some discoloured fungi and stuff it into their wide, lipless mouths. They were small-headed, with close-set eyes shadowed in deep sockets, slack, heavy jaws, and almost no necks. They did not speak or make any noise except for their shuffling footsteps – yet when the group of them came to a certain place in the forest they veered away, all together, as if at a soundless signal.

At that place stood an edifice whose walls – including the inner walls separating its various chambers – were formed from the petrified trees. There they grew even closer together, still rooted, but tightly intertwined and overlapping to form stony barriers. The whole structure was huge, sprawling out through the heart of the forest. And above it, as if further to prove it unique, loomed something wholly alien – an immense canopy made of dark metal, in the shape of a flattened and many-faced cone. The canopy hung or hovered motionlessly over the weird dwelling, serving as roof, not touching any of the trees nor supported in any visible way.

At the exact centre of the structure, in a clear area, stood a short man with an entirely hairless head and a brutal, beardless jaw, with thick black hair matting his chest and forearms where they showed past the collar and sleeves of his long fur robe. He seemed indifferent to the chill breeze gusting between the trees of his walls, or to the sound of rain on the canopy high above him. He stood still, wholly absorbed, his eyes – as fierce and bright and yellow as a raptor's – fixed unblinkingly on an immense stone bowl at his feet.

The bowl was full to the brim with a dark, shiny liquid on whose gleaming surface images formed – and shifted, dissolved, re-formed.

He had been staring for some while at a succession of these tiny, uncannily moving pictures. He watched as Red Cordell appeared from nowhere in the darkened street of Quamarr and drew his bright sword to defend Aurilia. He watched the flight of Vanticor, the hurled knife. His yellow eyes flared a little as he had watched Hallifort the Healer approach Red in the tavern, but still he remained unmoving as the images changed. He watched the discussions in the palace and Red's confrontation with the Barachi. He peered closer at Hallifort's intervention, then watched while the images changed once more – to show the flotilla of vessels on the river, the heavy pack-boats wallowing along behind the gull-winged royal barge.

For long moments he stared closely while the vessels sailed on. Then the image changed again, and his eyes blazed fiercely. The bowl was showing nothing but a slowly swirling, coiling, impenetrable cloud of smoke or fog. Yet now and then, through the veil, he could glimpse a blackness – something rearing up high and immense, shiny and gleaming, like a gigantic half-sphere carved from obsidian.

Slowly he turned away, leaving the dark images as they

were in the bowl. Faint light formed around his left hand as he made an abrupt, jerky gesture. On the far side of the clearing geometrical patterns appeared eerily on the flat lifeless ground. First a five-pointed star, then a pentagon around it, then a circle around that, finally a square around that. The man gestured again, speaking some words in a guttural, inhuman tongue. As he spoke, the air above the geometrical shape grew dense, whirled, formed a vertical spinning cylinder. Slowly the cylinder took on more substance and shape, until at once it became a tall and unnaturally thin figure, wearing a cowled robe of material so dark that its folds could not be seen. From the total blackness within the cowl could be seen two small points of red, like coals, and a faint sound could be heard that might have been the clashing of teeth.

The fur-robed man, his glowing hands rivalled by the fierce bright glare of his eyes, seemed unimpressed. 'Well?' he barked.

From beneath the cowl came soft, creaking laughter, sounding far away and ghostly. 'As you commanded, Magister,' said a voice as low and chilling as a whisper from a grave, 'I hurled all my power. The shielding deflected it and withstood it. I would think that its occupant would not even have noticed the attack, as he would not notice the sun's rays.'

'*All* your power?'

'All that I have been able to bring from my Realm.' The terrible creaking laughter sounded again. 'It is a shielding spell of the first magnitude, reinforced by other spells. Even if you were to risk summoning a score of powers like myself, I feel they could not break through. The spell would even resist the full extent of your *own* might.'

The man's yellow eyes darkened as he clenched his phosphorescent hands into fists. 'How could it *be* . . . ?'

The being within the patterns laughed distantly again. 'He is strong, Magister. And the defensive spells are always more potent than the attacking ones.'

'Do you now teach me sorcery, demon? If you're too feeble, I'll find another way. Begone – I banish you.'

The spectral figure began to fade, as if being washed out of

153

the quivering air. When it was almost totally gone, only the inhuman voice remained, the eerie creaking laughter.

'You should visit me in my Realm, Magister,' it said. 'I would teach you more than sorcery . . .'

Then the voice faded as well and was gone. The fur-robed man, seeming indifferent to the last remark, turned back to his scrying bowl, back to the image held there still – of the roiling fog, and the glittering black immensity looming within it. Slowly, as he stared, the image receded, showing that the fog and what it hid stood on the wild, rocky edge of an expanse of water, which stretched to a crimson horizon where the sun was setting.

Suddenly his face contorted with a mixture of frustration and towering fury. 'Misbegotten usurper!' he roared, throwing back his head like a howling beast. 'Your arrogant hungers will *destroy it all!*'

His glowing hands lifted above his head, clenching again into fists, muscular forearms bunching as the sleeves fell away. Beyond the weird dwelling the wind whirled and shrieked. Above, the giant metal canopy boomed like a gong. From the scrying bowl the liquid leaped like a fountain into the air, all of its images lost as it exploded into a cloud of inky steam that hissed like a snake as it fled as if alive out and away through the trees, to vanish at last amid the rain.

After many days of swift and uneventful sailing, the flotilla of boats led by the royal barge lay quietly at anchor, sails furled, on the vast, black, and gently heaving bosom of Lake Tenebrial, into which the River Tenebris flowed. The setting sun was disappearing into the taller treetops of the forest that clothed the lake's western shoreline. As the sky darkened and the clouds funnelling down were reddened by the sunset, Red stood at the rail of the royal barge, stretched and yawned, and thought wryly – not for the first time – that he had signed on for a war and had ended up on a cruise.

And a fairly boring one, at least in the daytime. Most people kept themselves to themselves. The prince seldom stirred from his cabin, nor had the mages made many appearances from theirs. The marshal tended mostly to stand, dark and brooding, at the bow next to the hawk-like figurehead, and Red thought they made a good couple. Sometimes Krost would wander by and chat, but the dwarf-giant had apparently worked on riverboats in his time and was more devoted to watching the processes of sailing the barge and, sometimes, joining in. And Aurilia came sometimes to spend a while with Red – but always the crewmen would look edgy and eye her warily, even in her elderly guise, until she would go back to her cabin just to put them at ease.

So he had spent his days staring or dreaming out over the black water, watching the Central Grasslands slip past along the river until they began to give way to more rolling, less fertile land further west. Or he had passed some time happily below decks with Grilena, grooming her in the cramped but tidy stabling provided for the horses. On some more restless days he had tried to find a semi-private place where he could put himself through some fairly demanding exercise routines, which amused Krost but startled any crewmen who happened along.

But mostly he had tried to keep out of the way of the crew, who seemed always to be rushing to reef this or belay that or whatever sailors did. Not that their busyness had seemed necessary, though, for the easterly breeze had blown merrily the whole time, keeping the gull-wing sails full and blooming, and the river's current added its impetus. It had therefore all been smooth sailing under a cheerful sun through all of those days. And so the boats had positively whisked down the river – the *upper* river, as it was properly called – and had surged out on to the lake in a thunder of dark foam.

Also, however, Red had needed to use some of the slow daylight hours of the voyage to catch up on sleep, for his nights were full of Aurilia. He had been assigned the smallest cabin of all in the barge's range of accommodation, so that he had only a narrow bunk, a stool, and a tiny all-purpose cabinet. But at least his cabin was set somewhat away from the others, so that his and Aurilia's daytime circumspection could be abandoned at night. And *abandoned* was exactly the right word.

Red had been a little surprised on the first night out from

155

Quamarr, when she had slid silently in through his cabin door wearing her wickedest grin, like a schoolgirl planning mischief. She was also wearing a silken wrap that clung to her closely enough to distinguish her beyond doubt from a schoolgirl, and to quicken Red's pulse considerably.

'Do you think it indiscreet, my coming to you here?' she asked, sliding her arms around his neck.

He lifted a shoulder in vague denial. 'I wouldn't want you not to. But is the prince a puritan who would object?'

She waved a hand airily. 'No – but his crew disapproves of me as it is, and I wouldn't want to embarrass Phaedran. Still, no one should notice. And the whole barge creaks and groans all the time, so we won't be overheard.'

Red smiled a wicked smile of his own. 'Even when we're creaking and groaning too?' he asked, reaching for her.

But she stepped back, holding up a hand in mock-seriousness. 'No – I'm here for a *purpose*!'

'I should hope so,' Red said, reaching for her again.

Laughing, she spun like a dancer away from his hands. 'I mean a proper purpose,' she insisted. 'One that might help to keep you alive.'

That stopped him. 'What do you mean?'

'Protection, Red. Against the possibility of sorcerous attack.'

He frowned. 'Is that likely?'

'It's quite possible,' she said, growing serious. 'We're getting closer to our goal every day. And though the Earth-magic wards that I can provide may not be the strongest armour you could have – certainly not against a strike from close range – they may fend off magical thrusts over distance. And they will be better than nothing.'

'If you say so,' he agreed. 'What do you have to do?'

The impish grin reappeared. 'First of all, I need you to take off your clothes.'

That made him laugh and comply without hesitation. And after an overacted, rolling-eyed portrayal of mock-admiration, she got down to business. Which consisted of removing a few hairs from the rich mass of her coiffure and tying them in intricate knots here and there on to Red's entire wardrobe, and the hilt and scabbard of the sword.

'How many of the others have you done this for?' he asked her teasingly.

Her eyes laughed at him, but her mouth was wry. 'The mages sneered when I suggested my wards for the prince – and the marshal said no quite rudely – and the captain looked terrified when I offered wards for his crew. I have only warded Krost, aside from you.' She smiled sweetly. 'And he was a gentleman, handing his clothing out from behind his cabin door, not standing brazenly before me as you are.'

'It'd probably be quite a sight if he did,' Red remarked.

She laughed and stood up from the stool where she had been sitting, reaching up for another of her long blonde hairs, twining and knotting it in among his tangle of red curls. Then she stood back and assumed her mock-solemn expression again.

'Perhaps I should tie wards into *all* your body hair,' she murmured.

Red raised an eyebrow. 'Is that necessary?'

'Perhaps,' she said gravely. 'There is a lesser spell that can turn a man's member into a living serpent.'

Then she laughed happily at his suddenly appalled expression and reached up to put her arms around his neck again, somehow contriving a sinuous wriggle that caused her single garment to detach itself and fall fluttering to the floor.

And that, or scenes similar to that without the preliminaries of the ward-knots, had been going on merrily every night during the down-river journey. So Red had felt no regret when their progress had slowed after they had sailed out on to the lake, losing the extra force of the river's current. He felt a keen anticipation of the action and excitement to come – but with Aurilia joining him on his narrow bunk every night, delicious and uninhibited, endlessly inventive and endlessly desirable, he was quite willing to let the other sorts of action and excitement come along later. Maybe a lot later.

Equally, the nights with Aurilia provided him with many a visual and tactile memory to be savoured during those even slower daylight hours when they were traversing the vast breadth of the lake. And some of those memories, along with imaginings about the night to come, were drifting peacefully

157

through his mind during that sunset, while the flotilla lay anchored on its approach to the lake's western shore. Yet even as he stretched and yawned, and silently encouraged the sunset to get on with it, he was also aware of a tiny but growing knot in his stomach – a bit like the twist in the entrails that he had always felt, momentarily, waiting for curtains to lift or cameras to roll.

Because the line of forest on the horizon, silhouetted then against the sunset, did not merely mark the western shore of Lake Tenebrial. Beyond it lay the Western Woodlands, the region that the Barachi called home. The region where the prince's enemy, the enemy of them all, might be lurking with a captive princess.

And from what Krost had told him along the way, the shoreline would also demand some very tricky navigation, which is why they had anchored at that point, in order to have full daylight when they progressed further. At its western perimeter the lake poured its waters out to form the lower stretch of the River Tenebris, which flowed on through the Western Woodlands. But the strait through which the waters left the lake was narrow and turbulent, with endless side-currents, backwashes, eddies, whirlpools . . . And over the centuries quantities of driftwood and other flotsam had collected, tangling together in the weave and spin of the weird currents – slowly gathering layers of mud and silt bound by drifting weed and eventually by the seeds of other plants. So what the strait contained was a large number of little islands that were not rooted, but were like natural rafts. They might extend to the breadth of the barge's deck or be no larger than a man's shirt. But most of them bore some form of plant life, and the larger ones even boasted shrubs, small trees, and forms of wild life like waterfowl and aquatic rodents.

They were called the Wandering Islets, Red had learned – and they were a riverman's nightmare, since of course no permanent channels through them could be charted. By necessity boats went through them by daylight, slowly and with care, to avoid the Islets themselves and also to take careful soundings in case of new sandbars or other obstructions created below the surface by the unpredictable movement of the waters.

In years gone by, Red had been told, the Islets had been a favourite spot for ambush by pirates who infested the lake and river. And though the pirates were long gone, that was another reason why the flotilla had stopped that evening – so that Wretifal and his cohorts could use their powers to look ahead at the Islets, to ensure that no enemies had set up their own ambushes.

If all was well, they would sail out on to the immensely wide, sluggish lower river – which would eventually divide into a myriad smaller streams that oozed and trickled on through the Woodlands towards the sea. But long before that, Krost had told Red, the expedition would disembark to proceed on horseback through the swampy forest to the southern coast near Claw Point. And Red was looking forward to being on land again, riding Grilena – though he also knew, with regret, that Aurilia would probably have to keep to herself at night during the overland march. One blonde or the other but never both, he thought, and sighed.

'Worrying about something, *Corodel*?' a voice asked him from a few paces away, sarcasm heavy in its pronunciation of the name.

Red swung around, knowing the marshal's voice and tone, expecting and finding the expression of dislike on the man's face. 'That's just Cordell, Marshal,' he said easily. 'And I try never to worry. Just hoping that things liven up a little before too long.'

Lenceon snorted. 'You might find things get *too* lively for you, shortly.'

Red smiled a derisive smile, raising one eyebrow, knowing from experience that it was one of his most annoying expressions. 'Too lively? That'd be interesting. I've never been anywhere that I found too lively.'

'You have never been in the Western Woodlands,' the marshal snapped.

'True.' Red maintained the derisiveness. 'And I'm sure you have. In fact you seem to have a *lot* of advance information about what it's going to be like, in there.'

It was a vague and general jibe, so Red was surprised to see the marshal's scowl turn into a look of unallayed, hate-filled malevolence. Not the first time, he thought, that Lenceon had over-reacted in a similar way. Red was even beginning to wonder if the man was somehow mentally disturbed – but he was unable to learn more, or provoke more, for Lenceon spun on his heel and marched stiffly off without another word.

His departure could have been partly due to Krost, who was ambling in their direction, peering from under bushy brows at the retreating marshal. 'Have you two been having words?' he asked Red merrily.

'Not really,' Red said. 'He just seems to like having enemies instead of friends.'

'I doubt if he knows about friendship,' Krost growled. 'But no matter. He should have enemies enough to keep him happy soon. And he is a good officer.'

'Bully for him,' Red drawled. 'What else is new?'

Krost smiled happily. 'The wizards have been labouring with all their spells of seeing and sensing and everything, and they say that the way is clear through the Wandering Islets.'

Red looked dubiously around at the distant line of forest, almost invisible by then as darkness settled on the lake. 'I wish Aurilia could do all that seeking stuff. I'd have more faith in her.'

'That is just because she is more beautiful than the mages,' Krost said with a chuckle. 'But Wretifal and the others are powerful, Red. They would know if any enemies are lying in wait among the Islets.'

'They were wrong before,' Red pointed out. 'Missing that barrier thing, on the coast.'

'True,' Krost said, his grin fading. 'But that was over a greater distance. Anyway, the prince has ordered them to continue their spells, without pause – to keep a constant watch on the Islets from now till we start through them in the morning.'

'What if they find something?' Red asked. 'What do we do if the Islets are crawling with enemies, come morning?'

Krost shrugged. 'Then we will have two choices – fight our

way through or try to bypass them on land. But those will be the *only* choices, Red. We will not turn back.' He scratched moodily at his tangled hair. 'I have seen Phaedran like this before. He is a strong-minded, stubborn man who can rarely be deflected from whatever he has decided on. Nothing will deter or turn him now. He intends to reach Claw Point, to see if it is the sorcerer Talonimal who lives there – and if Evelane is there. And he would go *alone*, if he had to, in the teeth of any opposition. Nothing will stop him now. Nothing this side death.'

At about the same time that evening, within the black structure that rose from the sea coast far to the south and west of
Lake Tenebrial, the silver-haired sorcerer stood with one arm
around the lissom waist of Princess Evelane, both staring
fixedly at the scrying stone where it jutted from the wall. The
stone showed the royal vessel rocking gently on the lake's
slow swell, trim and graceful with its sails furled like a seabird
in repose. But the two watchers were uninterested in nautical
beauty. There was an air of barely controlled excitement about
them as they watched, and perhaps also a tinge of savagery
in their eyes and smiles.

'Enjoy the peace of the evening, O Prince,' the man said
softly, gazing at the image. 'Tomorrow brings an end to
peace.'

The young woman stirred beside him. 'Nothing can go
wrong, can it?'

'Nothing,' he assured her. 'Everything is in place. In any
case, even if his entire force were to come clamouring to our
door, we are beyond their reach.'

She nodded, almost absently, and sighed. He peered
intently down at her, raising his eyebrows.

'What is it, my love? Surely you are not feeling some filial
guilt, some late twinge of conscience?'

'No!' She stiffened, moving a jerky step away from him,
facing him with a tight and angry expression. 'How could you
think that? I *want* him dead! I want your plans to succeed – I
want what you promised me when you brought me away
from that tomb of a palace . . .'

As her voice rose to shrillness he held out a pacifying hand,
his smile becoming oddly secretive. 'Then why do you seem
troubled, beloved?'

'Because it is to be so *easy*!' she cried, her mouth working.

'So *swift* – too swift to make up for the years of misery I went through, the humiliation of living with the witches while having no magic of my own, no more than one of their scullery-maids . . .'

'I know of your suffering,' the man cut in smoothly. 'And soon we both are to be avenged . . .'

'*No!*' she shrieked again. 'It's not *enough*! They will die out there, far away, and I will see only the soundless image of their dying on your stone . . . I wish I could *be* there, when he dies, when the witch-whore dies, and all of them . . . I want to *see* it, I want them to see *me*, to know the truth . . . I want to laugh in their faces as they die!'

The sorcerer had been nodding through the whole diatribe, the rising hysteria. And the secretiveness in his smile was more obvious by then, as was the cruel light in his eyes.

'Yes, Evelane,' he said soothingly. 'I understand. That is why I have kept . . . a small surprise for you.' His smile widened as she stared up at him, puzzled. 'I share your view that vengeance is far from sweet when it is indirect and far away. And besides, I have come to see that other *benefits* could be gained by postponing the final reckoning.'

'I don't understand,' she breathed.

He gestured idly at the stone, and the image vanished. Then he strode away a few steps, as if gripped by tensions that would not let him be still.

'The prince will not die in the morning,' he said, pacing.

'Will not . . . ?' she echoed, in a small wondering voice.

'Nor will the witch Aurilia,' he went on, as if she had not spoken. 'Some of the others also may survive, though I am less concerned about them. Certainly the mages must die at the first opportunity, since I do not wish to be distracted or wearied by magical battle . . .'

'But what of my *father*?' she asked insistently.

His teeth flashed in a grin that was both savage and self-congratulatory. 'He and the witch will be taken alive, and brought here to us. I have already sent instructions.'

Her mood altered instantly, like her expression, every remnant of hysterical rage vanishing to be replaced with delight. 'So then we can kill them here?'

'Even better, my sweet,' he said. 'So we can allow them to contribute to my . . . development.'

Understanding flooded through her, and the sound she made was a whimper of ecstasy. 'You will *offer* them!'

'Exactly. Consign them to the fire. Fittingly, since Aurilia would already have been offered if mischance had not intervened to save her.' His voice was fierce and intense as he paced. 'To partake of the powers of one of the Named Nine will advance me enormously, without question. As for Phaedran, and any others who may survive, even though they have no magical gifts their life-forces alone will be beneficial.' He glanced at Evelane, grinning again. 'Perhaps the one who walks the bridge will relish the royal flavour.'

She shuddered slightly, her smile unnaturally bright. 'And they will *know*, beforehand . . . They will suffer the anguish of knowing *who* has killed them, and why . . .'

'Exactly,' he said again. 'We shall ensure that they feel the torment of it fully, before the end.'

'Oh, my lord,' she murmured, moving to him. 'Oh, my Talonimal, thank you for this gift.'

'We shall share in its savouring, my sweet,' he said, stroking her hair as she clung to him. Then he moved her away, turning her so they were again both facing the blank surface of the scrying stone. 'Meanwhile,' he said, 'the alignments are forming, so that we can soon make use of our latest acquisition from Vanticor. With *her* witchpower, I should be at a new peak of strength by the time the prince is brought before us.'

He made a small gesture, and a picture formed on the gleaming stone. An image of the same dungeon-like chamber with glittering walls that had held the heavy, middle-aged woman in her transport of terror. But the new picture showed a different prisoner.

Nellann, lying on the stone floor with knees drawn up in a foetal position, her torn dress clutched around her.

The sorcerer stared at the image, wetting his lips as he studied the firm roundness of Nellann's body. 'We might have her bathed,' he said harshly, 'and brought to join us in your bed-chamber tonight.'

Evelane pretended to pout in mock-jealousy, then smiled, eyes glistening. 'And . . . and hurt her a while, as well?'

Talonimal chuckled. 'Ah, my dear, how swiftly and how well you have learned to appreciate the *subtler* levels of pleasure.'

'I have had a devoted tutor, my lord,' she replied archly.

'Then certainly you may practise on this one,' he told her. 'She needs merely to be alive for the Offering. Up to that point, my love, we may play with her tonight as roughly as we wish.'

Shortly after sun-up the next day, the prince's vessel was moving again, the heavy pack-boats in its wake. The morning was heavy and overcast, humid, warm, with scarcely a trace of breeze, and the entire flotilla had made as much sail as possible to take advantage of every stray breath. Even so, by the time Red emerged on deck – alone, for Aurilia always departed for her own cabin before dawn – the captain was preparing to rig a temporary boom for a jib, to gain extra sail.

'It is a delicate choice,' Krost explained to Red as they stood near the bow watching the crew at work. 'We must go through the Wandering Islets slowly, because of unseen dangers underwater. Yet if we do meet a sandbar or something, we need to have some way so we can break clear.'

'If you say so, admiral,' Red replied lightly, watching the tangled greenery of the lakeshore drawing near. 'And if we get hung up, we get out and push, right?'

Krost smiled. 'Only if you have webbed feet, my friend.'

Krost then went to see if he could help the captain, while Red wandered farther forward to find a vantage point, out of the way, from which to enjoy the slow approach to the Islets.

None of them seemed actually to be wandering, as the royal barge finally drew near. By then, even at its reduced rate of movement, the barge had forged well ahead of the much slower pack-boats. But no one seemed concerned about being ahead – and Red's own concern was with the fact that the shoreline did not look like separate islets but like solid ground, like a coast with many coves and inlets along its length. But as the barge drifted forward it soon became clear that they were actually the mouths of narrow channels, half-hidden by the lush greenery of the Islets on either side. The vegetation included clumps of coarse grass and a variety of shrubs, all made more tangled by profusions of strange flowering plants and ferns. The larger Islets even had slim trees, usually with leafy vines drooping from them – all nurtured by rich river silt deposited by the currents. And just then, as if for Red's benefit, the good-sized clump of earth and vegetation directly ahead of the barge suddenly floated away to one side, exposing a broad ribbon of clear water where it had lain.

That's handy, he thought. But it was also eerie, like a door being opened for them by an unseen hand. As the barge nosed forward into the newly opened channel, Red's instincts jangled with mounting wariness. The greenery was unnaturally silent. Maybe the arrival of the barge was silencing any birds or animals on the Islets, he told himself. But even so, he grew more tense and edgy as he stared around at the impenetrable shadows among the brush, and at the stretches of swirling, eddying black water ahead.

Behind him he heard a movement, and spun to see one of the crew doing something with a rope to put the final touches on the jury-rigged jib. The crewman felt his gaze, looked around and nodded carefully.

'Corodel,' he said in respectful greeting.

'That's—' Red began the automatic correction, but the man had turned back to his task and so he let it go. At the same time he saw Marshal Lenceon coming up on deck, striding forward towards the bow, obviously intending also to watch their progress through the Islets. Red turned away, not wanting to get into another exchange with him. They had forged some distance into the channel, even farther ahead of the pack-boats, and the breeze had vanished almost completely, intensifying the humid warmth, as the jungly greenness enveloped them.

'Oars!' he heard the captain shout from the wheelhouse amidships. He was about to turn and watch the preparations for rowing when he halted. Something had caught his eye. Something he had glimpsed, or thought he had, among the thick leaves of an Islet ahead and to their left: a movement, which could well have been some form of wildlife.

Except it had glinted . . .

Leaning forward over the rail, he strained his eyes, but saw only trailing branches and unmoving leaves. Yet his instincts were hurling warnings at him like electric shocks.

'Thinking of jumping overboard?'

He jerked convulsively as the crackly voice spoke next to him. Pulling himself back from his precarious position, he turned to face the wrinkled smile of Aurilia in her aged form.

'Thought I saw something shiny, over there,' he said tensely, aware that the marshal was standing not too far away, looking in their direction and openly listening.

Before Aurilia could reply, the marshal snorted. 'Are you seeing phantoms around you now, outlander?'

Red looked at him expressionlessly while he considered various replies, then thought better of them all and simply ignored him.

'Whatever you saw, Red,' Aurilia told him, also pointedly ignoring Lenceon, 'it couldn't be a threat. The mages have maintained their scrying watch all this while.'

The marshal snorted again, stepping towards them. 'His nerves are playing tricks on him, nothing more.'

Red watched him approach, still expressionless. 'I don't suffer from nerves that much, Marshal. Just from boredom. And I'm getting *really* bored with you.'

Lenceon's face darkened. 'There will be a cure for your boredom soon enough. If I don't cure it myself beforehand.'

'Whenever you feel like trying,' Red said through his teeth.

But Aurilia was stepping between them, green eyes ablaze in her lined face. 'Stop it!' she snapped. 'Will you brawl like children here, as we begin to cross the border of our enemy's domain?'

For a moment longer Red and Lenceon locked eyes, the marshal again wearing one of his expressions of malevolent hatred. Then he made a furious noise deep in his throat and turned to stalk away – until his stride became a stumble, nearly a fall, just as everyone on the deck suddenly lurched

167

and staggered. The air filled with a heavy grinding, scraping sound, and the barge came to an abrupt halt.

'Sandbar!' blurted the crewman with the rope, who had remained near by watching open-mouthed as Red and the marshal confronted one another.

'*Oars!*' Red heard the captain bellow once again, and turned to see the other crewmen breaking out the huge oars, hoisting them two men to an oar into the oversized rowlocks. While the Marshal hurried away, disappearing below decks, Red smiled to see Krost effortlessly hoisting another oar in one hand, slotting it into position so as to lend his strength to freeing the vessel.

'I should go and help,' Red said to Aurilia, taking a step towards the action. He staggered again as the barge lurched a little, as if struggling to free itself, and the nearby crewman also staggered, making a faint sound like a whimper.

Then the man toppled to the deck. Red saw with shock that something sprouted from his chest, like a small plant growing straight out from his shirt: a plant with a shiny-smooth stem and colourful leaves or flowers . . . But he heard Aurilia gasp and realized they weren't leaves or flowers but feathers.

On a Barachi dart.

Instinctively he whirled round, staring at the tangled foliage of the Islet – but he needn't have bothered. From hiding places around every one of the Islets within sight, heavy dug-out canoes surged into view, each of them overflowing with the massed bodies of howling, snarling, dart-hurling Barachi.

SEVENTEEN

Red and Aurilia stood rooted, dazed with the shock of seeing hordes of enemies where they could not conceivably be. Aside from the random dart that had slain the crewman, the royal barge itself was not at that moment under attack. It was the slower pack-boats, far behind as they pushed turgidly through the Islets, that took the brunt of the first assault.

Yet the pack-boats were not so far back that Red could not see and admire the professional speed with which the militia went into action. Crossbow bolts began streaming through the air, replying to the darts. But darts were still flying, and militiamen were falling – and though Barachi began dropping as well, there were so many more of them that it hardly seemed to matter. They were using leather thongs like slings to get more distance and power with their darts, and to hurl fire-darts. In moments smoke swirled here and there on the pack-boats as sails and decks ignited. Then the first waves of canoes reached the boats on every side – and the Barachi swarmed up the sides like malformed apes, while the outnumbered militiamen who were still standing reached grimly for their swords.

None of the attacking Barachi wore cloaks or other covering, and Red felt a resurgence of the revulsion he had felt when he had first seen their squat bodies, their scabby dead-looking skin, their reptilian faces. Most of the attackers carried spears as well as darts, as long as they were tall, with metal heads flat and sharp-edged like sword-blades. Then as he watched the hand-to-hand fighting on the pack-boats, a blazing fire-dart thudded into the planking of the deck two paces from him. He chopped at it with his sword, which he had no memory of having drawn, and whirled towards Aurilia. But she was already moving – in youthful form again, wearing her buckskin tunic – dashing towards the hatchway that led

169

down to the cabins. Heading for the prince, Red guessed, feeling pleased that she would be safe from stray darts for a while. Then more darts whistled past and he dropped to a crouch behind the rail. Several canoe-loads of Barachi were swinging their craft towards the barge.

In the bow of the barge he was in as good a defensive position as any – or as bad. Five more bodies, including that of the captain, had fallen under that last hail of darts. He could hear Krost bellowing from the stern, on the far side of the wheelhouse, where it seemed he and some remaining crewmen were still trying to use oars to force the stranded vessel free of the sandbar. That reminded Red of his thought that Krost could probably pole the barge like a punt, and he was smiling faintly as the first wave of Barachi came over the side, lizard-eyes glittering, saw-teeth flashing as they opened their mouths in eerie battle-howls.

They arrived amidships, not within reach of his sword – and as they arrived, the three wizards burst wildly out of the hatchway from the cabins, their hands glowing with the phosphorescence of their power. From the hands of Wretifal twin bursts of magical light and flame erupted, and two Barachi fell back shrieking from the ship's rail. Then more blasts came from the hands of the other mages, searing into a cluster of monsters clambering over the rail. But as they fell, more followed – and more darts hurtled through the air from other canoes hurrying towards the barge.

Wretifal was surrounded with a filmy glow that seemed to be protective, for darts were curving around it without striking him, as if diverted by some magnetic field. But Ahnaan and Inchalo appeared to lack the power or the concentration to create such a shield while at the same time giving battle with the explosive magical flame. As they flung more blasts from their bright hands, darts suddenly flowered all over their upper bodies – and both mages collapsed, their glow extinguished.

But Red did not see them fall. More Barachi suddenly appeared on the gunwale at the bow where he crouched, and he was no longer a spectator at the battle. He lunged towards them, noticing strange designs like warpaint on the grisly

170

grey skin of their bodies, but more concerned by the weapons being swung at him by their long-reaching arms. He flung the first few back easily enough with well-placed kicks. But then there were nearly a dozen more, swarming at him with spears and stabbing darts. They tried to get around him, to attack from two sides, but his wild counterattack was too swift. Spinning and twisting, he struck and parried and dodged and struck again – still flinching inwardly at how easily his sword's unnatural sharpness sliced into flesh. But he fought grimly until at last only one Barachi faced him – and it desperately flung its spear before diving over the side to escape. He fended off the spear with his sword, and spun to check on the rest of the battle.

With a terrible inward jolt, and bitter acid rising in his throat, he realized that he could see no one else alive. And the barge was afire – sails and yardarm enveloped in flame, more flames leaping up at the stern and along the port side. His guts twisted when he remembered that Krost had been at the stern and found he could no longer hear that defiant roaring. Nor was there any sign of Aurilia, the marshal, or the prince. Wretifal, too, had finally fallen with his colleagues, a small huddled heap with a Barachi spear jutting from his back. Probably he had expended too much energy, weakening his defences, for there were dead Barachi heaped all around him, proof of his indomitable last stand. Other heaps of Barachi corpses half-blocked the hatchways leading below – and horror clawed at Red again as he heard the muffled squealing of terrified horses below decks, and knew that more Barachi were down among them.

He wanted to leap forward, to hurl himself below in defence of his beloved Grilena. But was unable to move, paralysed by despair, by the feeling of being the only survivor on a ruined vessel in the midst of a Barachi victory. By then all resistance on the pack-boats had ended, all the militiamen lay sprawled in death among the Barachi they had killed on the blood-reddened boards of the decks. Some of the boats were listing as if damaged below the waterline, some had run aground on to Islets, all were afire. And from all the wrecked boats the

171

surviving Barachi were leaping back down into canoes, turning as one towards the royal barge.

And we're still stuck on the sandbar, he said to himself. And I'm alone.

He remained motionless, watching the canoes with their howling occupants drawing nearer. This is really it, he thought, no escape, the final scene, *exeunt omnes*. He tasted the acid of nausea again and spat, wondering if he was going to be sick, if he was going to collapse into a snivelling panic. But it didn't feel like that. Maybe the nausea was a reaction to all the blood and guts and having spilled his share of them with an irresistibly lethal sword. Otherwise, he found with a bleak sense of pride, he felt only a mixture of fatalistic anger and bitter regret.

I would have liked more time with Aurilia, he thought. I would have liked to go drinking again with Krost. I would have liked to ride around this weird land with Grilena. I would have . . .

Then regret fragmented and fled as he saw the first wave of howling, blood-frenzied Barachi reach the barge. I would have *really* liked a machine-gun, he thought fiercely, and was smiling a small smile as he readied his sword and braced himself for the action that was to be his last.

But action exploded from elsewhere.

First, with a roar, Krost burst into view around the side of the wheel-house, moving at a lumbering run towards the midships rail. In one hand he gripped his iron quarterstaff, while in the other he lightly balanced one of the barge's huge oars. As he came to the rail he turned slightly sideways, poised himself, and launched the oar like a javelin. It curved up into the air and down again, crashing into a Barachi canoe, punching a hole in it and spilling its occupants into the water.

As Krost then set himself at the rail, ready to use the iron staff against attacking Barachi from the other canoes, Red sprang to join him, grinning with delight at the reappearance of his friend. In that instant Aurilia sprang out of a hatchway, hurdling a heap of Barachi dead, with the prince, his two servants, and the marshal appearing behind her. All the men had drawn swords, and the prince's blade was dripping, indicating that some Barachi had indeed got below decks but had not lasted long.

'Hold them off!' Aurilia shrieked – at Red, at Krost, at all of them. 'Hold them as long as you can!'

Her voice was frantic but commanding. Instantly the men obeyed, dashing to the rails as a new wave of Barachi stormed up the sides of the barge. Red turned to join them more slowly, jolted with astonishment, for he had seen Aurilia run towards the centre of the deck, to stand with feet spread wide and braced, ignoring the attack, face lifted to the sky, her hair coming undone by itself around her. And as she raised her hands above her head, fingers curved as if beckoning, she began – uncannily, crazily – to sing.

But he heard a croaking snarl beside him, and wheeled in time to bring his sword up to block a clubbing blow from a Barachi spear. As the unbreakable blade resisted the impact, he slashed savagely across the monster's bulging eyes. Several Barachi lunged at him together, and he met them in a blur of speed – twisting and dodging, stabbing and hewing, avoiding spears or parrying them. At the rail the bellowing Krost swept Barachi aside with his staff as if clearing weeds with a scythe. Behind him Red heard a gurgling cry that sounded like one of the prince's footmen. Then as he hacked at a Barachi neck before pivoting to drive a boot into the belly of another he heard Aurilia's voice rising higher, echoingly, piercingly.

He looked to see her standing alone, unharmed – not screaming but still singing, her clothing rippling and flapping, her hair streaming out around her as if in the grip of a furious gale. Yet there was no breath of a breeze on that deck, within the Islets' shelter.

Swiftly he turned back to face the Barachi – to be almost fatally distracted when, from nowhere at all, a gust of shockingly cold wind whirled across the deck and struck them like a wall of ice.

Luckily the Barachi around him were even more taken aback. He recovered first and used the sword to clear a space around him. As he did so Aurilia's wind whooped down on them again, stronger and icier. In the water Barachi canoes were being swamped by sudden waves, the occupants swimming frantically for the nearest Islets. On the barge, the flames at the stern and on the great winged sails flickered and went out like blown candles, while the whole ship quivered and strained as a captive strains against shackles that bind his legs.

The wind rose to a monstrous shriek, the mast groaned, the ragged remnants of the charred sails filled and lifted, and with a stomach-twisting crunch that spoke of rending wood the barge broke free from the sand-bar.

Slowly Aurilia lowered her arms, her eyes wide and fathomless, while the wind struck like a mighty battering ram, screaming at near-typhoon force as it flung the barge ahead. Distantly Red could hear the raging, wailing cries of the Barachi as they were left behind. He saw the rootless Islets around them flung this way and that, smashing into Barachi canoes, sweeping them aside. He saw Krost, wild-eyed, rush for the wheel-house, and he turned then towards the bow to see the barge shoulder its way grindingly between two Islets, forcing them aside, driven by the thrust of that unbelievable wind. Beyond them he saw open water. Then they were through the Islets, through the strait, the wind flinging them like a waterborne bullet out on the vast black breadth of the lower river.

By then there were no Barachi left alive on the barge, and no longer any in sight among the rapidly receding Islets astern. Yet still Red and the others were not out of danger. The barge was listing badly as the wind-spawned waves pounded it, sinking lower in the water as the river poured in through wounds in the hull. Fighting for his balance on the titling deck, Red knew that if the wind continued the barge might easily heel all the way over, maybe turn turtle. As again he heard horses screaming below, a coldness lanced through him that had nothing to do with the typhoon.

'You have to stop it!' he yelled at Aurilia. But the wind took his words and made them soundless and Aurilia continued to stand unmoving, staring up at the sky, where incongruously the sun had broken through the wind-shredded clouds. Maybe she can't stop it, he thought wildly, maybe she only *starts* winds. He stared around, wondering what to do, or if

174

anything could be done. He glimpsed Krost in the wheel-house, scowling and intent, spinning the wheel as if aiming to turn to the nearest shoreline before the barge sank in the middle of the immense river. And then he saw the prince, standing like a captain by the mast, taking control.

'Cut the stays!' Phaedran was shouting, his voice slicing through the scream of the wind. 'Bring the mast down or we'll go over!'

Good thinking, Red said silently. He sprang towards the dense and orderly tangle of ropes and lines at one side of the bow – and then hesitated, not knowing which to cut. In that moment he heard the prince yell again, and Aurilia, their voices wild and desperate, yelling his name.

Whirling, he saw that the marshal had also leaped to cut ropes at the bow, on the other side. But he had hewed through a main support of the heavy boom that had been rigged for the addition of the extra sail, the jib, by then burned away. And the warning cries were just too late.

The jib boom had begun to sag, coming free, swinging lazily on its swivel. Swinging with deadly accuracy at Red, by the rail. Turning, he saw it only at the last minute – but still tried to dodge, though not quickly enough. The boom caught him a glancing blow and flung him, just as the barge heeled a few more degrees, into the black, wind-whipped river.

As Aurilia's wind had gripped the barge, so the seething water grasped a man. In the lower stretch the sluggish current contained its own myriad of swirls and roils and eddies, so that the water seemed to fold in and around and back upon itself. And all the conflicting forces were magnified and made more unpredictable by the battering of the storm on the sur-face. So the water took Red and dragged him down into its inky depths, flung him around and back and forth until he was dizzy and helpless. He no longer knew which way the surface lay, and a deadly ache was starting in his chest. Yet still he tumbled uncontrollably in the interweaving of those deep twists and whirls. He fought to free himself, flailing and threshing, but he had no hope of swimming against the frenzied water. He was sure he was being dragged farther down, as if sucked down a gigantic drain. He dimly knew that he still clutched his naked sword in the locked grip of his right hand, but even the luminous blade could cast little light through the blackness of the water. His struggles grew weaker, the pain in his chest more fiery, and panic clutched at him with fingers of searing cold.

How stupid, a part of his mind said, to survive a battle against the odds only to die by drowning. Aurilia will blame herself, her wind. He spoke her name again, inwardly, as if in farewell, while his struggles grew feebler. And in his mind's eye he saw her as he had last seen her, alone and magnificent on the besieged barge, summoning her gale, her hair like golden flame ablaze with magic.

Auriflamme, he said, as he sank. Auriflamme. And his lips moved slightly as if he sought in those depths to speak her Name aloud.

In the next moment a long lithe shape, pale and bright, lanced through the blackness above him like a thrust of sunlight.

Aurilia, answering his call.

Naked and glistening and beautiful, she was a beacon in the blackness, her hair streaming out, one end of a slender rope twisted twice around her wrist. Her eyes were wide with anxiety as she reached him and swung it around his chest where her magic knotted it. At once it tautened – and as the last shreds of Red's consciousness left him, he felt himself and Aurilia being jerked swiftly through the water like fish on some enormous line.

A strange, flickering, broken dream began then to drift through his mind. A dream that was partly memory, of a long-past day spent water-skiing – only in the dream he was being towed by some unnaturally fast boat and also, weirdly, towed underwater. Then the dream changed, so that he was flying through the air as if the water-ski run had led to a jump. But there was no sense of landing, just an endless floating – and then another related dream-memory, of a long-before time on a sandy shore, when a leggy starlet had slid out of her bikini and on top of him like an eel, kissing him as if she meant to swallow him whole.

He lifted his arms, which felt strangely leaden, and without opening his eyes wrapped his arms around her and kissed her back.

The kiss was abruptly broken. And a familiar voice, smothering a laugh, said: 'He's breathing now.'

'Is that what you call it?' said another familiar voice, deep and hoarse and also amused.

He opened his eyes. He was not on a beach but on hard boards, tilted at an odd angle. Kneeling beside him was Aurilia, wearing her wicked grin – and nothing else, though her dripping hair hung down over her body as a fairly adequate veil. And near by stood Krost, grinning, nodding at him in friendly greeting.

'He was probably awake for some time,' Krost suggested. 'Just enjoying being kissed.'

'If so, he wasn't breathing at the time,' Aurilia pointed out. She reached in an unconscious gesture to push the hair back from Red's forehead – then caught herself, and instead stood slowly up. Her body shimmered, and then it was the ancient Aurilia who smiled down at him, respectably clothed in her long grey gown, white hair tidily up in its involved coiffure.

Red propped himself up on an elbow, looking around, feeling bruised and exhausted. As far as he could see the river was placid and sluggish, there was no more than a breath of breeze in the sun-warmed air, and the barge – heeling steeply over – was drifting slowly towards a nearby shingly shore, with the tall shadows of a tangled forest looming beyond it.

'Where . . . ?' he began, then caught himself before he could complete the hackneyed question. Krost, grinning, answered it anyway.

Krost had steered the wind-driven barge towards the beach, trying to reach it before the vessel sank, while Aurilia had gone overboard in an arrowing dive a second after Red had fallen, taking with her a rope that she had managed to conjure down from the rigging and tossing one end to Krost. By the time she had found Red down in the roiling depths the wind had died away as suddenly as it had arisen. So Krost felt the weight come on the rope, and hauled it in with its catch as swiftly as his great strength could manage – finally hoisting both Red and Aurilia up on to the deck of the stricken barge. Aurilia had provided artificial respiration until Red had come around and turned it into something else.

Red looked wordlessly at the old woman, aware that his hands were trembling slightly, that there was a tightness in his throat. 'How could . . . How did you find me down there, in that water?'

'You spoke my Name,' she said simply. 'And you had your sword in your hand.' She gestured to it, where it lay shining beside him. 'I saw its light.'

They gazed at each other for a long silent moment, during which Red was scarcely aware that she was in her aged guise – for the green eyes never altered. Then Krost grunted and turned away. 'Brace yourselves,' he rumbled. 'The barge will go aground any moment.'

A sudden memory stabbed Red with guilt. 'Grilena!' he said. 'The horses . . . !' He tried to rise, then winced at a stab of more physical pain in his side.

'The others have gone down to see to them,' Aurilia said. 'Even the prince, with his one remaining servant, and Lenceon.'

'Good old Lenceon,' Red muttered.

'Your mare is unharmed,' Krost assured him. 'And my Wolle, and the others. We will unload them and the supplies . . .'

Then they were all flung sideways. With a grinding crackle, echoing the sound when they had struck the sandbar, the barge's forward momentum halted. For a moment it tilted dangerously, as if trying to topple on its side, but then settled back with a hollow crunch.

'Good,' Krost said, peering around. 'It should hold in these shallows while we unload.'

'But you will come with me,' Aurilia said firmly to Red. 'That boom may have cracked a rib where it hit you. I will have to mix a poultice . . .'

Red shook his head, getting carefully to his feet. 'I think it's just bruising,' he said, prodding at his side. 'Doesn't feel like a rib.'

Krost laughed. 'Then you are lucky, my friend. A cracked rib can interfere with all *sorts* of activities.'

And he winked hugely at them and strode away, chuckling.

Red sighed. 'Does everyone know about us, or just Krost?'

'I have no idea,' the old woman said, eyes twinkling. 'Such secrets are always hardest to keep in close quarters. Do you . . . feel compromised?'

'No,' Red said quietly. 'I feel proud.'

Her smile was brilliant as she reached out a bony hand to take his hand, partly to help him as he moved forward in a hunched shuffle. And the pain in his bruised side made him think of the heavy jib-boom swinging inexorably towards him, from where the marshal had severed one of its restraining ropes.

'I think I want a word with the marshal,' he said through gritted teeth. 'To see how much he knew about what he was doing when he cut that rope.'

She glanced at him with troubled eyes. 'Surely he couldn't have *intended* such an unlikely accident?'

Red shrugged, then winced. 'That's what I plan to ask him. Pointedly. When there's a quiet moment.'

She turned slowly, staring out at the ominous, silent shadows of the forest waiting beyond the shore. 'Red, there are only the six of us here, probably only the six of us left alive from the entire company. And we have been stranded on the shores of the Western Woodlands, home of the Barachi and perhaps of our sorcerous enemy. There may not *be* any quiet moments for a long time to come.'

EIGHTEEN

Aurilia's examination of the injury, in her cabin, involving some fierce prodding by bony old fingers and disdainful sniffs at his grunts of pain, confirmed that it was only extensive bruising rather than a damaged rib. She mixed an acrid-smelling salve that went on to the bruise with a sudden soothing coolness, then gave him a slightly fizzy drink that almost shockingly swept away the after-effects of his exertions and near-drowning, leaving him feeling restored and renewed.

'You should bottle that,' Red told her. 'It'd make a fortune in my world.'

'The Sisterhood does well out of it here,' she told him.

On deck again, they found that the others had laboured heroically. All the unloading – the horses and as much food and equipment as they could carry – had been accomplished. And Red was impressed to see the prince working steadfastly alongside the others, making bundles of necessary supplies and fastening them on to the spare horses, those which had belonged to the three wizards and the prince's second servant.

The surviving servant was toiling at his master's side, though he looked to be almost out of his mind with fear. He was young, round-faced and puffy, and was also still ashen and trembling from the effects of the battle, the typhoon, and the menacing dark silence of the forest around them. He was wrestling weakly with an awkward bundle that looked like part of the royal wardrobe. What the well-dressed prince wears when pursued by monsters, Red thought flippantly, and in the flush of his own renewed vigour he jumped from the barge, waded to the shore and went to help the servant, dredging the man's name from his memory.

'Let me take this one, Ulniss,' he said.

The man jumped as if struck, then looked abjectly grateful. 'Oh . . . Lord Corodel . . . thank you . . .' he babbled.

Red swung the bundle up on his shoulder, amazed again at the total absence of pain from his bruised side, thanks to the magical salve. As he moved to one of the pack-horses, he let the bulky bundle swing aside awkwardly, and slammed it into the back of Marshal Lenceon, who was adjusting the saddle of his own black stallion.

'Sorry, Marshal,' Red said cheerfully as the man grunted and staggered under the impact. 'Lucky we're not on the barge – you might have fallen overboard.'

Lenceon threw him a hate-filled glower but said nothing, turning his back and stalking away. Red grinned, then winked at Aurilia who by then had also made her way to the shore and was shaking her head at him as a parent will with an unregenerate child. But then Red himself received a sharp push in the back, barely managing to keep his feet, then whirling – to be transfixed by the large brown eyes of Grilena, clearly demanding to know where he had been when she needed him. As she nudged at him again with her nose, he laughed and evaded it, putting an arm around her neck.

'This is better, isn't it, my love?' he said to her. 'Solid ground underfoot. Now if only there was a nice meadow . . .'

'We will see no meadows for some time, Corodel,' said Phaedran's dry voice behind him.

Red turned with an easy half-bow. 'Just Cordell, sir,' he said firmly.

'Of course,' the prince said with a flinty smile. 'Though the other name would not be inapt, after your display of prowess on the barge. I am glad to see you have suffered no ill effects.'

'Thanks to Aurilia,' Red said.

Phaedran nodded. 'Quite so. We all owe thanks to Lady Aurilia, for that timely wind that took us out of danger.'

'Took us *into* danger, more like,' the marshal snarled. 'Nearly sank us.'

Krost gave him a withering look. 'Would you have rather stayed at the Islets with the Barachi, Lenceon?'

Once again Red saw the marshal over-react to a minor barb with furious malice which Krost failed to see, having already turned back to the others.

'The horses are ready, Highness,' he said. 'Do you wish me to lead the way?'

Phaedran nodded. 'None of us has your experience of wilderness, Krost. We rely on you.'

'Excuse me,' Red broke in, 'but just where are we heading?'

'Home,' the prince said briefly, 'to raise another force, and then return.'

The marshal snorted almost inaudibly, and for once Red almost agreed with him. 'Let's try to bring better wizards next time,' he said sourly. 'Ones that can *tell* when an ambush is waiting.'

'The Barachi were protected, at the Islets,' Aurilia said quickly. 'They had powerful wards on their skin and clothing that balked the spells of seeing and the rest. It was no fault of the wizards.'

Red remembered the weird designs painted on the attacking Barachi, and felt glad to know that the mages hadn't failed – especially Wretifal, who had turned out to be quite a tough little customer after all. 'All right,' he said, 'but now what do we do when the Barachi come after us and set up another ambush?'

'As they surely will,' the marshal snarled, while poor Ulniss looked as if he would be sick.

Krost was nodding solemnly. 'The wind will have done them little harm, since they are at home in water, and canoes can be refloated. Oh, yes, they will come after us. While others who were not at the Islets may be waiting for us, in the forest.' He waved the iron staff in a sweeping gesture at the trees.

'That's not really too encouraging,' Red muttered. Then he glanced at Aurilia as another thought struck him. 'Then there's this sorcerer who *put* the wards on the Barachi. What's going to stop him from using his magic to do his own seeing or whatever, to know just *where we are* at any time?'

Ulniss looked even sicker at that, but the others merely nodded as if the thought had already occurred to them without troubling them.

'I'm sorry, Red,' Aurilia said. 'I sometimes forget that you are unused to magic. It's quite simple. The sorcerer can see

182

us with his scrying power only if he *knows*, beforehand, more or less where we are. If we should ever get away somehow, so that he *lost track* of us, he would have to reach out with spells of seeking and so on, to range over a considerable area, to relocate us. Which would be wearisome for him, and perhaps unsuccessful.'

Red blinked and frowned, aware that Krost and the prince were nodding as if it was all elementary. 'So how *could* he lose us? How could we ever hope to get away?'

She smiled. 'We may already have, since my wind brought us to this wilderness shore at some speed. But even if he is watching us now—' a thought that made Red's skin crawl, and made poor Ulniss turn paler— 'I think I can thwart him. The Earth-magic offers a form of *veiling* that I can use. It lasts only briefly each time, but it may serve. If the others here will let me fix ward-knots on them, as I have done for you and Krost, Red, they will help to reinforce the veil. When we ride from here, our enemy will think us invisible.'

'We shall certainly accept your wards, Lady, with gratitude,' the prince said at once.

So Aurilia applied herself to tying some of her hairs – the white ones apparently as effective as the golden ones – on to the outer clothing and weapons of the others, ignoring a few angry mutters about 'witchery' from the marshal. And Red went to help Krost, who wanted to try to heave the barge out of the shallows so it would float downstream and be found elsewhere, as a false trail.

Red was actually very little help, since his strength had minimal effect on the vessel's vast weight. But Krost used heavy ropes to hitch his pony Wolle to the barge's bow, and used one of the huge oars as a lever to pry mightily at the stern. And the barge luckily proved not to be wedged as fast as it might have been. Wolle heaved magnificently, teeth bared as if threatening the river – and Krost splintered two oars in a cascade of obscure oaths – and slowly, grindingly, encouraged also by the river's slow current, the vessel tore free and floated away, once Red had slashed the ropes with his sword to free Wolle.

Then they rejoined the others, where Aurilia was singing

again, a brief and quietly melodic chant. And when the song was done she gazed around at them all and nodded.

'We are veiled,' she said. 'We must ride now, while we can.'

Then she shimmered into her youthful shape, in serviceable tunic and leggings, and mounted her white gelding while the others climbed into their saddles. Red moved Grilena up to ride next to Krost, in the lead, as they moved away.

'Do you really know your way around in here?' Red asked Krost, peering around at the shadowed forest as it swallowed them up.

Krost shrugged. 'I have been in the Woodlands before. And in many other wildernesses, at other times.'

'Good thing one of us is a boy scout,' Red said. 'So what's our route?'

'We must get well away from the river, first,' Krost told him. 'And then, as the land allows, we will move in a wide curve, swinging south-east, trying to stay on the edges of the worst swamps . . .'

'Oh, yes,' Red interrupted. 'I forgot about the swamps.'

'It is best to avoid them,' Krost said with a grin. 'There are creatures in some of them that make the Barachi seem kindly by comparison.' He chuckled at Red's grimace. 'Then, when we are far enough south to have got past any Barachi coming from the Islets to seek us, we will swing north-east and make our way back to the Grasslands and the river.'

'Sounds good,' Red said, glancing back. 'From what you said before, I wondered if the prince might just want to go and attack this sorcerer anyway, the six of us.'

'Even Phaedran sees that it is better to raise another force,' Krost said. 'So we will be all right. We are not as badly off as we might have been.'

'Oh, no,' Red said ironically. 'We're fine. Just going for a nice quiet ride in the woods.'

'Where have they *gone*?' demanded Princess Evelane, sitting stiffly on the edge of her divan. 'How could you just lose *sight* of them? Find them – *find* them!'

'Evelane,' said the silver-haired Talonimal, looking irritatedly around from his scrying stone. 'The witch has managed some kind of veiling. But it has limited power, and when it fades away I am sure I can locate them again.'

'But what if you *can't*?' she asked, her voice shrill. 'What if they get away again?'

He narrowed his eyes, looking weary and annoyed. 'They will not. I have sent Vanticor with another company of Barachi to seek them. Even if I cannot relocate them at once on the stone, the Barachi will find them. No one can elude the Barachi in their own forests.'

Her laugh was high-pitched and mirthless. 'Your Barachi! They were eluded well enough at the Islets!' Her face twitched, and her hands writhed and tangled in the fabric of her gown. 'How could that happen, Talonimal? Your plans failing . . . everything going *wrong*!'

'Evelane, don't upset yourself,' Talonimal said firmly. 'My plans are not threatened . . .'

'But they are *escaping*, and your scrying is useless!' she shrieked.

'They are not!' His voice sliced through her rising hysteria like a blade. 'They cannot possibly escape! Nor is it just Vanticor and the Barachi who will take them – I have another in place, to do my bidding!'

She seemed hardly to hear him, her eyes wild, her body stiff and quivering. 'It *is* all going wrong – my father escaping, Aurilia's power balking you . . . You are *failing*, Talonimal!' Manic rage suddenly flared in her eyes. 'And I might have been *killed* in my own bed last night, when you also failed . . . When you were so overcome by the young witch's charms that you failed to notice her reaching for the dagger on the dressing table!'

'That is foolishness!' Talonimal snapped. 'The knife should not have been there – and she might as easily have threatened me as you. Besides, no one could have expected her to seek her own death that way, to escape the Offering . . . But come, Evelane, this outburst is no help to me.'

'*Help?*' she almost screamed. 'Help to *you*? Oh, how much like the prince my father, selfishly bent on your own wishes, your own way, indifferent to all around you . . . What of *me*, my lord Talonimal? What of helping *me*? What of your promise that I should have the gift of magic from you?'

'And so you shall!' he broke in, glowering. 'When my powers have increased to the required level, as I have so often told you—'

'Oh, indeed!' Small flecks of foam had appeared at the corners of her mouth. 'You have told me! But what if you are mistaken, as you have been mistaken about capturing my father – and about the docility of the witch-girl last night . . . What if you truly *cannot* give me a magical power of my own? My father's wizards always said it could not be done . . . But I believed they lied, at my father's wish, because he was afraid that I would be more magically powerful than his beloved wife . . .' She was babbling wildly, eyes bulging, fingers wringing the cloth of her gown with manic strength. 'And is that why everything is going wrong for us now, my lord? Do you *want* my father to escape? Do you not intend to keep your promises to me? Are *you* also afraid of how powerful I might become with my own magic?'

'Evelane!' His roar struck at her like a fist. 'Stop it! Stop these wild accusations! You know very well that I need Phaedran and Aurilia here, for the Offering, for *both* our sakes! And they will *be* here! Now control your foolishness, or I shall forbid you to join me here in my spell-chamber!'

At once her entire attitude and posture changed. Her wild eyes took on a knowing look, and her mouth writhed in the semblance of a smile. 'Why, then, my lord,' she said in a rasping whisper, 'you would not have me here to slake your lusts when they are stirred by your magics.' She leaned back on the divan and with a sudden jerk dragged up her skirts, baring the length of her slender legs. 'Are you aroused now by sorcery, Talonimal? Do you want me *now*?'

As if against his will, Talonimal's gaze slid downwards towards her thighs. And she smiled again, seeing that, and tugged her skirts higher still, revealing that she wore no underclothes. Talonimal twitched, then took a deep breath, visibly struggling against the mixture of fury and desire that showed in his face.

'There is no reason for you to provoke me so,' he snarled.

'Nor for your anxiety and mistrust. Your father and his companions will not escape, I promise you. All our plans and intentions will be fulfilled.'

'Another promise, my lord?' Her shrill giggle was like the cawing of a bird, as she let her bared thighs move apart. 'And will you then come to me, here, for *my* fulfilling?'

'Not until you are calmer,' Talonimal said through gritted teeth.

He raised his left hand, which glowed slightly, in a taut gesture. At once Evelane's eyelids drooped and she slumped back against the cushions, deeply asleep. For a moment Talonimal stared fixedly, avidly, at the exposed length of her legs, the shadowed juncture of her thighs. Then he lifted his gaze – angry still, but then also with an edge of contempt – to her sleep-emptied face.

'See, my *dear*,' he snarled with bitter sarcasm, 'I *can* control my desires when necessary. Enough even to give you yourself to the Offering flame, if you grow more tiresomely unstable.'

NINETEEN

As Talonimal turned back to his scrying stone to seek his fleeing quarry, the objects of his search were riding steadily southward through the brush and ferns and tangled undergrowth of the forest. And at the same moment, far away from all of them in the city of Quamarr, as early evening descended, five men were gathered together in a locked room at the top of a windowless tower high above the thoroughfare known as Scholars' Way.

The five sat in ornate chairs placed in a vaguely oval pattern, which included two more chairs that stood empty, talking in low voices that strove for a semblance of casualness. They were all clearly well-to-do: they all wore rich, well-tailored clothing – elegant frock coats or decorated robes – with many prominent rings and other jewellery. Most of them were in late middle age, though two were definitely elderly and only one, with wavy hair, a smooth complexion, and an air of languid affectation, seemed still anywhere near youthfulness. By comparison with the men, the room seemed plain and sparsely furnished. But the abundance of parchments, odd implements, alchemical equipment, and the like revealed the tower as another spell-chamber of a High Adept.

None of them, however, was making any use of the paraphernalia around them. They continued to talk in slightly strained, tense murmurs, now and then glancing furtively at the two unoccupied chairs. And then, without warning, there was only one chair left unoccupied. The other was filled – with a faint *thump* of displaced air – by the figure of a short, bald, fur-robed man with burning yellow eyes, appearing out of nothingness.

The others merely blinked at his manifestation, then nodded in greetings that were as elaborately casual yet strained as their talk. 'Magister . . .' they murmured, in ragged unison.

The fur-robed man regarded them in thin-lipped silence, offering no acknowledgement. And as the silence grew, and the others shifted uneasily under his yellow-eyed scrutiny, the youngest of the group abruptly laughed, a short and nervous titter.

'Are we waiting for our errant brother to join us, Magister, before we begin?' he asked. 'Or is it *bad* news that brings you from the delights of your valley?'

The fur-robed man whom they called Magister fixed him with his hot gaze. 'Talonimal won't be joining us,' he rasped. 'He's lurking still behind his barrier, which resists whatever spell or power I send against it.'

'How *very* upsetting for you,' the younger man murmured insincerely.

'Then have you summoned us to conclave, Lebarran?' asked one of the older men, with an edge of nervousness. 'Do you want a concerted action against him?'

'No. That would be unwise, for many reasons. I'm here only to inform you of what's happening and what may happen, and to hear your thoughts on what indirect action we might take.'

'No doubt you are wise to be cautious,' the younger man said with a smirk.

'Surely, though,' the other elderly man said, his voice quavering, 'we have no certain evidence that there is a *need* for action. Talonimal may simply have gone into retreat behind his barrier. He would not be the first mage to do so. . . . We cannot know what he is *doing*, in his solitude.'

'Knowing Talonimal,' the younger one said, 'we can be quite sure what he is *doing*, endlessly, to the *princess*.' His snicker was echoed by some of the others – until they noticed that annoyance had begun to light a brighter fire in the eyes of the Magister.

'You'd know the present need, all of you, if age or indulgence hadn't addled your brains,' Lebarran growled. 'In his retreat, you fools, Talonimal has grown *stronger*.' The murmuring of the others, mingled with a gasp or two, held an

189

expression of both shock and doubt, and Lebarran's eyes flared. 'Look at the facts! His shielding spells are powerful, immense! He can't be stronger there without being stronger overall! And his creatures, the Barachi, are marauding in the city, to provide the *means* for his strengthening!' He glowered around with his livid eyes and saw most of the others quailing slightly, looking sick and appalled. 'So – now you're beginning to see what is there to be seen. I myself have no doubt of it. Talonimal is daring to perform the Forbidden Rite – to enlarge his power.'

'Sacrifice,' whispered the first man, looking revolted. 'The ultimate crime – the foulest breach of an Adept's code . . .'

'How could he risk it?' asked the other, his voice quavering even more. 'He must know that the rite exposes him to whatever demon or power he is invoking . . .

Lebarran shook his head irritably. 'There are certain potent spells that will protect him, if he can manage them . . . But I'm not concerned with how he shields himself during the rite. I'm concerned with his larger shielding – the huge barrier he has raised on the western coast.' He leaned forward, eyes aflame. 'I believe he raised *that* barrier to protect himself from *us* – from *me*. Because I don't think he's sacrificing to any lesser demon from the Realms. I think he has found his own way to the Void Beyond! I think he has invoked the Unformed, and is expanding his powers by making Offerings to it! To pre-empt the Apotheosis!'

A quivering silence fell upon the gathering as the other five stared at each other with expressions of horror. Then the younger one grimaced. 'I can hardly credit it,' he said. 'Talonimal is not a fool . . .'

'So you say, Yannahac,' Lebarran snarled. 'But he's also not the kind of man to go into a retreat, withdrawing from the world. And I *know* that he's behind the abduction of witches, which won't be merely to slake his legendary lusts. No – I'm sure he would risk reaching to the Void, performing the rite, if it furthered his ambitions.'

'He is not alone in being ambitious,' Yannahac muttered.

The Magister glared. 'True enough,' he snapped. 'All of us here have ambitions. Else we wouldn't have formed this

Order. And now we have to find a way to *protect* our Order, before Talonimal brings it down!'

'But you said you did not wish a conclave action against him, Lebarran,' another man objected.

'Quite uncharacteristically restrained,' said the younger man with another smirk.

'Restraint can be an act of wisdom, Yannahac,' the Magister rasped. 'Listen now. For a conclave, we'd need to travel to the west, in person, to be at full strength from close range. And that could *expose* us! Talonimal himself has been doing enough to stir up others, especially the Sisterhood. If we mount a magical attack on him from conclave, in the west, every Adept in the Continent and the witches too will know of it! Know of *us*!' His knotted fist crashed down on the chair arm, making the others jump. 'Right now, many powerful folk are already looking intently westward. The prince himself has marched against Talonimal, because of his daughter. If we also travel west, for our purposes, our Order risks being revealed – and forces might be marshalled against us!'

Most of the others were nodding and mumbling agreement. But the younger Yannahac, languid in his chair, still wore his provocative smirk. 'Also, of course,' he drawled, 'it *might* be revealed – most embarrassingly – that Talonimal has grown too strong even for a conclave led by the great Lebarran himself . . .'

That made some of the others sit up, frowning with sudden thought.

'And then some might wonder,' Yannahac went on, emboldened, 'whether they are *wise* to maintain the Order as it is. Or whether it might be wiser to throw in their lot with Talonimal, towards *his* Apotheosis.'

The arm of the Magister's chair crackled ominously as his hand gripped it, his eyes aflame with fury. 'Yannahac.' His voice had dropped half an octave, grating like a slab of stone shifting in some ancient tomb. 'You go too far. I'm not one of your half-mage admirers, applauding your limp wit. I am the Magister – I am the creator of this Order of the Apotheosis – and within it you'll be ruled by my word!' The others flinched as his hand grew white-knuckled on the chair arm, and the solid wood groaned. 'You'll show me *respect*, Yanna-hac! You'll be silent and *obey*! Or I'll cause you to be *brought to obedience* – by paths you wouldn't be pleased to travel!'

As he roared the last words he gestured, in a complex pattern, his hands glowing as fiery as his eyes. Instantly around the figure of Yannahac something like a huge bubble began to form. A bubble that was transparent, but solid and unyielding – and rising slowly above the chair, with the younger mage struggling inside it like a trapped insect.

'No . . . Magister . . . please . . . no . . .' Yannahac wailed, his voice thin and distant but clear from within the bubble.

As the bubble hovered, an opening formed in the floor below it – an opening into a shadowy dimness that was not only an absence of light but an absence of all that was stable, and natural, and bearable to human minds and souls. From the dimness a whining wind spread iciness through the chamber. And the aghast men in the chairs around Yannahac glimpsed macabre shapes moving in the dimness – shapes that lifted horned heads, that clashed fanged jaws or hooked beaks, that flexed clawed hands or taloned paws.

'Those who dwell within *this* Realm, Yannahac,' Lebarran intoned, 'could keep your very soul alive and in agony for centuries after your body became dust.'

As the bubble of force drifted down towards the opening and those half-seen horrors, Yannahac began screaming, wordless shrieks filled with pleading and desperate terror.

Then Lebarran snapped his fingers, the opening and the bubble vanished, and Yannahac alone remained in mid-air, knees drawn up, weeping.

Lebarran stared around, and the others flinched from the impact of his flaming eyes. 'Now that you're all aware of present events,' he rasped, 'we can simply watch and wait a while. To see what comes of the prince's intervention – or if the Sisterhood or some other power will take a hand. But in the meantime I've decided to send some of my . . . servants, to the Western Woodlands. To aid my watching, and to take any action that can be taken subtly, without risk to us. I'll inform you, in time, how *those* events develop.'

He glared around once more, then abruptly disappeared –

while the whimpering Yannahac crashed painfully down on to the chair where he had been sitting.

It has to be the bugs, Red thought miserably. Of all the things he hated in the soggy forest, the bugs took top place. They had descended in ravenous clouds on the horses and riders, as if ending a famine – tiny and black, with bites like stabs from red-hot, blunt needles. But of course other things were fairly close behind them in terms of hatefulness. Red had been carefully itemizing them all the rest of that day, ranking them in order. Things like the wet, clinging mud underfoot. The ground tended to be rolling, rising and falling, crests and troughs – and where the crests had splintery grey rock sticking out from them like rotten teeth, the troughs always held slippery mud and some ground water. And the six of them had been kept by Krost in the troughs, winding from one gully to the next, which caused many a reproachful backward glance at Red from Grilena as her slim golden legs turned steadily black with mire.

But they had no choice, if they wanted to stay out of sight as much as possible. Anyway, on his list of hatefulness, there were no paths in the wilderness, as if the denizens of the forest, Barachi or otherwise, never followed the same route twice. So they had to push through a jungle of dense and often brambly scrub brush that clogged the gullies, while also staying bent low in the saddle to avoid the lower branches of trees. Red recognized none of the trees or shrubs, though some looked vaguely like forms from his world – but anyway he did not want to know the names of the plants that were making travel so difficult. His thoughts tended more towards visions of bulldozers, or flame-throwers – though fire would probably not have helped, since the forest was so wet.

Its wetness was also increasing steadily, thanks to a penetrating drizzle that was doing a duet with dank, clammy mist. But those at least were not entirely the forest's fault – they were Aurilia's. Apparently mist and rain aided her magical veiling, so she had murmured a little witch-song to bring them along. Naturally, when they had been riding for some hours and the veiling had faded, or so she said, the rain and the mist seemed reluctant to go away.

Red felt a bit puzzled, and regretful, that her Earth-magic seemed unable to produce some useful way to drive off bugs, solidify mud, and the like. But he was reluctant to say so – partly because no one else seemed to be as troubled by the conditions as he was, and partly because of what he had learned, earlier, when he had asked Aurilia why it was that the veiling, once it had faded, could not be started up again at once, like a clock being immediately rewound.

She had shaken her head patiently and had explained that doing so would dangerously exhaust her. 'Working magic needs a special effort,' she said. 'It's like lifting a weight. At first it's manageable – but you can't hold it up for long without getting tired. And then you have to *rest* a while, to get the strength back to lift it again.' She had peered at him to see if he could grasp such a vastly complicated analogy. 'That is true of all magic, whether Earth-magic, wizardry, sorcery . . . Whatever level of strength a mage has, whether he lifts large weights or lesser ones, at some time he will grow weary in the same way.'

Red had nodded gloomily. 'So no hope of a dry place to camp tonight?'

But that remark had brought the marshal into the conversation, with a sneer about soft city folk who couldn't face the ordinary hardships of soldiering. And that in turn drove Red back into his miserable and irritated silence.

That was suitable enough, however, to the day and place. The forest itself was tomb-like in its own silence. No birds called, no small creatures scuttled through the ferns, even the insects did not buzz before they bit. The jingle of the horses' harness and the squelch of hoofs seemed grotesquely loud in that weird stillness, and Red reflected sourly that there seemed little point in staying out of sight when they were so clearly failing to stay out of sound.

Yet despite the silence the forest was not uninhabited. Or so Krost had made clear, telling him that birds did live there along with some small furry things and a multitude of snakes and lizards. But they were all driven into hiding and silence by the alien presence of humans on horses. And though Red peered around constantly into the shadowed greenery, he had not the smallest glimpse of fur, feather, or scale.

In fact as they rode on all through the day the silence grew, as unnatural silences will, more and more menacing and oppressive. And when the approach of twilight added its eerier quality they halted. It was not Aurilia's magic but Krost's woodcraft that found a comparatively dry place for their camp, in the heart of a thicket with clumps of tall trees forming an umbrella overhead. They could make no fire, for security, but it was a relief just to dismount and be free of the drizzle – if not the insects. Red also found it calming to be able to tidy Grilena a little, using a damp rag to clean most of the mud from her legs before rubbing her down generally. She seemed pleased enough by that, and by the fodder that he produced for her from the supplies, so he could leave her to her meal while he helped Krost tend the other horses. By then Aurilia was sorting out cold food for them from the bundles on the pack-horses, while the servant Ulniss struggled with the larger bundles that held their bedrolls and other necessities. Ulniss looked both relieved and scandalized when the prince came, quietly and without pretension, to lend a hand.

Phaedran also snapped an order at the marshal to bring him into the procession of chores. Lenceon had been sitting on one side, looking as if he was trying to rival the forest in being silent and darkly lowering – as he had been for most of the time since they had left the river. And when he rose to obey the prince, joining the others, he halted and scowled even more darkly. Because just then Krost was recommending to them all, firmly, that no one should ever leave the campsite unaccompanied, whatever their purpose, intimately sanitary or otherwise. Krost was also suggesting the likeliest pairings – Red with Aurilia, Krost himself with the prince, the marshal with Ulniss. And perhaps it was that last pairing that particularly fuelled the marshal's outrage.

'Who appointed you leader here?' he snarled at Krost.

Krost frowned. 'I have no wish to be a leader. I am making suggestions for our welfare.'

Lenceon snorted. 'Giving orders, more like . . .'

'Marshal,' Krost said, still calmly, 'I have been in these forests before, and have survived. That is the only important thing. We are not being soldiers here, with ranks and chains of command. We are trying to stay alive.'

'I know that,' Lenceon snapped. 'But I also know you are trying to enhance your position – taking command, pairing yourself with the prince . . . *You* should be paired with the servant, since you are little better than a servant yourself. Whereas I am commander of the militia, and of this expedition . . .'

'Which has all been destroyed,' Aurilia broke in acidly. 'Try to regain some command of *yourself*, Lenceon.'

'Indeed,' the prince said coldly. 'Stop this nonsense, Lenceon. Krost has the experience and the ability, and my fullest confidence.'

So that was an end of it, except that the marshal hurled more of his hate-filled glances at Krost and Aurilia and Red and even poor Ulniss. But he did help with the chores, as the prince had ordered, with some efficiency.

Ultimately, fumbling in impenetrable darkness that made the forest immensely more oppressive around them, they all tried to find some measure of rest in damp bedrolls. Krost had also advised that a watch be set, though Red remarked that in that darkness it would be more of a listen. Krost himself took the first watch – and Lenceon surprisingly volunteered for the later, pre-dawn turn, the worst one in the most dismal of spirit-sapping small hours. The others seemed to see that as the marshal's attempt to make amends, and were grateful.

Red slept fitfully, dreaming grisly dreams of biting insects as large as horses with huge fanged mouths and bulging reptilian eyes. When he awoke, it was to the sound of voices vibrating with tension. He struggled up from his bedroll, saw Aurilia emerging from hers – still in her buckskin-clad youthful form – and then saw Krost, the prince, and the marshal standing on the far side of their camp-site.

Where Ulniss lay. Not sleeping, but quite dead.

As they joined the group, Krost's brief gesture showed the

cause of death: a narrow red and green band wrapped around his forearm in a tight coil. When Krost prodded it with the iron staff, it removed curved fangs from the dead man's flesh and raised its head to hiss – a head less like a snake than like a miniature crocodile.

'Water viper,' Krost said calmly. 'Its bite is poisonous, and then it sucks the blood.'

Great, Red thought sickly. Not vampire bats but vampire snakes. Then a more relevant thought, or memory, stirred in him.

'Ulniss had the watch after mine,' he said. 'He was fine when I woke him – maybe even more scared than in the daytime, but healthy enough.'

Krost nodded, and Red saw that he was again looking at the marshal with the expressionlessly meaningful gaze. 'And did he waken you, Marshal, when it was time for *your* watch?'

'Of course,' Lenceon said firmly. 'So the viper must have bitten him after he returned to sleep. I would have heard nothing.'

'True,' Krost said slowly. 'But it is odd. It is a *water* viper. A swimmer in small pools, not normally seeking food on land.'

The marshal glared under Krost's scrutiny. 'So this one did. What of it? Are you now an expert on the creatures of the Woodlands?'

'No,' Krost replied levelly. 'I merely say that it is strange.'

'Strange and fatal,' Red muttered. He drew the glowing sword and prodded the viper as Krost had. When the grisly head came up again from its feasting, a swift flick of the blade severed it neatly. The body unwound from the corpse's wrist, writhing in its death throes until Red lifted it with the sword and flung it into the undergrowth. 'Let's bury Ulniss and get out of here,' he said roughly.

The shallow grave was easily dug in the soft earth, with water seeping slowly in as they lowered Ulniss, wrapped in his bedroll. Then Krost took his iron staff up to the top of a ridge and pried loose a man-sized slab of rock, carrying it effortlessly down to place it on top of the newly replaced earth.

'He will not be dug up easily by scavengers,' Krost said quietly, tamping the rock down with a heavy boot.

'But that nicety will leave a clear sign for Barachi,' the marshal snarled.

'Perhaps,' Krost replied, staring at him levelly again. 'But so will the hoofprints along our way. So would the noise we make, travelling. Or the very *smell* of us, alien to this place. Can you tell us how to avoid those problems?'

Lenceon did not reply, but merely wheeled away with another of his black looks. Red meanwhile was staring around at the forest again, feeling a chill of unease at Krost's calm catalogue of the ways in which they were making themselves vulnerable. And then the unease altered, transforming into a sudden coldly electric jolt of shock.

Because something in the distance had broken the silence with a scream – shrill, raucous, drawn out, falling away slowly into the counterpoint of echoes it had stirred.

TWENTY

Nothing lunged out of the morning mists to threaten them, nor was the scream repeated. None the less, the sound unnerved them all, spurring them to haste as they broke camp and flung their belongings on the pack-horses. There was another of those that morning, of course, since Ulniss was not there to ride his fat little roan. And it was a shaken, wordless, oppressed cavalcade of five that set off, southwards, that morning.

Red moved up beside Krost. 'What was that scream?' he asked uneasily.

The dwarf-giant shook his head, looking troubled. 'I have never heard such a sound in these forests. But it is peculiar. It is *very* like a sound that was once often heard in the Southern Highlands, on the plateaux of my people . . .'

'So there *are* things in the Woodlands that you don't know about?' interrupted the scoffing voice of the marshal, coming up to them. 'Water vipers feeding on land, nameless things that scream . . .'

Krost merely gave him one bleak look and then ignored him. And Red dropped back, not certain that his temper could put up with much more of Lenceon's sneering. He joined Aurilia at the end of the line, finding her singing softly as if to herself, obviously to gather another veiling around them. Red listened with pleasure to the last few melodic phrases, then moved Grilena closer to her horse, noting with concern how she seemed visibly wilted from her magical exertions.

'You'll wear yourself out,' he told her.

She gave him a tired smile and shook her head. 'I'm being as sparing as I can. I daren't exhaust my strength in case any of my other powers are needed.'

Which means in case we're attacked, Red thought darkly, and let his hand stray to his sword-hilt.

But when he looked all around, as he frequently did, the forest seemed no more silent and mysterious than usual. At least the new veiling had brought with it only more mist, instead of rain, making Krost and the marshal ghostly figures at the head of their line. The only things around here, he thought, that don't seem ghostly are the bugs – which had arrived for breakfast with voracious zest.

The horses trudged along, again growing progressively muddier as the morning wore on, while Red pondered some new worries that had occurred to him. First, the mucky ground and tangled brush kept them moving at a frustratingly slow walking pace, which was fine for keeping the horses fresh but not ideal for the swift escape from the forest that they had planned. Second, more immediately worrying, their food was spoiling. The stores had all been excellent, having come from the palace kitchens, but the damp murkiness of the forest was having its effect. The breads and rolls were developing alarmingly furry moulds, as was the dried fruit, while lurid green growths were appearing on their stores of cold meats and fowl. Just then such taints could still be cut away from the food. But at their slow pace, they would not be out of the forest before their food had entirely rotted. And Red did not feel keen on roast water viper for supper, ever. Also, of course, mould and rot were affecting the horses' fodder, and so affecting the well-being of their transportation.

So he went through most of that day in a troubled silence, chewing over the insoluble problems, matched by similar silences – for whatever reasons – from the others. Even the marshal abandoned his scorn and sneering to return to morose withdrawal. And the night came, with everyone taking turns to stand watch as before – and another dawn followed, without recurrences of snakebite or mysterious horror-screams in the distance.

On they rode through the next uneventful day and the next, always moving south and slightly east, always keeping to the muddy, squelching gullies, always plagued by insects and balked by spiky brush, at times veiled by Aurilia and shrouded by clammy mist – until on the fifth day those hardships proved to be greatly desirable compared to what now interrupted their journey.

The horses had been slightly tense and skittish the previous evening, but Red had put it down to the steadily worsening state of their fodder. All the same, he had kept the sheathed sword extra close to him in his bedroll that night. And he was glad of its comforting presence when he awoke with a jerk, with the sky showing only the first faint pre-dawn streaks of grey. He was sure that he had heard Grilena whicker from where the horses were tethered, and that her soft call had sounded urgent. But as he lay tensely listening, it was not repeated.

Must have been a dream, he thought. But even so he was wide awake, and so rose silently, pulling on his boots, buckling on his sword. The others seemed sound asleep, and he was unable to see the marshal, whose watch it was. Carefully he moved towards the horses, through the dimness of that pre-dawn, glad of the sodden ground where no grass could rustle or dry twigs crackle. In a fairly creditable soundlessness he crept across the campsite – and found the marshal, his hand clamped over Grilena's nose to silence her, peering into the misty darkness beyond the camp.

Reflexively, Red drew the sword – and the marshal whirled, harsh lines of tension showing in his face in the light from the blade. But he recovered at once. 'Corodel?' he said enquiringly, managing to inject a sneer into the name.

'Close,' Red said coolly. 'What are you doing with my horse?'

'Keeping it quiet,' the marshal replied. 'I thought I heard something in the forest.'

'I'd say she did too,' Red said. 'Maybe saw it and smelled it. Why didn't you wake anyone?'

'It might just have been some harmless creature,' the marshal said testily. 'Who are you to question me?'

But at that point Krost came to join them, followed by the others, roused by the voices. So Lenceon was distracted from his anger, and they all peered into the slowly lightening depths of the forest without growing any wiser. After a time, then, they turned instead to their morning chores – a few bites of whatever food remained edible for themselves and the horses, packing and saddling, resuming their journey. Throughout all that they exchanged very few words – the prince and Aurilia lost in what seemed to be gloomy reveries, Krost staring around at the trees or calming the still skittish horses, the marshal in another outraged sulk. And Red was silent because he was trying to work out a reason for what he had briefly seen, by the light of his sword, on Marshal Lenceon's face when he had whirled around from his position at Grilena's head.

Red had glimpsed for an instant the expression that would have been on Lenceon's face as he had peered into the darkness. Unmistakably, inexplicably, it had been an expression of intense *eagerness*.

By mid-morning, too many troubling theories had developed in Red's mind about the marshal. He really wanted to try them on Aurilia, but because of the possible threat that the marshal had claimed to hear at dawn, Aurilia had imposed a more prolonged veiling, which had left her slumped in her saddle, shaky and weak and half-asleep. It made Red wonder if it was really worth it. Or worth anything, he thought, given his new mistrust of Lenceon. So he urged Grilena forward, to go and put his ideas to Krost, who was riding in the lead as always.

As the golden horse took that quicker stride forward, Red heard a strange fizzing sound just behind his back, as if an oversized bumblebee had just whisked past. But it was followed by a wet thud, and a gasp of surprise from Aurilia.

Spinning in his saddle, Red saw – quivering in the bole of a tree an arm's length away – the feathered haft of a Barachi dart.

Grilena leaped forward at Red's wild yell. Sensing his need, she needed no urging, crashing past Krost's Wolle, plunging through the brush. Red had instinctively drawn his sword, and leaned forward to hack with it at some of the tangled foliage in their way. Behind him he could hear the others galloping on his heels – and then, when he was almost halted by a wall of briars, Krost and Wolle thundered past to take up the lead again. And that was better, for Wolle charged the brush like a massive dappled tank, his hide seemingly impervious, while Krost smashed leafy barriers aside with the iron staff. As they carved out the trail, the others were able to increase the speed of their flight.

Red had no idea if other darts were being flung or how many Barachi might be pursuing, if there was any pursuit at all. But he had no intention of stopping to find out. We need a fort, he thought crazily. Draw the wagons in a circle . . .

'There!' Aurilia shrieked behind him, as if responding to his thought. Half-turning, he saw her pointing to the side of the ridge above that particular gully. The ridge rose more steeply at one place, ahead – into a near-vertical cliff with a heavy overhang and a shallow cave scooped out below it in the shaly grey rock.

Not a fort but as good as we'll get, Red thought. And Krost clearly thought so too, for he wheeled Wolle and plunged through the brush towards it.

As they leaped from their horses Red saw that the cave or cleft was defensible enough, for it would force enemies to attack only two or three abreast, and the overhang would protect against darts from above. It was not a place to be besieged for any length of time, he thought, but that was something to worry about later. Swiftly they pulled the horses into the more protected depths of the cleft, while the marshal dragged a misshapen bundle from one packhorse and tore it open to reveal three crossbows and a supply of bolts. That raised Red's spirits, especially since he had improved his skill with the bow during his times with the palace guards. Lenceon took up one bow, arming it, and gave Red no more than a sour look when he sheathed the sword and reached for another, the prince confidently taking the third bow. Then, with Krost grimly hefting the iron staff, they took up positions within their narrow bastion.

And nothing happened.

No darts flew at them, no strange cries or any other sounds intruded on the silence of the forest. No movement of any sort could be seen beyond the cleft, not even a stirring leaf. The horses, which had seemed very nervous while being tucked into the safety of the cleft, visibly began to relax, nibbling at small weeds that grew from the near-vertical walls beside them.

'They're gone,' Red said at last in a near-whisper.

'Maybe,' Krost rumbled. 'If there was ever more than one. I saw only the one dart.'

Everyone agreed that they had seen only one dart, the near-miss that had flashed past Red. 'Perhaps just one wandering Barachi,' the marshal said. 'It may have been prowling around last night, and disturbed the horses.'

But that doesn't explain the eager look on your face, friend, Red thought dourly. Still he said nothing, knowing that he could hardly accuse Lenceon of anything on the basis of a facial expression.

'It is too soon for me to try another veiling,' Aurilia said with a note of apology.

'But we cannot stay here if there is no danger,' the prince pointed out impatiently.

Krost nodded. 'I will go and see.'

'I'll go with you,' Red said at once, all too glad of a chance to relieve his restless tensions. 'You said before we should stay in pairs.'

When Krost nodded happily, Red proffered his crossbow to Aurilia. 'You may need this here,' he said. 'Out there we'll just be looking, not shooting.' I hope, he added silently.

She looked at him solemnly, shadows of fatigue still showing under the green eyes. 'Go carefully,' she whispered.

'Count on it,' he told her – and crept out of the cleft after Krost.

Every bit of his skin felt tight and clenched as they advanced, waiting for the impact of a dart. But, again, nothing happened. They moved slowly, for the sake of silence – with Red marvelling at how Krost's great boots seemed scarcely to stir a frond, how his vast shoulders slid past shrubbery without troubling a leaf. And aside from the odd rustle or faint splash, Red felt he was doing quite well himself in the stealth department.

Krost seemed to be heading in a sweeping curve back in the general way that they had come. It made sense, if there were any Barachi coming along in pursuit of their headlong dash. For Red, though, the trail was not that obvious, since they were not following the actual path carved out by Wolle and the other horses, and in the forest generally one tree or thicket looked to Red much like another. But after some time he saw something that he recognized – a particular clump of smooth-boled trees with oddly bluish leaves, and heavy spreading branches down to ground level. He remembered that clump because it had been almost in front of him when that Barachi dart had been flung.

So they were just about back where they had started. Krost paused to scowl intently into the shadows among the trunks. Red still felt the same flesh-crawling tension, putting him on a knife-edge of alertness, and because of that and because he was looking more or less in the right direction, he saw the swift, jerky movement in the undergrowth – and lunged aside in a stumbling half-dive.

Once again he heard the soggy thudding sound, and saw a Barachi dart bury its spike deep into the tree beside him.

But this was no isolated attack. Around them the forest erupted with the rasping, growling cries of Barachi. More darts filled the air, and bit into the trees, as Krost – with a grunting roar like a challenge – grabbed Red's shirt in one hand and hoisted him like a child into the midst of the clump of trees.

Red pressed himself against one trunk, grateful to all the trunks that rose around him like protective pillars with their drooping spread of branches. And even Krost managed to get his bulk shielded, as the darts flew in and around and past. But then the hail of darts ended – and Red saw Krost grin, hoisting the heavy staff.

'They will have to come and fight us face to face,' the dwarf-giant rumbled. 'No more cursed darts.'

Red returned the grin, feeling his adrenalin surge again at the prospect of battle. The excitement was like wine in his veins as he peered past a leafy branch, and saw the enemy. Seven of them, he counted. Without the sense to surround them, but advancing in a bunch, wielding their sharp-pointed spears.

205

'Seven,' Krost growled annoyedly. 'Not even shares.'

'You can have the extra one,' Red said lightly. 'You're older.'

Krost chuckled. 'A mug of ale for each of them slain,' he rumbled, 'and he who kills least must pay for all.'

'You're on,' Red said – just in time. The Barachi raised their spears, howled, and charged.

In their charge they did at last spread out to attack from several sides. And then Red discovered what he might have realized sooner – that effective swordplay needs open space. The Barachi, leaping and howling around the clump of trees, could readily stab in among the trunks with their long-bladed spears, but Red and Krost could not reply. The tree-trunks that protected them also impeded them, impeded their own movements, the swing of the staff, the slash of the sword. Red and Krost had to use all their speed and skill merely to fend off the deadly spear-heads, without striking many blows of their own.

We could get killed in here, Red thought, blocking yet another spear-thrust with the bright unbreakable blade. But we could also get killed out there. And then there was no more time for thought or the weighing up of risks. He heard a roar from Krost that sounded as frustrated as he felt – and then he saw the massive figure leap out from the trees, laying about him with the staff. Red leaped as well, in time to skewer a Barachi aiming a spear at Krost's back, while the others stumbled away a step or two, startled by the sudden counter-attack. Red saw in one swift glance that Krost had felled two of them, which with his one left four to face them. And now they were out in the open, and the growling monsters were reaching swiftly to the pouches of darts at their sides.

No point running just to get darts in the back, Red thought. He measured the distance, poised himself for a leap that would take him in among the nearest group of Barachi, to take a few of them with him before the darts flew. And Krost was also readying himself, the quarterstaff poised. Right, Red thought fiercely. Charge . . .

But then his whole body convulsed as the entire sky above

them was torn apart by the loudest, most nerve-shredding scream Red had ever heard.

As he found his balance and looked up, as they all looked up, in awe and shock, Red saw that it had in fact been a chorus of screams. And some numbed part of his mind told him that it had been the same scream that they had heard before, in the distance.

The creatures were sitting on large branches among heavy foliage, so while there seemed to be a dozen of them there may have been more, hidden. They looked like huge birds, nearly the height of a man, with vast wings folded back. But they were not birds. They were monstrosities. They were scaly rather than feathery, greenish-grey and glistening as if coated in slime – their necks long and scabby, their eyes small and red-rimmed. They clutched their perches with talons resembling iron hooks, and their beaks were like long curved daggers.

And as the two humans and the Barachi stared incredulously up at them, the horrors screamed again like a million ungreased hinges and unfurled the great stained sails of their wings. Red flung himself to one side, sword ready, with a choked yell at Krost who seemed to be standing as if paralysed. But the winged monsters ignored them both. Claws reaching, beaks agape, their screams and the thunderclaps of their wings filling the air, they fell upon the Barachi.

As far as Red could see, as a dazed spectator, only one of the Barachi managed even a half-hearted upward stab with a spear. The rest of them turned, howling, and tried to flee. But the winged monsters were on them before they could take a stride – and the slaughter, for it was no battle, took very little more time. The wings crashed and stormed, the talons tore and the beaks ripped, and within a sickening moment or two there were only gashed and shredded portions of Barachi scattered on the ground, their blood soaking into the soil.

Shaken and nauseated, Red stared wonderingly as the winged things simply returned to their perches in the trees. And he wondered even more at Krost, who still stood unmoving, staring up at them.

'*Zhraike*,' Krost said. Or so it sounded to Red, though Krost had spoken in his hoarsest whisper.

Then cold shock blasted through Red all over again, for the monster on the branch nearest to them fixed them with an evil red eye, opened its blood-wet beak, and *spoke* – in a voice that was a quieter but still raucous version of its scream.

'We have leave to take Barachi, here,' it said. 'You are not Barachi. You go.'

Red stared, and Krost stood as woodenly as ever. Then, slowly, his giant forearm knotting with the tension of his grip, he raised the great iron staff. '*Zhraike!*' he said again, his voice choked with outrage. 'How come you here?'

Many of the creatures stirred on their perches, snapping their beaks. And the one that had spoken tilted its head to peer down at Krost. 'You speak as one of our enemies of old,' it grated. 'Yet you do not look as them. And you are not Barachi. So you go. Go.'

'Krost, come *on*,' Red said in an urgent half-whisper, tugging at the dwarf-giant's arm. 'While we can.'

Krost turned slowly, blinking at Red as if surprised to see him there. Then he glanced back at the winged monsters and nodded slowly as if confirming something for himself, before following Red into the forest. When Red looked back, the monsters were merely watching them go, impassively, from their high perches. Then the foliage closed in so that they could no longer be seen.

'And what in hell were *they*?' Red demanded at last.

Krost was staring blankly ahead as if caught up in the toils of some dire vision. 'Zhraike of the crags,' he growled. 'Creatures of the Southern Highlands, that some say are half-demon. Savage killers, with some intelligence, the power of speech.' He rubbed a hand down over his face as if to erase its ravaged expression. 'My people, the giants of the plateaux, fought them endlessly for years . . . for generations. In the end we drove them from the plateaux, and some thought we had slain them all. But others believed that a few survived, gone to live elsewhere in the South, in more remote mountains. And so it seems to be.'

'And now they live here?' Red asked.

'They are here,' Krost said doubtfully, 'but I cannot believe they *live* here. They are creatures of the crags, the heights – not swampy forests.'

'Maybe they just like the taste of Barachi,' Red said wryly.

Krost managed the ghost of a smile, which quickly faded. 'The one spoke as if they were controlled. Saying they had *leave* to take Barachi.'

'Seems to me,' Red said, 'that if whoever controls them doesn't like Barachi, he's on our side.'

Krost, frowning, said nothing for a moment, as they retraced their path back to the others. And before he could comment further, an outburst of sound in the distance stopped them in their tracks.

The sound of horses squealing in terror or rage – mingled with a wild human shriek, and a sudden unmistakable outburst of more Barachi howls.

TWENTY-ONE

Red yelled 'Aurilia!' and launched himself into a headlong dash through the undergrowth, oblivious of branches clawing at his clothing or slashing at his face. Krost ran with him stride for stride, charging the brush as indomitably as his pony had earlier. But it was Krost who kept his wits about him as they drew near to the cleft where the others had remained. He grabbed Red's arm, pulling him back so powerfully that he was lifted from the ground in mid-stride.

'Slowly,' he muttered. 'See what is there before you charge.'

It was sound advice, and Red clutched at some scraps of self-control and crept silently forward after him, up along the side of a nearby ridge, from which they could look down at the cleft from above, or at least as much as they could see of it past the overhang. When they eased forward among the ferns and twisting briars, they found that they could see all that they needed to see. Though not what they wanted.

They had heard a horse squeal, before, but by then there was no sound from where the horses had been placed in the cleft. Also, there was no sign of Aurilia or Phaedran. And Red had to clench his teeth till his jaw hurt to keep from crying out with fury at what he *could* see.

Marshal Lenceon, mounted on his black stallion. In the company of four spear-carrying Barachi.

Not as their prisoner or opponent, but as their ally.

And all of them, marshal and monsters, seemed to be searching for something in the brush growing all around the mouth of the cleft. The Barachi were beating at the brush with their spears, growling, while the marshal was leaning from his saddle to slash at the foliage with his sword. And he was doing so frantically, it seemed, muttering words that sounded like 'where . . . where . . .'

Red and Krost exchanged grim nods, surged to their feet

and hurtled down the slope. As they did so Krost bellowed, a mighty battle-cry that hurled its shockwave down to grip the enemy in an instant of paralysis. At their speed an instant was all that Red and Krost needed. The Barachi were only starting to reach for darts or to raise their spears when the iron staff swept furiously down, splintering two spear-hafts and smashing on to crush the skulls of their wielders. At the same time Red smoothly side-stepped a spear, sliced the throat of the Barachi who held it, half-pivoted to parry another spear and to drive the sword into the chest of the fourth Barachi. And for the first time, in his rage, he felt not the smallest inner flinch at the sudden death that his blade had meted out.

The marshal had wheeled his horse, pale and shocked at the onslaught and the death of his four Barachi. But he had also drawn a crossbow from a sheath on his saddle, and held it drawn and levelled. In the fact of that threat, Red and Krost halted, waiting.

'You betrayed the prince and Aurilia?' Krost asked, his tone almost conversational.

Lenceon's grin was vicious. 'The Barachi have your prince – and the horses. Though they will eat only the horses. My master has more interesting plans for Phaedran, and the witch.'

'I thought there was something fishy about you,' Red said, sliding one foot forward as he spoke.

'Stand where you are!' Lenceon snapped. 'You have no chance against the bow – just as you will have no chance in the forest, afoot.'

'Right,' Red drawled. 'A water viper or something might get us.'

Lenceon laughed harshly. 'The viper was meant for Master Krost. But it was not easy to carry, in the dark – and it wriggled free, and dropped on the fool servant.' He bared his teeth. 'I wish it had been *you*, first, Corodel.'

'Missed your chance, friend,' Red said.

'It will not matter,' Lenceon snarled. 'The Barachi will find you. They may even take you alive, as the master has asked us to do if possible, so that you may join your prince again.'

'And your master *is* Talonimal?' Krost asked, in the same casual tone.

'Of course he is,' Lenceon spat. 'I have maintained contact with him for years, ever since his banishment. He has promised me proper recognition, and position, when he has achieved power.'

'That is what he is doing, is it?' Krost asked. 'Achieving power? With the princess as his prisoner?'

Lenceon grinned tightly. 'Your questions will all be answered in time, monster. I would enjoy killing you both, here, but at least I have been promised that if you are captured alive I may watch you die.'

You couldn't kill us both, here, Red suddenly thought. Not with one bolt. That's why he didn't shoot as soon as he pulled the bow out. Shoot one of us, and the other would get him before he could reload. And . . . he might miss.

'What you're saying,' he drawled, stepping forward, 'is that you don't have the guts to shoot. Typical officer – needs others to do the killing . . .'

The marshal's face twisted with rage and his trigger-finger tightened. But then he controlled himself. 'Save your brave words, Corodel,' he sneered. 'Save them for when the Barachi come to find you – and for when we meet again, in the Dome.'

And he wheeled the stallion and galloped away, the forest closing behind him.

Red started instinctively forward, but halted as the horse and rider disappeared from view. Turning, he saw Krost staring thoughtfully at the ground around the cleft.

'At least our horses will leave a clear trail for us,' Red said.

Krost shook his head slowly. 'When we follow, we will choose our own path. But first there are puzzles to be solved here.'

'Such as?' Red asked, moving forward to join Krost as the dwarf-giant walked towards the cleft.

'Such as what they were looking for . . .' Krost began. But then he stopped, partly at the sight of another crumpled Barachi corpse lying inside the cleft – and partly because of a hazy, tremulous shape that suddenly appeared on the overhang above them. A shape that swiftly gathered substance, and became Aurilia.

Even in her younger form she looked drawn and almost haggard with exhaustion, her tawny hair half-fallen from its elaborate arrangement. And Red changed his shout of gladness, at the sight of her, to a leap that took him up the slope to her side, in time to support her as she sagged.

'Are you hurt?' he demanded urgently. 'Where . . .'

But she shook her head with weary slowness. 'Veiling . . .' she said.

He snarled at himself for not guessing sooner. *She*, hidden by her magic, had been what they were looking for.

Carefully he helped her down, to a point where Krost could reach up and lift her the rest of the way like a doll. He lowered her till she was half-lying on the turf, supported by Krost's mighty arm. And Red knelt beside her, anxiously seeing that she was as pale as if her very life's blood had ebbed away.

'Working magic acts like a drain on the life force,' Krost said quietly. 'Or so they say.'

'It does,' she whispered. 'But I will be all right . . . soon.'

Red stared around, in hopes that some of their supplies – a canister of water, a flagon of wine – might have fallen from the packhorses. But there was nothing in the cleft except the dead Barachi. Aurilia saw him looking at the corpse and smiled a faint smile.

'That was Wolle,' she said. 'The other horses were frightened, but he was enraged.'

Krost looked proud. 'He will be sorry to have killed only one.'

'We tried to fight . . .' she went on weakly. 'But there were too many . . . Perhaps two dozen – and led by . . . Vanticor.'

'I wish we'd stayed around,' Red snarled.

'Then Lenceon aimed his bow . . . at the prince,' she said, 'and forced us to surrender. But when they were gathering the horses . . . I brought a veiling around myself . . .'

Her voice faded. Red took her hand, alarmed to find it so limp and cold, watching worriedly as her eyelids drooped. But Krost nodded, looking untroubled.

213

'She maintained her veil too long,' he said, then lowered her gently. 'Sleep will restore her.'

'Phaedran . . .' Aurilia mumbled.

'They will not harm him,' Krost told her. 'It seems he is wanted alive. When you are yourself again, they will not be too far ahead.'

Her eyelids closed, her breathing deepened. As Krost got to his feet, Red let go of the sleeping woman's hand and rose to join him.

'Are we really going to go after them?'

Krost peered at him from beneath bushy eyebrows. 'He is our prince, Red. We have a duty – at least to *try*. But . . . perhaps you do not . . .'

Red shrugged. 'I signed on for the whole trip. Besides, where would I go in this place, alone? And most importantly – they've got my Grilena.'

Krost laughed. 'Good reasons – Corodel.' He prodded Red's chest with a stocky forefinger. 'And when we find them it will be the same arrangement as before, with the mugs of ale. You already owe me, since I have killed four today to your three.'

'If you say so,' Red agreed. 'Though I think Vanticor and Lenceon should be worth extra.' He glanced over at the cleft, and the corpse on the ground. 'We owe Wolle a mug, as well,' he said, gesturing, 'for that one.'

'So the witch and the others have escaped?' Evelane said tartly. Once again she and Talonimal were in his shadowed spell-chamber – where the scrying stone showed a number of huge flying creatures swooping high above a forest's dense greenery.

'Evelane,' Talonimal said warningly. There was annoyance in his eyes, but something else with it – a shakiness, as if something had unnerved him. 'The Barachi will gather them up before long. And we have Phaedran . . .'

She stamped her foot pettishly. 'Yet I am not permitted to *look* at him,' she snapped. 'I want to see his *face*, I want to see his *fear* – not these foul birds!'

'I have good reason for changing the image,' the sorcerer

said, the shadow of unease darkening in his eyes. 'I explained about the Zhraike . . .'

'You cannot *know* they are from the Magister!' she told him.

'I know,' he said bitterly. 'They now live among crags above his valley, and have come to serve him as do the stunted ones who wander his stony forest. They are here to watch me, Evelane – to harry me, to seek a way to breach my shielding. I *know* that. They may even be here as a spearhead, an initial probe, before Lebarran *himself* moves against me!'

Evelane paled, silenced as if realizing a cause for fear beyond her own preoccupations.

'You will have opportunity to watch your father,' Talonimal went on, 'and savour his downfall . . . And that of the others, when the Barachi take them. Meanwhile I must keep watch on the Zhraike. And—' he tugged at his beard thoughtfully— 'I might try to speak to Lebarran, through the scrying stone. Try to lull his suspicions, forestall him a while, perhaps learn what he and the Order are planning.'

'They cannot attack us, can they?' she asked shakily. 'Not even with these . . . Zhraike?'

He rubbed his eyes as if suddenly weary. 'I feel sure that they could not breach the Dome, even in conclave. Such shieldings are far harder to break down than to erect. And I am stronger now than when I first contrived it – so that *it* grows stronger too, each time I repeat the spell that reinforces it.'

She moved towards him, a wistful look in her eyes. 'If only your plans were further advanced, my beloved. Then you could use your power to . . . to do as you promised, and give *me* the gift of magic.' Her voice became a lilt, her eyes shone. 'Then I could stand at your side, adding my strength to yours, against our enemies . . .'

He sighed, his mouth tightening. 'That of course would be a boon, but it is not possible. I have *told* you, time and again, what an enormous outlay of strength and concentration would be required to infuse you with a magical gift. Obviously I have no time nor strength to spare at this moment – and even if I did, you would need a long period of study before you could begin to *use* your gift!'

The last words were spoken in an impatient snarl. And she drooped, tears glistening in her eyes. 'Yes, my lord . . . I'm sorry . . .'

Talonimal sighed again. 'Come, my dear,' he said, softening his tone, 'I do not mean to distress you. You must merely be patient. My powers have grown and will continue to grow. Before long, when the alignments are in order, I shall send your father and the witch and whatever others across the threshold. And then I will be enormously stronger still.'

She looked up, tears drying, being replaced by a hopeful glitter in her eyes.

'Then I may have become strong enough,' Talonimal went on, 'to bring *Adepts* to the fire, not merely witches. Perhaps even some of the lesser fools of the Order itself. So that I shall continue to grow, and grow!'

She stared beyond him at a vision that only she could see. 'And we shall rule?'

'We shall.' His voice grew sonorous, incantatory, as if repeating words spoken ritually many times before. 'I shall give you your power and train you in its uses . . . And we shall rule, together, the Most Supreme – destroying those who like Lebarran might oppose us. Taking more power, more life-force, from High Adepts given to the fire . . . We shall rule, a sorcerer king and queen, unchallengeable. We alone shall have the strength and the courage to summon the Unformed, without constraint. And finally – to achieve the Apotheosis.'

She had drifted close to him as he spoke, making small wordless sounds in her throat, reaching blindly out to him. So they stood for a silent moment, staring at the scrying stone as if seeing images of the unguessable future that he had described.

'Oh, my beloved,' she murmured, leaning into his embrace, 'it will be glorious.' Then she glanced up at him with a suddenly cruel smile. 'And what joy it is that we should be able to hasten that day – by taking our vengeance at last upon my father!'

Red and his companions travelled steadily for several days without overhauling the Barachi led by Vanticor. They were held back a little by a reluctance to overtax Aurilia – though she was steadily recovering her normal strength and energy. But mostly their progress was slowed because they were travelling through undergrowth parallel to the trail left by the horses, not following it where the enemy might have left traps or ambushes; and it seemed that Vanticor was pushing the Barachi along as fast as they could go – which was considerably, since the creatures seemed swift and tireless in their own wilderness.

'Vanticor must be riding one of the horses, to keep up this pace,' Aurilia said at one point.

'It would be good if he tried riding Wolle,' Krost growled.

Red did not pursue the subject, not wanting to think too much about the horses and what Lenceon had said about the Barachi's plans for them. By then, he assumed, the marshal would have joined that group on his own horse, so it was likely that Aurilia was right about Vanticor being mounted too. Maybe the scarred man would ride Grilena, Red told himself, and so might keep her from being butchered. If not, he vowed savagely, he'd do some butchering of his own.

By then the landscape had begun to change. The forest remained no less dank and oppressive, its shadowy depths no less ominous with potential hidden menace. But the rolling ridges and gullies gradually gave way to a steady downward slope, which led into a vast basin – where they found the swampland that Red had been told about. That meant stretches of murky water of unguessable depth, interspersed with isles and peninsulas and hummocks of slimy, muddy land. It meant unsightly plants, growing from both land and water, bent and gnarled into disturbing shapes – or scrawny, twisted trees whose bark looked leprous and whose leaves were the colour of dried blood, festooned with trailing streamers of moss like torn shrouds. It meant even more heavy, humid air, foul and almost choking. And that which lent a further element of oppression to the atmosphere of the place, which seemed both sullen and somehow expectant, as if the swamps themselves were preparing some unimaginable fate for the three intruders.

And where, earlier, the forest creatures had been silent and shy, the swamp creatures were much less reluctant to show themselves. The numbers and varieties of snakes were bewildering – from slow-moving monsters, endlessly long and as thick as Krost's arm, to tiny writhing things as greyish-pink as diseased skin, along with plenty of the ugly water vipers that Red had seen around the wrist of the unlucky Ulniss, and other serpentine things that wriggled or slithered past too swiftly for clear identification. Such presences, mostly in the water along with unknowable other forms of life, made the three humans all the more careful, even when they had to take a long way around, to stay on the most solid ground they could find.

So they forged on as best they could, chafing at the reduced pace, oppressed by the stinks and menaces all around them, troubled as well by constant hunger and thirst and weariness. Of course they had no supplies, which had all been carried by the horses. And even Krost's wilderness skills could find little that was edible for them in the swamp. But he knew ways to filter some of the less foul water, using cloth from a petticoat of Aurilia's older form, though the result was a gritty, evil-tasting liquid that they drank only when desperate. As they had to be to eat the few bitter roots that Krost dug up, now and then, which kept them only hungry rather than ravenous.

As for weariness, that was also only slightly eased by their rest periods, at noon and by night. Lying uncovered on oozing mud that smelled of rot did not induce restful slumber. Nor did the quiet squelchings, the stealthy bubblings, that filled the darkness around them at night – as if nameless horrors out of the foul water were creeping slowly upon them. Yet nothing attacked, though Red and Krost alternated on watch during the nights, letting Aurilia sleep to regain her strength.

So day followed day of slogging on, finding them always mud-smeared and clammily wet, always hungry and tired and on a vibrating edge of apprehension and dread that grew worse with every southward step. They recalled only too well Marshal Lenceon's threat that the Barachi would come after them – and so with every step they took on that grim pursuit they wondered if *that* was the bush, or *those* the fronds, from which a storm of Barachi darts might come.

Yet, inexplicably, as they struggled on, no attack came. But Red was willing to put up with the mystery, not wishing to tempt fate by discussing with the others where the Barachi might be. In fact the three of them talked very little during those days – being too focused on the gruelling effort of travel in the swamp, and too concerned otherwise with silence and alertness. Eventually, however, the puzzle was solved for them, gruesomely.

One murky dawn they were all dragged abruptly from sleep or wary watchfulness by a nerve-grinding series of screams in the distance. More of the screams of the demonic bird-things, the Zhraike. Coming from the south, directly along the route that they planned to follow that day. They were more alert and cautious than ever as they set off in the heavy clinging mist of that dawn. But when the mist's curtain had drawn back, an hour or so later, they found the cause of the Zhraike screams, and also the effect. It was on a long extension of land like a dike between cloudy breadths of dark water. On the dike, among torn and trampled ferns, they found a scene of slaughter like the one Red had seen before: the scattered, mutilated remnants of Barachi, lying on blood-soaked mud. Red realized sickly that no one would be able to put the jigsaw together to know how many Barachi there had been, for it was clear that large portions of the corpses were missing, presumably devoured.

'Told you those Zhraike were on our side,' Red said, trying to sound lighthearted.

'It is hard to imagine Zhraike doing good,' Krost said

dubiously. 'They are half-demon, Red. Whoever they serve, here, will not be a force for good.'

Aurilia nodded. 'If they have been given *leave* to kill Barachi, as it seems, why might it not be from a sorcerer? Demons will serve sorcerers, often.'

'You mean someone who's got it in for Talonimal?' Red asked. 'Sounds good. Let's hope they fight to the death and it ends in a draw.'

Krost shook his head. 'It would do *us* no good to be in the middle of such a struggle.'

'But it could help,' Aurilia said, 'if we need a distraction.'

'It's already helped,' Red pointed out, gesturing at the dismembered bodies. 'These were probably coming after us.'

Krost nodded. 'Most likely. So we need not fear attack, for a while – until the enemy learns that these have been destroyed.'

'Then we can move more swiftly for that while,' Aurilia said, and trotted off at a brisk pace, ignoring the lumps and shreds of Barachi in her path.

As the others followed, Red could not help glancing down at the torn flesh. 'At least the Zhraike are getting enough to eat,' he said sourly.

'May their appetites remain hearty,' Krost replied, 'when the next troop of Barachi come to seek us.'

Krost's doubts about the benevolence of the Zhraike failed to diminish Red's hopeful feelings, that day. The killing of their Barachi pursuers was good news in any terms, and definitely lifted his spirits. But then he had been aware all along that his spirits had *never* been as depressed as he would have expected. Not even in the midst of a stinking, deadly swamp, in a land swarming with enemies, on the way with only two companions to where a murderous super-sorcerer lurked. Those were good reasons for any man to feel a little gloomy, he thought. Yet much of the time, when he paused to look within himself, he found that he was, weirdly, feeling . . . exhilarated. Almost happy.

And by then he knew why. He was finally living on a level of intensity that he had, it seemed, always been craving.

Apparently, it took a promise of violent action, an atmosphere of supernatural menace, and a constant threat of death to make him feel wholly alive.

His instincts might always have known that, but at last his conscious mind had learned it too. And perhaps that was the very definition of an adventurer. Even of a hero, though he mocked himself for using the word. Yet even as he mocked he inwardly saw an image, like a memory he could not have, of a heavy-shouldered man in a leather jerkin with the glowing sword in his hand. And he would salute that image with a wry inner smile, knowing very well that if the adventurer-swordsman-hero Corodel had been in that swamp, in those circumstances, he would have been feeling exactly the same exhilaration.

Naturally, he said nothing of that to his friends – not sure how they would react if they knew that in some part of his being he was actually enjoying himself. But he was quite unaware that in some moments, the more tense times of creeping through particularly tangled areas that reeked of ambush, when his enjoyment showed; when his hand moved eagerly to his sword-hilt and his mouth smiled a hungry smile. And he was also unaware, at those times, of how Krost and Aurilia would exchange a glance that was both knowing and half-exasperated, before all three strode forward to confront what might be waiting for them.

But nothing ever was. And so for two more days they toiled on through the expanses of gluey mud, watched by slithery things with too many teeth – or through stands of the gnarled, leprous trees where fungi oozed corruption and dangling moss dripped slime. During those days they kept up their accelerated pace while also striving to raise their levels of caution and watchfulness. And it was that full alertness that brought Red to notice something peculiar lying at the edge of a muddy pond at one side of a strip of land they were following. They paused briefly to inspect it – and discovered in it a new cause for sick revulsion.

The peculiar thing looked like a corpse, lying half in the water. But when Krost distastefully used the iron staff to lift the thing clear, they saw that it was only half a corpse, with nothing of it left below the hips. The upper body and head had also been damaged, as if gnawed by whatever had consumed the lower portion. But though bare bone glinted wetly through the ripped skin of the head and face – and though the torso was extensively chewed, and slashed open so that the chewer could get at the entrails – enough remained for identification. Fragments of clothing, which had once been a heavily decorated grey-blue tunic. Along with the angular jawline, and some patches of iron-grey hair, it was clear that the corpse was that of Marshal Lenceon.

'I had hoped to kill him myself,' Krost rumbled disappointedly.

'At least he doesn't seem to have passed away peacefully,' Red commented.

'This perhaps is his punishment for failing to capture me, with the prince,' Aurilia said.

Red raised his eyebrows. 'Old Talonimal has a unique way of terminating a man's employment.'

'Never mind,' Krost said. 'There is still Vanticor to kill, when we catch them.'

As he spoke, as if in an uncanny response to his words, the wind shifted. It had been blowing lightly from the west for some days, bearing the usual array of swampland delights, the fetid stinks of foulness and decay. But in that moment it swung around to blow more from the south to bring nostril-cleansing odours of ozone and of brine.

The three of them went still, looking to the south, then at each other. 'The sea,' Aurilia murmured.

'Then we *must* be getting close to them,' Red said.

'Pray that we are,' Krost growled. 'Pray that we can catch them, before they reach Claw Point.'

Though their alertness did not waver, though they sought cover where it was available, they still managed to accelerate their pace – even while climbing the steep incline that was the southern side of the immense swamp basin. Two days later they reached the top of the incline, the basin's rim, and stared down a steeper slope through tangled foliage at a narrow beach, and beyond it a flat, empty sea.

Where the enemy lives, Red said to himself. And looking just the sort of place to make an evil sorcerer feel at home, he added, using the sarcasm to deny the fact that he was trying to keep from shivering. He had seen many seashores in his time, including some of the more polluted tourist beaches of his own world. But he had never seen one that looked less appealing.

Trees grew almost all the way down to the waterline, a density of small dark conifers, stunted, stumpy, and deformed by the sea's proximity. In their midst the undergrowth thinned, leaving only tall, dark grass sprouting in tufts. The sea itself lacked any hint of blue or green, showing no clear line where its blank surface made a horizon with the grey overcast of the sky. No waves or foam disturbed its greasily glistening surface, only slow undulations, unpleasant flat heavings as cloth might heave with something slithering beneath it. And where they stood on the ridge the breeze that had borne the scent of brine carried the reeks of decaying fish and rotting rafts of seaweed, essences of slime and foulness.

Just above the sea's surface, like ghostly but ill-formed vessels, floated swaths of mist and fog, clouds descended to walk upon the water. Now and then the breeze stirred these clusters of vapour, though they parted only to coil back and re-form. And it was one of those brief movements and dissolutions that caught Krost's eye – causing him to point wordlessly and Aurilia to take a quick sharp breath and touch Red's arm.

In the distance – too far away and mist-shrouded to be seen in complete detail – something rose from the water at the edge of the shore. Or, Red thought, peering, from a spit of land that thrust out into the water from the shore. The re-gathering mist showed only a glimpse, but the shape had to be immense. It was very dark against the grey of sea mist, dark, curved, and unnaturally shiny. And it had small weird shapes swirling around and above it, looking like wind-blown leaves.

As Red opened his mouth to ask a question he was jolted into silence. From the tangle of conifers below them, between the ridge and the shore, they heard the low, nervous whinny of a horse.

Silently they slid back over the ridge on to the safer side, crouching to peer carefully down from heavy cover. I bet that was Grilena, Red thought irrationally. And then he thought how lucky they were that the wind was blowing from the sea, so that their scent was not carried down to the horses – and perhaps to the Barachi.

Aurilia leaned close, pressed her lips to his ear. 'Krost wants to get closer,' she whispered.

He nodded, then with infinite care crept up and over the ridge with the others, on their bellies at first, then rising to a low crouch as they moved down among the interwoven branches of the conifers. It was a taxing, step-at-a-time pro-gress that left Red sweaty and agitated within a very few minutes. And they might never have managed it if the sound-less Krost had not shown them, at every moment, where to place hands and feet, how to slide under or around branches.

But they needed no signal from Krost when, after an age of silent creeping, they were brought to a heart-lurching halt. Not by a horse, that time, but by a human voice, raised in a snarl of anger. Red had no trouble identifying it. When he had last heard it, in the Catacombs beneath Quamarr, it had been calling for his death.

'I told you,' snarled Vanticor, 'we got to *wait*! We can't go near with those things flying around!'

In reply, Red heard other sounds that he also recognized – the low, rasping croaks of Barachi, in their tortured version of the human tongue.

'How do *I* know how long?' Vanticor replied. 'Go over to the Dome, why don't you, and ask the devil-birds when they're leaving!'

The *Dome*, Red thought. That huge curved shape in the mist . . . Marshal Lenceon had said something about a Dome, just before he ran for it, but Red had not thought about it since. But a Dome would be a likely shape for . . . a barrier. For Talonimal's sorcerous protection.

And the leaf-like things they had seen circling it were of course Zhraike. Making themselves useful again, he thought. Keeping Vanticor and the Barachi away from the Dome.

Vanticor's words had caused a burst of growling and croaking among the Barachi, and Red smiled to himself. Not worried about noise, he thought. The Zhraike are too far away to hear – and obviously Vanticor doesn't dream that anyone else is around. He thinks we're back in the swamp, either dead or captured by those other Barachi. Surprise, Vanticor, Red thought. Here we are, in one piece and right behind you.

And then he shivered as the breeze again exposed part of the mist-shrouded, looming monstrosity of the Dome, as if to caution him against tempting fate.

The shiver became a twitch as Aurilia leaned against him, her lips at his ear to impart another almost-silent message. Turning towards her, he stiffened, eyes widening. Krost was not there. Red had heard and sensed nothing, yet the dwarf-giant had moved away, as if he had flown on the breeze.

'Krost is having a look at them,' Aurilia whispered.

Red nodded, wishing that his woodcraft was good enough to let him go as well. Almost at once he began to feel fretful and impatient, anxious for Krost to return undetected and with encouraging news. But when the bulky man did reappear – emerging from the thickets with a silent suddenness that made Red start – his grim expression showed that the news was not good. And it was not difficult for him to find sound-less sign language to say what he had learned about the enemy force. He merely had to extend his ten spread fingers – four times.

Forty Barachi, Red thought, appalled. Where they had expected a much smaller force. And that explained why Vanticor's company hadn't been attacked by Zhraike, as the other, smaller groups had been. But it means our luck has finally run out, Red said to himself, sagging like a deflated balloon. We either let them take the prince into that Dome-thing, or we commit suicide trying to stop them.

He watched Krost whispering inaudibly to Aurilia, and then her lips touched his ear again. 'Krost says we must now wait, and watch, for a little. And hope for a chance.'

Fat chance, he thought. But then he turned to put his mouth to her ear. 'What about doing a veiling – so we could sneak in among them and get the prince away?'

She shook her head. 'As soon as I veiled Phaedran as well, they would know. We would be hard pressed to get *out* from among them, then.' She leaned back to look at him, then forward to whisper in his ear again. 'But I will do that, if necessary, as a last resort.'

Red grimaced. 'Last' would be the word, he thought. And meanwhile, like Krost says, we wait. Which, he thought, with an inward sigh, is one of the things I'm really not much good at, at all.

At much the same time, far away in a secluded valley, someone else was finding his patience tried. Under the hovering canopy of his weird dwelling, the man named Lebarran Magister sat staring once again at his scrying bowl. The dark liquid had been restored, its surface as smooth as ever, shiny as black glass. Yet the tiny images on that surface rippled and shifted as if the liquid was being furiously agitated – fragmenting again and again with minimal gestures of Lebarran's hand, while his unblinking yellow stare grew ever more fierce.

He saw an image of a dark and shadowed place: a sudden hue and cry, where reptilian man-things struck with spears at three persons, one with a glowing sword, until all three finally fell into pools of their own blood. He saw the image

226

tear apart to be replaced by one where the same three persons prowled endlessly, hopelessly, around the outside of an immense structure like a dome, that seemed to be made of glittering obsidian. He saw that image shift into a succession of rapidly altering scenes in a place where black fog drifted in corners, where unrecognizable bodies lay curled in a room like a dungeon, or floated in mid-air, or toppled into silvery-blue flames. More and more images followed, once again involving the three persons seen before but also including a silver-haired sorcerer, his slim young mistress, a cold-eyed prince, a scar-faced man in green and black. All switching and shifting through what looked like a crazed sequence of scenes from a drama, with the same group of players taking a thousand roles . . .

Lebarran snarled and muttered, glowing hands jerking in angry gestures, rage twisting his features and igniting a more volcanic fire in his eyes. For the scrying spells he was forming sought to carry his sight into the *future*, to see what lay ahead for Talonimal and his royal captive, and for the three who had come unseen and unexpected to within sight of the sorcerer's lair.

Yet not even the Magister – not even the gods themselves – could ever see with certainty which one of all those images of the future, all those shapes and scenes of *possibility*, would eventually be brought into reality, as the advancing point of present time chose its one sole path.

So Lebarran finally gave in, cursing. One glowing hand swept the surface of the bowl clean – the other placed new images upon the shiny liquid. Images of the present – of Red and Aurilia and Krost, crouched among the dark conifers only a short distance from the forty Barachi with Vanticor and the prince; and a long way from them, along the shore, the looming shape of the Dome showing through the mist, with Zhraike swooping tirelessly around it.

And the Magister recalled one particular scene, from his views of the range of possible futures, that had appeared many times in many patterns, over and over. A scene of high probability, then, he knew, seeing it again in his mind's eye – the three persons, two men and a woman, walking fearlessly

227

in through the gleaming wall of the Dome, unseen, unchallenged.

'Very well,' Lebarran rasped aloud, angry muscles jumping in his jaw. 'I have besieged him and unnerved him, with my creatures. Now let us see what the witch and her cohorts can do.'

He raised his hands high, as the images winked out from the scrying bowl. His face grew taut, and the brightness of his hands flared as he flung his power out across the enormous, intervening distance.

'Return, my Zhraike,' he muttered. 'Leave the way clear . . .'

The waiting was no more pleasant than Red expected, nor did it come to a swift end. All the rest of that day they crouched among the conifers, listening to the sounds of their enemies, with tension and frustration attacking them even more troublingly than the whirling clouds of insects. As the hours edged towards nightfall, they sometimes heard the sudden squeal of a frightened horse, and Red's imagination filled with ghastly images of slaughter and feasting. Also, only once, they heard the sharp, frigid tones of Prince Phaedran raised in some angry exchange – and Krost's grip on the great quarterstaff tightened to such a massive pressure that it threatened to reduce it to iron filings.

But they did not move, except with extreme slow care now and then to change position and relieve stiffening limbs. They did not move even when full night brought silence to the Barachi camp. Nor did they sleep, that night, not knowing whether Vanticor might send out scouts in the darkness, or an outer perimeter of sentries.

But the assassin and his creatures were apparently feeling confident in their camp. No one emerged from it during the night, nor did they stir too early after first light. So the three watchers near by, still alert at dawn as they had been at sunset, were the first to see what had happened in the first glimmering of morning.

The Dome was shrouded even more thickly in dark mist: but there was nothing else around it. The Zhraike had gone.

It took nearly until sun-up for the Barachi to stir enough to notice. Then there was a great burst of croaking – and a frightening near-miss. Vanticor clearly suspected a Zhraike feint, and sent a squad of ten Barachi to range through the conifers, to be sure that the winged monsters were not merely trying to lure them out of hiding. The ten Barachi passed within an easy dart's throw from where the three watchers had flattened themselves in the long dark grass.

But they remained unseen, and before long the ten Barachi wandered back to their main party to announce that they had seen and heard nothing, that the way was clear. That caused another burst of croaking, which cut off when Vanticor snarled his orders.

'Right, we can move. The way in'll be clear now. But some of you'll probably have to go back to the swamp, see what's keeping the other bunch who went after the witch and her friends.'

That, Red thought, would be the Barachi band who lay in shreds on the dike. And the Barachi response, a new flurry of croaking and growling, did not sound as if they were eagerly volunteering.

'Maybe you *can* have your feast before you go,' Vanticor shouted into the midst of the outcry. 'It's not up to me. If the master wants you to go, you argue with *him*.'

That reduced the noise to a very low mutter of discontent, which went on along with the noise of the Barachi getting ready to move out, a muffled clattering of weapons and equipment, a few more squeals from the horses. Then the whole party set off, looking tense and wary in the glimpses that Red caught of them through the trees. And he and his friends drifted silently along after them, wary enough in their own way.

'I wish about half of them would go back to the swamp now,' Aurilia whispered.

Krost nodded. 'Then we could go among the rest, veiled, and see how many we could kill while the veiling lasts.' He glanced around at the others. 'We might do that anyway.'

Red looked interested in the idea, but Aurilia shook her head doubtfully. 'Forty could be too many, if they scatter.

And we don't know what Vanticor might do to the prince if we attacked. Best to wait and see what happens between here and the Dome.'

Wait and see, Red thought with an inward sigh. And what will the plan be if *nothing* happens on the way to the Dome? He doubted if Krost and Aurilia would let the enemy take their prince inside Talonimal's stronghold without a good try at rescuing him, whatever the odds . . .

As he crept silently on with his friends, he felt again the electric surge of excitement through his veins, and mentally urged the Barachi to greater speed, to hurry them all to the denouement.

By then the sun was well up, only half-covered by some patchy clouds that were being shredded by a gathering breeze. The same breeze was also dealing briskly with the floating galleons of mist on the greasy sea, as well as the clouds enveloping the Dome. As they drew nearer, Red stared at it with awe, finally getting a clear picture of just how big it was. The jut of land that was Claw Point reached out into the sea for some distance, but Red could see none of its natural shape, for the Dome covered it entirely. It rose to an impressive height, as well, perhaps four storeys. But it was not size alone that made it awesome. It was its solid and featureless black surface, shiny and gleaming as if oiled. An armoured shell with no visible openings – like a monstrous dark imitation of a jewel.

'How do they get in?' Red whispered, staring wide-eyed up at the immensity.

'Vanticor spoke of his master opening the way,' Aurilia said. She too was staring up at the Dome, but assessingly, not looking very impressed at all.

By then Red was feeling as much oppressed as impressed – for he was inwardly confronting the fact that the Dome was not only a vast monstrosity of a structure, obscenely out of place on a wild sea coast. It was also a product of sorcery – brought into being by the dark magic contained within one man.

And we're thinking of challenging him, Red thought. We must be out of our minds.

But still he felt the battle-surge within him, still he stared hungrily ahead to where Vanticor and the Barachi were making their unhurried progress. And, eventually, that company arrived – grouping themselves loosely on a narrow stretch of open, shingly beach at the foot of the Dome, staring idly at the unbroken curve of shiny black soaring up in front of them, now and then glancing back as if to be sure that no dagger-beaked Zhraike were coming screeching out of the forest.

These backward glances forced the three watchers to remain crouched low in a shadowy thicket, silent and alert. Through the screening foliage they could see the prince in the midst of the group, looking haggard but coldly calm, wrists fastened behind him and always with several Barachi watching him with spears ready. The three also saw, with relief, that Grilena and Wolle and the other horses were still unharmed. But it looked beyond hope, Red thought, that they could stage a rescue, even with Aurilia's powers. They would need a miracle, he thought. But no miracles came along that morning. They waited for a time that seemed endless, while Vanticor and his Barachi milled around on the beach, staring hopefully at the Dome. And finally, in their thicket, Krost drew in a great breath and released it slowly.

'Veil us now, Aurilia,' he rumbled softly. 'We have no choice. We must strike before their master lets them in.'

Here we go, Red thought exultantly, reaching for his sword-hilt. But to his surprise Aurilia held up her hands to stop them.

'Wait,' she whispered. She was staring at the Dome with fierce intensity, brow furrowed. 'Perhaps we *do* have a choice . . .'

Then she stiffened, as if startled. And Red blinked, and stared – because something odd was happening to one small area of the Dome.

The affected area was at ground level, near the waiting Barachi. But it was not in the form of any kind of recognizable entrance. Red saw the gleaming black surface of the Dome at that spot suddenly grow dull, as if smeared. But then the smear took on a different texture, like that of black smoke or fog, and moved outwards, swelling a little, gathering into a heavy cloud that stood out from the Dome, thick and impenetrable, untroubled by the sea breeze.

'That will be the doorway,' Krost muttered.

Aurilia nodded tensely. 'And I think,' she whispered, 'that when they go in, we should go in *with* them. Veiled, of course.'

Krost and Red stared at her. 'That's crazy . . .' Red began. But she raised a hand again, silencing him.

'We may have a better chance, inside,' she said quickly. 'The Barachi will be scattered, no longer watchful, probably fewer of them guarding Phaedran. And it will probably be dark inside, which will help if the veiling wearies me. And . . . and we might have a chance to find Evelane, too, if she is here.'

Krost was nodding thoughtfully. 'We might even get the horses . . .'

'And go for a swim, and have a picnic on the beach?' Red asked sardonically. 'You've lost your minds, you two. Even if we weren't caught in there, rescuing people, how would we get *out* again? Ask old Talonimal to make another opening?'

Aurilia smiled. 'I don't think we would be discovered easily. It would be the *last* place anyone would expect us to be. As for getting out . . . The great spells of shielding known to the Higher Magic create barriers against any object or energy coming from the *outside*. The Dome might not bar our way, coming from inside.'

Red rubbed his eyes. 'That's a lot of ifs and might-nots.'

She shrugged. 'It still seems better than attacking forty Barachi out here.'

By then Krost was nodding more convincedly. 'There is something in that. Especially if we could bring the princess out as well . . .'

Then he halted, for a sudden burst of croaking from the massed Barachi alerted them that something new was happening. Peering through the branches, Red saw that the cloud of misty blackness that had extruded from the Dome had begun eerily to move. Not drifting vaguely like fog or smoke but in a more controlled way – spinning around upon itself in a circle, like a vertical whirlpool. And as centrifugal force drew the black fog to the edges of that circle, it formed a dark vortex – like the mouth of an unfathomable nightmare tunnel, leading into the Dome.

It was not an unduly large vortex, however, so it seemed that only one person, or creature, could pass through at one time. And that was confirmed when the Barachi, not seeming particularly surprised about a phenomenon they had obviously seen before, began jostling themselves into a ragged single file. Then, as one of them moved towards the slowly revolving vortex, leading a reluctant horse, Krost turned to face the others.

'We have to decide now,' he growled softly. 'Would you be able to keep us veiled for long enough, Aurilia?'

She lifted one shoulder in a half-shrug. 'I'll do what I can. It will depend on where they take Phaedran.'

'That's still a lot of unknowns,' Red put in, 'that we're *depending* on.'

Aurilia raised an eyebrow. 'When did you start worrying about things like that – Corodel?'

For an instant he scowled at her. Then his face relaxed, and he smiled – the battle-smile that was tinged with eagerness. 'Oh, I'm not *worried*,' he said easily. 'Go into a magic Dome and snatch a pair of prisoners from a super-sorcerer with an army of monsters? What could be simpler?'

The others grinned back at him. 'Let us go, then,' Krost said. 'Before the entrance closes.'

'Let's,' Red said. 'I'll be interested to see what this place looks like on the inside.'

Of all the weird, improbable things that had happened to Red Cordell since his arrival in the Four-Cornered Continent, perhaps the weirdest of all occurred then: when he and his two friends simply walked out of the woods and down on to the beach, where forty armed and deadly enemies were gathered, and not one of those enemies even glanced at them.

Aurilia's veiling seemed one hundred per cent effective, Red thought gleefully, only just restraining himself from making childish faces at the nearest Barachi. Despite the weirdness and the tension he was enjoying himself hugely, enjoying the sensation of power that realized everyone's dream of invisibility. And apparently there was a double level of safety in Aurilia's veiling: in the way of the Earth-magic she had exerted her power on elements of nature, doing something to the air and the light. Red hadn't fully understood her hasty explanations, but apparently somehow light rays and sound waves and air and everything passed around them without touching them. So they were soundless as well as invisible. And they were each separately veiled, not as a group – though Aurilia had said it was less of a strain for her if they stayed fairly close.

So they walked up to the straggling line of Barachi and stood there quietly, waiting for a space in the line to step forward into the vortex. Then Red saw that their arrival had not gone entirely unnoticed. Grilena and Wolle were pricking their ears and snorting, not seeing but obviously somehow sensing their masters. But that was just seen as more of the horses' nervousness, and not even Vanticor himself seemed to have the slightest suspicion.

Then Krost nudged Red. A gap had in fact opened up in the single-file line – a gap just behind Wolle, since no Barachi wanted to stand too close to the pony's lethal hoofs. And the

Barachi in front, leading Wolle, was nervously doing so on a very long rope. So Krost, unseen, was able to step in by his pony's head. Wolle snorted again, softly, and the Barachi must have thought that he had become suddenly docile, as he followed Krost unresistingly into the vortex.

By then Red and Aurilia were behind the pony, striding forward to keep ahead of the following Barachi. And if the awareness of being invisible seemed peculiar, it was nothing compared to the ghastly sensation that overtook Red as he stepped into the vortex.

The ground beneath his feet seemed to fall away, and he bit back a sudden cry. His entire body seemed to fly apart, cell by individual cell, as if some monstrous inner explosion scattered him into millions of fragments. Covered in icy sweat, he stumbled forward – and felt Aurilia reaching to grasp his hand with supportive strength.

'Don't be distressed,' she said. 'The transition won't harm you.'

Shakily Red nodded, finding his balance. Around him the blackness continued to form its featureless tunnel, as dense and swirling as ever. He lurched blindly on, clinging to Aurilia's hand, fighting the sense of inner dislocation, until abruptly he was on solid ground again, the tunnel of black fog behind him.

Dazedly he stared around. They were still enveloped in shadow and silence – and his mind filled with wild thoughts of what menaces might be gathering, what horrors looming unseen around them. He had a sudden despairing sense that they had destroyed themselves, that they had entered a deadly sorcerous trap from which there would be no exit.

But then Aurilia pulled him aside, out of the path of the next Barachi emerging from the vortex, and he realized that they were quite safe and unassailed. As fright and foreboding receded a little, he found within himself a thread of exultation. Because they had done the near-impossible. Unseen, unharmed, they had penetrated the Dome.

Still veiled, they hurried away over the rough sand and shingle covering most of the spit of land called Claw Point.

They flung themselves down behind a low dune topped with clumps of dead grass, and Aurilia released the veiling power from around them and lay gratefully back on the sand, panting slightly from the strain.

But they were well enough hidden, all the same. The interior of the Dome was in darkness, as if a late twilight had descended upon them without preliminaries. Red could only vaguely make out the moving shadows that were the Barachi and the horses as they massed near their entrance. It seemed that the Barachi could to some extent see in the dark – but then a torch suddenly flared into life in the midst of the crowd. It was held by Vanticor, who obviously did need artificial light, and who held the flame up to peer with a cruel grin at the expressionless face of Phaedran.

'Be welcome, O Prince,' Vanticor said, his mocking voice carrying easily to the three watchers. 'You will meet many surprises and terrors here in the Dome, before you finally meet your end.'

The prince merely gave him a withering glance, then looked away. Vanticor laughed, before spitting a mouthful of quick orders at the Barachi. Some of the creatures began to trudge away with the horses – it took three of them on the rope, this time, to overcome Wolle's reluctance – while the rest gathered around Phaedran and followed Vanticor and his torch in a different direction.

When they were far enough away, Aurilia rose to her feet. 'Follow them,' she whispered. 'I must look at the inside of the Dome, and then see where they take the horses. I will find you.'

Red nodded, the gesture unseen in the darkness. Now that they were in, she was going to try to secure their way out.

'And stay well back,' Aurilia added. 'I must save my strength, so you are not veiled.'

That announcement tightened Red's stomach a little, but he rose at once with Krost and crept off in the wake of Vanticor's torch, clearly visible ahead. Not being veiled meant that they could be heard, he knew, and his stomach clenched even tighter when he found it impossible to walk on the sand and pebbles without muffled crunching noises. But of course,

236

ahead of them, a crowd of Barachi were carelessly crunching along as well, and were hardly likely to be listening for pursuers, there under the Dome. So Red and Krost moved along steadily, keeping the flickering torch in sight.

As far as Red could see in the uncertain shadows, Claw Point seemed to widen out a good deal at its far end, where it curled back to form the claw-shape. The Dome was not a perfect hemisphere but fitted sorcerously on to the exact shape of the whole spit. Nice trick, Red thought, trying to find a sardonic note that would ease his tension and hold back his fears . . . But they swarmed furiously when Krost stiffened and abruptly halted. Nerves ablaze, Red reached for his sword-hilt. But Krost was looking up, pointing.

He was looking at several small lights in the blackness beyond where Vanticor's torch was moving. But not only ahead of Vanticor – high *above* him as well. They were small, orange-red lights, moving and wriggling, flames or lamps hovering in the air, neither rising or falling. Talonimal's answer to street lighting, Red said to himself, still trying to untighten his nerves.

'Castle,' Krost rumbled briefly.

The single laconic word changed Red's perception completely. The outlined shapes of dark towers and battlements assembled themselves, looming out of the blackness, dimly lit by the suspended orange-red glows that, he realized, were only high windows with lamps or candles behind. He felt comforted, in a small way, to have this proof that Talonimal was after all human, that he allowed some lighting and warming of the tomb-dark shadows within his Dome.

'They must be taking Phaedran in there,' Krost said. 'We must not follow too closely when we go in after him.'

I'm in no hurry, Red thought silently, as they crouched watching the torch-lit mass of Barachi crowding along towards the castle. It was not immensely large, he saw, though imposing enough. Its central keep was no more than two storeys high, for all its length and breadth. And only four towers rose from it, one at each corner – widening out a good deal at their tops, so that they looked top-heavy on spindly stems.

'Like a long-legged beast lying on its back,' Red murmured.

Krost gave a quiet snort of amusement. 'And a very danger-ous beast,' he said. 'Come – we can explore a little until Aurilia finds us.'

That comforted Red a little more, both Krost's apparent lack of tension and his confidence that Aurilia would return to them. They moved away, at an angle – but halted again at a new burst of croaking from the Barachi group ahead. The creatures seemed to be forming another line, and Red could make out – in the torch-light – another of the spinning vortices shaping itself against the castle wall. Slowly the Barachi filed through, with Phaedran in their midst and Vanticor bringing up the rear, the light from his torch extinguished as if a switch had been thrown.

With the enemy safely inside, Krost and Red were able to move a little more easily, though still not carelessly. They crept closer to the wall of the castle, aided by the dim light reaching down from the high slit-windows of the nearest towers. But up against the solidity of that dark stone, it became clear to them that this was no ordinary castle built by some lord to be a home as well as a defence, with some thought for the normal comings and goings of people. There was no way into Talonimal's castle – save by the sorcerous vortex.

And the immediate surrounds of the castle offered them little more encouragement. The building rose on the very end of the spit of land, so that its far side almost touched the curving sweep of the Dome. And there the surface of Claw Point altered from sand to mostly solid rock, with nothing but smears of dark lichen and streamers of long-dead moss to cover its bleak nakedness. That jut of rock might well have become an island, Red guessed, if the sea had worn away the looser gravel and shingle that linked it to the mainland. But the Dome was preventing that, as it prevented so much else.

Circling around to inspect the castle's farther side, Red and Krost came upon a small collection of half-ruined buildings, which would have been no more than sheds or huts when they were new. Krost guessed that they had been made long in the past, before the castle was built, by fisherfolk striving to establish a base on the coastline. Until, doubtless, the Barachi drove them off or killed them off.

But the collapsed ruins became useful just then for one last time, as a shelter. The two of them heard the unhappy neigh of a horse in the darkness behind them, and had just time enough to duck away behind the nearest crumbled wall. They heard the crunch of feet and hooves on gravel, then their clatter on rock, and saw the outlines of the other, smaller group of Barachi moving towards the castle, leading a single horse. And the savage eagerness in the croaking voices of the creatures left no doubt as to the fate that awaited the horse within the castle walls.

Red narrowed his eyes and tilted his head to see the horse more clearly through the shadows. 'Not big enough to be Wolle,' he whispered anxiously to Krost as the group of Barachi reached the castle. 'Do you think . . . ?'

'It's not Grilena either,' Aurilia's voice said, startlingly, next to them.

Red whirled as Krost choked on a muffled oath. 'Where did you—' he began, then realized that she would have been veiled, soundless and invisible, as she approached.

'I found the horses,' she said, her voice sounding weary. He saw her only as a vague shadowy form, but he had the idea that she was carrying something, as she sank down to the ground beside them, slumping back against the wall. 'They've been tethered in a copse of dead trees not far from here, where there's a small spring that will give them water.'

'Keeping them alive for feasts to come,' Krost growled.

'No doubt,' Aurilia said. 'And the horse they've chosen to start with is the fattest – the roan Ulniss rode. Grilena and Wolle are fine. And I rescued some food and water from the packs, for us. The Barachi threw everything away among the trees.'

Red was feeling hugely relieved to know that it wasn't Grilena that had been led into the castle to the slaughter. And he felt better still, to be able to sit there quietly and chew a bit of hard and probably mouldy bread and sip lukewarm water from a flask. 'All I need now,' he muttered, half to himself, 'is to be able to see what I'm eating.'

239

That made him think with some longing of the fact that he carried his own special light source, which had been so useful in the Catacombs. But as his hand strayed unconsciously towards the hilt of the sword, he heard Aurilia hiss and Krost grunt in warning.

'That would be an unnecessary risk,' Aurilia told him.

'And would destroy our night vision,' Krost added.

'I know,' Red said defensively, withdrawing his hand. But he was smiling to himself, thinking of himself and the sword the last time they had been in blinding darkness. It's always nice, he thought, to know that you'll be able to see who you're fighting.

Then Aurilia pushed herself away from the wall, took a deep breath as if to drive away her weariness, and offered another morsel of encouragement.

'I can tell you,' she said, 'that the Dome is not a barrier at all from the inside, as I hoped.'

'Then we can get out?' Krost asked.

'Easily. The shielding is exactly the one-way protection that I expected – so Talonimal's magic can pass out through it, and his Barachi, and ourselves.'

'So why don't we move?' Red said. 'Go and find Phaedran and the girl if we can, and get *out*.'

Krost's grin was a dim flash of white. 'Such impatience. Are you ready, Aurilia?'

She shrugged. 'I had to veil myself before, so I'm not as strong as I might be. But I'll be all right.'

'No need for veiling yet,' Krost told her. 'There are no sentries.'

'There's no door, either,' Red reminded him.

'They used one of those spinning openings,' Krost told Aurilia. 'Maybe they appear when people approach the wall.'

But he proved to be wrong. They approached the castle wall – at the place where Vanticor and the Barachi had disappeared – and no vortex greeted them. They pushed and prodded and even quietly tapped the great blocks of stone, over a large area, and nothing happened.

'How do they make it?' Krost growled, frustrated.

And Red had an inspiration. 'Maybe a code word,' he said. 'Open . . .'

He had been going to say 'Open Sesame', but his mind could find no version of the second word in the language he was speaking. Yet as he hesitated, all three of them suddenly jerked back, tensing, as part of the surface of the wall began to move. It was a door-sized part, shifting and rippling, transforming into another patch of the smoke or black fog, which gathered into a ragged circle and began without sound to revolve, creating another vortex like an entrance to a ghostly tunnel.

'So simple,' Krost muttered. 'Just the word open.'

'Too simple,' Red said. 'The spider ushering us into his parlour.'

'I have no sense of an *active* spell, here,' Aurilia whispered. 'It's as if the opening is an automatic response to the word.'

'It could still be a trap,' Red pointed out.

'Then let us find out,' Krost said, and unhesitatingly strode into the vortex.

Aurilia followed immediately, with Red at her heels – flinching when his body again suffered the wrenching horror of that inner, cell-by-cell dislocation. But as he moved forward, gritting his teeth, he emerged from the vortex into what looked like a broad, dimly lit clearing amid a dark and unnaturally orderly forest.

'We're veiled now,' he heard Aurilia say, sounding like she too was clenching her teeth with strain. 'This must be some kind of main entrance hall or the like. Are those stairs over there?'

Red gazed around, realizing that the clearing was a sweep of stone flooring, and the forest was a regular array of pillars in a cloister effect all around the chamber. From one spot among the pillars a dull red glow emerged, as if from a light burning some distance along a corridor, though there was no way of telling how many other corridors might also open among those cloisters. The light failed to reveal the height or nature of the entrance hall's ceiling, but it did reach far enough to illumine what Aurilia had seen – a wide and grandly curving stone staircase rising on the far side of the hall.

'I hope all the doors in this place aren't those spinning things,' Red muttered. 'I *hate* that feeling.'

'The stairs look normal,' Aurilia said. 'Let's go.'

As they moved silently across the hall, Red saw that some of the black fog that had formed the vortex opening seemed to stay with them. Then, peering through the darkness, he saw that it infested the whole building – drifting along the floor at ankle-height, collecting and slowly seething in the corners and around the bases of the pillars. And because of it they reached the bottom of the grand stairway before they noticed a narrower, less imposing flight of steps behind it, leading downwards into impenetrable blackness.

'That goes below ground,' Krost rumbled, as if to himself.

'Castles sometimes have dungeons,' Aurilia said quietly. 'For prisoners.'

Krost nodded, hefting the great staff. 'Let us begin there.'

'Always start at the bottom,' Red said wryly, as they moved to the descending stairway.

It was one thing going down, one slow step at a time, staying pressed against the wall in total and blinding darkness. It was quite another thing to stand at the bottom of the stairway with no idea at all of what lay around them or ahead.

'Red,' Aurilia whispered, 'let's risk some light, just for an instant – from the sword. Then I'll veil us again.'

Red was only too willing. Gripping the hilt, he drew the blade slightly from the sheath, so that a narrow beam of light spilled out, illuminating their surroundings. They saw a short, narrow corridor of harsh, blank stone. Leading to a featureless wall – a dead end.

As Red released the tense breath he had been holding, and glanced around to see how revealingly the light from the sword shone back up the stairs, Aurilia stepped up to the dead-end wall. 'Open,' she commanded.

Nothing happened. The wall remained solid. And Krost growled with disappointment as he moved up with her, prodding moodily at the unrelenting stone. 'Why would they build stairs down to nowhere?' he asked.

Aurilia shrugged. 'It can't be a dungeon without an opening.'

242

At once, to everyone's amazement, the stone of the dead-end wall began to be transformed, as if it was evaporating into black fog that roiled and seethed and began to spin.

'So which word *was* it?' Aurilia asked wonderingly.

'No matter,' Krost rumbled. 'Such a doorway would make a secure prison – for a prince.'

'For us, too, maybe,' Red muttered. But he knew very well that having come that far, nothing would stop his friends going through that vortex too, whatever might await them, in case their prince was there. So, with the blade still slightly drawn, he moved forward to join them. But he was still some paces behind them when, without a backward glance, they walked into the vortex, Aurilia leading the way.

As they vanished into the dark swirl, Red strode grimly up to the opening. But then for a fateful moment he hesitated. It was a reflex hesitancy, born of his knowledge of how it was going to feel, the dislocating sensation within the cells of his body. And it was no more than a second, perhaps two. But it was enough.

Before he could take a stride into the spinning tunnel-mouth, the dark fog of the vortex began to contract and fade.

And then it simply vanished – to leave Red staring in total horror at a blank stone wall.

TWENTY-FIVE

In that moment his mind went as blank as the wall that barred his way. Some saving instinct kept him from shouting aloud – but nothing could keep him from flinging himself at the solid stone, hammering at it with his fists, clawing futilely at it until his nails splintered. In his mindless attack he was gasping and snarling deep in his throat, his panic emerging as fury. But then he stopped, silenced, as sudden new dread poured over him in a wave.

A piercing, echoing scream filled the castle around him. In sudden icy fright at first he thought it was his own voice, out of control at last, but even before the reverberations began to fade, he recognized the scream, and realized why it had been been sharply cut off.

It was a horse, not too far away in the corridor leading from the entrance hall: Ulniss's horse, in an extreme of anguish and terror, as it went to the slaughter for the Barachi feast.

It was followed by a burst of Barachi howling, muffled by the intervening space but audibly gleeful. Red, shaky and sweaty, leaned back against the stone and gave silent thanks that the Barachi had been fully occupied with their rituals and had not been wandering past where they might have heard his frantic assault on the wall.

But his rational mind, back in control, knew that the Barachi preoccupations with feasting would be the only advantage he had. He had to assume that he was no longer veiled – that Aurilia, wherever she was, would probably not still be able to reach him with her magic. Only darkness cloaked him at that moment, since he had resheathed his sword fully. And darkness would be little use against the Barachi nocturnal vision, if any of them were to come his way.

So he was exposed, and alone, in the enemy's stronghold. With no way of knowing where his friends were or what had befallen them. If they were unharmed, he knew they would be trying – with all their considerable resources – to find their back to him. But meanwhile, he did not care for the idea of waiting indefinitely in the dark dead-end.

He turned to face the wall, fighting for calm. 'Open,' he said softly.

The wall's stone face remained unchanged. He fought down an urge to strike it again, and struggled to think of the exact words that Aurilia had used to create the vortex. Something about 'no dungeon without an opening', he thought. But when he muttered those words aloud, the wall remained as it was.

For a moment he felt almost dizzy with frustration and despair. Maybe the magic has to recharge itself or something, he thought. Maybe it only works at certain times – or for certain voices . . .

But there were too many maybes, and he felt too ignorant of the workings of magic. Whatever was the truth about the vortices, he knew that he was stuck there, at least for a while. All he could do, then, was to wait – in hopes that the vortex might eventually open, and re-unite him with his friends. Because without them, he had little chance . . .

He pushed that thought away, to balk another wave of panic. Think, think, he told himself desperately, breathing deeply, clenching his bruised fists, digging broken nails into his palms so that the small pain might keep his mind clear. If they come back, he thought, I have to be somewhere near by, so they can find me. But not here. Find a place to hide, he told himself – a waiting place.

He steadied himself, used a finger's width of sword-blade to light up the corridor for orientation, then crept back towards the staircase they had descended. Silently he moved up the steps, back to the great entrance hall ringed with its cloistering pillars. There the dim red glow from the side corridor still reached out into the shadows – and with it came the muffled sounds of Barachi, along that corridor, croaking and snarling at their feast.

Briefly he glanced across the breadth of the hall to the blank wall where they had formed the vortex that was their

245

entrance. But he dismissed the thought. He did not want to be outside the castle if his friends reappeared – especially not if they were in some kind of trouble when they did so. Anyway, he had had enough of vortices for that day. And then his skin prickled with new dread as a fearsome thought occurred to him. What if the openings were *not* automatic, as Aurilia suggested they were? What if they were manipulated every time by Talonimal? What if the sorcerer had simply lured them in, captured Krost and Aurilia – and was then playing a tantalizing terror game with him, laughing at his feeble attempts to get through a solid wall like a fly buzzing in a jar?

He stared fearfully around. Suddenly he could almost feel Talonimal's brooding, darkly magical presence – in every block of stone, in all the inky spaces between the pillars, in every drift and coil of the black fog that thickened the shadows. The feeling turned his legs to water, so that he had to lean against the wall for support, staring at the darkness wildly as if waiting for a sudden monstrous assault. But as he remained alone, in silence, unharmed, his strength and his reason slowly reasserted themselves. No, he thought – surely if Talonimal *had* captured Krost and Aurilia, he would have no reason to close the dungeon wall and leave Red wandering free around the castle.

Not that *free* was exactly the right word, he thought grimly. And in that moment he heard a new and louder burst of croaking howls from the Barachi down the corridor – an outcry that sounded almost as if they were emerging from their feast. He knew that the dim light from their corridor shone its dull redness on him, where he crouched at the top of that one narrow stairway, near the first steps of the larger stairway's upward sweep. He also knew that he did not want to try hiding among the pillars on that ground floor where the Barachi were.

So, with another deep breath, he turned and fled silently up the curving breadth of the main staircase.

On the way he kept the sword-blade firmly in its sheath, feeling almost glad of the shadowed dimness. For the banisters of that stairway were decorated with a series of carvings in dark metal – depictions of ghastly and twisted forms, human and not-human, involved in the most repellent variety of perversions and sadisms. Feeling sickened, keeping his gaze averted, he climbed unseen.

There was enough of the dim light to confirm that he had reached the upper floor of the keep, and that he stood on a broad, stately balcony, or perhaps a gallery, with a carved stone balustrade, running all the way around a central opening or well that looked down on to the main hall. Tall, ornate doors stood at intervals all around it, obviously leading to unknown upper chambers. And there were also heavy, decorated draperies or hangings at each corner – which, he guessed, probably covered some kind of access to the castle's four towers.

He paused briefly at the top of the stairs to study the layout, listening hard for threatening sounds. But when only silence and shadow prevailed, he began slowly to prowl along the gallery, staying near the wall away from the balustrade so as not to be seen if anyone looked up from the hall below. Again he was glad of the lack of light as he dimly glimpsed more grotesque works of art along the walls, paintings and tapestries, monstrous and perverse. He passed the tall doors nervously in his prowling, willing them to remain shut, but began to think that one of the sets of hangings at the corners might offer the best hiding place. They would allow him to peer through a small gap in their draperies, watch the gallery and perhaps not be trapped. So he crept on, teeth gritted, trying to breathe deeply to steady his clamouring nerves, and reached out to one of the sets of hangings.

Just as other hangings, at the directly opposite corner of the gallery, were flung aside with a sudden snap and rustle. And someone began to step out.

Red dropped with instinctive speed, shock racing through him like cold flame. He crouched behind the stone balustrade, staring through a gap between its carved supports, trying to identify the shadowy figure that emerged. Then the other person – who had, thankfully, failed to notice him in the dimness – reached the top of the staircase and was touched by more of the red glow from below. And Red had no difficulty recognizing the lank yellow hair of Vanticor, even though the poor light hid his scarred face and black-and-green garb.

Vanticor seemed totally at ease, not looking around as he started down the stairs. He even seemed to be smiling to himself. Looking happy, Red said to himself. Maybe he's heading down to join the Barachi for dinner. Or maybe Taloni-mal has been telling him he's a good boy for bringing in the prince. But it's interesting that the servants used the stairs, not magic openings.

And then he went suddenly very still, hardly breathing. *Servants*, he thought. Where are they? He recalled the busy, liveried people scurrying constantly to and fro in the prince's palace. Yet in the sorcerer's castle, he had seen none. Was that luck, he wondered, or weren't there any? He somehow doubted if the savage Barachi would be much use at washing, dusting, and general housekeeping. Maybe a super-sorcerer does all that by magic, he thought. I hope so – because I really don't want to run into the butler.

Cautiously, chilled again by that thought, he reached out as before for the hangings at the corner. At least, he told himself, I know where one of the bad guys *isn't*. And if Vanticor *was* visiting his boss over there on the far side of the gallery, then I can be fairly sure that neither of them is in here.

Nerves vibrating, feeling that he would give anything to have Krost and Aurilia there to help him know what to do, he drew the hangings aside and stepped through – into total blackness. Holding his breath, hand on sword-hilt, he peered uselessly around, waiting, listening, even sniffing the air, poised to fight or flee. At last he felt sure, as sure as he would ever be, that there was no one in that lightless space with him. So he gathered his courage and his battle-readiness, and again slid from its sheath a narrow portion of the glowing blade.

Its comforting light showed him to be totally alone. Ahead he saw a short narrow passage, almost an alcove, with a small flight of steps at the far end, leading to another ornately carved door reinforced with dark metal. He wanted very much to stay just where he was, within the shelter of the alcove behind the hangings. But he knew that the door spelled danger, if someone was to come out of it while he was hiding there. The alcove could not be his hiding-place, he knew, unless he first went to see what, if anything, might be seen beyond that door.

He moved to the steps, then to the door, gripped its handle, took a deep shaky breath, resheathed the luminous sword, and turned the handle with agonizing slowness. Pushing the door gently open a crack, he saw only more unrelenting blackness. But in a moment or two his eyes began to adjust again from the effect of the sword's light, and he saw that there was some sort of light source beyond the door. He shrank back a little, new tension clutching at him – but his other senses detected no movement or breathing on the far side of the door, and no odours except a faint, slightly rich sweetness. Slowly his returning night vision began to make out shapes within the blackness, until he suddenly realized that he was looking at the bottom of a spiral staircase, with dim light filtering down from the top of it, and no one else in sight.

Relief made him almost gasp aloud. Of course he might have expected stairs, he thought, since this had to be an entrance to one of the towers. And again, though the idea filled him with new dread, he faced the fact that he had either to learn whether some danger lurked at the top or to find a different hiding-place. I suppose since I've come this far, he told himself shakily. I doubt if I'll be much safer creeping around somewhere else.

He forced his reluctant feet to the spiral staircase, set them to climbing silently, strove to shut down the clamour of his fear. This could lead to a place of safety, he told himself. No reason why not. At least there was a chance. And he had spent his whole life being ready to take chances.

At the top of the stairs he found a narrow door, standing half open, with brighter light – flickering like candlelight – pouring through it. Hardly breathing, moving with concentrated care, Red peered around the door's edge and saw a narrow room full of furniture that looked like some kind of sitting room.

It was empty of people – he made sure of that first, in the

golden glow from the one small lamp, its flame enclosed in translucent crystal. And he saw that the furnishings were luxurious to the point of opulence, but also undeniably distasteful. The air was heavy with the over-sweet perfume that he had detected from below, the walls held pictures and hangings with abstract patterns that somehow troubled the eye, and everything was unpleasantly dark, including the purplish-black carpet with another ugly pattern and the wood-panelled walls that seemed to absorb the light.

Weird, he thought. And it was weirder still when he saw that the hangings were actually drapes, floor-length, pulled partly across slit windows with deep sills like stony window-seats. And through the nearest window, just visible as the lamplight reached out to it, he could see what looked like some kind of slightly curved wall, no more than an arm's length or two away. Which had to be the Dome, he realized – the upper curve, the inside surface.

Only then did he gather his nerve and creep into the sitting room. And the change in the angle of his vision showed him the bright crack outlining one section of the panelled wall – which looked like the tiny space around another door, leading to an adjoining room. He edged forward, boots silent on the thick carpet, taking desperate care not to touch any furniture on the way. Through the crack of the door in the panelling he peered through into a smaller room, just as lavishly furnished, dominated by a huge bed with silken coverings of dark purple and a heavy black canopy swooping over its carved posts. Again the carpet was thick and the walls panelled – again one small lamp did what it could to hold back the shadows – again the room seemed deserted.

Red took several moments to open the bedroom door, braced against a hinge's squeak. Safely inside the bedroom, noting that it too had slit windows with hangings drawn partly over them, he focused mostly on the evidence that it was a woman's room. The sickly perfume seemed even heavier there, articles of feminine clothing were scattered on the bed and elsewhere, unmistakable containers of cosmetics and the like cluttered the top of a dressing table with a tall mirror above it. So Talonimal has a playmate in his castle, Red thought – and his heart sank, knowing that he could not remain in that tower, in case the sorcerer or his lady decided it was time for bed.

And even as the thought formed, a sudden sound behind him made him leap like a terrified beast.

Reflex turned the leap into a lunge for safety, behind the nearest set of floor-length drapes half-covering a window. And luck made it a silent leap, with no scrape of the sword's scabbard against stone. In the shadowed alcove behind the thick cloth he turned, heart hammering, to peer through a narrow gap in the drapes and see what had made the terrifying sound.

It had been the clatter of yet another door, he saw – an even narrower opening in the bedroom's panelling. At first the person who had opened the door was just a silhouette, framed against candlelight from the room beyond, where Red saw a basin and the edge of a crude water closet much like the dubious amenities in the palace. Then the person closed the door, standing for a moment as if lost in thought, and Red could see her clearly. She was worth seeing, too, he thought – young, slim, with a heart-shaped face, smooth pale skin, long dark hair. Girlishly attractive, almost beautiful – except perhaps for the hints of something like petulance and tension around the delicate mouth.

The young woman moved further into the bedroom, glancing idly around, while Red held his breath. In front of the mirror above the dressing table she studied herself, twirling the long skirts of her gown. It was a sweeping, floor-length gown of pale mauve, much embroidered, with a round collar that showed off the smooth throat just as the well-fitted bodice showed off the small round breasts beneath it. But then her thoughtful expression became a scowl. She whirled from the mirror and almost startled Red into another leap – by speaking, sharply, to the blank panelling of the wall nearest her.

'I want a *black* dress instead,' she said, her voice almost shrill. 'More low-cut than this, not so loose-fitting. Elegant and simple.'

She went silent then, apparently waiting, visibly growing impatient as the seconds passed, while Red watched with

251

puzzlement. But then a garment materialized in mid-air, against the wall where the young woman was staring. It was a long gown made of iridescent purple silk, with flounces on its full skirt, ruffles on its sleeves, a floppy bow on its neckline.

So the sorcerer's lady is magical too, Red thought. That sorts out the question of where the servants are, here. Even if she's not too good at it. And he almost smiled, despite his tension, to see the sudden wrath that twisted the young woman's face as she glared at the purple dress.

'No!' she shrilled. 'I said *black*! And I don't want *this* – or *this* . . .'

With each word she stabbed a finger furiously at the dress, and with each stab a feature of the garment changed. It became a gleaming black, its flounces and ruffles and other embellishments vanished. Finally, when it was narrowed and refined to a smooth, narrow, graceful sheath, she grasped it from where it hung in mid-air and flung it on the bed, before turning back to her mirror.

'Remove these things,' she snapped. Again nothing happened, for several seconds. Again her face twisted in fury. 'Clothes!' she spat. 'Remove my *clothes*!'

Suddenly, electrifyingly, she was naked. And Red stared, transfixed, as she stood unselfconsciously studying herself in the mirror, her slim shapeliness painted golden by the lamplight. Then she sat down at the dressing table, picked up a hairbrush and glared at it.

'I'm not trusting *you* to work for me today,' she said tautly. For a moment or two she attacked her long hair with the brush – but then, abruptly, flung it furiously across the room.

'Why can't I have some *maids*?' she wailed at the mirror.

At once she seemed to shrink, to cower, to look around like a nervous, guilty child. But when her outburst received no response, she turned back to her preparations – touching her face here and there with cosmetics, touching her body with the stopper from a vial of the heavy perfume. For a long motionless moment she examined the effect, then rose to her feet again, moistening her lips, running her hands lightly down over her breasts, smiling an unpleasantly knowing little smile at her reflection.

'Now,' she snapped, 'underclothes, then the black dress.'

For several seconds once again, nothing happened, while her face began to clench into another mask of fury. But then, in an eye-blink, she was fully clothed, the black gown sheathing her in a smooth and perfect fit. She leaned forward to make some minimal adjustment to the revealing neckline, but stopped, again unmoving. And Red just managed to avoid clutching at the drapes to support himself, amid a new wave of fear.

The mirror no longer showed the reflection of the young woman standing before it. It showed the image of a man with silver hair and a high-collared robe, gazing steadily out at her with deep-set eyes. And Red was jolted again when the image spoke, in a resonant baritone.

'I fear I shall be delayed a while, my love,' the image said.

The young woman scowled and pouted. 'But Talonimal . . .'

'I hope not to be long,' the image in the mirror said firmly, while Red stared through the drapes, studying the face of the enemy. 'But I have arranged that . . . *contact* which I mentioned before, and I cannot postpone it now. You must rest a while, to be fresh for our important encounter later.'

The words were meant to be soothing, but the young woman was not to be appeased. 'I'm not in the *least* tired!' she said shrilly. 'And I'm all *ready* – despite the fact that all the servitor spells you gave me are growing *weak* again!' She paused, looking suddenly tense and afraid. 'Are you . . . have you overtaxed yourself?'

'Not in the slightest,' the image said, sounding annoyed. 'They merely need reinforcement, as spells often do. I shall attend to them soon.'

'If you would give me my *own* magical power,' the young woman flared, 'I could attend to them myself!'

The image glowered. 'I have no time for that argument again, Evelane. I shall join you shortly, when we shall go together to confront your father.'

The image vanished, leaving the young woman glaring pettishly at herself in the mirror. Turning away, she snapped a stream of angry orders at the empty air, which eventually resulted in her being reclothed in a filmy nightdress and her bed being turned down. But Red scarcely noticed. Instead, he was leaning shakily back against the stony edge of the window, behind the hangings, trying to come to terms with what the sorcerer's image in the mirror had revealed.

TWENTY-SIX

Evelane. The name was echoing in his mind. The *princess*? Not an abducted captive but a pampered resident, entirely at ease and at home in her dark tower. Being called 'my love' by Talonimal. And apparently going with him at some point to confront the prince her father, who certainly *was* a captive . . .

It was too much for him to take in. He peered out again, in time to see her turn down the lamp before climbing into bed with a petulant flounce. So she *is* going to have a nap, Red thought. To be fresh for . . . whatever they're planning. And he settled grimly back, mind awhirl, to wait for her to go to sleep.

It took less than half an hour before Evelane was breathing deeply and regularly, with occasional delicate snores. But Red felt as if a month had passed when he finally crept slowly out and across the room, then through the sitting room and out of the door. Swiftly he descended from the tower, back on to the gallery, back to creeping through shadows. And all the while his thoughts were in turmoil as he wondered how he could tell Aurilia and Krost – if ever he found them – that they had risked their lives to come and rescue a princess who didn't need rescuing.

By then the appalling truth that he had learned was making him deeply angry – so much so that he was growing less careful, more reckless, as he renewed his search for a place to hide. Not only did he open some of the doors around the gallery, but he peered in and around by the light of his blade. Luck kept him undiscovered, but brought him no obvious place of safety in the dusty, obviously seldom-used chambers. Eventually it occurred to him to try a third tower, for if Evelane was in one and Talonimal was in the other where Vanticor had been, then the further two towers might be empty. The logic was less than sound, but in his careless, angry mood it was enough. So he crept past another set of hangings into another alcove, past another ornate door, and up another spiral staircase. He paused, half-way up, noticing another faint gleam of light reaching out towards him from the door at the top of the stairs. Not empty, then, he thought angrily – and kept going up, determined to have a look at whatever new shocks this tower held.

But at the door he paused, listening. From the chamber beyond the door he could hear a voice raised suddenly, in apparent anger. A voice that he had just heard coming weirdly from a mirror in Evelane's bedroom. Talonimal's voice, then, sounding almost smug within its anger.

So he had been wrong, he thought sourly, about the tower where Vanticor had been leaving. But then this one could easily be somewhere that the sorcerer had magically shifted himself, for whatever dark purposes. He said something to Evelane about a *contact* – and whoever he was talking to, he sounded as if he didn't like them much. But not Phaedran, for he had said they would see the prince later.

The thought struck him that the sorcerer might have Aurilia and Krost in that tower, as the target for his smug anger.

Slowly he crouched at the top of the stairs, putting one eye to the crack of the door where the light dimly gleamed. As he did so he heard more clearly not only the voice but the words of Talonimal, beyond the door.

'—do well to remember,' he was saying, 'that you are here in this manner by sufferance, and are in no position to hurl threats.'

Sufferance? It seemed an odd word to use to a prisoner. But in his belief that his friends might be there, his reckless courage bypassed such thoughts. He began carefully to turn the door handle, a hair's breadth at a time, at last pushing the door slightly open. The hinges made no complaint, the whole operation was as soundless as one of the wisps of black fog. But any noise from Red might well have been covered, as it happened, by the sound of another voice, replying to Talonimal. A voice that seemed oddly hollow, as if from the bottom of a well, yet that was strong enough and filled with rough anger.

'If you keep on refusing to answer my questions, Taloni-mal,' the voice said, 'you'll find that my threats aren't empty.'

By then Red had edged forward into a position where he could see through the partly open door. And before anything else, disappointment struck him like a club as he saw no sign of Aurilia or Krost within the room. But also, with the disappointment came astonishment and a new wave of fear.

His first glance showed him that it was a large room, occupying the entire breadth of the tower rather than being divided into rooms like Evelane's. The place was furnished with a variety of tables and cabinets and the like, which contained an orderly profusion of books, papers, peculiar implements, things that looked like old-fashioned chemical equipment, and many more things that Red only glimpsed and mostly failed to recognize. But in any case his attention was focused on the tall, silver-haired figure of Talonimal standing at one end of the room, quite alone, speaking in his confidently angry, resonant voice to . . . a picture on the wall.

It was a bright picture, the main source of light in the room, but what stirred Red's amazement and fear was that it was moving – and speaking, with the harsh voice he had heard before – very like a television screen. So it had to be magic. Then he peered more closely, and was further unnerved. The picture showed a man – stocky, bald, wearing a fur robe, sitting in a sort of forest. And he wasn't looking *out* of the picture; he was looking down at a huge bowl at his feet – a bowl filled with a dark shiny liquid. On its surface Red could see a tiny image of the silver-haired Talonimal, just as he was then, speaking to his wall.

Red vaguely grasped what he was seeing. Talonimal had conjured up a picture of someone on his magic screen. The someone had called up a simultaneous picture of Talonimal in a magic bowl. In that way they had formed a connection like a TV link and could speak to one another.

Equally interestingly, they were not having a friendly chat at all.

'You can deny what you're doing all you like, Talonimal,' the fur-robed man was growling. 'But I'm not a fool. I've *seen*.

257

I know you want the leadership of the Order. I know why you've been abducting the women—'

'You do not *know* these things, Lebarran,' Talonimal interrupted smoothly. 'You merely surmise them. You send your monsters, your Zhraike, to harry me and kill my servants on the basis of wild suspicion alone. It is unjust. It is the act of a tyrant. You—'

'Tyrant?' roared the man called Lebarran. 'You forget yourself! I am the *Magister*, creator of the Order of the Apotheosis – which you once pledged to serve, and to obey!'

So you're the one who sent the Zhraike, Red thought. Go to it, then. Any enemy of Talonimal has to be a friend of mine.

'I have never denied your power or pre-eminence,' Talonimal calmly replied. 'As I have told you, I have simply absented myself from the Order for a time of contemplation and study. I am not the first High Adept to do so . . .'

Lebarran snorted. 'Lies. Why should you raise such a powerful shielding, if you're just *studying* behind it?'

'You know very well,' Talonimal said with a cool smile. 'Princess Evelane has chosen to join me here, without her father's permission, and Phaedran is a vengeful man who has hated me for years. I believe he has actually launched a force against me, which will prove the value of my protective Dome.'

'I'm sure *you* know very well,' Lebarran rasped, 'that Phaedran's force was destroyed on Lake Tenebrial. By a remarkable typhoon, it seems. Though I happen to know that the prince and his royal barge escaped destruction. And I'm sure you know exactly where Phaedran is at this moment.'

'Wandering in the Woodlands, no doubt,' Talonimal said with an elaborate shrug. 'I am not much concerned. Not enough to waste time and strength on spells of seeking.'

Lebarran's hot eyes flared. 'Really? But you seem to have such strength to spare, Talonimal. Especially when you can muster such high spells of shielding to raise this Dome. Why, it's almost as if your powers have . . . grown.'

Talonimal's smile was dismissive. 'I suggest that you have always underestimated my powers. From the vantage point of your own great strength, Magister, it cannot be easy to assess other Adepts accurately.'

Lebarran leaned forward, glaring. 'Give me no more lies and evasions. I know what you're doing. Just as I know that you created this Dome to protect yourself against *me*. You knew you'd face my wrath when I learned the truth about you. That's why you fear to face me now, but allow only my scrying sight to enter your lair.'

'Why should I invite you in person,' Talonimal replied coldly, 'when you have without provocation sent your Zhraike to attack me?'

'Provocation?' Lebarran's voice dropped to an ominous, hollow bass. 'Let's set out the facts – or perhaps the charges. Your Barachi creatures have been roaming Quamarr, abducting women of the Sisterhood . . .'

'So I am now also a kidnapper?' Talonimal broke in. 'But there are no Sisters here, Lebarran. If the Barachi have been stealing women, it may be to feed their own distasteful appetites. I shall certainly reproach them.'

'Lies.' Lebarran's distant voice sounded like a murmur from a grave, and Red shivered at the door where he crouched and watched. 'The witches have *been* here – and if they're here no longer, I know where they've gone. You've used them in the most forbidden extreme of the dark side of the Art. The foulest, most dangerous act in all of the Higher Magic. You've used them in *sacrifice*.'

'You have no evidence for such an accusation,' Talonimal said, his own voice as icy as a polar wind. 'Beware, Lebarran. One of the risks of supreme power is that its holder can fall victim to delusions of plots and persecutions . . . seeing perils where none exists . . .'

'*Lies!*' Lebarran bellowed. 'You *are* sacrificing, to enlarge your magical strength! You're making offerings and partaking unnaturally of what is offered! Do you think I don't *know* about such things? Every mage has peered briefly at the forbidden texts, has felt the temptation . . .'

'You have no evidence,' Talonimal repeated tensely.

'And which Power,' Lebarran went on, as if the other man had not spoken, 'are you offering to? To some petty, treacher-

259

ous demon from a farther Realm, as too many misguided fools before you have done? Oh, no. I think the real reason why you're hiding here behind your Dome, fearful of my wrath, is that you've found your own way to the Void Beyond and have succeeded in invoking the Unformed!'

Talonimal nodded stiffly. 'Now we come to it, do we not? You fear that you will be displaced. You fear that *I* might gain pre-eminence in the Order and in the world.'

'I'll tell you what I fear.' Lebarran's voice had dropped again, into a deep grinding resonance like a tremor in the earth's bowels. 'I fear that you won't be able to control what you've begun. I fear the truth that every mage in the past who risked the forbidden act of sacrifice has been destroyed by it. Which is *why* it's forbidden. Fool, do you think I formed the Order of the Apotheosis because I *enjoy* sharing power? I gathered you all because I knew the risks! Even *I* felt unable to control the might of the Unformed, alone, without others to help impose restraints in conclave!' He pointed a thick finger at the image of Talonimal in his scrying bowl. 'But now *you*, with your private greeds and lusts and ambitions, are putting it all at risk. Fool, can't you see? Your sacrifices can make the Unformed stronger too, as well as yourself! If you go on with this madness, the threshold won't contain it! You'll bring the One Beyond ravening from its bridge prematurely, before it's formed! And it could destroy the world!'

Talonimal stood motionless, staring coldly at Lebarran's image. In the silence that followed the outburst, the dire last words of the Magister seemed to echo around the chamber. And Red found that he was clammy with sweat and shaking with impending horror.

'Is that really the danger that you see, Lebarran?' Talonimal said finally. 'Or are those merely the warnings that you brandish at your acolytes in the Order, to keep them cowed while you plunder their strength to fulfil your own ambition? In any case, be advised that I am an acolyte no longer, and your threats do not trouble me.'

'No?' Lebarran asked in that cavernous voice. 'You'd best be very sure of that, Talonimal. I'll test your Dome tirelessly. And if I find any weakness, where I can thrust in with more than a scrying eye, I'll bring your protection down like a wall of straw and crush you as I would a beetle underfoot!'

Talonimal's face contorted with fury. 'Lebarran,' he snarled, 'it may be that before long I shall see fit to emerge from my Dome. And when I do, you would be well advised to restrict your crushing urges to insects!'

'Say you so?' Lebarran's eyes were volcanic, but he was smiling a terrible slow smile. 'Then, by all the Realms, you've proved the case against you. You *must* be striving to grow, by sacrifice, if you've started dreaming dreams of challenging *me*. So I'll be waiting, fool, whenever you choose to come out and offer that challenge. Except I don't think you ever will. Because if the Unformed reaches across the threshold before its time, you and your petty dreams of power will merely be the first things to be destroyed.'

Talonimal's laughter was tense and mirthless. 'You may cling to that hope, you and your Order of idiots, until I come among you to take my rightful place. Until then, go back to ranting among your dead trees. This discussion is at an end.'

He waved a hand, and the image on the scrying stone vanished.

'And I promise you, *Magister*,' he added, almost spitting the words at the blank stone, 'that you will not wait too long for me. The alignments are gathering – and before long I shall be more powerful than you dare to dream.'

He wheeled away from the wall, dark robe flaring, and stalked to one of the cluttered tables. Snatching up a faded parchment, he frowned down at its pages. 'Yes, it is certain,' he muttered. 'Only this day . . . then midday of the following . . .'

Suddenly he stopped and straightened. The frown on his face gave way to a look of astonishment combined with savage delight. At the door some instinct raised an alarm within Red's mind, so that he began to turn, to leap . . .

But the sorcerer gestured, one hand aglow. The door was flung open with a crash, and something like invisible bands of metal clamped around Red's body, holding him motionless.

'Corodel, is it not?' Talonimal drawled with a savage smile. 'The young outlander wearing a dead hero's name? Yet quite heroic enough yourself, it seems, to roam my castle alone and even find your way to my spell-chamber, undiscovered! And after the witch and the dwarf-giant *assured* me that you died in the swamps.'

He waved his hand briefly, and the unseen bands around Red seemed to lift him, to hold him floating lightly above the floor.

'Let me make you welcome, young man,' the sorcerer went on. 'You cannot know how pleased I am that you have presented yourself in time to join the others – in the fire.'

Red scarcely heard the sorcerer's final words, and had no idea what they might mean. He was too occupied with his soul-shattering capture, and Talonimal's indication that Aurilia and Krost were also captives, or worse. Held floating there by immovable, unseen bonds, Red felt strength draining from him with the despairing knowledge of how hopeless it had been all along to think that the three of them could hope to penetrate the Dome undiscovered and oppose such magical might.

He saw the sorcerer beckon with a glowing finger, felt himself float across the room, to dangle in the air in front of Talonimal. He strove then with all his will to summon some courage, or at least bravado, to return the other man's scrutiny with an unwavering gaze.

But Talonimal simply studied him as he would a specimen, smiling his cruel smile. After a moment he reached out to grasp Red's jaw in his hand, turning his face this way and that. 'Good-looking enough, in a common sort of way,' he said musingly. 'An athletic and boyish appeal, certainly, though somewhat in need of bathing. I wonder if my beloved would find it exciting if I were to bring you into our bed tonight.'

Red did not move his body because he could not, but his eyes and his grimace were full of revulsion. 'You'd have to kill me first,' he said hoarsely.

Talonimal laughed a cold laugh, withdrawing his hand. 'No, no, young man. I know of course that you would not be so sophisticated as to be willing – but I could make you so. I could twist your mind and soul, Corodel, so that you crawled to me *begging* to be seduced, afire with corrupt cravings.' He laughed again at Red's sickened expression. 'But do not fear – I shall not. I must abstain a while from such delights, to ready myself for a supreme ceremony. In which your death will be of far more value to me than your violation.'

Red did not respond – but the sorcerer's eyebrows lifted at the change in his captive's face. 'Well, well,' he said ironically. 'The threat of death seems to disturb you *less* than my first suggestion. But it might be otherwise if you had understood anything of what you clearly heard here just now.'

'I understood enough,' Red snarled. 'Enough to know you have a powerful enemy who scares you.'

'Lebarran?' Talonimal curled his lip. 'You understand nothing. For all his power, he cannot reach into the Dome . . .'

'He got his image in,' Red said quickly.

'I *allowed* the scrying contact,' the sorcerer snapped. 'And only that, fully protected by shielding spells. No, he cannot touch me and I do not fear him. And you and your friends, Corodel, will in fact aid me to reach a level where *he* will come to fear *me*.'

'Don't be too sure,' Red said harshly. 'Remember that *we* got into your Dome easily enough . . .'

'And showed me how to stop it happening again,' Talonimal said. 'That vortex, which opens through the Dome itself, can no longer be activated by any one but me, directly. I am grateful to you for showing me that possible weakness.'

Red forced himself to remain silent, realizing that there was no point in debating with the enemy. So he merely watched with a sick emptiness as Talonimal moved one glowing hand – and the belt and sheath that held the sword of Corodel came away from Red's waist and floated over on to a nearby table.

'I am also grateful to you for providing me with such a glamorous and legendary blade,' the sorcerer said with a smirk. 'I shall enjoy having it. And while I can use any blade in the ceremony to come, it will be amusing, tomorrow, to use this one. For a purpose that would incalculably affront the witches who created it.' He raised his hand. 'Now be gone, Corodel. Join your friends, to expand their sense of helplessness and loss of hope. I shall visit you all soon, to offer some foreglimpses of what awaits you, and to introduce you to my beloved. That should plunge all of you into the deepest of desolations – from which, I promise you, you will never recover.'

Laughing his coldly cruel laugh, Talonimal gestured abruptly. Red braced himself, not knowing what to expect but feeling certain that he would not enjoy it. The bands of unseen force around him seemed to shift their grip, he could see a strange haze gathering around him, the separate cells of his body seemed to quiver towards a dislocation like that caused by the vortices . . .

And then he was standing on a cold stone floor, in a bare room with walls that glittered eerily. When Aurilia and Krost and Prince Phaedran turned to look at him, astounded.

Red stumbled slightly before finding his balance as the invisible bonds released their grip on his body. In the next instant he was clasped again, almost as firmly, by the smooth strong arms of Aurilia in her younger form. For a long moment they merely clung to each other, while Krost hovered and the prince watched with visible regret in his eyes.

'I thought I would never see you again,' Aurilia said, her voice muffled against his chest. 'And yet I would wish that you were not here, but elsewhere and safe.'

'There was never much chance of that,' Red said bleakly.

By then Krost had looked him up and down. 'You no longer have the sword, Red . . .'

'Friend Talonimal took a fancy to it,' Red replied, trying for a light tone.

Aurilia pulled back to look at him. 'You saw him when he captured you?' she asked. 'How did it happen?'

Red glanced briefly at the prince, wondering how he was going to manage to tell the Evelane part of the story. 'Tell me what happened to you, first,' he said.

It was a brief enough tale, he found. Aurilia and Krost had stepped through the vortex to find themselves in that chamber, which was indeed the castle's dungeon, with the prince there before them. And somehow Talonimal had been instantly aware of their arrival in the dungeon, and had shut down the vortex so that they were trapped. Then the sorcerer himself had magically materialized in the dungeon to gloat briefly over their capture and his triumph, and to promise that they would not have long to wait before his triumph was made complete.

'He said something about how we would meet our destiny by helping to fulfil *his* destiny,' Aurilia concluded. 'I imagine that means he'll kill us in some unpleasant way . . .'

Red grimaced, admiring her matter-of-fact tone. 'Maybe I can throw a little light on that,' he said.

As briefly as possible, then, he told them about his adventures – a sketchy account of his wanderings in the castle, sidestepping his discovery of Evelane in her tower to focus instead on what he had heard of the confrontation between Talonimal and the man named Lebarran Magister.

'*Sacrifice*.' Aurilia's eyes were wide and horrified, as if looking at some unnameable monstrosity. 'I can hardly believe . . . how could he *dare* . . .'

As words seemed to fail her, Phaedran nodded gloomily at Red. 'Lebarran is of course the mightiest mage in the Continent, the most powerful that this world has ever known. He is also moody, stormy, perhaps even unstable – and many people breathed more easily when he appeared to go into retreat, as a recluse, in some remote valley in the Southern Highlands.'

'The people of the Highlands were not pleased,' Krost said darkly. 'Yet we believed that he had kept to himself. No one guessed that he had recruited the Zhraike to his service.'

'No one seems to have known that he was setting up a power base, either,' Red said. 'With this Order that Talonimal seems to have resigned from.'

'The Order of the Apotheosis.' Aurilia repeated the words slowly, as if weighing them. 'But Apotheosis means a transformation on to a divine level – achieving the position and power of a *god*. Surely Lebarran cannot contemplate . . .'

And then she fell silent again, ashen with perceived horror.

Red frowned. 'What's most worrying here isn't Lebarran, it's Talonimal. Trying to make himself stronger, magically, by making these sacrifices to something evil. He's sacrificed all those Sisters, and – now it's our turn.'

'Doubtless the madman has also sacrificed my daughter,' Phaedran said tonelessly, holding himself very still.

'No, sir, he hasn't,' Red said, and watched the prince's eyes grow bright with hope.

'You *know* this to be true?' Phaedran asked quickly.

Red swallowed, glanced around as if looking for help, then decided to sidestep again. 'All I can tell you, sir,' he said vaguely, 'is that I'm sure she's alive and well inside this castle.'

The prince looked anxious to learn more, but Aurilia forestalled him, reaching to clutch Red's arm. She seemed not to have heard the exchange about Evelane – her eyes were still wide and unseeing in the grip of her private nightmare.

'Sacrifice,' she breathed again, her fingers steely on Red's arm. 'The most depraved and forbidden path for an Adept . . . But it is the only way that a mage can enlarge the magical power he was born with. Some have tried it, tempted by the vision of power, but none has ever succeeded. All have in the end been destroyed by the very evil to which they made their foul offerings . . .'

'Good,' Krost growled. 'So Talonimal will be destroyed too.'

'Probably not in time to help us,' Red said.

Aurilia stared at them, her eyes bright in her bloodless face. 'He will kill us in some ceremonial way, to offer up our life forces to the evil Power. And the ceremony will enable Talonimal as well to partake of a share of our life forces.'

'Like a magical cannibal,' Red muttered.

Aurilia went on, unhearing. 'A mage's magical power is bound up with his life force, inextricably. As Talonimal's life force is enlarged, by partaking of these offerings, so is his sorcerous gift. Especially when he has been offering . . . others who possess magic. Like the Sisters he has taken.'

'Then he will be glad to have *you*,' Phaedran said bluntly.

'Oh, yes,' she whispered. 'As one of the Named Nine, I may be the most powerful one that he has yet offered. His magic will be enormously enhanced. As it will be to some extent by *your* life forces – those of two strong warriors in their prime, and a prince of the blood royal.'

'He has not killed us yet,' Krost growled.

267

Aurilia gazed at him for a long moment, her distraught stare slowly coming back to focus, her painful grip on Red's arm loosening. 'No, he hasn't,' she agreed quietly. 'And . . . we may not be totally without resources to thwart him, even here.'

Krost nodded firmly. 'We are not defeated while we still live.'

'That is not what I meant,' Aurilia said. She smiled at them all then, a sweet sad smile that erased the look of horror from her face. 'Even in our defeat, now, we have some limited choice. Talonimal could not offer us in sacrifice if . . . if our life forces had already fled.'

Red began to frown, then understood. 'You mean we should *die*?' he asked angrily. 'Kill ourselves off so we don't become a main course for a supernatural cannibal? Seems a little hasty . . . And how would it work? I strangle you and Krost does the prince and then Krost and I draw lots or something, and the last one standing hits his head on the wall?'

'Even if it was only I who died,' Aurilia said stubbornly, 'the loss of my magic would be a huge setback for Talonimal.'

'Only until he grabbed a few more Sisters,' Red pointed out.

'None of us should think of dying,' Krost put in firmly, 'while there is still hope that something – an accident, a mistake – might offer us a chance to escape.'

'And I shall hold to life to the very end,' Phaedran snapped, 'in the hope of freeing Evelane from this evil place.'

Aurilia shook her head quickly, as if disposed to argue. But she had no time in which to make her point. They all were silenced in that instant by a strange disturbance in the air, near one end of the dungeon, midway between floor and ceiling. Red's heart lurched as he saw it, thinking that a vortex was forming, bracing himself to leap out through it or to confront whatever might be coming in. He felt the others grow tense as well, saw Krost's great muscles roll and bunch.

But it was more a stirring of the light, as if something was being shaped. It began to move faster, shimmering, then with shocking suddenness two human figures appeared, standing calmly and motionlessly in mid-air and looking down at the four prisoners with dreadful smiles.

The four stared back, numbed and speechless. Until at last Krost, before any of them, broke the silence.

'By all the Realms and Spheres!' he said, half-choking. '*Evelane!*'

Filled with grim compassion, Red looked around at the others. They all, especially Phaedran, looked paralysed with shock and incomprehension. Even so, he saw, Aurilia had for some reason gone through her shape-shift into her aged, grey-gowned form. But then Red's attention was drawn back to the two floating figures, fully clarified by then, full of gloating and cruelty.

'Greetings, father!' Evelane said with a shrill giggle. 'How nice of you to come so far, at such great cost, to *rescue* me!'

Phaedran paled under the impact of his daughter's malice. 'Evelane, dearest . . . I don't understand . . .'

'Of course not,' the young woman spat. 'When did you ever understand me, or seek to? You either sent me away or ignored me. Should you expect me in return to be a dutiful daughter? Oh, no, father dear. I have renounced you! Your foolish ill-fated rescue had no point from the start – for I am here because I *choose* to be!'

Phaedran flinched as if struck. In the same instant Krost growled and lunged forward – or tried to lunge. But he was mysteriously halted, as if his legs would not move. And Red tried to move his own feet, only to find that they were held rigid as if encased in stone.

'I thought it best to immobilize you,' Talonimal said, his evil smile broadening, 'during this little visit. You will also find that I have removed the feeble little witch-knots placed on your person. And the walls of this chamber—' he gestured at the strangely glittering stone— 'are themselves warded against any power that *you* might bring against them, witch. I would not want you to have any illusions about your help-lessness.'

Krost growled again, in fury, as Phaedran turned shakily to Aurilia. 'He has placed a spell on her, has he not? Controlling her mind . . . Or perhaps this is not my daughter but some demonic simulacrum . . .'

'I fear not, prince,' Talonimal told him. 'This is Evelane, her mind is free, and she is here because she wishes to be.' His gloating smile broadened as Evelane looked up at him with over-bright eyes.

'I'm sorry, sir, but it's true,' Red broke in flatly. 'I didn't know how to tell you . . . But I got into her tower, earlier, and watched her when she didn't know I was there. And – she's not a prisoner.'

Evelane, staring at him, giggled shrilly again. 'In my tower, watching me? Did you like what you saw?' Then she swung her fevered gaze back to the others. 'But you may believe it! I was not abducted – I was *rescued* from your ghastly palace, with its empty promises and suffocating memories . . . Talonimal visited me often, magically, in my chambers, though no one knew it – and always he was kind, concerned for *me*, as no one else was in that place of ghosts . . . He gave me gifts, used his power to take me places . . . told me tales of the past, how he too had suffered in the palace . . .' Her eyes were wide and rapturous. 'And then he offered me his love – and with it offered me so much, much more – and finally brought me away, brought me here, and became my lover, my wonderful tireless lover, who will make me his *consort* when he has conquered the world!'

In the echoing silence that followed those revelations, Phaedran groaned hollowly and Krost reached out a supporting hand towards him as he seemed to sway. But Aurilia had not taken her eyes from the face of Evelane, and her sudden harsh laugh struck like a whip.

'You fool of a girl!' she said fiercely. 'Succumbing to a seducer's false promises like any dairymaid . . .'

'They are *not* false!' Evelane shrilled. 'Talonimal loves me, and I love him! But what would you know of love, you who are both withered hag and scarlet whore . . .'

'Evelane!' Aurilia's voice lashed out again. 'I know more of love than Talonimal could ever teach you . . . And I know something of *him*, as well, just as your father does! Listen to me, child! Even before he was possessed of the evil that has

270

driven him to this Dome, Talonimal was known to be self-seeking, grasping, ruthlessly ambitious. Never, *never*, a man who could truly love another . . .'

'No!' Evelane shrieked. 'He loves me! He *does*!'

'It is not in his nature,' Aurilia said, her own voice rising furiously. 'Listen to me! Lust, yes, but not love . . . He brought you here, Evelane, to avenge himself on your father – and to impose his lust on you as he could never do on your mother, to whom he made advances many times in vain . . .'

'No!' Evelane raged. 'He loves me! *Me*!'

Through the storm of emotion Red saw that Talonimal was content to remain silent, smirking coldly at the strength of Evelane's devotion to him and the pain it was visibly causing to Phaedran. But the smirk began to fade at Aurilia's next words.

'If you believe in his love for you,' Aurilia said, 'then you would expect him to remain faithful to you. But that is not his *nature*, Evelane. Watch him. Watch his eyes.'

And she suddenly transformed herself – into her voluptuous younger form, hair tumbling down her back, wearing a long sheer gown as clinging and translucent as gauze. Red saw how Talonimal was at once betrayed by his own urges, how an ugly hunger appeared in his face as he stared at Aurilia's beauty.

But Evelane did not see it. She merely laughed, her shrill giggle. 'Foolish hag,' she said to Aurilia. 'What does it matter to me how he looks at others? We have often taken the young and pretty witches into *bed* with us, while they were prisoners here, to add to our own pleasures!' As Phaedran groaned again, anger returned to her face. 'But not *you*, old whore! He would not sully himself on *you*!'

Only then did she turn to Talonimal, who had had time to control his expression and was looking at Aurilia with a sneer.

'Quite so, witch,' he said. 'Your overblown charms hold no appeal for me. And my Evelane knows very well the depth of my feelings for her.'

The princess whirled back to look at Aurilia, triumph glittering in her eyes. 'You *see*,' she hissed, 'how your lies are exposed! You cannot turn me against him! We are bound together for ever, he and I – and when he is able to give me the gift of magic that the witches and my father *denied* me, he and I will *rule* . . . !'

'Is *that* what he promised you?' Aurilia broke in, looking appalled. 'That he would give you magical power? Evelane, don't you know that it cannot be *done*? The gift of magic cannot be conferred by *anyone*, not even the most powerful mage who ever lived!'

Evelane laughed harshly. 'So the Sisters told me, so my father told me. But I do not believe them! Talonimal *will* give me the gift, as he has promised – when he has grown so mighty that he has reached the level of a god . . .'

'Evelane,' Phaedran said brokenly, *'please* . . .'

'And you cannot make appeals to me, father!' she spat, turning her glare towards him. 'Would you have me return to be the forgotten, abandoned princess in that desolate place? Never! I was of no importance to you – and now you are as nothing to me! Except in one way, for one purpose!' Her eyes were bulging and flecks of foam showed at the corners of her mouth. 'Instead of a princess, I shall be a *queen*, Talonimal's queen, the consort of a god! And you will hasten that day, father, you and these others! You will help make him more powerful, so that none can stand against him! And you will do so because of the way that you are going to die! Painfully, horribly, *die*!'

TWENTY-EIGHT

As Evelane's last word rose into a hysterical shriek, Talonimal clamped a hand on her arm to quieten her. Slowly she subsided, with eyes still glaring wildly as she took huge shuddering breaths.

'The princess speaks the simple truth,' the sorcerer said coldly. 'As I'm sure the would-be Corodel has already told you. The alignments are gathering – and very soon you will all finally be of some value, by providing what I need to rise to an unheard-of level of power!' He glanced at Evelane, sagging slightly beside him as if spent, then turned back with a savage smile. 'I will explain more fully at the time. I would not want you to be spared the crushing anticipation of what is to come.'

'We know what is to come,' Aurilia snapped. 'And it is you, Talonimal, who will be crushed for your folly, dabbling in the evil of sacrifice.'

The sorcerer raised an eyebrow. 'Such bravado from one so helpless.' Unobserved then by Evelane, his gaze roved hotly over Aurilia's body, and his skin seemed flushed. 'But I do not *dabble*, witch, not in anything I do. You have learned that you will be sacrificed – but you cannot begin to conceive of the terror of the One who will receive the offering.'

Red's mouth tightened. 'Are we supposed to start grovelling and begging for mercy?'

'Perhaps not yet,' Talonimal said, smiling. 'But you may come to do so. When you meet the One who awaits you in my Tower of Invocation.'

'If it comes to that,' Krost growled.

The cruel smile broadened. 'Are you fools enough still to harbour dreams of escape? Abandon them, abandon hope. For all the witch's magic or the dwarf-giant's strength, you are truly powerless. You cannot possibly oppose me, or free yourselves.' He laughed once, harshly, mirthlessly. 'Now we shall leave you a while, so that you may begin to contemplate your dissolution. But rest assured – I shall not keep you waiting long.'

His hand, glowing, made a negligent gesture, and he and Evelane grew hazy and vanished.

As they disappeared, the magical paralysis suddenly ended. The prince lurched briefly before finding his balance, then turned stiffly away from the others as if to hide the visible signs of his pain and grief. Krost looked at the other two, shook his head, then went to Phaedran to offer what solace he could.

Aurilia sighed. 'I would never have imagined . . .'

'Good point,' Red interrupted, glowering. 'Why didn't anyone ever think of the possibility that Evelane might have left of her own accord? She seems to think she has good reason . . .'

'Not reason enough to give herself to Talonimal,' Aurilia said. 'Not reason enough to want to see her father die.'

'Well, maybe *reason* isn't her strong point just now,' Red said flatly. 'All that hate and spite and everything seems to have pushed her over an edge.'

'I do not believe so, Corodel,' said the prince icily, and Red jumped slightly. Phaedran had regained some control, and had heard his last remark. 'I cannot believe that is truly how my daughter feels. I am certain that Talonimal has imposed his sorcery on her, literally to charm her, so that she believes she loves him and hates me. So she *has* been abducted – her mind twisted by magic, her body violated . . .'

His voice broke, his face twisted, and he turned away again, stalking across the room to stand stiffly facing the wall, one hand to his eyes.

The others looked sadly at each other. 'Could he be right?' Krost asked.

'I fear not,' Aurilia said softly. 'I had no sense of a spell operating to control Evelane.'

'Then how could she become . . . what she is?' Krost growled.

Aurilia gestured helplessly. 'It might have been foreseen from the nature of her childhood – and those difficulties being harder on her because she was by nature sensitive and highly strung . . .'

'And now she's totally unstrung,' Red muttered.

'Besides,' Aurilia added, 'everyone underestimated how much her lack of magic affected her, how deeply, so that it above all has helped to damage the balance of her mind.'

'So there we are,' Red said bleakly. 'That's what all those men died for, on the lake – and what we'll die for, it seems. A half-crazy girl who's been seduced by a power-mad sorcerer with a hyperactive libido.' He sighed wearily. 'Seems kind of a rotten ending to the story of my adventures.'

'Red,' Aurilia said softly, reaching out to him, 'I'm so sorry. If I hadn't summoned the sword . . .'

He put his finger lightly on her mouth. 'If you hadn't, you might have been here sooner, and already sacrificed. No, *I'm* sorry, to sound like I was regretting . . .' He let his fingers trail gently along her cheek, down over her throat. 'I don't regret *anything* that's happened to me in this world. Certainly not meeting you . . . I wouldn't have missed it for . . . for all the Realms and Spheres.' He smiled his ironic smile. 'And I definitely wouldn't regret getting a chance to spoil Talonimal's big plans for us.'

'That is exactly right,' Krost growled fiercely. 'A *chance*. Perhaps we cannot hope to oppose him, as he says. But that does not mean that we cannot *try*. We will have nothing to lose – and some chance might favour us . . .'

Red nodded. 'We'll need one, if we're to fight him. But you're right. No point being lambs at that slaughter.'

'And who can know what might happen?' Aurilia said determinedly. 'For all his power, Talonimal is human – he has weaknesses, he can make mistakes . . .'

'He's as good as beaten already,' Red said sardonically. 'But I just hope he gets *on* with it. Sitting around here, waiting, is going to be the tough part.'

And so it proved to be. Red's remark seemed to put a conclusion to the talk, so Aurilia turned away with Krost to see what they might do to ease the prince's misery while Red wandered aimlessly around the dungeon, peering at the glittering solidity of the walls, prodding with a toe at the stone flags of the floor. If we do get a chance, he thought gloomily, it won't be here. And he thought then of the others who had been there before him, the women of the Sisterhood – and in particular, Nellann. Would she also have been *used*, he wondered, as a sexual plaything, in the ugly way that Evelane had talked about? I might have tried to do better for you in the Catacombs, Nellann, he said silently. Though it probably wouldn't have made much difference, in the end, to either of our deaths.

Eventually he went over against a wall and sat down, settling himself, trying to achieve a relaxed calm so as not to drain his energy in pointless agitation. It took a considerable effort, mainly to block the sense of desolate hopelessness that threatened to overwhelm him, but also to quell his imagination, which was producing a range of fearsome ideas of the sacrificial process awaiting them. In his inward struggle against his emotions and imaginings, he looked for a diversion by recalling and savouring good times. And, doing so, he discovered something remarkable. The good times he had had in that strange land, and with Aurilia and Krost especially, were among the very best of his life. What he had said to Aurilia was literally true: he had no regrets about being there. If his sojourn led to a dungeon and the promise of terrible death, that was simply the price to be paid.

And the really remarkable thing was: it was worth it.

He felt slightly startled to be thinking along such lines, and rather pleased with himself. In his rare past moments of painfully honest introspection, he had always viewed his lifestyle as shallow and trivial, his so-called wild rebelliousness as basically childish and petty. But in his brief, hectic time in the Four-Cornered Continent he had begun to develop another view of himself. He had learned that he had true courage, not just a crazy recklessness. He had learned that he was capable of true commitment – to the extreme of putting his very life on the line, for a friend like Krost, a lover like Aurilia . . . even for a cause, of sorts. In short, he had proved himself capable of living and behaving, for a while, like a *real* hero. Not playing the part of one for a camera.

It's been good, he said to himself in silent affirmation. I've never felt so alive before. And if being here, a short time away from death, is where everything has always been leading, then so be it. I'd do it all again . . .

Then he became aware of Aurilia, lowering herself gracefully beside him where he sat propped against the wall. 'Where are you?' she asked. 'Lost in gloomy thoughts?'

He smiled at her, taking renewed pleasure in her nearness, the faint spicy perfume of her hair, the richness of her body in the gauzy gown. 'No glooms,' he said quietly. 'Just thinking it's better to be totally alive for a little while than half-alive for a lifetime.'

Her smile was luminous. 'All dungeon-dwellers should be so philosophical.' Then her smile faded, and she reached for his hand. 'I'm glad you're not hating me for bringing you into all this.'

'Hating? No – quite the opposite.' He reached with his other hand to caress the firmness of her shoulder. 'I just wish . . .'

'I know what you wish.' The green eyes danced. 'And I share the wish. But we cannot embarrass Krost and the prince.' Her grip tightened on his hand. 'We will just be as we are, together and close and quiet – and compose ourselves, prepare for whatever is to come.'

Red nodded silently as she leaned in against him, and as the calming silence wrapped around them, he deepened his breathing and began his own inward preparation. But it was not a seeking after serenity before death. It was a process learned from his martial-arts studies. An internal gathering, a tuning and refining, that was partly to do with relaxation but more to do with focusing an inner force. So that he would be ready, poised to strike like an arrow on a drawn bow, if the smallest chance presented itself.

The process was rather like the first stages of self-hypnosis. All traces of fear, despair, rage, regret, or other hampering emotions gradually fell away, leaving his mind as still and cool as an underground lake. Perhaps that stillness communicated itself, for before long he heard Aurilia's own breathing deepen, sensed her relaxation against him as she slept. Then he may have slept as well, or else remained in a light state of mental suspension that was as effective as sleep. Certainly he no longer had any sense of the passing of time, or any concern for it. He might have stayed peacefully against that wall, with Aurilia beside him, for eternity.

But time did pass, and in the end Aurilia woke, to blink and smile at Red. Shortly the others stirred as well, expressing amazement that they could have slept in such circumstances. As they rose to stretch stiffness from their limbs, Krost discovered that some time during their sleep two objects had magically arrived next to them: a loaf of coarse bread and a flask of water. So they eased what thirst and hunger they felt, amazed again that they could manage to feel such common-place things.

'He is keeping us healthy,' Phaedran said sourly as they ate, 'so we will be satisfactory offerings.'

Krost shrugged. 'We need our strength for our own reasons – if chance is kind to us.'

Red said nothing, knowing that Krost was right, knowing that they had to maintain their physical well-being just as he had to hold on to his own internal readiness. And perhaps again his inner-focused clear stillness communicated itself to the others. They seemed to find their own forms of inner calm, so that something very like peace descended within that bleak prison, and though time continued to pass with tortuous slowness, none of them suffered unduly from that torture.

Their imprisonment ended with sudden shock. The roiling black fog of a vortex appeared from nothing against the end wall, offering its eerie opening towards the unguessable, and as they rose cautiously to their feet and stared into its spinning tunnel, the voice of Talonimal startlingly filled the space around them.

'Your time has nearly arrived,' the voice boomed. 'Please join me in my Tower of Invocation, where I shall be happy to explain what awaits you.'

The false courtesy in the voice was a mockery. The four

prisoners looked at one another, peered warily into the vortex, and did not move.

'Are you reluctant?' Talonimal's voice said, with an edge of cruel laughter. 'Then I must *urge* you into the vortex.'

Around them, on all three sides of the dungeon other than where the vortex whirled, the stone walls burst into bright yellow flame. Its brightness was dazzling, its heat overpowering. Though it was a magical flame, the four of them were in no doubt that it was deadly. Slowly they began to back away – towards the vortex – as the flame crept towards them, enclosing them, leaping and crackling from the bare stone floor.

'Enter the vortex one at a time,' Talonimal's voice ordered. 'His Highness first, then her ladyship, then the false Corodel, and the dwarf-giant bringing up the rear.'

Driven by the flame, by then fiercely threatening to blister their skins, the four moved reluctantly into position, stepping one at a time into the black opening. Red saw Aurilia glance briefly back at him, her eyes wide with apprehension – and in turn he glanced back before he entered, nodding at the look of grim determination on Krost's face.

Then his body went through the familiar dislocating wrench, and he was standing in a gloomy, dank room that was almost empty save for a few articles of furniture near by, with the prince and Aurilia next to him – Aurilia having along the way returned to her form of an aged crone.

The room was not especially large, he saw, but was impressively high, its ceiling invisible in the shadows above, which also contained the usual trails of drifting black fog. And despite the room's bareness Red saw its general resemblance to the place where he had first seen Talonimal, which the sorcerer had called his spell-chamber. So this must be the fourth of the castle's towers, he thought. The Tower of – what had he called it? – Invocation.

By then Krost had joined them, and they were all looking around with differing degrees of tension. They were standing on a sort of raised stage at one end of the chamber – half a man's height above the stone floor, with some broad steps leading up to it at one side. The vortex had left them grouped near the top of the steps, while on the other side of the stage stood the only furniture: a huge, heavy table and two sumptuously cushioned divans. The table contained several candles that were the chamber's only sources of light, as well as a scattering of manuscripts, books, implements – a smaller display of the kind of paraphernalia Red had seen before. There were a few gestures towards decoration, in the form of weirdly colourful hangings interrupting the high blank surfaces of the walls, but there was nothing else in the room. Certainly nothing like an altar, Red thought, or any similar sort of place . . . where sacrifices might be made.

He narrowed his eyes, trying to peer through the darkness to see the far end of the chamber. The wall appeared to be interrupted – what was it, that shadowed patch? And then he realized, with a clench of nerves. The patch on the far wall was a door. Which was opening.

And through it stepped the green-and-black-clad figure of Vanticor, scarred face lit by an ugly grin as he stared at his prisoners. And behind him, croaking quietly among themselves, crowded a group of nine Barachi with their long-bladed spears, wearing long cloaks or robes with heavy hoods shadowing their faces, like the garb of those that had guarded Aurilia when Red had first arrived in Quamarr. Ceremonial costume, Red thought grimly. But the spears aren't symbolic . . .

Vanticor led the nine Barachi along the length of the chamber, still grinning, and halted at the foot of the steps leading up to the stage. Red measured the distance between them, then studied them carefully. Vanticor was wearing his two blades as usual, while the Barachi could well have their pouches of darts hidden under their robes, besides their spears. But in those circumstances, he thought, they did not look particularly on guard. A sudden attack with Krost, grab a couple of spears, and the four of them might reach that door . . .

But as he threw Krost a meaningful glance, Vanticor saw it and laughed. 'Don't get ideas, hero. You'd never get past us. Just stand there and wait. That's all you've got left to do.'

Red barely listened, continuing to plot the series of moves

that would have to be made faultlessly and at blinding speed to have even the smallest chance of success. This might be your last fight, he told himself. Make it a good one. And, unconsciously, he began slowly to smile his hungry battle-smile.

Vanticor saw that as well, and his own expression turned equally eager as his hands reached to the hilts of his two weapons. But the blades were not drawn, nor did Red move. And the scarred man laughed aloud, and relaxed, as he saw Red's smile vanish with sudden shock.

He had been immobilized, with the others, by the invisible force that had gripped them all in the dungeon. As it closed around them, the air above the stage shimmered and Talonimal materialized, with Evelane beside him, standing in front of the two divans.

'Are you such fools,' the sorcerer snarled at the four prisoners, 'that you cannot accept defeat?' His cold gaze swept over them. 'You will remain restrained, then, until the ceremony begins. And even then you must face reality. You will never leave this Tower. If you offer resistance of any sort during the ceremony, Vanticor and his Barachi will deal with you.'

Red and the others remained silent, watching as Talonimal stepped to the huge table, briefly surveyed a frayed parchment, then studied a flickering candle that was marked with regular lines to indicate the passing of time.

'Excellent,' he said at last. 'The time grows near. But a while remains for me to . . . enlighten you. It will be pleasing, at last, to have victims who can properly *grasp* what I have achieved and will achieve. The minor witches who preceded you were always too terrified, and too ignorant.' He let his cold gaze settle on Aurilia, and Red was sure that he saw a flicker of disappointment as Talonimal surveyed the scrawny old woman. 'But at least you, my old shape-shifter,' the sorcerer continued, 'and possibly the prince, will understand fully and exactly what is to be your fate.'

'We understand, madman,' Phaedran said, his voice thick with icy rage. 'And we also know that it will surely bring your own downfall, before long!'

'Perhaps it might,' Talonimal said with a sneer, 'if I were less than I am. But in truth, prince, I am stronger now than *any* of the fools who attempted this enterprise in the past. And you four are about to make me stronger still.'

He stepped to the edge of the stage, gesturing grandly. 'Attend, now, my honoured and welcome guests. Shortly, when the alignments have come fully into place, I shall raise a fire in the midst of this floor. A fire that is a portion of the cold and deathless inferno that burns in some of the empty infinities beyond the Realms and Spheres. And then, I shall begin the invocation. A threshold will appear, within the flames, and beyond it a bridge. And along the bridge, towards the threshold, there will come a Visitation whose terror and ghastliness is beyond the reach of your imaginations. Who will come to receive the offerings . . .'

'Enough!' Phaedran shouted in regal fury. 'Do you seek to frighten us to death with talk of whatever demon you conspire with in your foulness? Or merely to *bore* us to death with your smug posturing?'

The sorcerer's smile vanished in a spasm of anger. 'Hold your tongue, prince,' he snarled, 'or I shall rip it from your mouth. Bear in the mind that I merely need you *alive* for the ceremony. Not necessarily whole or unharmed.'

Phaedran did not flinch. But when Aurilia laid a restraining hand on his arm he subsided into silent glaring.

Talonimal nodded, regaining a chill half-smile. 'There is no point in railing. If you wish to avoid unnecessary pain, hold to your silences, all of you, while I continue with my discourse.' His eyes glittered in the candlelight. 'Until the moment arrives when you may begin to die.'

Red glanced at the others – at Krost's fearlessness, Phaedran's cold anger, the look of concentration on Aurilia's lined face. All ready, he thought calmly. He said he'd release us when the ceremony starts, so that's when we go. All-out, full speed, and see if luck's with us. Maybe Aurilia can veil us or something, to give us an edge. Because we'll need one . . .

Then his thought broke off. As the sorcerer re-examined the candle and his other materials on the table, Red noticed a familiar sheath among the folds of the dark robe. Talonimal was wearing the sword of Corodel. Now that, he thought, would be perfect. With a veiling or some kind of diversion, I might get to it . . .

Talonimal turned back to face them. 'To proceed,' he said briskly. 'The prince could not be more mistaken in his belief that I make my offerings to some mere *demon*. The One who receives what I offer does not dwell in any of the Realms of Darkness or the Spheres of Light. It dwells in the terrible domain that lies past the outermost boundary of the farthest Realm of all.'

'The Void Beyond,' Aurilia whispered.

'Very good, my lady,' Talonimal mocked. 'You are quite extensively learned, for a witch.'

'But the Void is empty, lifeless,' Aurilia said. 'An infinite expanse of . . . of nothingness.'

'True, and yet not true,' Talonimal replied. 'The Void is actually a remarkable paradox, being both a place and a non-place, empty and yet not empty. *Things* can be found there, which are alive in their own ways, though not as we experience life. They are without true form, and are mostly mindless, purposeless, inanimate. Yet they can be awakened. And when they are aroused, they have *power*.' He fixed them with his glittering gaze. 'The One to whom I make offerings is vastly more powerful even than the highest demon from the darkest Realm.'

Red felt his skin crawl at the words, but remained silent, held as if hypnotized by the sorcerer's fervour.

'The first contact with this greatest of beings Beyond,' Talonimal continued, 'was made by Lebarran *Magister*.' His lip curled as he pronounced the title. 'His power took him exploring into the Void, where he encountered those who dwell there – and found that the encounter not only awoke them but awoke *in* them a monstrous hunger. You can perhaps deduce that they hungered for that portion of a human being that they so markedly lacked. The true life force.'

He paused, watching for their reactions. But when all four expressions remained unchanged he smiled in disdain and went on.

'Lebarran's protections kept the creatures at bay – but farther into the Void he encountered a being who was nearly too powerful even for him. An immense, monstrous, formless power – which not only shared the hunger of its lesser fellows but which, when awakened, displayed a separate driving force of its own. An awesome, relentless urge to dominate, to *rule*.'

He glanced briefly at the parchment and the slowly shortening striped candle.

'Lebarran believes that being, which he calls the Unformed, to have power comparable to a god's. And after that first encounter he devised a means of *invoking* it, with suitable restraints, seeking to understand it and communicate with it. As time passed, and he gained greater insight into the two-fold hunger of the Unformed, and its titanic power, Lebarran developed his plan. He began to seek ways to bring the Unformed fully into this world and to give it, here, the substance and form it craved. He believed that when it was formed he could control and use its power to enhance his own, to raise himself to unimaginable heights. Leading in the end to his ultimate and total mastery of this Sphere, and no doubt many others.'

'Madness,' Phaedran growled, and Aurilia's hand tightened on his arm.

Talonimal seemed not to hear. 'Lebarran called his plan the Apotheosis, reflecting his view of the god-like power that both he and the Unformed would wield in this world. Yet even the great Magister himself was not wholly certain of his ability to restrain the Unformed indefinitely. After all, *he* did not seek to enhance his power, beforehand, by sacrifice.' His smile was a mockery. 'No – instead, Lebarran gathered other mages, including me, and formed us into his Order of the Apotheosis, to combine our powers in conclave towards this goal. And he intended to launch the first stages of his plan at this year's autumn equinox.' The smile widened. 'Except that, some months ago, I pre-empted him.'

From the divan where she half-reclined, Evelane tittered, shrill as a seabird's cry.

'Lebarran did not imagine,' the sorcerer went on, 'that any of us might dare a betrayal, or be capable of it. But I had spied on him, undetected, and had discovered the secret rituals by which he reached out to the Void and invoked the Unformed. In the course of striving to master those rites, I learned that the being is quite indifferent as to how it satisfies its hungers in this Sphere, or through whom. So I erected this Dome to protect myself from Lebarran and the Order, and any other force that might be brought against me in this land. And I began to adapt Lebarran's plan to my own purposes – while first adding my special refinement.'

'Sacrificing Sisters,' Aurilia said, almost casually.

'Indeed. Of course anyone with any life force will do as victim, but my strengthening is accelerated when they have some magical gift of their own.' The savage grin flashed again. 'Think of the benefit, then, of *your* powers, my lady. They will hasten the day when, as I have vowed, I can wield my invincible strength and offer up Lebarran Magister himself!'

The words left a frozen stillness in the air of the chamber, broken after a moment by an equally frosty snort from Phaedran. 'Most reassuring, Talonimal. I see that your ambition has led you not only into unspeakable evil but also into megalomania. Which will certainly destroy you, in time.'

The sorcerer went rigid with anger, but before he could speak Evelane half-rose from her divan, flushed with rage.

'That is a *lie!*' she shrilled. 'Talonimal will prevail! It is *you* who will be destroyed – and we shall rule, my lord and I . . . !'

'Exactly so,' Talonimal hissed. 'And now there can be an end to words.' He looked once more at the striped candle. 'The patterns are aligning, the time is nigh. We may begin.'

He moved towards the table to frown down again at the parchment before picking up two small objects from among the assorted materials. As he strode then across the raised stage, Red was aware of Krost briefly straining against the invisible grasp that confined him. But the restraints held, and Talonimal did not even glance in their direction as he passed. Descending the steps, he stalked to the centre of the chamber, the drift of black fog sweeping aside to reveal the expanse of the bare stone floor.

There he raised one of the objects brought from the table – a tiny vial that seemed to be carved from crystal. From it, with glowing hands, he scattered a dark powder on to the floor, while muttering rhythmic words in a guttural, unintelligible language. And from the similar vial in his other hand he sprinkled droplets of a colourless liquid, with more incantatory muttering. Then, putting the empty vials in a pocket within his robe, he reached for the hilt of the sword and drew the luminous blade.

Red tensed as he did so, and Talonimal turned to smile his cruel smile. 'Bid farewell to your borrowed sword, young man. Its glamour is eminently appropriate here.'

He turned back, reaching down with the blade-tip to the dampened powder on the floor. The steel made a faint metallic rasp as the sorcerer trailed it over the floor in criss-crossed, interwoven lines. As he did so, the phosphorescence of his hands growing brighter, he continued to chant in the strange harsh tongue – more loudly, his voice forming eerie discords and broken rhythms that lifted the hairs on the back of Red's neck. And though he did not press down with the sword, so that even its magical edge could not have marked the floor, the movement of the blade began to leave weirdly glowing patterns on the smooth stone.

As the sword continued to move, the patterns grew – extending from the centre of the floor along to the edge where

286

they met the front of the stage. At that point it seemed that the patterns were complete, for Talonimal stood back, sheathing the sword – though not pausing in his weird, harsh incantation. He climbed back up the steps to the stage, and as he passed the captives Red could see lines of strain marking his grimly intent face. Moving again to the table, the sorcerer took up a small ceramic urn, and turned with it to stand at the very edge of the stage. As his unmusical chant rose in volume to a rasping shout, he took a handful of the urn's contents and flung them in a cloud of flaky ash out over the patterns magically inscribed on the floor below. The strange fluttering cloud floated slowly down. And as they reached the floor, and settled, the complex patterns suddenly, shockingly, burst into flame.

But it was sorcerous flame, as unnatural as its origins. Its tongues leaped from bare stone where no fuel fed it. It burned with a chill silvery-blue light, leaving no mark on the floor, creating no sound as it blazed, emitting no heat at all. In fact, Red thought, it made the chamber feel even colder.

Taking a deep ragged breath, Talonimal halted his incantation and turned to stare at Vanticor and the Barachi. 'Vanticor,' he grated, 'I shall now pronounce the Invocation. So I must release the restraint on the prisoners, to give my full concentration to the rite. When I do so, *watch* them. If they attempt to flee or to resist, you and the Barachi may cripple them, hamstring them, maim them as you will. But you *may not kill them*. If you fail me in this, you will take their place in the fire.'

Vanticor, looked paler than usual, swallowed and nodded – and he and the Barachi glared at the captives with new ferocity. But Red scarcely noticed. The unseen bonds that had held them had suddenly disappeared, and they could move again. And the fact that Vanticor and his spearmen had to keep them alive would provide them, he thought, with a very useful edge. In that moment of freedom, his battle-readiness straining at its leash, Red turned with his small hungry smile to look at Krost.

Until he felt Aurilia's bony hand clutch his arm, and saw her other hand grip Krost as fiercely.

'*No*,' she whispered, almost soundlessly. '*Wait*. This is not the moment. Follow my lead.'

Red tensed and twitched, barely able to restrain himself. But he saw Krost nod the smallest of nods, and so – reminding himself that Aurilia knew about magical rites and what sort of moments might be expected – nodded as well, reluctantly.

Talonimal had seen nothing of the exchange. Still at the edge of the stage, he had raised his arms high and had begun another chant in the unknown tongue, his voice rising and falling, loud then soft, high-pitched tenor or rough baritone, harsh and discordant. The glow intensified around his up-reaching hands as he exercised the full extent of his power, spreading his arms wide, fingers splayed and clawed. His chant rose into higher registers, and higher still until he was screaming at full pitch. He held that raucous, shrieking note, his hands flaring as if they too had burst into unnatural flame, until the precise instant when the time-keeping candle on the table burned down completely and winked out.

In the same instant, above the tongues of flame on the floor, a strange pale glittering cloud began to form, as if the air was condensing. The cloud expanded, and slowly within it shapes began to appear, without ever solidifying into complete clarity. But Red could make out the hazy image of tall columns supporting a high-arched pediment, forming an entranceway that was outlined with an eerie green incandescence. And beyond it stretched the equally hazy image of a bridge, whose arches apparently rested on nothingness, the whole structure extending to the far wall of the chamber where it did not terminate but merely faded mistily away into invisibility.

Talonimal slowly lowered his arms, a glint of sweat visible on his brow, and turned to the young woman on the divan.

'The stage is set,' he said hoarsely. 'The One who walks the bridge approaches. Now *you* may choose, Evelane my dear, which of these should be first to fly to Its embrace.'

Evelane licked already wet lips, her eyes bright and staring. 'My father!' she said eagerly. 'I want to see my father burn!'

Talonimal looked displeased. 'But no, surely, we can prolong his anguish and our vengeance if we keep him till *last* . . .'

And Red jerked with sudden surprise as Aurilia burst into a screeching cackle of laughter.

'Now I see why she believes your lies, Talonimal!' she cried. 'She's just as stupid and greedy as she ever was, when the Sisterhood was trying in vain to educate her!'

Evelane's mouth fell open and her eyes widened. Suddenly chalk-white in wild fury, with two spots of red burning on her cheekbones, she lunged up from the divan, one shaking finger pointing at Aurilia. 'No, *her* first! Let me see the old witch-whore burn! Burn her, *burn* her!'

'Very well,' Talonimal said soothingly, pushing her gently back, calming her. 'She is exactly the right choice. And then the others in their turn . . .'

Aurilia's bony fingers were like thin bands of steel on Red's arm, and on Krost's. 'Wait for the moment,' she whispered urgently. 'Follow my lead. I *know* what he will do.' And then she released her grip, let her hands fall by her sides, put a bleak flatness into her expression and her voice.

'*Let* me be first, then,' she rasped at Talonimal. 'Do your worst. I am weary of this charade.'

As she hobbled forward, looking suddenly older and more frail than ever, Talonimal showed her his savage grin. 'You will not be weary for much longer, witch. And it might rouse you, even in that shape, if you were to enter the flame in the same costume that so many of your Sisters have worn before you.'

He gestured, and abruptly Aurilia's long grey gown and all her other garments vanished. Red drew in his breath with a hiss, feeling almost ashamed to be looking at the withered breasts, the sagging wrinkled skin, the scrawny boniness of the old woman.

But Aurilia lifted her head to stand as straight as her aged body would allow. 'If it gives you some perverse enjoyment to gape at this old flesh, so be it. I am willing to leave the world naked, as I entered it.' But then the green eyes sparkled, and astonishingly she smiled, almost teasingly. 'Still,' she added, 'if you wish to take me now, my lord Talonimal, you might prefer me otherwise.'

Her body shimmered through its metamorphosis and in

place of the old woman stood Aurilia in her younger form – completely, breathtakingly naked. Her honey-bronze skin looked oiled, its rich gleam a total contrast to the cold blue flames that still leaped from the floor below. Her breasts thrust forward temptingly, her belly curved invitingly, her splendid thighs tautened as she stood with them slightly apart, flaunting the blond curls at their juncture. The brightness of her eyes and the glint of her smile offered both challenge and invitation. And as she took a step towards Talonimal her thickly piled hair came loose, tumbling and rippling down her back almost all the way to her knees.

Talonimal stood staring, as if paralysed – as did every man in the Tower at that moment, under the impact of her overpowering sexuality. Even Red, though he was no stranger to her body, stared stupefied. And below the stage the Barachi watched silently from beneath their hoods, stirred by uglier hungers.

In that frozen instant, if they had been able to rouse themselves from that fixity, Red and Krost could have launched their desperate bid to escape. But there was only one person in that Tower who was not immobilized: Evelane, looking disturbed and anxious as Aurilia took another swaying step forward and Talonimal stared. The princess was slowly beginning to rise from her divan, to reach out a hand towards the sorcerer. But then she halted. And in that moment all possibility of movement was halted.

Drawn by atavistic awareness or compelling dread, everyone turned towards the hazy threshold whose columns rose above the flames, and the unending bridge that stretched beyond it. Where something moved.

Towering, gigantic, shapeless, composed of roiling grey-black shadow like the clouds of an ultimate storm, it advanced – to push at the threshold with a terrible, unseen hand, to rest on the gathering an awareness like an unspeakable eye.

It paused there, looming, waiting – filling the Tower with its unholy, imponderable might and evil, and the enormity of its hunger.

THIRTY

Talonimal was first to recover from its effect. Everyone else was still transfixed with horror when he swung back to look again at Aurilia with glittering eyes, moving his tongue slowly over already shiny lips with an expression of boundless greed aroused not only by Aurilia's sexuality but also by the imminence of her sacrificial death.

The sorcerer's movement, the impact of his eyes, in turn tore Aurilia's attention away from the horror at the threshold. Though she was ashen, somewhere she found the strength and courage to recover her challenging smile, to display herself as temptingly as before.

'Do you want me now, Talonimal?' she asked, her voice again heavy with the double implication.

Her voice also seemed unnaturally loud in the silence that still quivered through the Tower. It jerked Red out of his paralysis, pulling his gaze away from the threshold in time to see Aurilia take another step that brought her almost within arm's reach of the sorcerer. In that instant he guessed something of what she intended, and cursed himself for the slowness of his response.

He began to turn towards Krost, to alert him. As he did so Talonimal made a low growling sound in his throat and moved towards Aurilia, hands reaching.

At the same time Evelane came to her feet by her divan, eyes wide and desperate. 'My dear . . .' she said tremulously.

The sorcerer seemed not to hear. His hands descended on to Aurilia's smooth bare shoulders, on either side of her flawless throat. They lingered there a moment, then slid downwards as if moving of their own accord, to trail fingertips over the upper curves of the firm breasts.

'Talonimal!' Evelane cried, as if stricken. 'Stop! *Beware* her!'

If the sorcerer heard he did not respond. His hands moved

to clamp themselves painfully over Aurilia's breasts, but she did not flinch. Holding his gaze with her own blazing eyes, she widened her smile into a grin of triumph. And one long, rippling tress of her hair rose up in the air by her side, coiling, serpentine, before it struck – lashing down to twine around Talonimal's wrist, binding itself into the witch-knot that Red had experienced – the irresistible magic bond of desire.

By then the others were aware of the drama on the stage, diverting their attention from the ghastly presence at the threshold. Yet the overwhelming waves of sexuality emanating from Aurilia remained almost as immobilizing as the terrible visitation. For everyone except Talonimal.

And as he moved, he was no longer the powerful, coldly arrogant sorcerer. He became a rutting beast, tethered and compelled by Aurilia's magic. The witch-knot aroused all the lust that had driven him throughout his life, bringing it surging through his being more powerfully than ever before. Wild-eyed, drooling, panting, and grunting wordlessly, all his senses focused exclusively on Aurilia, he dragged her towards him with one hand into a brutal embrace, his other hand groping frenziedly at her body, while from the far side of the stage Red heard Evelane whimper.

But Aurilia was using all her lithe strength to push Talonimal away, to keep out of his arm's savage clasp, even as her witch-knot drew him to her. As they swayed and staggered and struggled there in the centre of the stage, her right hand darted down in a blur of speed – to snatch the sword of Corodel from its sheath at the sorcerer's side.

Half twisting, she flung it wildly towards Red.

And Evelane screamed.

The scream shattered the hypnotic stillness gripping the chamber. As the sword arced through the air towards him, Red heard a burst of snuffling growls from the Barachi at the foot of the steps, and a hoarse grunt of shock from Krost beside him. But he was intent on the sword as he caught it clumsily by the hilt's guard and quickly shifted his grip. More than anything he wanted to leap forward and use the blade on Talonimal. But he heard the Barachi snarl, heard the choked yell of warning from Krost, and whirled just in time to deflect the stabbing head of a spear wielded by one of the Barachi leaping up the steps at him.

Metal clashed on metal as he parried with the unbreakable blade, clashed again as he blocked another spear. He heard a roar like a battle-cry from Krost, and at the edge of his vision saw the dwarf-giant grasp the haft of a thrusting spear and tear it from the hands of its wielder. He spun away from another spear, and another, trying to find a way past the thicket of stabbing weapons, trying to turn defence into attack. He heard Krost roar again, heard a snap that sounded like a spear-haft breaking, and from the far side of the stage heard another shrill scream. And in that moment the forest of spears threatening him parted – and confronting him stood Vanticor, sword in one hand and long dagger in the other, scarred face contorted with desperate fury.

Red's glowing blade flashed as he parried Vanticor's first wild sword-slash, and he just managed to twist aside from the following lunge with the dagger. Then both men seemed to settle, as savage battle-fury gave way before the watchful control of practised swordsmen. For Red all else on the stage faded away – how Krost was faring, what was happening between Talonimal and Aurilia. All he could see was the two skilled blades opposing him, the lethal patterns they were weaving, the flickering colours of his own blade as he blocked and parried and counter-thrust.

And all he could think, as they fought in that first blindingly swift exchange, was that Vanticor was the more skilled of the two of them. He would have been dangerous with just one blade. With two, he was deadly. Red could only defend, desperately – and even then, as he dodged and parried and retreated, he knew he was slowly being driven back towards the edge of the stage, where the terrible cold flames burning below would finally halt his retreat.

He chopped at the other man's sword, trying to spin away, back to the centre of the stage. But the move left his side open to the dagger. As he tried hopelessly to evade it, he felt the shorter blade rip through his shirt and slice along his ribs like a line of fire. Yet he pivoted away despite the pain, pivoted again, and whipped his leg up and around in a sweeping kick. Had he been a fractional instant quicker, he might have taken Vanticor's head off. But the scarred man jerked back in time, leaping away from the slicing edge of Red's sword.

For a moment he paused, a flicker of puzzlement showing on his face at Red's unorthodox footwork. And in that briefest of respites Red saw Talonimal still entangled with Aurilia, oblivious of anything else around him. Bruises and red scratches showed on Aurilia's naked skin where he had madly clutched and clawed at her flesh – by then even more bestial, eyes bulging, body jerking, grunting savagely as he struggled to draw her to him while trying to tear away his own robes. But in his clumsy mindlessness Aurilia was able still to resist him, so that they swayed and stumbled in a terrible mockery of a dance. While Evelane half-crouched by her divan, eyes crazed and huge, hands shaking, mouth writhing as she whimpered incoherently. By the side wall Krost had a Barachi spear in each great hand, slashing and battering with them at the hooded monsters assailing him. None of them could get past the tireless curtain of steel that he had created – and three who would no longer try lay crumpled in their own blood.

And at the back of the stage, looking as desperate and ashen and wild-eyed as anyone, Prince Phaedran was moving towards the far side where his daughter was – slowly edging along the wall so as not to attract the eye of any of the Barachi.

Red had no wish to turn to look at the centre of the chamber, where the terrible being still hovered monstrously at the threshold. But in any case he could no longer divert his attention, for the brief instant's pause came to an end. Vanticor came at him again, no less coldly furious but perhaps slightly more wary – attacking in a smooth rush and a treble strike, sword-slash, dagger-thrust, sword-lunge. Red's injured side flared with blazing pain as he parried the sword – and perhaps the wound slowed him slightly as he tried to sway aside to evade the dagger-thrust at his groin. The thrust missed its target, but stabbed deep into his thigh.

Fresh agony almost cancelled out the pain of his gashed ribs. Even so, as Vanticor jerked the dagger free with a snarl of triumph, Red swung the sword in a flurry of blows to drive his opponent back. But the blood was pouring down his leg and side – and as he tried to move out of danger he slipped in his own pooling blood and half-fell to one knee.

Vanticor's eyes flared as he raised his sword, poised for the kill.

'I'll bet,' Red panted as he tried to raise himself, 'you've forgotten you're supposed to keep us alive.'

Vanticor stopped as if struck, the fear erupting into his expression showing that he had indeed forgotten his master's order. Then his eyes narrowed with new determination, and he sprang forward.

Red struggled upright just in time to meet that flashing attack. Vanticor's sword and dagger flickered and stabbed as if they were themselves cold silvery flames – and Red barely managed to parry or evade the endless, snake-quick blows. Yet he could sense that he had gained some small portion of an advantage, for Vanticor seemed no longer to be trying to kill him but only to *disarm* him, which was far more difficult.

Even so, it was also growing more difficult for Red to resist, as his dripping wounds began to drain his strength. His parries and counter-thrusts became weaker and more desperate – and Vanticor was grinning, gloating, as he pressed the attack. Finally Red's sword was moving only in half-aimless flailing, his movements turned to limping, staggering lurches. Vanticor sprang at him with a powerful flurry of blows and Red stumbled back, frantically beating at his enemy with his sword, trying to lash a kick with his wounded leg at the other man's knee.

Too slow – the kick missed. For an instant Red was off balance, exposed. And Vanticor yelled aloud, a victory cry, and lunged to drive his blade into his right arm, to make him drop the sword.

As he began the lunge, he met Red's gaze. In that splinter of a second, seeing the tautly focused concentration in the pale blue eyes, the scarred man knew his mistake. Some of the fumbling weakness had been feigned – to *draw* him into that triumphal, careless lunge.

Red did not even try to avoid the blade. Instead, he simply moved his right wrist, just enough, to just the right angle. As

295

Vanticor's sword bit deep into Red's shoulder, the impulse of his forward lunge brought him smoothly on to the waiting point of the luminous blade.

Vanticor made no sound as the blade drove through his heart. He stared wonderingly, the dagger dropping from his hand. Red moved back unsteadily, his sword held ready as the enemy's blade was pulled, crimson, from his shoulder. But all life and awareness had fled from Vanticor's eyes. He remained on his feet, an upright corpse, for another second. And when he finally fell, Red was already turning away – towards the sound of muffled screaming.

The sound was from Evelane, screams like loud, choking sobs. Red saw that by then Talonimal had torn aside most of his robe and the sight had apparently jolted Evelane into action. She was clutching and tugging at the sorcerer, trying to drag him away from his struggle. Aurilia had begun to tire from the unequal conflict, though the witch-knot remained firm and her green eyes still blazed with fierce determination. But inadvertently Evelane was aiding her, partly holding Talonimal back. And only then did Talonimal become aware of her, because she was trying to balk his uncontrollable rut. Turning slightly, his face twisted manically, he swung a vicious backhand blow that smashed into the side of her face and flung her back into a heap on the floor where she lay dazed.

In that instant Aurilia renewed her struggle. Blood gouting from three wounds, Red began stumbling towards them – and saw Phaedran moving in the same direction, from where he had been edging stealthily along the back of the stage.

Then Evelane went into a convulsion, her body jerking and bucking, foam flecking her lips, raising clawed hands high as she screamed – an echoing, crazed screech that rose and rose as if it sought to break through the shadowed ceiling high above.

And in its wake, invisible havoc stormed into the chamber.

The huge table leaped as if something unseen tried to over-turn it. Everything on its surface, books and parchments and candles and implements, flew into the air like dry leaves raised by a gale. The table itself cracked and shattered, its fragments joining the whirling storm of objects. Even the corpses of Vanticor and the fallen Barachi were flung around gruesomely. Red barely lurched aside in time as a spear flew past him, to plunge into the flames where the formless Being still loomed at the threshold. In the same instant the heavy divans were swept up into the air as if they were no more substantial than the parchments – and one hurtled across the stage and crashed into the howling Barachi, still in battle with Krost, slamming them forward into a sudden heap with Krost somewhere beneath them.

Red stumbled another step forward, not sure whether he was going to Krost's aid or Aurilia's. But his desperate move to evade the spear had been too much for his wounded leg. It crumpled beneath him, sending him sprawling into the gathering pool of his own gore. On the other side of the stage, Evelane collapsed into unconsciousness, her eyes rolling up in her head – and at once the storm of flying objects ended, all of them dropping to the floor in a harmless clutter.

And from where he lay, struggling to rise, Red saw at last what Aurilia was trying to do.

She was not just trying to control Talonimal and simultaneously fight him off. With all the strength of her splendid body, she was trying to force him *backwards*. Towards the edge of the stage – where the deathly fire burned.

Overwhelmed by the power of the witch-knot, the sorcerer seemed unaware of her intentions. The diversion created by Evelane had allowed Aurilia to push him back quite close to the edge of the stage. And there she continued the struggle, with waning strength but with undiminished will.

Red fought to muster his own will, fought to rise despite pain and weakness that were bringing shadows on to the edges of his consciousness. He saw with terrible clarity that Aurilia was not intending to force Talonimal alone over the edge of the stage. She seemed unwilling to release the witch-knot or her own grip on him – as if afraid of freeing Talonimal's mind, and power. Red remembered her calm willingness to die, to thwart the sorcerer's plans, and understood that she was not going to push him into the fire – she was going to *take* him.

That awareness brought Red at last to his feet, swaying, bleeding, trying to stagger forward, dragging his injured leg. He saw Aurilia gather her strength for one last mighty effort at the stage's edge – saw the smooth muscles of her legs and back leap into definition as she moved farther into Talonimal's maddened embrace and clamped her arms around him.

'No!' Red tried to yell, his voice crackling and weak. 'Don't – Auriflamme!'

He hardly felt his leg giving way under him again, hardly noticed his collapse. His gaze was fixed on the struggling couple – and on the fierce green eyes of Aurilia, looking towards him at the sound of her Name, filling with shock and concern and indecision. In that frozen instant, distracted, she might have lost the initiative, and the struggle.

But Prince Phaedran appeared as if from nowhere at her side. His face a stony mask, he clamped his sinewy hands on to the sorcerer and tore him away from Aurilia's grasp, from the witch-knot. With a surge of astonishing strength, fuelled by the immensity of his rage, he lifted Talonimal's feet from the floor and hurled him into the cold blue flames.

Aurilia slumped to the floor, gasping for breath – yet staring fixedly into the fire, as the prince stared, as Red stared despite the dimming of his vision, while wishing he could look away.

Talonimal had not fallen to the floor from which the flames rose. He was held suspended within the fire, his body twitching and quivering, his mouth agape in a terrible soundless scream. His robe was burned away at once, not even a fleck of ash remaining. And then the silent inferno assaulted his naked flesh. His skin darkened as it began to char, distending in places where bulges like huge bubble-blisters formed beneath. As the swellings extended and spread, the flesh sagged and slid as if melting, drooping down into the flames in great stringy globules that grew more and more viscously fluid, darkening further to black and bubbling fiercely in a slow, grisly dissolution. In a moment more the flesh was entirely gone – and the bones too, still held suspended, slowly flaked and crumbled away, finally disintegrating into a dust that flared briefly and vanished into nothingness.

Yet at the end something remained – like the barely visible

essence of smoke. It hovered and trembled for a moment within the flames, and then it moved. It hurtled at speed towards the hazy columns of the threshold, drawn there by inexorable compelling power, an unnatural summoning suction – and finally pulled through the opening, into the engulfing maw of the shapeless waiting horror on the bridge, to be consumed.

In the next moment the Presence began to withdraw, back into the distant mistiness. When it could no longer be seen, both bridge and threshold began to fade, disappearing from sight. And the silver-blue flames in turn sank low, flickered and died.

And Red, nodding once in grim satisfaction, let himself sag down to the floor, into the thickening pool of his own blood. A small smile curved his lips as he looked once more at Aurilia, kneeling in her exhaustion, cloaked by the rich fall of her hair, alive and intact. He tried to speak her name, but his voice and his strength failed him. Behind him he heard a sort of choked roar, as if from a great distance, but before he could identify it a blackness deeper than the Tower's black fog swept down to envelop him.

After an age of peaceful oblivion, sudden pain flared in his wounds to drag him back from darkness to light and agony and failing life. Krost was looming over him, grim-faced, covered in blood none of which seemed to be his own, binding tight pads of cloth over Red's wounds – with Aurilia hovering beside him, still in her younger form but clothed by then in tunic and leggings. He saw her stricken expression, tried to smile at her, tried to speak, but could produce no movement or sound except a faint groan when Krost abruptly lifted him from the floor, draping him over one shoulder.

'I'll take him,' he heard Krost growl. 'Help the prince with Evelane.'

At that point Red drifted back to unconsciousness, and drifted in and out several times in the next while. So he was only vaguely aware that no one, surviving Barachi or otherwise, tried to block their passage down from the Tower and through the castle. He was not conscious when they emerged from the castle, nor when they made a swift detour to collect their horses. He was dimly aware when they passed easily through the wall of the Dome, as Aurilia had thought they would on the outward journey. And when he came awake again they were on a gravelly beach, under an overcast sky, with light and air and the smell of the sea all around.

In waking he found he had somehow left pain behind, that he felt as if he was floating, weirdly, unable to move or speak but fully aware of what was happening. Aware also that he was dangerously weak from loss of blood, but remarkably unconcerned about it. Krost was crouched over him again, doing something to his wounds, while near by Aurilia was rummaging through a saddlebag on the back of her white horse. Red was comforted to see Grilena with the horses, looking unharmed. And at the edge of his vision he could see

Evelane, sitting motionless and blank-eyed on the sand, with the prince standing anxiously at her side. Red saw that the prince had the sword of Corodel thrust through his belt, and felt pleased. That'll help you fight your way back to Quamarr, he thought distantly. Even if it won't help me.

'He's started bleeding again,' he heard Krost say, anguish in his voice.

'I have herbs that might help,' Aurilia said, coming away from her horse with a small bag in her hand. 'But it'll be hard to prepare them properly here.'

'We must do something,' Krost rumbled. 'He's fading . . .'

Then he broke off with a sudden grunt of surprise, while Aurilia's eyes went wide – and the prince took a startled breath and snatched at the hilt of the sword.

'No, wait!' Aurilia said quickly. 'We know him . . .'

And Red heard a soft, high-pitched voice that he had heard before.

'I am alone and intend no harm,' the voice said. 'I am here to help.'

'How came you here?' Phaedran demanded, his voice ragged.

'I . . . was in the vicinity,' the other voice said. 'And I see that I have come just in time.'

The speaker moved closer, framed against the grey sky as he came to stand next to Krost, and Red stared wonderingly up into the purple-and-white eyes of Hallifort the Healer.

Kneeling beside him, Hallifort placed his small hands on the blood-soaked bandages over Red's wounds. With his touch, the floating painlessness within Red's body vanished – restoring the fiery agony in his torn flesh. But it lasted only an instant, followed by the equally sudden spread of a cool softness like an ineffable balm. With it, life and strength and vigour flowed back into Red like spring rainfall into a dry riverbed. Calmly, easily, Red sat up and peeled the bandages away from wholly unmarked flesh.

The others stared speechlessly. 'A great power . . .' Phaedran breathed.

Red got to his feet, almost overwhelmed by how entirely whole and well he felt. 'His name is Hallifort,' he told the prince. 'He healed me before, when I first arrived – and helped me against the Barachi in the Rookeries.'

'And the gods be thanked that he is here again,' Krost rumbled, 'by some strange fortune.'

Hallifort looked at him with an odd expression, which became a gentle smile as he turned then to see the tears of gratitude in Aurilia's eyes.

'I don't know where you came from, friend healer,' she said softly, 'but I'm glad to see you.'

'As are we all,' Phaedran said. 'We owe you a great debt of gratitude, Hallifort, and I will readily reward you, in whatever—'

Hallifort held up a small hand. 'Thank you, Highness, but I have everything I need. I heal for fulfilment, not for gain. In any case . . . my task here is not yet done.'

He glanced aside, and the others followed his gaze – towards where Evelane sat, unmoving, staring out at the sea with empty eyes.

'Can you help my daughter?' Phaedran asked urgently. 'She has suffered no more hurt than a blow to the face, yet she seems . . . mindless . . .'

Hallifort moved towards Evelane, touching his fingertips gently to the side of her face where Talonimal had struck her. When the swelling bruise had faded and vanished, he moved his hands to rest on either side of her head, and frowned slightly.

'She has suffered an extensive mental collapse,' he murmured. 'Apparently involving the release of a destructive poltergeist force.'

'That was *her*?' Red asked incredulously. 'All those things flying around, even the furniture . . . ?'

'So it seems,' Hallifort said. 'It is often the case, with a young and – forgive me – unstable woman. But the outpouring of psychic energy was too powerful, too damaging to her. Her mind has retreated, deep within itself. And there is more . . .'

'What more?' Phaedran asked.

'Deep within her mind are terrible rifts and lesions,' Hallifort said sombrely. 'Much inner scarring, and mental barriers

302

raised – all psychic wounds formed and deepened by the circumstances of her young life.' Red saw the prince's face tighten, but no one spoke. 'These are not wounds of the flesh that can be healed at once with a simple laying-on of hands. Here, now, I can only ease them, to call her mind back from its retreat. The healing must take a longer time, in a more tranquil place, with the princess's active involvement.'

'But can you *do* it?' Phaedran rasped.

'Perhaps,' Hallifort told him. 'But only if she permits, and participates.'

'Then,' the prince said fervently, 'I would be willing to reward you with everything I have.'

Hallifort shook his head. 'As I said, I seek no gain. The healing itself is my reward.'

'But why *us*?' Red asked suddenly. 'Why did you travel all this way, alone, probably at great risk, to find *us*? Did you *know* things were going to end this way? Can you see the future as well as heal?'

'No one can do that with certainty, Red Cordell.' Hallifort said quietly. 'Even the greatest power, seeking to look ahead, can only see the myriad of pathways with differing degrees of likelihood.' Intensity brightened his strange eyes. 'But one thing has been clear for some time. Your destiny, Red Cordell, and the destinies of all of you here, are closely bound up together – and bound up also with the future peace and well-being of this Continent, this entire Sphere. I cannot see the exact nature of that binding, but I have no doubt of it. And so . . . I came here to ensure, as best I can, that you fulfil your destinies.'

'Just as well, too,' Krost rumbled. 'So why do we not leave the philosophy aside and ride on, before more Barachi come along to put an end to our destinies?'

But the others still stared at Hallifort, as if trying to fathom the depths of meaning within his words.

'You are unlike any other healer I have known,' Aurilia said thoughtfully.

'Unlike any *person*,' Red growled. 'I owe you my life yet again, Hallifort – and there are no words for my gratitude.

303

But there's too much mystery. I need to know. Who are you, really? *What* are you?'

A look of terrible desolation swept over Hallifort's face – exhibiting such a depth of grief and loss that Red found himself wanting to reach out to the little man. But then Hallifort's face smoothed, and he sighed a faint sigh.

'I cannot tell you, Red Cordell,' he said softly. 'Yet it is my belief that you may be led by mischance to learn the answer to that question, by yourself, before this time of violence and peril comes to an end.'

He turned then and moved slowly away, as if burdened. The others looked at each other, all save Evelane – seeming troubled and shaken in varying degrees, yet remaining silent, though hosts of doubts and questioning swarmed behind their eyes. Then they simply gathered themselves up and wordlessly followed the small figure of Hallifort, walking away along the shore.

Charles de Lint
Yarrow £4.99

A new tale of enchantment and wonder from the author of *Moonheart* and *Greenmantle*

Cat Midhir lives in a land of dreams, crossing nightly over the borders of sleep into a magic realm.

YARROW

A land where gnomes hide among standing stones and selchies dwell beneath the waves, where the harper Kothlen tells tales of the ancient days and the antlered Mynfel walks by moonlight . . .

When Cat wakes she weaves stories around the Otherworld. Her books are labelled as fantasy, but Mynfel's domain seems more real to her than the humdrum streets of the city.

Until a thief comes stalking – and steals Cat's dreams away . . .

'You open a de Lint story, and like the interior of a very genial Pandora's box, the atmosphere is suddenly full of deep woods and quaint city streets and a magic that's nowhere near so far removed as Middle Earth' JAMES P. BLAYLOCK

'The storytelling lyrics of folk music lie at the tender heart of Charles de Lint's fictions. His work reaches to the very heart of humanity' FEAR MAGAZINE

'Classical folklore with modern settings full of power and beauty . . . one of the most gifted storytellers writing fantasy today' LOCUS

Kate Elliott
Jaran £4.99

'Well-written and gripping' KATHERINE KERR

Tess is cursed by an accident of birth. Her brother led Earth's rebellion against its alien conquerors. Defeated, but honoured, he was given a dukedom for reasons only the aliens know.

Tess is his only heir, a daunting position she wants nothing of. She flees to one of the remote worlds in her brother's domain where she discovers love with Ilya, leader of a nomadic tribe, and a terrible secret which draws her into a vicious interstellar political game.

Whether it is her brother or the aliens that win Ilya and his tribe must adapt or face extinction . . .

'Impressive . . . a very strong debut' LOCUS

'Sweeps the reader along like a wild wind across the steppes' MELANIE RAWN

'A rich tapestry of a vibrant society on the brink of epic change' RAVE REVIEWS

'A bright new talent' JUDITH TARR

Dwina Murphy-Gibb
Cormac the King Making £9.99

Continuing the glorious saga of Cormac mac Airt, greatest of the High Kings of Ireland.

'And so the one-eyed man has come. And so the KingMaking has begun.'

Heralded by a druid prophecy at birth, all the mystical signs point to Cormac's greatness. Now the time has come for the young Cormac to assume the mantle of kingship.

But with enemies both far and near mere signs are not enough. Cormac must learn to fight for his throne, under the tutelage of the forbidding one-eyed warrior Goll mac Morna.

In the arduous rituals that lie ahead of him, Cormac must learn not just how to kill but how to lead men, before he is fit to rule over a land made for heroes.

Also available book 1 Cormac The Seers

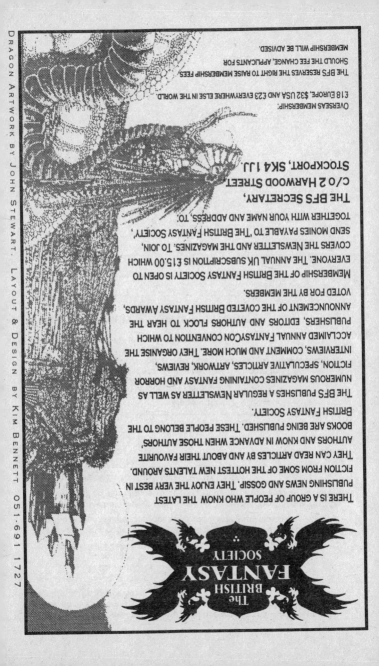

All Pan books are available at your local bookshop or newsagent, or can be ordered direct from the publisher. Indicate the number of copies required and fill in the form below.

Send to: Pan C. S. Dept
            Macmillan Distribution Ltd
            Houndmills Basingstoke RG21 2XS
or phone: 0256 29242, quoting title, author and Credit Card number.

Please enclose a remittance* to the value of the cover price plus: £1.00 for the first book plus 50p per copy for each additional book ordered.

*Payment may be made in sterling by UK personal cheque, postal order, sterling draft or international money order, made payable to Pan Books Ltd.

Alternatively by Barclaycard/Access/Amex/Diners

Card No. | | | | | | | | | | | | | | | | | | |

Expiry Date | | | | | |

Signature:

Applicable only in the UK and BFPO addresses

While every effort is made to keep prices low, it is sometimes necessary to increase prices at short notice. Pan Books reserve the right to show on covers and charge new retail prices which may differ from those advertised in the text or elsewhere.

NAME AND ADDRESS IN BLOCK LETTERS PLEASE:

Name _____

Address _____

_____

_____

_____

_____

6/92